MYSTIC
WIND

JAMES BARRETTO

MYSTIC WIND

A LEGAL THRILLER

OCEANVIEW ⬡ PUBLISHING
SARASOTA, FLORIDA

ISBN 978-1-60809-496-7

Published in the United States of America by Oceanview Publishing

Sarasota, Florida

www.oceanviewpub.com

10 9 8 7 6 5 4 3 2 1

PRINTED IN THE UNITED STATES OF AMERICA

This book is dedicated to my late friend and former colleague, Assistant District Attorney Paul R. McLaughlin, who was murdered in 1995 in the line of duty by a gang leader whom he was scheduled to prosecute on the following day.

ACKNOWLEDGEMENTS

With a grateful heart, I wish to thank my writing group, which was founded by Kelly Tate and included Sibylle Barrasso, Gary Chafetz, and the late Jeremiah Healey, winner of the prestigious Shamus Award and former president of the International Association of Crime Writers. These talented writers pored over each of my original scenes and put me on the road to publication.

I express my sincerest appreciation to *New York Times* bestselling author Joseph Finder, author of twenty-plus novels, two of which have been adapted as major motion pictures. Joe encouraged, advised, and cheered me on for a long time. He never gave up on me. Not once. He also invited me to the 2019 ThrillerFest XIV in New York City, sponsored by the International Thriller Writers, where, as fate would have it, I met Bob Gussin, cofounder along with his wife, Dr. Pat Gussin, of Oceanview Publishing, who both saw merit in my project. Without their willingness to take a chance on me and my story, you would not be reading this book.

I am also indebted to B.A. Shapiro, *New York Times* bestselling author who first told me I have a book in me and to a quartet of talented editors: Francesca Coltrera, Ellen Clair Lamb, Tiffany Hawk, and Jeff Gerke, author of *The First Fifty Pages*.

I thank, among others, two dear colleagues: Judge Laurence Pierce of the Massachusetts Superior Court and Judge Daniel Roache of the Massachusetts Juvenile Court for their encouragement and for balancing my reliance upon more than a modicum of fictional license with real-life trial practice norms. Any deviation from the law as portrayed in this novel was made in the service of entertainment and is my sole responsibility. Thanks also to my friend, attorney, and retired U.S. Navy Commander Emery L. Haskell, veteran of the Iraq and Afghanistan Wars, who provided insight into Matt Marino's military background.

A loving thank-you to my late mother, Florence, who was the first to read to me and in so doing lit a fire, whose flames continue to burn today. And to the men in my life, past and present, who were there for me: John Barretto, Saul Lerner, Frank Finocchio, Tony Rubbicco, Judge Paul J. Cavanaugh, Hon. A. Joseph DeNucci, and David Barretto. I have loved them all. I thank my sons, Christopher and Matthew, who have made my life truly special. Keep swinging for the fence, guys.

Finally, and most importantly, words cannot express my appreciation to my partner and the love of my life, my wife, Luann, for her infinite patience, keen intellect, and unending support. Without her, I would be nothing.

MYSTIC WIND

PART I

MURDER & BETRAYAL

AUGUST 1980

CHAPTER ONE

It always began in the same terrible way: first the shakes, then the roiling sickness. And the only way to stop it was the booze. That worked. For a while, at least.

Sweet Jesus, Nora thought, wiping the sweat off her forehead with a filthy hand. Maybe the wine she'd found near the train tracks earlier that night had been tainted. Or too old.

Nora sat down and took a long breath to settle her stomach. The air smelled of sulfur as a summer wind swept in from the nearby Mystic Creek. Ghostlike flashes of heat lightning illuminated the desolation around her.

Nora dropped her head between her legs, into the wild brush that lined the abandoned tracks of the old Boston & Maine Railroad spur. Long blades of grass, the color of wheat, swayed in the night breeze and caressed her face.

The moment Nora raised her head, her world began to spin.

Then Nora heard the voices. Not the ones in her head. These were real.

"Put your fuckin' face on the ground. Or you ain't gonna have a face."

Nora peered in the direction of the voices into a darkness punctuated only by the spill of pale yellow from spotlights high up on the old factory behind her.

Three men gathered in a tight knot on the raised railroad bed that supported the tracks. They seemed close, maybe fifty feet away, but the bushes, thorny bramble, and grass concealed her. The tracks hadn't been used for years, which was why the area had made such a good home for her and others in her world. Until now.

The men all appeared to be young, one with blond hair kneeling facedown on the ground, his face pressed into the dirt and crushed stone. The second was an intimidatingly large man, equal parts brawn and beer belly. Another man, dark-haired and much shorter, stood nearby.

The shorter man had a gun.

Nora put her hand to her mouth, so she wouldn't heave. The impulse stifled, she took a deep breath.

"And you, ya fat shit." The man brandishing the gun gestured wildly at the biggest of the two. "The fuck do you think you are, screwin' with us? Huh? Think you saw some things and now you got a big mouth." He pistol-whipped the man he called a fat shit across the side of his head.

Making no effort to protect himself, the big man absorbed the full force of the blow. Blood ran down his face. Nora cringed as he fell to one knee and began to cry. "Please. I've got kids."

"To hell with your kids. After we're done with you, we'll kill your kids and make your wife watch."

The guy they called a fat shit began to wail. "I'm sorry. Please . . . I told you I'm sorry."

"Get on your knees. The hell were you thinking? Gonna shake us down?"

Despite the order to kneel, the other man tried to stand. "Please," he begged.

The man holding the gun hesitated, then laughed, breaking the tension. "All right. Wanna live, shit for brains?"

The man paused. "Yes. Please," he repeated, breathless, tears running down his face.

"Then kneel back down," said the man with the gun.

As he knelt, Nora could make out the silhouettes of two more men who'd appeared on the tracks. Unblinking, she watched as the big man looked up at them and pleaded, his voice filled with hope.

"Help me," he gasped. "He was gonna kill me." He reached toward the men.

The man with the gun just stood there.

The larger of the two new arrivals reared back and struck the big man across the face with something dark and hard, the sound of broken bone slapping off the building behind Nora. Another blow followed. Beaten down to one knee, the big man reached up toward his attackers in supplication.

The men yanked him to his feet while the young blond remained prostrate on the ground.

Nora looked up at a night sky that trembled with bone-white flashes of lightning. Maybe it was all a dream. She was going to be sick. That much was real.

She looked back, the wash of light from the steel foundry allowing her to see everyone clearly. It was no dream.

And that was when the realization hit her.

Nora stared in disbelief, adrenaline electrifying her frail, malnourished body. Still unbelieving, she blinked, wiped the sweat from her eyes, and looked directly at all of the men. At the hunting party.

It was true.

Bloodied but conscious, the big man pleaded for his life in loud, plaintive sobs. "Why? No. No. Please—don't—don't—"

The sound of the gunshot punched a hole in the night, as Nora watched the big man collapse.

The night sky began to spin out of control. It was all too much. Nora's hand came to her mouth too late as she retched.

"The fuck was that?" one of the men said.

"Jesus, someone's in the grass," another yelled.

The men fanned out, searching the area. Nora could hear the dry grass swishing as they made their way toward her.

She thought about fleeing, but it was no use. She couldn't run. Hell, she couldn't even stand.

But she could crawl. And if she could crawl far enough, she might be able to reach the creek.

Nearly invisible in the darkness, a thin finger of the Mystic Creek lay hidden only yards away in the weeds and brush at the side of the tracks. Nora could smell it, a stench carried on the back of a gusting wind. The creek was open here. Another few feet beyond, it entered a culvert under the tracks, carrying globs of illegal waste and raw sewage to the larger Mystic Creek proper.

If Nora could reach the culvert, they'd never find her. No one would.

Her stomach turned at the thought.

As footsteps closed in on her, Nora dragged herself forward on her elbows through the brush to the edge of the creek. The smell of the sludge burned her nostrils. Sharp, jagged thorns ripped her flesh, cutting her face, her elbows, her arms, anywhere her body was exposed.

Reaching the creek, she lowered herself into the effluent, her arms and face streaked with blood, clenched teeth forcing a moan back into her throat. The men were almost on top of her.

"Where the hell?" one of them screamed.

The odor was like nothing she'd ever experienced. Driven by instinct, Nora found refuge in the oil black of the culvert directly under the tracks, her head held just above the surface. As she inched still deeper into the tunnel, a sudden, excruciating pain surged up her leg. She grabbed at her calf and felt something frightening brush up against her. Exhausted and overcome, Nora pressed her body against the cold aluminum sides of the culvert and clamped her hand over her mouth to stifle a cry from the animal's bite.

For too long, Nora thought, the railroad tracks had been her home. But the tracks—and the sewer and waste that ran beneath them—would always belong to the rats of the Mystic Creek.

CHAPTER TWO

Though he was in a courtroom, in a place he loved, surrounded by memories of past victories, thirty-four-year-old Assistant District Attorney Jack Marino was so damp with cold sweat that his shirt clung to him. He turned and stared at the defendant, one of Boston's most notorious gang leaders and drug traffickers.

The defendant was accused of the crimes of Kidnapping, Assault with a Dangerous Weapon, and Mayhem for maiming a young woman, Ms. Maria Lopez, who worked as a prostitute for him and his gang. She'd made the near fatal mistake of telling the gang leader that she quit, that she was out of the life. For good. Worse, she'd had the temerity to say it in front of several other prostitutes who worked along with her.

The defendant had decided to make an example of her. He'd killed before and gotten away with it, but this time he wanted a daily reminder—a reminder written in flesh and blood—an example for all the other girls. Something that would be remembered.

So, he'd ordered several of his lieutenants to find her and bring her to the deserted three-family tenement that served as the gang's headquarters. When she arrived, the defendant was ironing a shirt on an old-fashioned, pull-out ironing board. And smiling.

Moments later, her screams were unearthly as he finished his ironing.

If she survived the horrific third-degree burns to her breasts, she could do nothing again but turn tricks for her boss—but only with her shirt on. For the defendant, it was a statement worth making.

Given the defendant's lengthy criminal record, replete with multiple convictions for drug trafficking and crimes of violence, a conviction on any of the crimes would take him off the street for at least ten years, maybe thirty if he were found guilty on all indictments.

The trial had gone well, but the victim had failed to appear during the first week of the trial. Without her, the prosecution could not prove its case—so Jack, head of the District Attorney's Urban Gang Unit, was forced to juggle, explaining to the jurors that they would hear the witnesses out of their natural order. While everyone waited for the victim to arrive, Jack laid the groundwork for conviction, but the most important piece of the puzzle was missing.

He was worried. And out of time.

Judge Carolyn McCormack had given him the weekend to locate the witness. Jack would have to call his witness or rest his case.

He and the victim witness advocates had worked with the victim for months. She'd promised to testify but stopped answering their calls. The DA's office had sent a police cruiser to her home over the weekend, but no one answered her door.

"Mr. Marino," the judge instructed, "call your next witness, please."

The jurors watched Jack Marino with anticipation.

Behind him, the gallery was packed—not only with the usual onlookers—press, witnesses, his colleagues—but with gang members as well, who made no pretense of hiding their identity. Their colors, their tatts, their body language—all silently screamed malevolent intent, an expression of intimidation to anyone unfortunate enough to be called as a witness. They stared at Jack, and like a prize-fighter, he stared back, his eyes locked on the evil that sat before him.

The Trial Court had pulled out its biggest guns to ensure security. Court officers were stationed throughout the courtroom. The Boston Police Department had sent a contingent of officers, who unlike the court officers, were armed. The head of the trial security department, a tough-as-nails former Army MP, eyed the assemblage, ready for anything.

Jack couldn't bring himself to respond to the judge's inquiry. Instead, he turned and stared at the defendant, who sat at one of the two mahogany attorneys' tables, a smug smile on his face as he turned to exchange looks with his fellow gang members.

"Mr. Marino, I've put a question to you," Judge McCormack said. "What are your intentions?"

Outside the old courtroom, storm clouds had gathered, summer rain clicking against the thin glass that separated this house of justice from a city outside that saw little of it.

Jack bit his lower lip. "To do justice, Your Honor . . ." He paused. "However, I'm afraid the Commonwealth's identification witness has failed to appear, and I regret to say that I don't have an expectation that she'll be arriving any time soon."

"Does that mean that the Commonwealth rests its case-in-chief?"

Daniel Vega, the defendant's high-priced defense attorney, saw his opportunity. "Your Honor, in light of this development, the defense moves for dismissal for lack of prosecution." His smirk presaged an easy win.

"Counsel, jeopardy has already attached. A dismissal for lack of prosecution is not appropriate. You know better than that."

"Then I move for a required finding of not guilty."

"Your motion is premature. The Commonwealth hasn't rested its case yet." The judge turned back to the prosecutor. "Mr. Marino, if you have no further witnesses, is the Commonwealth going to rest?"

Jack stood silent, as a silver, metal electric fan oscillated back and forth, the fan's rhythmic sound filling the courtroom.

Judge McCormack tapped her fingers loudly against the polished surface of the judge's bench. She glanced at the clock. "Mr. Marino?"

Jack was out of time.

The only thing he knew above all else was that the defendant belonged in hell. Jack Marino detested those who preyed on the weak, and all he'd ever wanted was a chance. A chance to make the streets safe, to use his trial skills to pursue justice. Maybe even make a better world. He drew a long breath.

"Your Honor, the Commonwealth can proceed without our identification witness."

Judge McCormack looked surprised. "Really?"

"May I approach sidebar?" Jack asked.

"I'll see both counsel."

The attorneys approached the side of the judge's bench farthest from the jury, out of their earshot.

Jack kept his voice low. "Judge, the Commonwealth has a 911 tape in which the missing witness identifies the defendant by name as her attacker. I'd like the opportunity—outside the presence of the jury—to demonstrate to the court that the 911 call is an Excited Utterance and therefore an exception to the hearsay rule."

Vega was apoplectic. "Judge, this is ridiculous. The witness isn't here. Anything on that tape is obviously hearsay and is inadmissible. Not to mention my client has a constitutional right to confront the witnesses against him. I strongly object."

Judge McCormack held up her hand. "Hold your fire." She turned to the jurors, her voice calm. "Members of the jury, it has become necessary to hear and determine a motion outside your presence. So you know, the reason for hearing this matter outside your presence is not to keep relevant evidence from you. It's just the opposite: It is to make sure that what you hear is relevant to this case and that the evidence is presented in a way that gives you a fair opportunity to evaluate its worth."

"Okay," the judge said once the jurors had been escorted from the courtroom. "I'll hear from Mr. Marino. But, Mr. Vega, let's get something straight. A first-year law student understands that an Excited Utterance is an exception to the hearsay rule. I won't prejudge the issue, of course, but don't presume to tell me what an Excited Utterance is." The judge turned to the prosecutor. "And, Mr. Marino, you well know that this issue should have been brought to the court's attention prior to trial. Not moments before you rest your case—whenever you get around to doing that."

"Your Honor, we've had a fully cooperating victim and absolutely no reason to believe she wouldn't appear for trial. Neither the State Police assigned to my office nor the Boston Police can find her. At this point, I'm concerned for her safety."

The judge turned to defense counsel. "Do you know anything about why the victim has failed to appear?"

Defense counsel shook his head. "I was looking forward to cross-examining her myself."

Judge McCormack looked down at the defense attorney. "I'm sure you were."

With the Court's permission, Marino played the tape. Between the words was a wailing unlike anything he'd ever heard. What was clear was that she said her boss and his goons had kidnapped her and maimed her breasts with a scalding iron. The incredible thing was that she'd somehow made the call from a public telephone only a few feet from where they'd dumped her. How she got the strength to make that call, Jack would never understand.

"Your Honor, the victim's 911 call clearly expresses intense emotion," Jack said. "It was made in the immediate aftermath of a horrific attack, and it's obvious that she remained terrified. Her call was a call for help, not the product of reflective thought."

Vega jumped in. "Judge, I've heard the tape, which was provided in discovery. First, we don't even know if the voice on the tape is that of the alleged victim. She never identified herself. Second, the confrontation clause as interpreted by the United States Supreme Court in *Crawford vs. Washington* bars the admission of statements of a witness who does not appear at trial unless he or she was previously available for cross-examination."

Marino wasted no time. "Your Honor, *Crawford* only bars testimonial statements, and under the primary purpose test created by the Supreme Court there can be no doubt after listening to that tape that the victim's call was an effort—a heroic one at that—to report an emergency. Her statements are clearly non-testimonial, and for that reason, they're admissible."

Judge McCormack delivered her ruling with precision. "I find that the 911 tape is self-authenticating based on circumstantial evidence, its content is non-testimonial, and that it constitutes an Excited Utterance and therefore is admissible as an exception to the hearsay rule. The 911 call will be admitted into evidence for its full probative value."

Jack unbuttoned his suit jacket. *Thank God.*

Moments later, with jurors in the jury box again, Jack pressed the button on the tape recorder, and the 911 recording began to play. Not a single juror would ever forget what they heard that day.

The jury deliberated nearly three hours.

"Madam Foreperson, has your jury agreed upon a verdict?" Judge McCormack asked, once the jury had returned.

"Yes, we have," said the foreperson, a slight woman with salt and pepper hair.

"What say you, Madam Foreperson, as to the indictment charging Kidnapping, Assault and Battery with a Dangerous Weapon, and Mayhem. Is the defendant guilty or not guilty?"

"Guilty on all counts," said the foreperson as the rest of the jurors looked at their shoes, their legal pads, anything but the defendant.

The defendant dropped to his seat, his hands curling into fists.

The drug kingpin's lieutenants shouted an ugly chorus of obscenities. A phalanx of court officers and Boston Police moved in, lining the gallery with a show of force.

Judge McCormack pounded her gavel. "Silence."

The defendant's eyes cut sideways to his associates, his face betraying an ice-cold hatred, his eyes an obsidian black. Turning to the associates nearest him, the defendant brought his hand to his neck, palm down, and drew it from left to right.

The judge sentenced the defendant to thirty years in state prison.

The defendant's fellow gang members watched helplessly as Jack Marino was mobbed by a horde of Assistant District Attorneys, congratulating him, shaking his hand, clapping him on the shoulder. Next stop was the 21st Amendment, a popular Beacon Hill watering hole where Jack would be the guest of honor.

Just as he was leaving the courtroom, an administrative assistant approached. "Sorry to rain on your parade, golden boy, but you've got to cancel. There's been another shooting."

"Not Maria Lopez?"

"No. Hours ago, someone found a young man down by the old railroad tracks behind the projects near the Mystic Creek. Shot in the head. Police think it's gang-related, and the DA wants you on scene. Now."

CHAPTER THREE

By the time Jack rolled up to the crime scene in nearby Mystic, the rain had stopped.

He noticed a brown, four-door Chevrolet Caprice station wagon parked slightly canted to the left, its nose butted up against the side of a long-abandoned maintenance shack near the railroad tracks. Two Mystic police officers busied themselves examining the car. The wagon's windows were partially clouded up as if parked at a lovers' lane.

Jack flashed his DA badge and the police nodded, allowing him a better look. Careful not to touch the car, Jack peered through fog-shrouded windows to see a set of keys on the floor in front of the driver's seat. His eyes moved to the rear of the car, where a dirty blanket in the rear cargo space had slipped away to reveal a single bloody arm.

Mystic, Massachusetts, a working-class city of thirty-five thousand souls, sat just north of Boston at the confluence of the Mystic River and the Mystic Creek. The city was no stranger to trouble, but murder was still a big deal.

A gleaming black SUV, outfitted with emergency blues and takedown lights, pulled up and skidded to a stop. Throwing open the door, the driver jumped out with the agility of a cat. He had dark hair, worn straight back, and a three-day growth of beard, like those sported by undercover detectives. He wore black jeans with a dark blue sport coat over a pressed white shirt. Jack figured him for five ten, probably 170 pounds, fit for a guy in his forties.

The man shook his head in disgust. One of the uniforms was wiping the rear glass of the Chevy for a better view. Another was trying to access the locked car. A loose pack of civilians stood nearby, eyeballing the scene.

"Clear the area," he barked at the patrolmen. "Take your hands off the car and chalk a perimeter."

The man turned to Jack. "Unbelievable. I've got to tell my own how to run a crime scene. My apologies." He extended his hand. "Mystic Police Commissioner Jeff Knight."

Jack shook his hand. "Jack Marino, head of the DA's Urban Gang Unit."

"Sure. I've seen your name all over the place."

"Hopefully it's not graffiti."

The commissioner laughed. "No. It's all good, but I don't envy you. You've got a dangerous job."

"Not as dangerous as yours."

The commissioner smiled. "Appreciate your help. The gangs are out of control here."

Jack nodded. "I think we're turning the corner." He looked up at the sky, which had cleared. It was already hot as hell again.

Jack turned and stared in the direction of the nearby creek.

"What're you looking at?" the commissioner said.

He pointed at the coal-like sheen of industrial waste in the canal that paralleled and then crossed under the railroad tracks. "See that. That tributary empties into the larger Mystic Creek and eventually Boston Harbor."

"It's a poisoned blight. A sewer."

Jack shook his head. "Hard to believe that the Mystic Creek was the sight of the first naval battle of the Revolutionary War."

"Can't say I knew that," the commissioner said.

"Gets lost in the shadow of Concord and Lexington. Bunker Hill, too. But it's true.

"And somewhere before the creek bleeds into the Mystic River lies a sunken British warship, the HMS *Diana*. Still undiscovered to this day."

"Bit of a historian, huh?"

Jack shrugged. "Not really. I grew up around here, and I guess I read a lot."

The commissioner cocked his head, reappraising Jack. "My money says not many like you made it out of this place."

Jack ignored the implication. Instead, he looked beyond the creek and across the railroad tracks at a ruby red neon sign that winked above an exotic dance club named The Treasure Chest. Despite broad powers granted to the police commissioner by Mystic's mayor, the local news had reported Knight's losing battle to shutter the strip joint. Jack winced as the electric silhouette of a young, naked, busty woman flashed on and off around the stem of a cocktail glass intended to be a stripper's pole—or, maybe, something else.

To his left, Jack eyed a group of homeless people in tattered clothes huddled across the railroad tracks, not fifty yards away—a portrait of the poor, the powerless, the dispossessed.

The commissioner yelled to his officers again, pointing at the group. "Move 'em outta here." He turned to Jack. "I don't want this crime scene tainted."

The officers began to march toward the group. One shouted a sharp warning to clear the area, while other officers rested the flats of their palms on their holstered sidearms. The group began to disperse, several of them folding ragged pieces of cardboard they'd used to sit on. They moved faster than Jack thought possible, except for one—an older Black man, his emaciated arms failing him.

Jack turned to the commissioner. "Give me a moment, would you?"

The commissioner held his hand up, his face betraying his frustration.

Jack walked to his car, reached in, and grabbed an unopened bottle of spring water from the console. He crossed the tracks and knelt to offer the man a drink. "Go ahead. You'll feel better."

The man took the bottle from Jack and began to gulp from it, his hands trembling as he drank, Jack's hand resting on his shoulder.

Mystic police officers stood in a semicircle behind Jack, the wind kicking up and throwing litter and debris all around them.

Turning away from the wind, Jack stood and removed his wallet, then his business card. He scribbled the name of a homeless shelter on the back of the card and handed it to one of the officers. "Call this number. Mention my name, and they'll send a van. They'll help him."

The officer glanced at the card and threw a look back at the commissioner, who nodded his head. "Roger that," the officer replied.

As another Mystic patrolman measured the distance between the car and the field house, the commissioner radioed the desk sergeant at headquarters downtown, reeling off instructions. Jack was impressed.

Within an hour, the crime scene swarmed with personnel from multiple law enforcement agencies. State Police assigned to the District Attorney's office joined the macabre choreography, following their own protocol. Commissioner Knight radioed the Department of Public Safety's main crime lab in Boston for a forensic expert and other crime scene technicians as well.

Before long, the area in front of the maintenance shed was dressed in the somber attire of a murder scene. Bright yellow crime scene tape fluttered around the station wagon, an island frozen in time.

Evidence markers were placed down. Uniformed officers stood at the front and rear of the vehicle. A detective busied himself interviewing the man who'd found the car while walking his dog. A hundred yards away, two blue-and-white Mystic police cruisers were parked grille to grille, like opposing sentinels, preventing unofficial traffic from entering the paved stretch that dead-ended at an old field shack, the railroad tracks behind it, and a corpse.

The rear door to the station wagon was swung open for the police photographer to take photos of the blanketed victim from every possible vantage point.

Twenty feet behind the station wagon, a white Ford minivan from the coroner's office rolled to a stop. A man in a rumpled white lab coat and charcoal gray slacks stepped out of the van, clearly the Medical Examiner. He was tall, over six feet, with longish curly brown hair, a narrow face, strong jaw, and pronounced Adam's apple. He had the harried look of a state-paid medical professional with too much work and too little time. Trailing in his wake were two assistants.

The M.E., whose embroidered coat read Dr. Neil J. Backman, shook hands with Knight and Jack. "What've we got?" Backman nodded toward the station wagon.

"Male. Caucasian," the commissioner said. "Found this morning by a man walking his dog. Apparently, the foggy windows piqued his interest, and when he walked over, he saw congealed blood that had leaked out of the back of the wagon."

"Anyone touch the body?"

"No one," Knight said. "Car was locked until one of my officers opened it with the Slim Jim."

Backman grunted, still eyeing the wagon. "Let's get started."

The man's body lay in the back of the car. The victim's head was streaked by long purple-brown smears of blood mixed with what appeared to be dirt. On one side of his face, a scar, ragged and ugly, ran from his mouth to his cheekbone. A tuft of thick brown hair was matted over his forehead, his lips purple, his eyes, particularly the right one, swollen shut in death. The victim was north of 250 pounds, maybe even 275. He wore a red T-shirt, sweatpants, and lay stomach down, his head closer to the back seat, legs and feet near the rear cargo door.

Jack knew the routine. Backman worked it methodically, ordering his assistants to remove the blanket and instructing the photographer to capture the original position of the body.

Before Backman authorized removal of the body, he gave a State Police chemist a chance to pick and pluck, nudge and scratch. With tweezers and magnifying glass in hand, the chemist gathered samples from the crime scene. Even clumps of dirt and what appeared to be regurgitation were carefully deposited in separate vials. After securing the caps, the chemist scribbled identification marks on each one.

With the body stripped of its death secrets, assistants from the M.E.'s office pulled a gurney to the rear of the station wagon and removed the victim.

For Jack, visiting a murder scene was like hell week for a Navy SEAL candidate: it triggered bone-deep exhaustion. Every time. So, an hour later, he decided to call it a day. As he drove away, beyond his view, a black Cadillac Eldorado coupe, its windows tinted raven black, purred to life and pulled slowly behind him, splashing through the rain puddles that dotted the barren landscape.

CHAPTER FOUR

That evening was like any other one—until it wasn't. Jack and his wife, Abby, had made reservations at Maison Robert, a swanky French restaurant tucked inside the ornate Old City Hall building on School Street in Boston. It would work out great, she said, because they could celebrate his win in the mayhem case.

Once home, Jack tossed his keys on the granite desk tucked behind the arch of the entranceway. The living room smelled of wild-cut flowers that Abby had placed in each room. She loved this place and had put her signature on everything. To Jack, their unit, nestled on the thirteenth floor of a palatial high-rise building on Atlantic Avenue, was a balm from the gritty reality of his job—and from the even grittier reality of his youth.

He grabbed the newfangled remote control and clicked on the TV that sat on a mantel above a gas insert that housed a gorgeous, odor-free fire. A news junkie, Jack scanned the television channels and settled on his favorite new station: a twenty-four-hour cable news channel called CNN.

Jack had no sooner thrown his battle gear—suit, briefcase, tie— onto the couch when the doorbell rang. As Jack opened the door for his wife, someone kicked it in the rest of the way. Something cold and hard, like steel rebar, hit him in the sternum and knocked him to the floor. His breath left him in one painful gush, the pain so intense he teetered on the edge of consciousness.

Later, it would astonish him how a single moment could change his life permanently, a blur of time and events that forever established a *before* and *after*. In those first few seconds, his mind unable to keep up, Jack managed to register a few things. A man in a ski mask rushing in. Two men, also masked, following on his heels. The door closing behind them.

Jack was sprawled on the carpet, as the three men began to kick him viciously. He rolled into a fetal position, tried to cover up, still unable to breathe from the pain in his chest. Powerless, his face grew wet with a river of blood. For some crazy reason, he worried about the carpet that bloomed scarlet beneath him. Through watery eyes, Jack strained to get a look at his three assailants. Their powerful physiques suggested they were young, each sporting similar jackets and dark, nylon ski masks.

The first of the home invaders, apparently the leader, waved a gun. He was the one who had speared Jack in the chest with the gun barrel. He finally spoke. The smell of cigarettes wafting forth as he did. "Get up, asshole. You the one in trouble now. How's it feel, motherfucker?"

Jack tried to lift himself, but his body shuddered, failing him.

The other two men dragged Jack up and threw him down on the sofa, his blood dripping onto the white cloth of Abby's new Donatella couch. He tried to open his mouth, but before he could, another kick, this one breaking his nose, sending more blood streaming down his face.

Out of the corner of his eye, Jack tried to focus on something. Anything. He willed himself to stay conscious. He eyed a photo of Abby set in a silver frame on the table beside the couch. He concentrated on her face. Then the clock on the wall. She'd be home any minute now. Jack shuddered at the thought of what would happen to her if she walked through that door.

"'Specting someone?" The leader pointed the gun at his wife's photo. "Where's she at?" The man who spoke gestured toward one of the others, who withdrew plastic ties and adhesive tape from his pockets. "Tie the motherfucker up."

Jack refused to offer his hands.

The third man struck him across the face with a fist wrapped in brass. Jack felt a new gash open in his left cheek. He fell off the sofa to the floor again and looked up, the room spinning relentlessly. From his awkward angle on the floor, all he could see was the wall clock. The pendulum swinging. The second hand ticking. Soon, he would no longer have a choice. Or chance. Abby would be home any minute. Even if she survived, life as she knew it, as she'd become accustomed to living it, would be over.

The two men grabbed his wrists and began to force Jack's hands behind him as he lay on the floor, his heart pounding against his chest. He had only one choice.

With all his strength, Jack lunged for the man with the gun.

A single shot rang out, and Jack's ears exploded with a piercing, shattering roar. He was hit. But breathing.

He hoped people in the building heard the gunfire. But during construction, Abby had insisted on soundproofing their walls, so she'd never hear their neighbors. Jack had welcomed the change order; he'd spent his childhood listening to his neighbors arguing through his bedroom wall. Now, he prayed the sound protection wouldn't cost him his life and wished with all his heart that those same neighbors were still behind that wall. Still arguing. Jack had only one chance left. If he could reach it. He extended his hand as far as he could and, in the chaos, pulled a fire alarm. Another ear-piercing sound that would rouse the entire high-rise building.

Startled, the leader looked down at Jack. "Lucky motherfucker." He turned to the other men. "Let's fly." Looking back at Jack one last time, he said, "We ain't far. 'Member that before you try to do us again."

* * *

Three months later, Jack's recovery reached what the doctors called an End Medical Result, at least on paper.

In a way, he'd been fortunate. Although he'd needed plastic surgery to close his facial lacerations and had suffered a concussion, the bullet had only grazed his kneecap. A talented orthopedic surgeon at the New England Baptist Hospital had been able to reconstruct it instead of replacing it with an artificial one.

The bad news was that doctors told him that recreational running, one of his greatest passions, was over.

Except for greeting the occasional visitor, Jack spent most of his days holed up in his home office. But his home was no longer a safety net. Instead, everything about it served as a grim reminder of the savage attack—and a cruel reminder of all that he'd been before he opened that damn door.

Because the faces of his attackers had been covered, Jack had been unable to identify his assailants. Detectives kept the case open, but they were at a dead end. He'd prosecuted God knows how many criminals, so the list of people he'd "wronged" was long.

When he began to venture back into work, Jack didn't have the concentration to review his cases, which he'd parsed out among the Assistant District Attorneys who worked for him. A few weeks later, once he transitioned back to full-time work, he assumed an administrative role as head of the gang unit, subject to an upcoming meeting arranged by the DA. He stopped appearing in court. Rarely ventured into the field. After work and on weekends, he walked his neighborhood, but always looking over his shoulder.

A phobia is interesting to read about, but hell to live through. Jack was in a maximum-security prison cell, walls of invisible cement and steel pressing in on him. No matter the time of day. No matter where he went.

At night when sleep finally came, his attackers were waiting for him. Jack would wake with a start, his T-shirt soaked with sweat. When his tossing and turning woke Abby, she'd ask him if he was all right, and he always said the same thing: "I'm fine."

It was one hell of a lie.

CHAPTER FIVE

Deep in the confines of the old courthouse, Jack waited in the office of his boss, legendary District Attorney Trevor Cameron. The rumor was the DA was going to give him a commendation for his dedication, recognition of the injuries he'd suffered in the line of duty.

Dozens of framed black-and-white photographs adorned the walls, a shrine to a career of influence and power, ambition and prestige. The collage documented Cameron's rise from the maelstrom of Boston's machine politics: from South Boston precinct captain to ward boss, City Councilor, State Representative, and State Senator.

An early photo showed Cameron in his late thirties standing beside newly elected President John F. Kennedy, their vitality and youth frozen in time. Photos with governors, congressmen, and United States senators chronicled Cameron's decades in public service. White, toothy smiles everywhere. An older Trevor Cameron, with a shock of premature white hair, celebrating his election as District Attorney.

A shot taken inside Charlestown District Court reminded Jack of the white metallic sign hanging outside the frosted glass of his first office. A younger Jack Marino sat behind a gunmetal-gray steel desk—an underpaid, inexperienced, and dedicated Assistant

District Attorney whose day had started much earlier, gathering facts, interviewing civilian and police witnesses in preparation for the day's nearly endless trials and pleas.

If you could survive the Charlestown District Court, Jack thought, you could succeed anywhere in the DA's office. Charlestown was a rite of passage, trial by fire, far more important to an assistant DA's career than class standing, law review, or any other classic markers of early prosecutorial success.

It hadn't taken Jack long to catch the attention of the District Attorney himself. In 1976, Cameron had sauntered through the squealing doors of the Charlestown courthouse to take a personal look at his rising star. "You should be on our team," he said, extending his hand. Soon after, Jack had been reassigned to work under Cameron where he'd begun prosecuting major felonies—armed robberies, rapes, and murders—with a vengeance.

Jack had found a patron and a future, which he was eager to embrace. Finally, he'd become someone.

The door to Cameron's office opened and the past disappeared. Jack turned as the DA strode into the room as confidently as ever with his $100 haircut and custom-tailored suit.

Following behind him was his right-hand man, First Assistant District Attorney Bradford Sears, the Commonwealth's winningest prosecutor: a rare bird, who had never lost a homicide trial in his career.

Cameron waved off the hand Jack extended. "Ever hear the name Julia Gibson, Jack?"

Cameron's demeanor, cold and unapproachable, jolted Jack who had been expecting a warm welcome. "Who?"

"You heard me. Do you know who Julia fucking Gibson is?" Cameron looked directly at Jack.

"Yeah," Jack said." Everybody does. She's a columnist for the *Boston Tribune*."

"Talk to her recently?"

Jack looked away for an instant. "How do you mean?"

"This is what I mean." Cameron slapped a copy of the morning's *Tribune* onto the polished walnut conference table with a fury Jack had never seen before.

Jack looked down at the paper. An above-the-fold headline read "District Attorney Would Rather Play Midnight Basketball."

"Midnight basketball, Jack? That's what you told them we do here? Play midnight basketball with gangbangers?"

"They're not all gangbangers," Jack said, almost to himself.

"Actually, you're right. Some of them are just plain fucking murderers." Cameron picked up the newspaper and waved it in Jack's direction. "You know the office policy. No interviews."

Jack shook his head. "It was supposed to be off the record."

The DA pointed to the newspaper resting on the conference table as if it were a live hand grenade. "Off the record? Jack, nothing is off the goddamn record."

"She promised me. It was just background. I was home recuperating. Said she was doing a story on urban violence and wanted to make a difference. She'd heard you did, too."

"She made a difference all right." Cameron turned to his first assistant. "Brad, tell him the difference she made."

Brad Sears looked at Jack. "The Governor knows an opportunity when he sees one. His first campaign commercial, which is scheduled to air this week, quotes you."

"Jack," said Cameron. "You're the chief of my goddamn gang prosecution unit. I've been going from newspaper to newspaper, editor to editor, bragging about the work you're doing." He tapped his chest. "The work *we're* doing. Jack, I trusted you. You're about the best attorney I've got, and I imagined you by my side in a big way."

Sears flinched, apparently insulted by the would-be competition.

Cameron shook his head at Jack. "And this is how you pay me back? Just as I kick off my candidacy against the Governor? To a person, the editors have been telling me Boston is overrun by gangs, and the problem's getting worse. If I don't succeed with these stuffed-shirt pinheads, I don't become Governor. Understand?"

Jack glanced at Sears, who nicely fit Cameron's description of a pinhead.

"Poll numbers don't lie," the First Assistant District Attorney added, as if reading Jack's mind. "The gang problem—and criminal justice, in general—are the keys to this election. We have to look strong."

Jack felt a stab of anger, incredulous that his loyalty would be questioned. "Exactly," said Jack to Cameron, ignoring Sears. "And there I was, sitting in bed for weeks after taking a bullet for this office, and I've finally got the time to think about what we're doing here. I've been putting these guys away for years now, but in truth, we're not even making a dent, Trevor. Hell, I'm prosecuting some of their kids. Think about that. There has to be a better way."

"Okay, I hear you." Cameron sighed. "But let's say I referee some games. Give out free friggin' sneakers to half the city. Say it buys us some respite from the violence. What happens to my gubernatorial campaign? The public doesn't want me lacing up some asshole's sneakers. They want blood."

Jack thought of the endless blur of gang prosecutions he'd pursued. "But blood doesn't work, Trevor."

"You know something?" the DA said. "Maybe it doesn't, but if that's the kind of governor they want, that's what they'll get."

Jack felt his defenses rise, a bloody mix of fear, embarrassment, anger. "So, this is about your political career?"

Cameron slapped the table. "You're damn right it is. Jack, I molded you for that unit. You wanted trials. I gave you trials. You wanted murders. I gave you murders. And after I did all that, I built our entire gang unit around you. I gave you assistants. I gave you staff. So don't presume to question my motives."

Jack's heart pounded. Was this his respected mentor talking—so much more than a boss, a friend even? "And I did right by you. I won those trials. I convicted those murderers. Remember?"

"My point exactly," Cameron replied. "No one knows that unit like you. That's why we've been so patient with your recovery. But now you're falling down on the job, Jack. The case backlog is piling up. Younger assistants who work for you are telling me that your hands shake when you're in court."

Jack couldn't pretend he wasn't slipping. "Trevor, I was attacked, for God's sake. I was beaten and shot. My wife could have been raped." Jack's left knee throbbed, the pain a constant reminder of his ordeal. "Look, I'll work in any unit except gang prosecutions. I'll even write appeals if I have to."

Cameron rubbed the back of his neck. "I get it, Jack. I do." For an instant, he seemed to be seeing reason. "But the last thing I need is another egghead scribbling in a law library 'til midnight. I can get a freshly minted ADA to do that for next to nothing. No, Jack, I need a trial chief who'll put these animals away for me, where they belong. And someone who knows enough to keep his mouth shut when the press comes calling. You want that job, it's yours."

Jack hesitated, his face burning with humiliation. "Either of you know how it feels to be looking down the barrel of a gun?" Jack asked. "Can you even imagine that as you sit in this plush office of yours, with a battalion of State Police outside your door?" Jack took a breath.

"For God's sake, Jack," Cameron said. "Pull yourself together. You need to see a damn shrink, see one. But in the meantime, you want to work in this office, you show up for the work we hired you to do."

Jack sat down and ran his hand over his hair. There was no point in pretending. "I can't prosecute gangbangers anymore, Trevor. I can't do it."

Cameron didn't blink. Sears shrugged, a cold, indifferent gesture that suggested Niagara Falls would slow to a trickle before they'd change their minds.

"So that's it?" he said quietly, dabbing a line of perspiration from his forehead with a bent finger.

Cameron avoided eye contact.

"Got a feeling you can get a plush job with your wife's daddy," said Sears.

"You're an asshole," Jack told him.

"Cut it out. Both of you." Cameron tapped his watch. "Look, Jack, we'll issue a press release saying you're pursuing other opportunities. Extolling your contributions to the office. Yadda, yadda, yadda."

Jack's throat closed. He couldn't believe this was happening. The DA's office was all he had. He turned to Cameron. "I broke my ass for you for nearly ten years. I was almost killed for you, for this goddamn office, for this apparent stepping-stone of yours."

"Jack, you were a good prosecutor, but things have changed. You've changed. You said it yourself that this job isn't for you. Look, Jack, the Governor is kicking my balls in. And quite frankly, you're helping him do it. He says I'm soft on crime. Me. The fucking County District Attorney. People are buying it, Jack. They're believing it." Cameron pointed at the paper lying on the table. "Even if you *did* have the best intentions, I'm going to lose ten points in the polls over this. Maybe more, once that damn commercial comes out. This is not about you—it's about me. And if you're not going into court with guns blazing, then you're not on my team."

Jack drew a long breath. "I'm a career prosecutor, Trevor. This office is all I know." He let the breath out. "There has to be a place for me."

The District Attorney cast his eyes toward the plush blue carpet beneath his feet. "Not anymore."

Jack spoke slowly and deliberately. "What happened to you?"

Cameron gave Jack a look somewhere between compassion and curiosity but didn't answer. Maybe he couldn't answer. Instead, the DA turned his back and walked out of his office as quickly as he'd come in, his Rottweiler not five paces behind him.

Leaving Jack Marino alone, still standing before the wall of photos, his body a boiling cauldron of blood and shame.

PART II

THE APPOINTMENT

FALL 1982

CHAPTER SIX

His heart racing, Jack stared up at the regal French Provincial chandelier that hung above the bed. Matching wall sconces were dimmed to reflect a diffuse, romantic splash of yellow.

"I'm sorry, Abby," he said, perspiration dotting his face. "I don't know what's wrong." Jack rolled over, tossing the satin sheets aside. The attack was more than two years ago, but it felt like it was two weeks ago.

Abby propped herself up on the crook of her elbow, sighed, and gave her husband a look.

How Jack had come to hate that look. He hadn't seen it during their engagement or the first whirlwind year of their marriage.

Jack met Abigail Thorn, daughter of one of Boston's last legal titans, in the District Attorney's office. Abby had been serving her six-month rotation through the Boston Municipal Court as part of a pilot program that placed associate attorneys from some of Boston's largest law firms in the DA's office to gain much needed trial experience.

Jack had been dating a secretary within the office at the time, but it hadn't been long before Abby brought an end to that relationship. In a big way. Everyone in the DA's office treated Abby like royalty. She and Jack developed an easy rapport, sharing jokes and pushing each other to excel at work. Lunches led to drinks that led to what should have just been a drunken one-night stand. Before Jack realized what happened, he was confessing his infidelity and dumping his girlfriend. The most confident and impressive woman Jack had ever met, Abby began spiriting him away, flying as passengers in her father's private helicopter to lavish, lazy, sex-filled weekends on Martha's Vineyard and Nantucket.

In less than six months, Jack proposed. It was a society affair. The talk of Boston. The upcoming marriage of Abby Thorn, daughter of a powerful Boston legal baron, to Jack Marino, a handsome but little known, up-and-coming Assistant District Attorney. Conspicuously absent was any mention of Jack's family pedigree. Because he had none.

Their photo had appeared everywhere. The *Tribune*. The *Record*. Five hundred people had attended the wedding, almost all invited by Abby. Jack hadn't known a soul except a few of his closest colleagues from the District Attorney's office. His brother, Matt, the only living member of Jack's family, hadn't been able to attend. Jack had stood beside his new bride, smiling and accepting congratulations meant only for her.

Lying on the bed, Jack wrapped his face in his hands. "Maybe it's the job."

"'The job'? Are you crazy? You're doing great at Daddy's firm."

"Not that job," Jack replied. "I'm talking about my old job with the DA's office."

"Shit." She sighed. "We've gone over this a dozen times. Jack, the DA's office was what, two years ago? It's ancient history. What's to miss? The thirty-something thousand you were making as a senior assistant? You're making five times that now. If we play our cards right, our combined salaries will be well over a million dollars a year. Not to mention what happens when Daddy, shall we say—'retires.'"

Jack sat up in bed. "I wasn't at the DA's office for the salary, Abby. I was there because I was making a difference in people's lives. And it might be ancient history, but I was once one of the best damn trial attorneys in Boston."

"Look where it got you. You were nearly killed. Another ten minutes, and I'd have been home and who knows what would have happened to me. Thanks for the memories, but I'll pass." She slapped his leg.

Jack caught his breath as pain shot down his knee.

"Come on," Abby said. "We'll try again. If you're good, I'll wear something nice."

Jack looked into his wife's eyes, trying to disguise his fatigue and lack of interest. "How about tomorrow morning? You love morning sex."

"I love anytime-sex, but, Jack, it's the second time this week that this has happened."

It was Jack's turn to sigh. "I know. I think a lot of it has to do with the attack."

Abby flipped away the sheets, revealing a body pampered by some of the best spas in Boston. Rising from the bed, she wiggled into a thick terrycloth robe. Against the lush white cotton, her skin glowed from a recent business trip to Jamaica.

"Look, Jack," she finally said, "maybe you should talk to someone. A professional? I want you better before our next trip."

"I'll be fine."

Abby grimaced. "Jack, it's all about you lately. How you were beaten. How you were fired. How you're not happy at Daddy's firm. You talk about the DA's office as if it were the magic fucking kingdom. Well, we're not in Kansas anymore. And that's fine with me."

"Let me pour you some wine," he said. He'd never met anyone as iron-willed as Abby Thorn. Except, he supposed, her father.

"Jack, do whatever you need to do. 'Cause I need to get the man I married back into my life." Abby slipped out of her robe. In seconds, she freed the belt from its loops and snapped it out in front of her, hitting him in the butt, laughing. "And back into me." She paused, her expression changing on a dime. "Because I didn't marry a loser, Jack."

CHAPTER SEVEN

Brad Sears, First Assistant District Attorney and most trusted confidant of District Attorney Trevor Cameron, took a seat at the mahogany conference table in the DA's office and surveyed the room where he'd spent so much time over the last twelve years. He hoped this was his last year and the first year of something bigger—much bigger.

The DA set his glass of Glenlivet with a flourish on the mantelpiece of one of the few remaining working fireplaces in the old County Courthouse. As a practice, he kept this luxury to himself. But on this occasion, glasses had been placed before the two men seated at the mahogany conference table in his office.

"Gentlemen," he began, striking a pose next to the fireplace. "Tomorrow, after three terms as District Attorney, I enter the last phase in my campaign for Governor of Massachusetts. You've both played a crucial role in my pursuit of that prize. And, if our polling is accurate, you'll play equally important roles in my administration."

Brad Sears raised his glass, unable to keep a self-satisfied smile off his face. Next to him sat Jeff Knight, the police commissioner of the nearby City of Mystic.

As the civilian head of Mystic's police department, Commissioner Knight was an odd bird of sorts: part politician, part law-enforcement official. He'd been appointed by the crusty longtime mayor of Mystic, one of the last of the old-breed Suffolk County power brokers. It had taken Knight time to earn the respect of the rank-and-file cops in the department. But he'd done it.

Knight's aggressive broken-windows approach to crime fighting had slowed gang violence and closed numerous bars and other establishments known to be dealing in drugs. Cameron and Sears thought his endorsement would go far since many in Boston, still awash in crime, wanted to emulate Mystic's approach.

And now his endorsement was a key piece of the law-and-order platform Trevor Cameron believed would sweep him into the Governor's Office.

Brad was as eager to make that happen as anyone. He tired of fighting that battle one criminal at a time. They could make a much bigger difference in the Governor's Office. Not to mention raise his own profile. It was thrilling to think of moving from litigation to policy making, from the county level to the state, and who knows from there? But first they had to get Cameron elected.

Cameron locked eyes with both men. "You've both made an extraordinary contribution to this campaign. And I can tell you this: Our time is now."

Brad smiled inwardly. He'd even predicted the phrase Cameron would use.

"But there's a problem," the DA continued. "Here we are in October, only a month out from the election, and because the Governor signed the first death penalty statute in Massachusetts in fifty years, the polls show we're falling behind on an issue we should be dominating: criminal justice." He paused. "We've got to own that issue. *We* have to be the ones people see as tough on crime."

For Brad it was simple. Though the death penalty statute had passed the Legislature by a single vote, they were in the middle of the Reagan Revolution, and capital punishment was an issue that cut across party lines. And for good reason. People didn't feel like they could walk down the street at night or send their kids out without worrying.

Cameron sat down with a sigh of frustration. "So, what have you two got for me?"

Brad Sears cleared his voice. "If I may. The commissioner and I have been thinking about something. The Governor *signed* a death penalty bill, but we could be the first to actually *use* it." He turned to the District Attorney, who looked to be considering the idea.

"It could work," said the commissioner.

The DA nodded his head, pondering. "Huh, that's not bad." And by the time the idea sunk in, he looked like he'd won the Publishers Clearinghouse Sweepstakes. He seemed a man transformed. "The first person put to death since the 1938 execution at the old state prison in Charlestown. Grim, but it'd be a hell of a headline."

"I can see the poll numbers climbing now," said Brad, trading a satisfied look with the police commissioner. "The commissioner and I have taken the liberty of researching eligible cases." Brad shuffled through a pile of files spread before him. "We've got three unsolved homicides that might fit the bill. First is a Harvard Law School professor. Walking near his Beacon Hill home at night, next thing anyone knows, there's a six-inch blade sticking out of his chest. Poor bastard crawled to a doorway and died on the steps. But it's dead ends everywhere. Boston Homicide Unit's checked out everything. No motive, no eyewitness. Nothing."

"What else we got, Brad?" Cameron asked.

"Got a doctor. Found dead in her car. Not a clue, so probably not our best bet."

"The hell we've got here? Open season on professionals?" Cameron said, looking over his shoulder.

"Watch your back, boss," Brad said with a wry smile, as he opened a thick black three-ring binder. He began to rifle through the pages, nodding as he did so. "Here's the one Commissioner Knight and I think is our winner."

The commissioner looked over at the file. "Thomas Regan, a father of three, murdered in my city. Case is a bit more than two years old now. And we finally have someone in custody."

Sears continued to read the index. "Definitely a murder that's eligible for the death penalty under the new statute."

"Kids look great before the cameras," said the DA.

"Case is almost trial-ready," Sears said, pushing the binder toward his boss. "Only problem, the defendant has refused to meet with an attorney, insists on representing himself. The assignment judge has given him a series of continuances, but she's ready to go with the next court date and simply appoint standby counsel to monitor the case."

"Just in time for the election," said Cameron, looking satisfied. "Jeff, what can you tell us about the defendant?"

"As far as we know, he's a nobody. Project kid from Mystic. Name's Lamb. David Lamb."

Brad Sears pushed away a legal pad that had been sitting on the table in front of him. "He's perfect. A no-name defendant, someone without the resources to fight this, so it won't bog down in endless pre-trial litigation."

"Someone no one will give a shit about," added the District Attorney, almost to himself. Cameron looked over at the fireplace, then refocused on the men before him, his voice turning somber. "The case would have to be delivered on a platter."

"Got that covered," said Sears. "Originally, as the commissioner knows, there were two suspects. A strip club owner, Mickey Nolan, and David Lamb, his employee. Truth is, either one of them could have done it," Sears continued, tapping a finger against the page as he skimmed his notes. "In fact, it's quite possible they both did it. But to break the case, we needed one of them to flip on the other. This strip club owner must have some big bucks because his attorney is Teddy Smith. We sought a grant of immunity for her client in return for his cooperation. And got it."

"Ah, Teddy." Cameron smiled. "She's made a great living fighting us. And we haven't exactly made it tough on her."

Brad had to admit the witness and immunity deal she brought forward felt a little convenient, but he wasn't going to look a gift horse in the mouth. One way or another, they would be getting a scumbag off the street, and another conviction would make others think twice before committing crimes. Then, if it helped them get elected, they'd be pushing policies that could make a *real* difference. He wondered if it was vain to enjoy the thought of getting credit for all that? He had, after all, spent the last twelve years working his ass off for this community. "There's a problem, though," said Brad. "With appeals, the actual execution could drag on 'til after the election. Maybe well after."

The District Attorney waved away the objection. "We don't need to fry the defendant before the election. We only need bragging rights. They can execute him whenever they get around to it. By then, I'll be Governor."

Sears and Knight nodded in agreement.

"All right," said the DA. "To get this case into court, he needs an attorney. An attorney who'll do just enough work to defend the case but not enough to win it."

Brad waved his hand in dismissal. "Most public defenders are overworked and underpaid. What's the chance he gets a competitive defense?"

The District Attorney slapped the table. "Problem is, as much as I hate to admit it, some of them are good. Really good. No. I've got the perfect attorney for this case. And the last time we saw him, he walked out that door." The DA pointed toward the entrance to his office.

The First Assistant District Attorney stared at his boss. "You can't mean who I think you mean. Jack Marino is so screwed up he couldn't try a case for us with an army of State Police protecting him. You think he's going to jump back into this?"

"A tad harsh, Brad. The man just didn't want to prosecute gang-bangers who'd almost killed him. Frankly, who the hell could blame him?"

"You did," Brad responded. "You fired him."

"Let's not forget, Bradford. It was on your recommendation. And when it was finished, not only had we unloaded someone who could no longer get the job done, but you no longer had someone snapping at your heels."

"Whatever. Marino will never qualify for the murder list."

Cameron shook his head. "The murder list isn't the issue. He's tried dozens of murders for us. They'll put him on the list in a heartbeat. Problem is, he'll never knowingly take on a death penalty case. My sources tell me he's barely a shadow of the attorney he once was."

"So, he won't know it's a death penalty case that he's taking," said Brad.

"And exactly how are we going to pull that off?" the DA asked.

"We don't tell him right away. Under the new death penalty statute, we have until the last pre-trial appearance to give notice that the Commonwealth intends to seek the death penalty. He won't know what hit him. And by that time, the judge will never let him out of the case. Not to mention it'll be too late to properly prepare the case," Brad said, pausing. "No. The larger problem is—what if he's not interested. Isn't he making big bucks at his father-in-law's civil firm?"

"All in the invitation," the DA said. "Marino was always a sap about loyalty. And very close to Judge McCormack, who, as you will recall, was his supervisor before she was elevated to the bench. Credits her with his early training. All that warm and fuzzy shit. Believe me, if he needs convincing, she can do it. She trusts me. She'll think she's doing him a favor."

CHAPTER EIGHT

"Look down there." Abby Thorn pointed through the floor-to-ceiling glass of her office, the rhythm of Boston's city life pulsing beneath them.

Jack obliged, his gaze falling thirty-seven floors to the street below.

"We're on top of the world, Jack." Abby came alive whenever she spoke about her work and the legal empire her father had built. "Daddy's not going to run the firm forever."

Jack, on the other hand, had been working at his father-in-law's firm for two years and hated practically every minute of it. His professional life was now divided up, packaged, and sold in six-minute increments. Every minute recorded, typed up, and sent to the billing department—where they would manipulate and stretch the numbers in an endless pursuit of the bottom line.

"Abby. I've worked nearly seventy hours this week. For what? To grab four hours sleep a night to do the same thing again next week. And the week after that. Look at us. Neither of us has a life." He turned away from the window.

"I hate when you talk like that. Soon we'll be managing all of this and sending out the bills ourselves." She moved over to her desk and picked up a file.

"Abby, it'd be a nightmare to manage two hundred and seventy attorneys," Jack said. "We'd have heart attacks."

She rolled her eyes. "Members of the Thorn family don't have heart attacks."

"Really?"

"Yeah, really, Jack. We give them," she joked.

Abby's intercom buzzed. She picked up the handset. "Mmm. I'll let him know. Jack, Judge Carolyn McCormack's lobby secretary is on the phone. Apparently, the judge wants to see you today."

"That's strange. It's been ages. I'll take the call in my office," Jack said.

"Don't you need to be in Essex County Court today?"

Jack shrugged. "I can have J. Owen cover it."

"Can he handle it?" she asked.

"Blindfolded. It's a routine continuance."

"Just be back in time for my father's dinner tonight."

Jack threw a look back at his wife. "I can't wait."

And he was out the door.

CHAPTER NINE

Hidden behind the curved signature of Boston's Center Plaza stood the County Courthouse in Pemberton Square. A 21-story high-rise had been grafted onto the stately original courthouse, like a forced marriage. Getting off the elevator on the seventh floor, Jack rounded a corner and pushed open the swinging doors that marked the entrance to the First Session courtroom 704 where criminal assignments were handed out and bail was set. The courtroom stood empty but for a single assistant clerk magistrate, who was busy shuffling the mass of papers generated by the day's cases.

Here the county's regional administrative justice, acting as a judicial traffic cop, sent cases to the various trial sessions sprinkled throughout the building. Once assigned, attorneys entered their appearances, formally signaling their representation, and prepared to argue bail and other critical pre-trial motions, all leading to the big show: Trial.

"Excuse me," Jack said to the clerk, a ruddy-faced man in a beige sport coat and khaki slacks. "Is Judge McCormack available? She's expecting me."

"One minute, Counsel." The clerk disappeared through a door to the left of the judge's bench. In a moment, he reappeared, inviting Jack to enter the Judge's lobby.

Sitting at her desk jotting notes on a legal pad was County Court Judge Carolyn McCormack, one of a handful of women who had blazed a path to the bench. At forty-seven, she was paper-thin with an honest face and an intellectual air. Her hair had prematurely silvered, adding a judicious maturity to an otherwise youthful face. A decade earlier, Carolyn McCormack had served as chief of the trial bureau in the District Attorney's office. She'd taken a special interest in Jack, guiding his career, grooming him for the fast track, always demanding more from him.

"Judge, how are you?" Jack asked, smiling.

"Jack, it's good to see you, but if you call me 'judge' again, I'll start calling you Mr. Marino."

Jack laughed. "Understood."

The judge stood and shook his hand. "Please. Have a seat. There's something I'd like to talk to you about."

Reseating herself, Judge McCormack tapped the keys of a large, boxy Wang computer, among the first of a few such machines in the court system. Amber text rolled across a dark gray screen.

"Here it is. Commonwealth vs. David Lamb." The judge paused. "Jack, I'd like to appoint you to represent the defendant, who's indigent and entitled to public counsel."

"What's the charge?"

"Murder in the first degree."

"Carolyn, I've never defended a single criminal case in my life, let alone a murder."

The judge shrugged. "Before the Governor appointed me to the bench, I'd never judged a single case. Hear me out."

Jack nodded.

"It's a bit of an unusual case. The crime was committed in August 1980, near the Mystic Housing Projects, but the DA only recently returned an indictment following a grant of witness immunity."

"Actually, I remember the case."

"Oh really. Any conflict?"

"No. I visited the murder scene right after the guilty verdict in my last trial. The day of the home invasion. There was no case anyway. No defendant. No weapon. Nothing. When I left the office, the whole thing was dead in the water."

"Well, I've appointed two previous attorneys, but the defendant refused to speak to them. Instead, he insists on representing himself. He's been jailed for nearly a month without bail since his indictment. Since then, he's come unglued, telling everyone he's being framed. He's demanding to speak to the State Police, the FBI, basically anyone in a uniform. I thought he might be having some sort of breakdown, but I've had the court clinician evaluate him, and she assures me he's competent.

"My biggest concern at this point is that the DA might take the defendant up on his request to talk to the police and grab an incriminating statement. So far, they've held off because they know that I'm troubled by the defendant's behavior and the fact that he's not represented. The decision to hold him without bail was made without prejudice, so you can re-argue bail." She swiveled in her chair and looked out her window at the plaza below, then returned to Jack. "I'd like you to accept my appointment on his behalf and enter an appearance before he talks to anyone."

"Carolyn," Jack said, his mouth set. "I have a job. Besides, I'm not the right person for—"

Judge McCormack held up a hand. "Jack, you haven't been in a criminal courtroom since you left the DA's office. And—if I may be frank?"

"Of course."

"Some of us think it's time you get back into the fight."

Jack's face began a slow burn. "Why not appoint another attorney off the county murder list? There're dozens of lawyers who could handle this case."

"Because I can be sure he'll get a fair trial—or a fair disposition on a change of plea—if you're defending him. That justice will be done." Her voice was soft, measured, and distinctive; her eyes clear, resolute, unwavering.

Jack shook his head and fingered his day calendar. He looked at the judge. His former boss's eyes told Jack all he needed to know: she was concerned about him and wanted to see him back in the arena. Back in the criminal law.

"I'm sorry, Carolyn. But I can't."

Carolyn McCormack's gaze seemed to penetrate the very seat of Jack's personality as the two sat in an uncomfortable silence.

"Jack, sometimes in order to do what we love to do," the judge said, "we need to do what we fear to do."

Jack absorbed this truth like a blow to the body.

"Off the record, Jack?"

He nodded almost imperceptibly.

"This isn't exactly a high-profile case, and I don't think the DA's office wants to try it. I actually think the case could resolve fairly quickly. In fact—and this is confidential—I understand that the DA could be convinced to break the charge down to murder in the second degree on a change of plea."

"A plea?" Jack said more to himself than to the judge.

"It makes sense. The evidence isn't terribly strong. Plus, the Commonwealth can't convict solely on the testimony of an immunized witness. My guess: it's going to be a fifteen-to-twenty-minute change of plea to murder, second-degree, and you're done. But more to the point, you'll be back in the criminal law—where you belong." She looked directly at him. "Can I count on you?"

The judge might as well have added the words *to do the right thing*.

Jack looked away. He wasn't ready for this and hated himself for it. But just as he was about to decline again, something inside him began to rip. A part of his heart that used to be fearless. A part he didn't realize had survived the attack bubbled to the surface. This might be his chance to reclaim what he'd lost: the opportunity maybe to be the kick-ass trial lawyer he'd once been. The thought was so powerful, his eyes began to water.

Jack raised his head to face his former mentor. To say *no* for one last time. Perhaps it was a whisper, a cry for help, a tentative first step—maybe it was all these things—but what he heard next frightened him to the bone. "All right. A change of plea."

The words seemed to reverberate inside him, and he had to fight the impulse to reverse himself. He checked his watch and changed the subject. "But first I've got to get to a function—in less than an hour."

Judge McCormack beamed. "Could you drop over to the jail for a few minutes? Lay down some quick ground rules, so he doesn't talk to the police. And, Jack, don't take no for an answer when he insists he doesn't need a lawyer. The trial date has come and gone a number of times."

"When's the scheduled trial date?"

"A month from now."

Jack splayed his hands out on the judge's desk. "Carolyn, you know I can't get ready for a murder trial in a month."

"Not to worry. A quick trial date will actually facilitate a change of plea. Worse comes to worst, I'm confident—as new counsel— you could get one last continuance if you really needed it. So, how about this? My clerk will give you an appearance slip on your way out. While you're here, drop into the First Session and file it."

"I won't ask you if you think he's guilty or not."

"The beauty of this job is that guilt or innocence isn't an issue for me anymore. My job is to assign cases for trial and ensure that each defendant gets a fair trial. A level playing field. And that's where you come in." She hesitated. "I don't know a better trial lawyer."

Jack's eyes met his former senior colleague's. Rising from his seat, he shook her hand, hoping she didn't feel the tremor he fought hard to control. "He'll get a level playing field." Almost as an afterthought, Jack asked, "Who's the trial judge?"

"The only judge who has an opening right now is"—Judge Mc-Cormack fingered her court calendar—"Judge Marshal Stone."

Jack froze at the name.

CHAPTER TEN

Late that same afternoon, business had picked up in courtroom 704 where Jack Marino went to find his former colleague, First Assistant District Attorney Bradford Sears. Suffolk County's senior prosecutor could be found there most afternoons, reporting to the court on the status of cases scheduled for trial.

It would be a good time to make initial contact. Talk about bail. Feel him out. If Sears would agree to a reasonable bail, the judge would almost certainly follow a joint recommendation, and Lamb would be free prior to trial. Free to assist Jack in formulating his defense, free to discuss a plea, free to take him to the scene, free to help Jack redeem himself.

Sears himself probably had some serious doubts about this case. For starters, the immunized witness had plenty to gain simply by pointing the finger at Lamb. And what about the physical and documentary evidence—the lab reports, fingerprints, ballistics? Which way would those point? The credibility of Lamb's accuser would be badly damaged if the forensic evidence failed to corroborate what he was saying.

Jack surveyed the busy courtroom. The session clerk called out the trial list with a drill-sergeant cadence. Attorneys sat in chairs inside the mahogany rail that marked the border between the public and members of the bar.

Jack spotted Sears on the other side of the courtroom, standing near one of the court officers' desks. Next to him, a court officer dressed in regulation black slacks and white shirt stood facing the public gallery at the back of the courtroom. A two-way shoulder radio emitted a steady but suppressed drone of official chatter.

Known throughout the Commonwealth for his trial skills, Brad Sears had the longest-running streak of homicide convictions in the state. When he wasn't kissing the DA's ass, Sears was a loner, a legal gunslinger with a streak of independence. There was something about his Eagle Scout demeanor and his blue-blooded good looks that made juries trust him. But he could be vengeful, perhaps the only real chink in his armor. If you crossed him, he'd take you on, come after you, using up a lot of energy, maybe taking his eye off the ball in his fervor. That was where you'd find the opening. If you were lucky.

"Still putting the bad guys away?" Jack said as he approached Sears. "Have a minute to talk outside?"

"Never thought I'd see you back here again," Sears stoically replied, heading out of the courtroom.

In the corridor, Jack said, "Brad, I'm going to represent David Lamb, and I'd like to get him home to his family pending trial."

"Home with his family?" Sears forced a short laugh. "He's going to prison for life . . . Are you interested in life without parole?"

"The only issue right now is whether he'll show for trial. And I'll guarantee that."

"Are you seriously suggesting that someone who's looking at life without parole doesn't present a risk of flight?" Sears asked.

"Where's he going?" Jack said, frowning. "He lives in the projects."

"Sorry. No deal."

"Look, anyone with money would already be on the street."

"Fine," Sears said. "File a motion, and we'll have another bail hearing."

Sears turned toward the double doors leading back into the First Session. "Drop by my office," he said to Jack. "My secretary will give you the grand jury minutes."

"Police and forensic reports? I need them all."

"File the usual motions," said Sears, pausing at the entrance to the courtroom. "You'll get everything you're entitled to."

Without Lamb on the outside to assist him, Jack's job would be much more difficult—even if the Commonwealth could be convinced to accept a plea to murder in the second degree. "We need to talk about this case," he insisted.

Sears stared directly into Jack's eyes. "We just did."

CHAPTER ELEVEN

The District Attorney's office was on the second floor of the courthouse. Jack didn't need directions. Emotions rose as he remembered the countless mornings he'd come to work, marching through the same doors, day after day, week after week, year after year.

The two years dissolved the moment he opened the door to Brad Sears's office. But nothing prepared him for what he saw next. A slender woman with lustrous black hair and high cheekbones sat behind the front desk.

"Summer?" Jack asked, barely able to get her name out of his mouth.

Summer St. Cloud looked up from her keyboard. She, too, seemed uncomfortable with surprise but forced a smile. "Look who it is."

Jack returned her smile. He registered the absence of a ring on her left hand—and became self-conscious of his. Why had he looked? It was hard not to wonder where their relationship might have gone if Abby Thorn hadn't come along.

"It's good to see you," he said. "I didn't know you were working for Brad."

"We work well together, actually." She rolled her chair back and stood. "So, your first case against the office?"

"Hard to believe, right?" Jack said, looking around. "Brad mentioned that the grand jury transcripts in the Lamb case might be ready."

"The stenographer finished them yesterday." Summer tapped a towering stack of bound volumes to her left.

The transcripts would contain a record of everything that occurred in the grand jury room—or almost everything. The grand jury, whose job was to determine if there was enough evidence or probable cause to charge an accused with a crime, was a creature of the District Attorney's office.

The DA educated it, indoctrinated it, fed it, and attended to its security, comfort, and continued existence. And nowhere was that symbiosis more practiced, more entrenched, than in Boston, Massachusetts, birthplace in 1689 of the first grand jury in America.

"Gonna take a while to get through all this," Jack said, taking the transcripts in hand. He hesitated. "You know, we should catch up sometime."

Summer's face was unreadable at first. Then as it softened, she said, "Sure. I'm hoping to hear you're doing better since the . . ." She paused.

"Oh, yeah. Right. The attack. Not the way I thought I'd go out of here. I don't mind telling you about it. But it hasn't been pretty." He paused. "Summer?"

She nodded.

"Thanks for asking."

CHAPTER TWELVE

Visiting a client in lockup was an unsettling affair. Jack eyed the gray metal lockers running down one length of the processing center at the Suffolk County Jail, a short walk from the court. A glass-fronted command center occupied the width of the room. Behind thick glass, correctional officers watched over rows of benches clustered at the back of the room to seat the public—almost always wives and girlfriends waiting on sons, husbands, and boyfriends. Each bench was fastened to the floor with large, chrome hexagonal bolts.

A female officer who recognized Jack from his days as a prosecutor waved him to the counter. Penning his name and that of his new client, he slipped the request card into a mechanical drawer that swallowed it whole, then stepped back to wait.

The metal door in the corner of the room engaged with a loud click, the heavy door sliding on steel wheels, revealing a narrow entrance into the prison labyrinth. The door closed behind Jack, leaving him locked in a room small enough to be a diver's decompression chamber. A loudspeaker crackled in monotone: "Deposit everything metal in the bowl provided: rings, keys, coins, pens. When I give you the signal, walk through the metal detector."

After off-loading his personal items, Jack stepped through the metal detector. He walked to the interview room, where plastic chairs were positioned along a low counter. The room was a glass cage, its door wide open so no privacy was possible. Unseen men yelled from inside the jail.

Jack checked his watch as he looked around at the concrete walls. How the hell did he get here? A former prosecutor. A proud one. And now here he was, waiting on a Murder One defendant. With nothing but a faded yellow legal pad and a pen. What on earth had he done in taking this on? Worse, he was going to be late for Abby's father's dinner if he didn't wrap this visit up quickly.

Nearly forty-five minutes later, a correctional officer escorted David Lamb into the room. He shuffled in, ankles shackled, head bowed, his arms clutching a pile of manila envelopes and assorted papers. His blue-gray prison garb had the paper-thin, disposable look of hospital gowns. On his feet were open-toed, backless slippers.

The man standing before Jack appeared to be in his late twenties. His face was pale but handsome, with a thin, chiseled nose and deep blue eyes that contrasted with his blond hair.

The defendant stood hunched over, eyes bloodshot.

"Sit down," Jack said.

Lamb sat in a white plastic chair. He lowered his face, his eyes cast toward the floor.

"I'm Jack Marino. The Court appointed me to represent you."

Lamb looked up. "Already told them I don't need a lawyer. I need to talk to the police. I can explain this, because I'm innocent."

Jack studied him. "There's one thing you absolutely can't do, and that is speak to the police. Do you understand?"

"If the local cops won't listen, I'll speak to the State Police or the FBI." Lamb's voice notched higher.

An officer rapped on the glass, pointing at Lamb. "Want him removed?" came a disembodied voice through the loudspeaker.

Shaking his head, Jack turned back to his client. "Listen, the police don't give a shit about you. Do you think you can just call up the State Police or the FBI, and they're going to run down here to chat? Even if they agreed to talk, they're only going to give your statement to the prosecutor. You need to understand something: the police and the prosecutor are on the same team—they've picked their defendant, and it's you. As far as they're concerned, this crime is already solved. The only step left is your conviction. Start talking, and you'll play right into their hands."

Lamb stood, pacing crab-like in shackles. "But I'm innocent. I can make them understand." His voice began to crack.

"Look, if you're innocent, you don't have to worry." Jack cursed himself the moment the words fell from his lips. Like all criminal lawyers, he'd lost cases he should've won and won cases he should've lost, a frightening reality in the criminal justice system. He moved on quickly. "The police aren't going to make a deal with you. So, sit down and tell me what happened."

Lamb shook his head. "I've got to get home to my kids." He pounded his knee with his fist.

Jack sat unblinking, listening, evaluating. His client looked like someone who'd fallen through thin ice and was drowning. "I can call the jail psychiatrist and see if they can give you some medication—"

"No!" Lamb pleaded, cradling his head in his hands. "If you do that, they'll send me to the state hospital. Do you know what it's like there?"

"David, look," said Jack. "I didn't come here to argue with you. I came to help you, but I need you to answer my questions. Agreed?"

Lamb was silent.

"Are you married?"

Lamb shook his head. "No. The girls' mother's a junkie. Disappeared years ago. I don't even know if she's alive."

"What about your parents?"

"Just my mother. She's taking care of the girls. They're both nine—twins—and I have to be there for them."

"I'll need to talk to everyone."

"Don't drag them into this." Lamb looked scared as he said it.

Jack's pulse quickened. "David, are you being threatened?"

Lamb looked away.

"If you're being threatened, we can deal with it, but you have to tell me now."

Lamb shook his head. "What could you do about it?"

Jack had to think. Only the prosecution had the resources to protect its witnesses or place them in a witness protection program. The defense had no way to ensure the safety of a defendant. Or the safety of defense witnesses. Neither the cops nor the prosecution would lift a finger to protect them.

"We can ask for some kind of protection if you're being threatened." It was the second time Jack had offered assistance he couldn't provide.

Lamb's eyes turned wild. "From the same people you say I shouldn't speak to, right? The ones looking to put me away in a hole somewhere. Are these the people you're gonna turn to?"

Jack nodded.

"I've got two little girls out there," Lamb said, springing to his feet. "Little kids. How the hell are you gonna protect them?"

CHAPTER THIRTEEN

Abby Thorn sat next to her father at the front of the ballroom in the Parker House Hotel, trying to calm him down.

"Christ," Richard F. Thorn snarled, his face scarlet. "I can't believe your husband could screw this up so badly. On this night. Of all nights."

"Daddy, Owen was supposed to cover for Jack." Abby was just as pissed at Jack, but she needed her father to calm down. By not showing up at court—after she'd directly reminded him—he'd jeopardized one of the firm's most important clients. When they first met, he had so much promise. He dazzled her—and the other women in the office—with his striking looks and killer intellect. She liked that he was street smart and was certain she could smooth out his rough edges and turn him into a star. It had been harder than she expected. There were things he just didn't get, things that came naturally to the people in her world. She feared that she was so determined to prove his worth to her father that she had overlooked his shortcomings.

Richard Thorn shook his head. "At this point, Jack'd better come with an armed guard. So you know, Billings' company brings in two million dollars a year for us."

Abby fought the impulse to cry, something she hadn't done since she was a little girl, something she would not permit herself to do. She could barely hear the master of ceremonies as he began to introduce her father. This evening, the U.S. Bar Association would bestow on Richard F. Thorn the coveted Atticus Finch Award.

"Daddy, please calm down. You've got to go up onstage in a minute."

"Damn it. It was Jack's responsibility to anticipate every contingency. It's really simple. Money talks in this profession, and sons-in-law listen."

Abby took a deep breath. "Understood."

The emcee was calling her father up to the stage. The audience applauded.

Then came the transformation. Richard Thorn flashed a society-page smile for the packed audience. Before he left her to receive his award, the guest of honor turned back to his daughter, still smiling, and whispered in her ear. "He's fired, Abigail, and I'll make sure your fingerprints aren't anywhere near this thing. Even if they are."

CHAPTER FOURTEEN

With a sigh, Jack pushed one of the grand jury transcripts across his desk as the door to his home office opened. Abby stood at the threshold, an oblong splash of light slicing into the room. Even in shadow, Jack knew Abby was distraught.

"How in Christ's name could you have done this to me?" Abby asked, still standing in the doorway. "You missed a critical summary judgment motion. And the motion for summary judgment was allowed because no one showed up. Really?"

Jack stood up and moved toward her. "Abby, I arranged for coverage. I had no idea the judge would go forward on the merits."

"It was your responsibility, Jack. No one else's." Abby entered the room and tossed her satchel on the credenza. "Do you realize Daddy's firm could be sued for malpractice? Not to mention the fact that we've probably lost one of our most valuable clients."

Jack reached for her hand, but she turned away.

"Abby, Judge McCormack asked me to take a murder case. What was I supposed to do?"

"Easy. Say no. Is Judge McCormack paying your goddamn salary?"

"Abby, please. She's done a lot for me and has never asked for anything in return. Until now. As hard as I tried, I couldn't bring myself to say no to her. Or to myself."

Abby threw up her hands. "And to add insult to injury, you couldn't even bother to attend Daddy's award dinner. Where the hell were you, Jack? What's more important? Judge McCormack and this stupid case of hers, or me, your wife?"

"Abby, I wouldn't be where I am today without her."

"It was her *job* to train you." Anger flashed in Abby's eyes. "And do I have to point out how you really got to where you are?"

"That's not fair," Jack said.

Abby wasn't going to drop it. "'Fair.' Let me tell you about fair. It's not fair when the CEO of a major company we represent gets his dick handed to him because his attorney—who happens to be my husband—doesn't even bother to show up in court. And, Jack, judges are out the door at four thirty like clockwork. Where were you? You couldn't have been with the judge into the evening."

Jack looked at his wife. "Interviewing my client."

"Your client? Jack, you already have clients. We don't represent murderers at Thorn & Associates. In fact, we don't do criminal work of any kind." Abby put a hand to her hip. "So let me understand this. You were interviewing a murderer instead of representing your actual clients or attending my father's dinner." She shook her head. "What the hell is wrong with you?"

Jack felt a twist of regret, even shame. "Abby, I'm sorry. She put me on the spot. I couldn't let the judge down." It made no sense to tell Abby that he needed to do this for himself as well. He knew he'd messed up, but this was the first thing that felt real to him in a long time.

"There must be a hundred fucking attorneys she could've appointed to this case. Why does it have to be you?"

He sat back down behind his desk. He didn't know how to get through to Abby. "Maybe she's heard I haven't tried as much as a parking violation in I don't know how long and wants to help."

Abby's face contorted. "Jack, you yourself said you haven't heard from her in two years. Where was she when the District Attorney fired you?"

Jack took a breath. Abby had hit an exposed nerve. And she wasn't going to stop. She never knew when to stop.

With the swing of a brass pendulum, the sound of midnight reached them from another room.

Jack said, "The case is against my former office."

Abby came around behind him. "I don't think you understand the trouble you're in."

"Abby," Jack said. "Listen to me." He swiveled his chair to face her. "This case is different. Nothing the prosecutor put before the grand jury—the Medical Examiner's opinion, prints, ballistics—none of it connects the defendant to the murder. Yet he's locked up without bail.

"Of course he's locked up." Abby shrugged, her voice rising. "He's a murderer, Jack."

"No. You don't understand. I think I can prove he's not. All they've got is one so-called witness."

"You didn't go into court for one of my father's most important clients. I can assure you you're not going into court on behalf of a killer."

"Abby, it's too late," Jack said. "I already took the case."

"Well, untake it. You have a job. You have responsibilities. You can't take advantage just because I'm your wife. My father wants to fire you. If I'm a particularly good ass-kisser, I might be able to talk him into only suspending you. That would actually look pretty good, not to mention scare the shit out of all the other associates at the firm. That will drive our billables up, for sure. In fact, that's how I'll sell it to him. No favoritism here. Son-in-law does his sentence, so to speak. And then, with all the appropriate apologies, etcetera,

etcetera, I'll get you back—on probation." Abby turned to leave the room.

Jack stared at the wife he thought he knew. *Untake it.* He'd already lost his self-respect once, and she was asking him to give it up again.

PART III

PRE-TRIAL

CHAPTER FIFTEEN

"Your Honor," bellowed the session clerk, "the case of Commonwealth vs. Lamb in the matter of the defendant's motion for pre-trial investigative funds." With a shuffling motion, the clerk handed the case file up to County Court Judge Marshal Stone.

A former state representative and veteran of the trial court, Judge Stone had made his bones in the District Court and, later, sat for years in almost every session of the County Court in the state. At sixty-seven, he looked more like eighty-three. Crusty and gnarled, his snow-white hair long and unruly, he ruled his courtroom with an iron fist. His nickname was Poker Chip, an unaffectionate reference to his acrimonious ascent to the bench, propelled by a powerful Boston politician who'd held hostage a multibillion-dollar state budget until Stone received his judgeship. Ever since, Judge Stone had been tossing people in prison as fast as he could bang his beloved gavel.

Defense attorneys did everything possible to avoid him. Like every other prosecutor, Jack had always tried to get in front of him. Until the Latham case.

Jack advanced toward the bench alongside Assistant District Attorney Brad Sears. "Your Honor, Attorney Jack Marino. I represent the defendant in this case. I have a motion for investigative funds."

"I know who you are, Counsel." Judge Stone tilted back in his chair, his eyes fixed on Jack. "How much are you looking for?"

"The defendant asks for four thousand dollars, Your Honor."

"That's outrageous, Mr. Marino," said the judge.

"Not at all, Your Honor." Jack laid his motion on the table before him. "The defendant is indigent, as you know, and is being held in jail pending trial. His family has nothing, and they're powerless to investigate this case."

"Mr. Marino, I'll give you one thousand dollars." Judge Stone raised his gavel.

Jack leaned toward the bench. "Your Honor, the defendant is charged with murder in the first degree. He's facing life without parole."

The judge glared down at Jack. "I can read the indictment, Counsel. And I'm well aware of the punishment for murder. I've been sitting on this bench longer than you've been alive." Judge Stone pressed down on the old mahogany bench with the bony heels of his hands.

"But, Your Honor, one thousand dollars won't buy any more than ten hours of investigative services," said Jack. "That places an impossible burden on my client."

"Actually, the burden is on the Commonwealth." Judge Stone shuffled the papers before him.

Jack looked down at his motion papers and the supporting affidavits lying on the table before him. He held his tongue, reminding himself of the importance of these funds to his client.

"Your Honor, the Commonwealth has unlimited access to every possible resource: the State Police, local police, forensic labs, the list goes on. The defendant has nothing."

The prosecutor, Brad Sears, had no standing to oppose the motion but seemed eager to chime in. The judge's head bobbed slightly.

"What the DA spends his money on is his business. The state doesn't have unlimited funds available to it. Four thousand dollars is out of the question."

Jack locked eyes with the judge.

"Judge, if you can't allow a full four thousand, at least authorize three thousand?"

"I'll give you one thousand dollars. Not another penny." Judge Stone turned from one attorney to the other.

Jack refused to cede the point. "Judge, at a minimum, we need a private investigator and a ballistics expert to review the Commonwealth's findings."

"Why would you need a ballistics expert?" asked Stone.

"We need a ballistics expert to discuss, among other things, the implications of the entry and exit wounds. All of which are relevant to who shot the victim."

Judge Stone asked, "Do you consider the entry and exit wounds to be issues in this case, Mr. Sears?"

Sears looked pleased to have a reason to hear his own voice. "Not as far as the Commonwealth is concerned," he said. "It's an open and shut case. The defendant shot the victim."

"Judge, this is outrageous. It's not for the Commonwealth to decide what's relevant. A defendant who wasn't indigent would spend thousands on pre-trial investigation."

The judge tapped his watch. "It's now nine hundred dollars," the judge barked in a raspy voice, striking the bench with his gavel. "For every additional minute you stand here, it goes down one hundred dollars."

"This is outrageous. Note my objection," Jack said. "But I have a right to be heard on bail."

"No bail," Stone said. "He's charged with murder in the first degree."

"I wish to be heard," Jack insisted.

"Actually, I've heard just about enough from you. Mr. Clerk, call the next case."

*   *   *

Nine hundred dollars and no bail. The judge had gone out of his way to humiliate him, Jack realized, as the heavy courtroom doors swung shut behind him.

Jack's battle with Judge Stone stretched back seven years to the Latham case: a 15-year-old girl raped and murdered, the 26-year-old son of a senior state senator accused of the crime—a senator with whom Stone had served in the Legislature before he was named to the bench.

The Boston newspapers had covered the trial daily. It had been Jack Marino's first murder trial, and when the forewoman said "Guilty," the defendant's mother had screamed and collapsed. Stone, banging his gavel and calling for order, had sentenced the defendant to life imprisonment without any possibility of parole as required under Massachusetts law. When the lead defense counsel asked for a stay of sentence pending appeal, Jack had objected loudly, against Judge Stone's expectation. In the face of the objection, Stone was forced to deny the stay and sent his former colleague's son to prison. He'd never forgotten.

Nor, Jack thought, would Stone ever forgive him.

CHAPTER SIXTEEN

The law offices of Theresa "Teddy" Smith sat perched like a crow's nest at the end of a graying pier off Commercial Street on the edge of Boston's North End. Built on pilings, the old building faced a fashionable swath of Boston's waterfront, a stone's throw from The Old North Church, lights from which centuries earlier had warned Paul Revere that the British were coming. Rumor had it that Smith had taken the property as a fee for successfully defending murder charges brought against the son of a popular Boston restaurateur. Bay State law forbade criminal defense attorneys from using contingent fee agreements, and the Board of Professional Responsibility—the legal watchdog agency—would certainly have pursued this. But there was no proof. Nonetheless, many in the legal community agreed privately that Smith would be parking her law books on a far less pricey slice of Boston real estate had she lost that case.

Jack sat impatiently in the plush waiting room. For two days, a secretary had rebuffed his calls to the renowned attorney, who had represented bar owner Mickey Nolan in his successful quest for an immunity deal that fingered David Lamb.

What had happened before Nolan saw the grand jury? In Massachusetts, the law prohibited a defense attorney from accompanying a client into a grand jury room, except in the rarest of circumstances.

Jack had the transcripts, of course. But they wouldn't reveal what had taken place in the corridor outside the grand jury room, prior to Lamb testifying.

It wasn't unusual for a recently retained defense attorney to request a delay in testimony until lawyer and client had spoken. But Smith had arrived at the courthouse while Lamb was still testifying before the grand jury, stating under oath that he hadn't been there on the night in question, just as he and Nolan had agreed. And immediately after she arrived, Nolan had invoked the Fifth Amendment, his privilege against self-incrimination. Coincidence? Jack didn't think so.

Lamb should have taken the Fifth, too, but instead he lied about what had happened. By perjuring himself, he'd dug himself into a hole: It doesn't matter what the lie is. Once the prosecutor has you lying under oath—about anything—the DA only has to say in closing, "If the defendant lied about one thing, what else is he lying about?"

Jack had another reason to be skeptical about Mickey Nolan's immunity deal. Usually, when a witness clammed up before a grand jury, prosecutors tripped over themselves to force the witness to comply through criminal contempt proceedings. But no one had tripped over anyone in this case. There wasn't even a hint that the Commonwealth had sought contempt. Instead, after a two-year investigation that didn't produce as much as a single lead, Nolan got immunity and David Lamb was indicted for murder in the first degree.

No, more was here than met the eye. It would be worth the wait to learn what.

Thirty-five minutes later, the celebrated attorney deigned to make her appearance. "Awfully sorry," she said, strolling over to Jack with a look of practiced sincerity. "I've had some unexpected business to take care of."

"I'm sure you're very busy," Jack said, standing to shake her hand. "I won't take much of your time."

Once seated in a black leather chair behind a grand mahogany desk, Smith waved Jack to an overstuffed Queen Anne chair, then picked up a blinking light on her phone. "I won't be a minute. Emergency, I'm afraid."

Smith was a plump but attractive woman, somewhere in her early fifties, with the affable air of a person who could talk her way in or out of anything. She wore round tortoiseshell glasses, a sharp black suit with charcoal pinstripes, and a tan that looked a good two inches thick. Her hair was short and silvered on the sides.

Jack surveyed the overdone opulence of Smith's palatial inner office. Smith had stocked the place with a carload of antique furniture. Original watercolors occupied three walls. The fourth was devoted to engraved plaques of newspaper articles highlighting her victories. Plush Oriental rugs hugged the richly polished wood floors.

Smith must have sensed Jack's interest. "And they say crime doesn't pay," she said, hanging up the phone with a laugh.

Jack didn't laugh in return. He noticed Smith tended to look away when she spoke, a habit of so many attorneys.

"Weren't you a prosecutor once?" Smith asked.

"Yeah, though I've been out for a while."

"I'm surprised we didn't come up against each other."

"Most defense attorneys did their best to avoid me."

"Good at it, huh?" Smith used her hands a lot when she spoke, enough to show a gleaming, stainless-steel Swiss Tissot watch on her left wrist.

"I wasn't very kind with my sentencing recommendations."

"And what are you doing now?" Smith asked.

"Civil practice, mostly," he answered.

"Oh, decided to go for the big bucks, did you?" Smith said. "Let us lowly servants of the criminal law fight for the few crumbs that fall from your table."

"Something like that," Jack said. "I understand you represented Mickey Nolan before the grand jury in the Lamb prosecution. How'd you come to do that?"

Smith seemed unaccustomed to such direct questions. "Best as I recall, he just called me up. After you practice twenty-five years in this town, your name gets around."

"I'm sure it does," Jack said. "Nolan manages The Treasure Chest, doesn't he?"

"Actually, he owns it. Crazy places, those skin clubs." Smith whistled. "Sex always sells."

"I understand the case went well for you."

Smith shrugged. "Piece of cake. I was retained at the last second, as I recall. Talked to my client outside the grand jury room for a few minutes, told him to take the Fifth. Turns out the First Assistant District Attorney thought your guy was the shooter from the beginning. Before I knew it, I had the DA's office chasing me with an offer of immunity. What was I supposed to do? Turn it down?"

Smith rearranged some papers on her desk, revealing a brass desk blotter that gleamed like gold. "Are you appointed counsel or privately retained in this case?"

"Appointed."

Smith looked relieved, as if she could count on less of a fight from a court-appointed attorney like Jack. "Thought so. Your guy's a project kid, isn't he?"

"A single father raising twin girls."

"Tough place to grow up. I've seen a lot of kids go bad in the projects. Black. White. Hispanic. Doesn't matter. That's what happens when you grow up with no values. As I always say, big fuck-ups make little fuck-ups." The same laugh again.

Jack eyed Smith, who looked everywhere but at Jack. "Lamb says he arrived at the grand jury room with your client. Is that how you remember it?"

"I can't recall."

"Your guy kept his mouth shut for two years. Why didn't he spill the secret sooner if he knew who the murderer was?"

"Told me he was afraid of your client."

Smith leaned back, re-crossed her legs, her three-hundred-dollar Gucci pumps gleaming. "You know, if I were you, I'd look into a plea. Maybe Brad Sears would agree to murder in the second degree. That way, your guy would be eligible for parole in fifteen years—if he kept his nose clean in the joint and did his time right."

"Just in time to celebrate his forty-second birthday," Jack said.

"It's not like *you* have to do the time." The chuckle again, and a nod toward the clock. "I wish I could spend more time with you. But I'm afraid I've got a hell of an afternoon."

Jack figured he'd go for broke. "Risky business flipping a client, isn't it?"

Smith leaned forward. "No one flipped anyone," she said. "One needs to be careful when making certain accusations in this profession."

"I've heard that once you flip someone—you know, convince a client to inform on someone else—the wise guys on the street will never trust you again," Jack replied.

Smith spoke slowly. "Understand something. My client was never a suspect in this case. The way I figure it, the police were looking at your guy from the get-go. As you know, I've got an obligation to zealously represent my client." Smith's features softened, her demeanor reverting from machine-gun intensity to relaxed confidence.

"If I didn't accept the grant of immunity, I'd be guilty of ineffective assistance of counsel now, wouldn't I?"

"How do you know it wasn't your client who pulled the trigger?" Jack asked.

"You know that's a question we lawyers don't ask ourselves."

"I do."

She shrugged. "Not in his character. Look at his record. Guy's squeaky clean. Smith placed her hands on the arms of her chair, readying herself to leave. "I'm sure you're wishing you could say the same."

"Meaning?"

"I assume you've checked your own client's record by now."

"I was recently appointed," Jack said, caught off guard. "Of course, I intend to."

"I represented your client on a felony conviction for unlawful possession of a handgun. Fresh one, too. Not long before the murder."

Jack's heart sank.

"For my money, you're going to look pretty foolish arguing to the jury that Lamb couldn't possibly have done this crime. He's a felon with a firearm conviction."

Smith stood, grabbing her Hermes Birkin bag from her desk. She walked across the office and held the door open for Jack. "Don't worry. We've all been there. Remember, as defense counsel, we're all on the same side," she said, with the same laugh she'd begun their conversation with.

*   *   *

What a rookie mistake. Hours later, working alone out of his home office while Abby continued to negotiate his return to the firm, Jack still felt the sting of embarrassment. By failing to check his client's record, he'd broken a cardinal rule of defense practice: Never assume anything. Jack smelled fear, his constant, familiar foe.

Far from clarifying the Lamb case, his meeting with Attorney Smith had made things worse. In a brief phone call to David Lamb's mother, Ann, Jack learned that a lawyer hired by The Treasure Chest had pleaded Lamb out on the gun charge shortly before Tommy Regan's murder. Teddy Smith fit her description exactly. Why hadn't Lamb told Jack?"

Smith had made everything sound so simple, as though she'd been in the right place at the right time. Getting to the grand jury just in time to tell her client to take the Fifth. Catching a grant of immunity for Nolan offered by a willing prosecutor.

Determined not to fumble again, Jack checked Lamb's record with the Probation Department. Just six months before the murder of Thomas Regan, Lamb pleaded guilty to a reduced charge of unlawful possession of a firearm. Though he'd managed to avoid jail because of the charge concession, he still had a felony on his record. The only bright spot: A quick check of police reports revealed that the gun was still in police custody on the date of Regan's murder, so it couldn't have been used to commit the crime. But still, the conviction would haunt them.

According to Ann Lamb, her son had been working part-time at The Treasure Chest for at least a year before his friend's murder, washing dishes, mopping floors. Grunt work. One night after the club had closed, some local cops muscled their way into the strip club. Out of nowhere, it seemed, a cop had asked Lamb to consent to a search of his car, a faded-blue Ford Escort parked behind the bar. With nothing to hide and his boss, Mickey Nolan, looking over his shoulder, Lamb had given the go-ahead. Moments later, the officer thrust his hand under the seat and pulled out a nickel-plated .38-caliber handgun. Lamb was arrested, booked, and released from police custody later that night, still protesting that he'd never seen the weapon before in his life.

Lamb couldn't afford a private attorney so words couldn't describe his appreciation when his boss, Mickey Nolan, offered the services of an attorney. An attorney who'd promised to take care of everything. An attorney who proposed a plea bargain, telling Lamb that his own consent to the search had killed any chance to suppress the fruit of an otherwise illegal search and seizure of his car. Instead of receiving a mandatory one-year jail term for the unlawful carrying of a firearm, Lamb had pleaded guilty to the lesser offense of possession of a firearm. A felony, but it carried no jail time. Lamb went home to his kids. And happily agreed to continue working at a much-reduced hourly wage at The Treasure Chest to pay back Mickey Nolan.

Jack rose from his desk and moved to the double-hung windows overlooking Atlantic Avenue. Darkness had squelched the daylight, and storm clouds rolled in. Early evening traffic flowed below him.

Jack had envisioned painting Lamb as a man incapable of the gruesome murder of his friend Tom Regan. Though he had planned on a quick change of plea, it appeared he was looking at his first criminal trial in two years. His breath quickened and he felt a light-headedness descend upon him.

With a felony conviction, the case of Commonwealth vs. David Lamb had become considerably more complicated. An experienced prosecutor, Brad Sears would know his own case had a gaping hole: the police had recovered no murder weapon; the Commonwealth couldn't place a gun in Lamb's hands. A perilous problem for any prosecutor. But if Sears could question Lamb about his prior firearm conviction jurors would know that Lamb had carried a gun before the murder.

It was the next best thing to coming up with the actual murder weapon.

Keeping Lamb off the witness stand was one way to avoid this. But if Lamb didn't testify, the only complete story the jury would hear would be that of an informant. No, Lamb's best shot—if the matter went to trial—would be going one-on-one with the prosecution's star witness. A battle of credibility. Nolan's word against Lamb's. Even then, the trial would be a roller-coaster ride. But at least he'd have a fighting chance.

But Lamb could only testify if Jack excluded the firearm conviction from evidence. Of course, this put Jack and his client at the mercy of Judge Stone. And Judge Stone loved prior convictions: "Shortens things considerably," was how he'd once put it.

Jack sighed. Another confrontation with Stone, and he had no time to lose. Still on the list was finding an investigator who was willing to work for next to nothing—either that or end up doing the investigation himself, a daunting prospect he wasn't ready for.

Jack shut the door and headed to the elevator and the street below. He knew one thing: He needed to speak to his client, fast.

CHAPTER SEVENTEEN

"Absolute immunity? What the hell is that?" David Lamb asked from his metal chair in the interview room.

"A free ride," Jack replied. "All Nolan has to do is testify against you, and he's home free no matter what happens."

"Is this some kind of sick joke?" Lamb said.

"No joke." Jack struggled to maintain eye contact, the walls of the interview room closing in on him.

"He's free? He walks?"

"Free forever. If Nolan testifies in return for the grant of immunity, he can never be prosecuted for any crime regarding Tommy Regan."

"Even murder?" Lamb yelled.

"Even murder," Jack said. "That's absolute immunity."

Lamb's eyes filled. He wrapped his arms around his midsection, as if covering himself with a blanket. "Tommy was pressuring Mickey for money, so he killed him in cold blood. I was there. And now he's trying to kill me. Can't we appeal it?"

"David, if what you say is true, they've immunized the wrong man. Even so, it's irreversible. Once the DA seeks immunity and the court grants it, that's it. It's final. There's not a thing you or I can do about it except try the best goddamn case they've ever seen," Jack said. "It still won't put Nolan away, but it could save you."

Raw anger flashed behind Lamb's tears. "I should be getting immunity, not him. I want to make a deal. I want to talk to the police."

Jack leaned forward. He'd come too far to turn back. "The prosecutor and the cops have already struck the only deal they're going to make. And that's with Nolan. You're out."

Silence filled the small room, both men breathing with effort.

Jack spoke again. "Now tell me what the hell happened out there."

"You don't understand." Lamb's voice cracked.

"Actually, I do. I understand you're going to be convicted unless you start cooperating with me." Jack rose to his feet and looked at his client. "Why didn't you tell me you have a gun conviction?"

Lamb continued to hold himself, rocking back and forth.

As Jack waited on his client, a correction officer rapped on the door and entered the room, keys jangling.

"Sorry, Counsel." He looked at Lamb. "We're taking you down to ADMIN. You get one phone call. That's it."

"For what?" Lamb asked.

"You got a daughter, right? She's been messed up."

CHAPTER EIGHTEEN

The smell of Mystic Memorial Hospital jolted Jack: a mixture of solvents, of sickness, of institutional life, of sheet vinyl floors, of freshly bleached laundry. Rubber heels squeaking on linoleum floors. The clatter of medication carts. Patients moaning—all visceral reminders of his own hospitalization following his beating.

God, he hated hospitals.

"I'm here to see Wendy Lamb," he said quietly at the nurses' station on the surgical unit.

"Are you family?" a nurse asked.

"No. I'm an attorney and she's my client's daughter."

The nurse turned away. "I'm afraid if you're not related by blood or marriage, you can't see the—"

"Please," Jack interrupted. "Just for a moment. I know she's been hurt. I want to be able to tell her dad she's all right."

The nurse looked directly at Jack, holding his gaze. "She's a minor. And she's been hurt badly. But her grandmother is with her. She might step outside. She's been with the child for some time now. Room 32, just around the corner."

Seconds later, Jack looked through the open door. Wendy Lamb, a pretty nine-year-old wisp of a child, was lying in the nearest bed. Her eyes were shut, her right cheek swollen and red as if she'd been found frozen suffering from frostbite. Both legs were bandaged. Blond hair like her father's spilled out from a heavy layer of white gauze encircling her head. She appeared to be sleeping.

Ann Lamb, gray with streaks of blond, her face a mask of worry, stood on one side of the bed amid a tangle of tubes and other medical apparatus. Her head tilted down and to the side as she stroked a tuft of the girl's hair that had escaped from the cocoon of bandages. If Abby could only see this little girl, Jack thought, she'd feel differently about his decision to take this case.

Looking up, Ann Lamb noticed Jack. She left the bedside and stepped to the door. Another child, presumably the victim's twin, clung to her grandmother's waist.

"Can I help you?" she asked.

"Jack Marino. We spoke on the phone. I'm defending your son. He's beside himself with worry."

"Thank you for coming by."

"Do you know what happened?" Jack asked.

"From the little she told me on the way to the hospital, a car stopped by the side of the road. A man tried to grab her, and she turned to run away but ran straight into the street. That's when she was hit."

"Did she see him well enough for an identification?" asked Jack.

Ann Lamb turned to Wendy's twin. "Go ahead, Katie, sit down beside your sister. I'm going to talk to this young man." Ann Lamb stepped outside the door, dabbing at her eyes as she looked from Jack to her granddaughter in bed. "We don't know. She hasn't been able to talk since. Both legs are fractured, and she has a head injury. They say her legs will heal, but she's had three seizures in the last two hours." She turned away in tears.

Ever so lightly, Jack placed his hand on her arm. When he turned to leave, he felt sick. Who on earth would intentionally hurt a little girl?

And what in hell was going on here?

CHAPTER NINETEEN

She was Lakota, and her Native American beauty could steal a man's breath away.

Jack gestured to get Summer's attention amid the din of the crowded waterfront bar. As she walked to his table, several male patrons glanced her way.

Jack stood. "Thanks for coming," he said, her perfume, still familiar, reaching him before she took a seat. He was caught off guard by how nervous he felt. He'd told himself this was just two former colleagues catching up, and besides, if he could get any insight into the case, it would be worth Abby's wrath. Not that he could get out from under it anyway.

They ordered a carafe of wine, and Jack filled their glasses, trying to appear smooth and casual. A gentle Boston rain began, transforming the harbor behind the panes of glass into a runny blur of blues and grays.

"So, Jack, how *are* you?" Summer asked with a compassionate look that suggested more than small talk.

The question threw him off, but he knew what she was asking. "I'm okay. Well . . . not really." He brought her up to date: the fears; the places he couldn't go; the things he once took for granted but could no longer do. It felt good to share this with someone who would actually listen.

"Let's say I'm a work in progress," he joked.

"And Abby?"

"She's well. You know. Driven, on her way to the top." He thought about saying more but stopped himself. "How about you?"

"I'm good, thanks. I'm back in school. Pursuing a Masters."

"That's fantastic."

Summer raised her glass. "To better days."

They touched glasses.

She looked like she was about to say something but didn't.

"What?" he asked playfully.

The waiter placed a basket of thinly sliced Italian bread in front of them. They brushed hands as they each reached for it at the same time. Jack felt a shock of electricity before they both pulled away and laughed.

"You first," he said.

She smiled, but neither of them knew what to say. Was she thinking about Abby as much as he was trying hard not to?

As she tore off a piece of her bread, she turned back to office stuff. "I have to say I never thought I'd see you defending a case against the office."

"Not to mention a murder case," Jack said. There was another awkward pause as he searched for more to talk about. "I'm up against Brad Sears, of all people—who, it would seem, wants to bury my client in a hole for the rest of his life."

Summer said, "You know Brad. And that whole undefeated thing. That's all he thinks about." She sipped her wine.

Jack smiled. "I thought he might entertain a plea to something less than first-degree murder."

"I think they're planning to try this case." She paused. "Is the case defensible?"

"I think it might be." He told her a little bit about the case and about his visit to Mystic Hospital. "It's an immunity case."

"I know. Whenever the DA grants immunity, he assigns the case to Brad."

"It might sound cliché, but I've actually begun to wonder if this guy is innocent." With his own words, Jack felt the weight of his undertaking. "If he is, the office may have immunized the wrong guy. Worse, if my client is to be believed, Cameron and Brad immunized a killer."

"Is that even possible?" Summer asked.

"It's happened before. Remember that Norfolk County case? The jury convicted a guy of murder when the only connection between the defendant and the crime was the testimony of the Commonwealth's eyewitness, who'd been granted immunity in exchange for his testimony. After the defendant did three years in maximum security, the immunized witness came forward and confessed to the killing."

Seconds passed. "Am I putting you in a difficult position?" Jack said. He respected her and didn't want to get her in trouble, but at the same time, a man's freedom was on the line.

Summer smiled. "What do you think?"

"I'd be lying if I told you I wasn't curious about what happened before the grand jury in this case."

"You've got the grand jury minutes."

"I mean what really happened. The parts that aren't in the transcript. What you saw. What you heard."

Summer looked down at the table between them, then met his eyes and said nothing.

Jack refilled their glasses. "Were you there?"

She sipped her wine again. "I was."

Jack worried he was about to cross a line.

Summer looked out at the watery seascape, leaned back in the tufted black leather chair, and wrapped her arms around herself.

Jack stood, removed his jacket, and gently draped it over her shoulders.

"Thank you," she said. She took a long breath. "I don't know if I should be talking about this, but both witnesses arrived together: your client and the witness who was eventually immunized. Odd that they came together, because we subpoenaed them individually to arrive at different times."

"Who was scheduled to testify first?"

"The witness who eventually received immunity."

"Did they seem friendly?"

"Like they were going to a Red Sox game together."

"Could you hear what they said?"

Summer hesitated.

"Of course, I'm not asking about a private conversation. Only what was said aloud in a public building."

"Your client didn't want to testify. I remember he kept saying that. But he didn't have a lawyer, so Brad could speak to him directly. And they got into it. Pretty heated, as I recall. Brad kept telling your guy that if he had nothing to do with the crime, he had no reason not to testify."

"Did Nolan, the guy who got immunity, indicate he wanted to testify?"

"He kept going to the telephone, then coming back and saying he didn't want to testify. Finally, after one call, he said he would testify."

"Did Lamb ever go to the phone?"

Summer shook her head. "I don't think so."

"What happened then?"

"Nolan told your client to testify first. Said he would testify right after your guy finished."

"And when did Attorney Smith show up?"

"Oh, her?" said Summer, rolling her eyes. "She showed up while Lamb was in the grand jury room testifying."

"Summer, do you know if Nolan made a telephone call after Lamb went in?"

"Actually, I think he did."

"And Smith showed up shortly afterwards, right?"

Summer nodded.

He took a sip of wine and tried to act as casual as possible. "Did Brad know that Smith was going to show up and invoke her client's Fifth Amendment right not to testify?"

Summer drank more wine. "Please, Jack."

"If Brad knew that Nolan never intended to testify, then the whole thing was a setup to get Lamb to go on record first. Summer, I'm sure you can see that."

Summer said nothing.

"I'm probably going to find out anyway," Jack said. "He's obligated to turn over all correspondence between him and Smith in discovery."

She looked at him gravely. "You won't find any correspondence prior to the grand jury."

"Everything was on the telephone, wasn't it?" he asked.

Summer inhaled deeply and returned his gaze. Unblinking.

It was enough for him.

*   *   *

Jack dropped Summer off at the parking garage under Center Plaza. They stood there for an extra beat before Jack moved in for a quick embrace. So quick it was clear they were both self-conscious and unsure of what they were feeling. He was thankful for his workload. Otherwise, he might have invited himself to her place for another drink. Putting her in the position of rejecting him or being alone with a married man, a married man who was starting to remember just how much he cared about her.

He watched her walk away and considered the implications of her eyewitness account. And even more, what might have been. Clearly, the indictment had been a Teddy Smith–Brad Sears production all the way, fueled by the ambition of a DA hungry for a politically strategic conviction. Smith surely knew that Lamb couldn't afford an attorney to advise him properly. Shit, Lamb had been doing everything he could to pay her earlier bill. The case against Lamb was perfect: a one-horse race with Lamb never getting out of the starting gate.

The deal would not have taken long to set up. Smith would have approached Sears with the promise of a break in a long-unsolved case. Cards would be shuffled and laid out one by one until Sears felt certain Smith could deliver eyewitness testimony detailing the killing of Tom Regan. In exchange, Smith got Sears to guarantee that her client, Mickey Nolan, would receive immunity for rolling over on his would-be co-defendant. All in time for the grand jury to hear enough evidence to indict and for the newspapers to play up a tough-on-crime DA running for Governor.

The key to sewing up the case was getting Lamb to lie under oath, telling a story that was easy to disprove. After that, neither the grand jury nor the trial jury would believe another word out of his mouth. A lie, however insignificant, would be all the rope an experienced prosecutor like Sears needed to hang Lamb.

Getting Lamb to testify first would have been easy enough, Jack figured. From the moment of Regan's murder, most likely, Nolan had threatened Lamb or his kids. He'd surely threatened Lamb's job. Nolan would have assured Lamb that he'd be coming into the grand jury room next to testify to the same phony story they'd agreed on. And Lamb probably persuaded himself that the cover-up was no big deal. At least he hadn't killed anyone. Why would he worry?

Could Lamb truly be innocent? Jack wondered. An academic question for a defense attorney, sure, but one that had begun to stalk him. The case for the prosecution didn't add up. Why would David Lamb have killed Tommy Regan, someone he was close to, someone he worked with, someone he hung around with? Could Micky Nolan and David Lamb have done it together? If so, why? What was in it for Lamb? And for Smith? Turning—or flipping—a client to gain immunity could brand an attorney as a rat. The wise guys, those in organized crime, from whom she'd been known to make significant sums of money in the past, would shun that attorney. Or do worse.

A shiver ran down Jack's spine as he turned the car toward home. The October night was chill. Dark quarrelsome clouds capped Boston's jagged skyline. Atlantic Avenue was deserted except for the occasional pedestrian dashing to a late-night destination.

The digital clock on the dash of his BMW 320i, a birthday present from Abby, blinked nearly eleven. A heavy fatigue was pulling him home. But the jail was only a few minutes away.

What the hell, Jack thought. A late-night visit might shock Lamb into talking.

CHAPTER TWENTY

In Massachusetts, only two classes of citizens had access to prisoners, day or night: lawyers and legislators. The attorney-client relationship was so strong it could not be abridged at any hour. And legislators, acting as a check on the power of the government's executive branch, could inspect conditions within the Commonwealth's prisons at any time. Only rarely, however, did they bother.

Jack settled into a small interview room, readying himself for a long wait. The lighting was stark and antiseptic and reminded Jack of the operating suite they'd wheeled him into the night he was attacked.

Time was running short. Unless Lamb began to cooperate, they'd be steamrolled at trial. He absolutely had to get Lamb to talk.

An hour ticked away. Steel doors clanged, hinges squealed, phones rang. The heat was cranked up to a nearly unbearable level.

Fighting off fatigue, Jack was jarred out of his reverie by the noise of a moving elevator. Heavy stainless-steel doors groaned open.

What Jack saw startled him. At the rear of the elevator, the tallest of three correctional officers stood with his right hand clamped on Lamb's shoulder, firmly holding him in place. In front of them two other COs, resembling bulldogs on steroids, flanked a hospital gurney that carried a young Black man, motionless on his side. The inmate's head was wrapped in layers of heavy white gauze, bright red blood oozing through the bandages, his eyes staring blankly. He seemed conscious, but Jack couldn't be sure.

Oh God, Jack thought. Was Lamb involved in this?

The gurney came off the elevator first. The tang of male body odor and blood reached Jack through the narrow corridor and open doorway. The bulldogs parked the stretcher against the corridor wall. One of them ambled over to the control room and began scribbling paperwork. Finally, the CO who'd been holding Lamb's shoulder escorted him into the room.

"He's all yours," the officer said. "I'm locking you in, Counsel. I'll be right outside."

Jack felt a wave of guilt for assuming Lamb was responsible for the man's beating. In the harsh glare of the overhead lights, Lamb looked drawn and exhausted. He seemed thinner, and his skin had acquired a yellow pallor.

Jack extended his hand.

For the first time, Lamb shook it. "Thank you. My mother told me you went by the hospital to visit Wendy."

"No problem," Jack replied. "What happened to him?" He looked back toward the young man on the gurney.

"Guy from my cell block. They're takin' him to the infirmary."

"Did he fall?"

"Yeah. A bunch of times as they were beating the shit out of him."

Jack looked at the young man, no one moving to comfort him, the still-fresh blood forming a bull's-eye on the blue vinyl cushion beneath him.

"He inform on someone?"

"Are you kidding?" Lamb shook his head. "You rat on somebody, they'll slice your throat. He wouldn't give up his boom box."

"This was about a radio?" Jack asked.

"Nuh-uh. This was about saying no to the wrong guy—the leader of the Eighth Street Posse. Thing is, they gave him two chances."

"How's that?"

"The kid's either slow or retarded, 'cause the first time he said no they gave him a two-minute root canal right there in his cell. Tops and bottoms. Gone. Just like that. Spent two days in the infirmary and was back on the cellblock with a bloody mouth and no teeth." Lamb sounded even more tired. "After the first beatin', they could have just taken the damn box, but they wanted to make him give it to them. Fool said no again. This time at least three of the Posse stomped him for over five minutes before a guard came."

"Anyone charged?"

Lamb shook his head no.

"How does something like this happen without the guards knowing it?"

"It doesn't," Lamb said. "They heard it. Hell. Everyone on the cellblock heard it. The poor bastard screamed himself hoarse. You do what you gotta to get through it. Turn up your radio if you have one. Flush the toilet. The rest of the beating he couldn't scream no more, a little whimpering and the thuds from the kickin' is all you could make out."

Jack shook his head, an inner rattle spreading from head to toe. He felt guilty for not being able to get Lamb out on bail. He bent his attention to the reason he'd come.

There was no easy way to say this. "I think you were set up before the grand jury."

Lamb had a puzzled look on his face.

"Nolan had an attorney from day one," Jack said. "But he made you think he'd tell the same story you did, right?"

"Told me he would say the same things I did. That we didn't know anything about the murder."

Lamb's eyes met Jack's.

"Tell me. Who was out there that night, David?"

Lamb sank in his chair and began to weep. "They said they'd kill my kids. I know what they can do."

"But if you don't help me, I can't help you."

Lamb's eyes flashed. "My kids gotta walk to school every day. Look what's happened to Wendy."

"David, listen to me. At one time, I was a high-ranking Assistant DA, and I know some state troopers pretty well. These are guys who would do a favor for me. I'll ask them to watch out for your family. It won't be twenty-four-seven, but it'll be enough to send a message."

They sat in silence for a moment.

"David, if you really want to help your children, tell me what you saw that night."

Lamb let out a long breath. "Nolan told me to get down on the ground, to put my face into the dirt. Didn't see much of anything after that."

Jack's heart skipped a beat. All along, he'd assumed Lamb had witnessed everything. He rolled his head, trying to clear the accumulated tension of the night. This case was going to get even more difficult.

"You didn't see anything else?"

"I heard voices and footsteps coming toward us."

"How many people?"

"Two, three. I'm not sure. All I remember is Tommy asking for their help and then begging them not to shoot him."

"Try to remember, David."

Lamb stared at the cracks in the concrete floor. "It's all so jumbled. I can't be sure. I know I heard Nolan laughing, really weird like. But there was something else. I don't know exactly. It was like— some kind of electric sound."

"Electric?"

"I don't know how to describe it. Kind of like the zapping sound of high voltage wires."

"Like from an electrical substation. That sort of thing?" Jack asked. There was one not too far from The Treasure Chest, which could explain it.

Lamb nodded. "Something like that."

"What happened then?"

"I couldn't tell for sure. Nolan said if I looked up, I'd have my face shot off. I could hear Tommy. He was begging the guys who showed up. Then there was a commotion. Something went wrong. I heard the other voices. I didn't recognize 'em. Someone said, 'Do it.' Tommy started screaming, 'No, no.' Poor bastard started to cry. That's when I heard it."

"What?"

"A single shot," Lamb said, his whole body shaking. "There was no more cryin' after that."

"Do you remember anything else?"

Lamb shrugged. "I remember hearing someone gag. Out of the corner of my eye I thought I saw a shadow moving against the wall of one of the buildings back there." He slouched down in his chair. "That's when they hit me. I must have gone out cold."

"Where'd they hit you?"

"Back of the head."

"Did you see a doctor or go to the hospital to document the injury?"

"No."

"Take pictures? Anything?"

"No."

A long silence followed.

"I need more. I need you to ID the killers."

"I can't."

"David," Jack said. "The trial is coming up fast. If we can't identify the killers, the only thing the judge will be giving you is life in prison."

*   *   *

"Where the hell have you been?" Abby asked. She sat in the dimly lit kitchen, her blond hair falling loosely around her face. A crystal wineglass hung between the fingers of her right hand, classical music playing from recessed speakers. Neither the wine nor the music seemed to have soothed her.

Shutting the door, Jack placed his briefcase down and shed his coat. He looked at his wife. She was attractive in her signature chalk-white robe, its matching belt tied loosely enough so her robe barely covered her. Her expression was worried.

"You, okay?" Jack said.

Abby pivoted away from the table on her bare feet and moved toward the marble counter. "Someone followed me home tonight."

"Huh?"

"Jack, it's two in the morning. Where've you been?"

"Who followed you?"

"I called everywhere. No one had heard from you."

"Abby. Please." Jack tried to control his voice, hoping to deflect his wife's questions. "Are you all right?"

"Considering I had a strange car with two men in it shadowing me for miles, I'm fine." Her tone sounded less worried but more angry now.

"Look, maybe it just seemed like someone was following you."

"Six inches from the rear of my car." She placed her wineglass on the marble countertop, its base clattering a little against the polished stone. "Bastards tapped my bumper twice. Does that sound like my imagination?"

"I'm sorry. I didn't mean to sound dismissive. Did you get the plate number?"

"It didn't have front plates and never pulled in front of me." She took a breath. "Jack, I'm scared. It has something to do with this case of yours, I know it."

What Jack didn't say was he'd actually begun to believe David Lamb was innocent. Which, if true, meant someone else had murdered Thomas Regan, someone who had a lot invested in seeing Lamb convicted—and making sure Jack failed. But he didn't want to believe—and he certainly didn't want Abby to worry—that he'd somehow exposed them to danger.

"C'mon. We'll get through this," he said.

"A strange car—with two men in it—follows me home at night and *we'll get through it*?" Anger flashed in her eyes. "What haven't you told me about this case?"

Jack forced himself to speak softly. "Let me handle this, Abby. I'll call a State Police detective I knew from the DA's office and see what he thinks."

"Enough about the DA's office. If whatever you're doing is putting us in danger, I want you out." She narrowed her eyes. "You still haven't told me where you were tonight."

Jack paused. He'd always been faithful to his wife, but the evening with Summer had left him feeling guilty. "I had to meet a potential witness in the Lamb case."

"Since when do you meet a witness late in the evening?"

"Abby, it's a criminal case, not a boardroom dispute," said Jack.

Abby's voice grew determined. "And who was this witness?"

"Two people actually. Summer St. Cloud and David Lamb," he said.

Abby stood up. "The Summer you were seeing in Cameron's office?"

"Abby, she agreed to speak to me about a sensitive matter—at great risk to her own job security, I might add."

"Job security? For Christ's sake, she's a dime-a-dozen secretary." Abby flipped a strand of hair from her eyes. "And, Jack? Maybe it's your job security you should worry about."

CHAPTER TWENTY-ONE

The following morning, running late, Jack muscled his car in and out of traffic, heading down Beacon Street. His destination, a well-advertised breakfast fundraiser for District Attorney Trevor Cameron. Brad Sears would be there.

A little girl. In serious condition. It was time Sears understood what was really happening in this case.

What would Sears think now of the nest of vipers surrounding his star witness? Would he take a second look at this prosecution? Perhaps see it in a different light and realize that the office had moved too aggressively on this one. Maybe even made a mistake. Jack hoped the case hadn't hurtled past the point of no return.

He nudged the accelerator harder. Turning onto Boylston Street, Jack caught sight of the Prudential Center, pierced in the middle by Boston's first true skyscraper, a blue and white steel monolith that pushed back the Boston sky for fifty-two stories. Tires squealing, Jack plunged into the underground garage and snatched a parking ticket from the machine. He parked against a concrete wall marked in red letters: RESERVED FOR GUESTS.

Jack took the escalator three steps at a time, emerging into the money-green marble lobby of the Sheraton Boston Hotel, polished chrome and brass gleaming under designer lights, employees rushing around in blue uniforms. A long rectangular table stood outside the entrance to the ballroom where District Attorney Cameron would be spooning out promises as smoothly as waiters served up smoked fish, cheeses, and egg specialties. Behind the table sat two well-dressed women, one taking checks, the other writing out name tags.

Jack marched past the table, ignoring their protests. Inside the function room, a huge crystal chandelier, brilliantly lit, hovered above round tables that seated the crowd. The scent of coffee and bagels and lox mixed with the air of political expectation, the clatter of dishware and utensils floating above the din of conversation. At the front of the room, the DA stood at the dais, his familiar voice lambasting those who would be soft on crime.

Spotting Sears at a table of major contributors, Jack scribbled a note and handed it to a staffer, asking him to pass it on to Sears.

Pacing the rear of the room where attendees were sparser, Jack felt like he no longer belonged.

Sears stood, scanning the room for Jack. As he moved to the back of the hall, everything about him signaled self-regard.

"Jack, I'm in the middle—"

"This can't wait. One of my client's daughters was nearly killed yesterday."

"What?" Sears looked rattled.

"She ran into the street after breaking away from a man who tried to abduct her."

"Slow down. What makes you think this is connected to the case against her father?"

"David Lamb practically told me it would happen, Brad. This is why the guy won't talk. How am I supposed to prepare a murder case if the guy won't speak to me?"

Sears shook his head. "I don't know. Defendants say all kinds of things. So do kids."

"Please," Jack said. "This isn't a coincidence."

"Right now, it's speculation, Jack. Tell you what. I know the Mystic Police Commissioner. I'll make sure he puts someone on it. Has she been able to ID anyone?"

"She can't ID anyone right now. She's unconscious Brad, I need you to convince the DA to continue this case. Just enough time for all of us to take a second look."

"Are you kidding?" Sears said. "The case is ready for trial. You know the system. I've got my indictment. You've got your defendant. If he's innocent, a jury will say so."

"Look," Jack shot back. "You know anything can happen in a jury trial. Anything at all."

It was true. A single muffed response to a critical question, one of hundreds asked over the course of days, could flip the outcome. He'd seen a clever closing argument change everything. From not guilty to guilty in a heartbeat. He'd seen jurors refuse to be swayed no matter what the evidence showed. Worse, most jurors didn't have a clue how frequently trials were scripted. How witnesses practiced everything. What the jury saw was too often nothing more than a play performed by actors called witnesses.

"Sorry," Sears said. "This one will be decided by twelve in a box."

Jack stabbed the air with a forefinger. "Weren't we taught that a prosecutor's first duty is to pursue justice, not simply to prosecute at all costs? You're not seeking justice. You're trying to win another case." He stopped to catch his breath. "Worse, my gut tells me you want one more first-degree murder conviction before the election."

"Great speech, Jack." Sears clapped Jack on the back and moved to walk away.

At the front of the room, Cameron had finished his speech. Applause rained down as he worked the crowd, pumping hands, slapping backs, circling ever closer to the two combatants.

Traveling ahead of the candidate capturing crowd reactions, Boston 9 TV reporter Alexa Metranos and her cameraman reached the back of the room in time to get an earful as Jack and Sears squared off. Petite and attractive with short-cropped dark hair, the reporter turned to both men.

Jack looked Sears up and down. "How can you sleep, Brad, knowing that you may be putting an innocent man away for life. And as I see it, you've immunized the real killer. What's Cameron promised you?"

"What?" Sears asked.

"If he's elected. What's it going to be? Secretary of Public Safety? Department of Corrections? Or do you want to go to the bench?"

"Get the hell out of here," Sears said, trying to keep his voice low.

"Did you really think I'd just lay down on this one?" Jack asked.

Sears bit off every word carefully. "History usually repeats itself, Jack."

*　　*　　*

Jack's blood boiled. He should have known better. The County DA's office was set up to prosecute. The office camaraderie that Jack missed instilled a pressure to convict at all costs. At every turn, the incentives were to force a plea or go to trial. Worse, added to this already combustible legal atmosphere was a group of ambitious overachievers—all of whom would hurl themselves off the granite snout of New Hampshire's Old Man of the Mountain if it would advance their careers.

When a case got a rare second look, the question was usually "Will the office look bad if we can't convict?" not "Is justice being served by bringing this case in the first place?" Jack couldn't recall a single instance during his tenure when an Assistant District Attorney expressed the opinion that it was simply wrong to pursue a particular case. No one had shown the courage necessary to stop a borderline case. Including himself.

Sears's eyes had told Jack all he needed to know. The senior prosecutor was preparing for trial. And Jack had better do the same.

But he couldn't seem to focus. Judge McCormack had been wrong about this one: there would be no plea bargain. They had their killer, and it was Lamb.

He could think of only one way to get at the truth: convince an insider to speak to him—again.

CHAPTER TWENTY-TWO

Ninety-nine-point-nine percent of all successful criminal defense attorneys were drowning in paper. Juggling hundreds of cases, they scramble from one to the other, dousing brush fires like human fire extinguishers. "Trial preparation" was an oxymoron. The question was not whether everything could be done to prepare for trial, it was how much time could be stolen from a hundred other cases to get ready for this trial.

But Jack had a few things going for him.

First, he'd always been masochistic in his preparation for trial. He worked when his opponents ate and drank, when they slept, or played with their kids. If he had to, he could go completely without sleep.

Second, he had no other cases now that his father-in-law had fired him. Abby had pushed like hell to get Jack back, but he couldn't bring himself to grovel.

And, finally, Jack had another advantage: the gift of language. Since childhood, Jack could read well over a thousand words per minute, forward or backward, with near perfect comprehension. He'd prepared for the bar examination—a six-week process at a minimum—in ten days and passed it. He ate law books and the le-galese of appellate opinions for breakfast. When he showed up in court, no one—not even the judge—knew more than he knew.

Packed into a beaten-up, plastic milk crate, the Lamb file grew heftier by the day. Dozens of folders formed a motley collage: "Grand Jury," "Defendant Info," "File Memos," "Legal Memos," "Photos," "Statements," "Police Reports." And more. Although the autopsy report had yet to arrive, Sears was flooding Jack with the usual paper-based detritus of a murder case: police interviews with Nolan, Lamb, other witnesses; memos from the Mystic Detective Division to Commissioner Knight; evidence reports; the indictment; a pre-trial conference report.

Separately, the First Assistant District Attorney had sent over a stack of crime scene photographs. By long-standing tradition, blood and gore were generally admissible in evidence, a prosecutorial advantage Jack had profited from on many occasions. The gruesome photographs would be a powerful stimulant for conviction. Jack could imagine Sears's pleasure when he introduced them into evidence.

The jury would never forget them.

Sears had also sent a fingerprint report that compared Lamb's fingerprints taken at the time of his arrest with latents found in Regan's vehicle. They were a match, proving that Lamb had been in the vehicle. No surprise there. Lamb and the victim were close friends, traveling together frequently. Jack would have been surprised if Lamb's prints hadn't appeared in the victim's car.

Jack emptied the crate, spreading its contents over the condo's granite peninsula that he was using as a conference table. He grabbed his micro-cassette recorder, popped a cassette into the machine, and began dictating what would eventually become his opening statement. He focused on finding inconsistencies that would help him expose Nolan's testimony as a pack of lies. If Jack could convince the jurors that Nolan was lying, the next outsized hurdle would be convincing them that the District Attorney's office had granted immunity to a killer.

He created a chart the size of a pin-up poster, tacking key statements from Nolan on the left, then an inconsistent statement, along with its source, on the right.

Problem was, Jack found precious few inconsistencies.

And another big hurdle: Lisa Regan, a widowed mother of three young children, could easily trump minor inconsistencies. And a widow who believed her husband's good friend had pulled the trigger would be a very persuasive witness for the prosecution. The Mystic Police had had months to convince Lisa Regan that Lamb had killed her husband. How could Jack neutralize that?

Sears couldn't instruct Mrs. Regan not to speak with the defense, but the DA had taught every assistant how to accomplish the same thing: point out to witnesses how speaking with the defense might jeopardize the Commonwealth's case. And leave the decision to them. Jack was certain Mrs. Regan would be dialing 911 the moment he set foot on her stairs.

But even Sears wouldn't think to warn her about a call from someone else. Someone who wasn't on the defense team.

Lamb's mother.

Maybe Jack could convince her to reach out to Lisa Regan? Face to face, mother to mother. If Ann Lamb could get in that house, it might be possible to get over the firewall the prosecution had erected around Lisa Regan—and with luck, to win her over.

Finally, there was motive. The good news was Lamb didn't seem to have one.

Legally speaking, Sears wasn't required to prove motive. But jurors always expected the prosecution to make sense of it all, to justify the terrible finality of both the crime and their verdict. From experience, Jack knew that few people, if any, killed for no reason. Absurd or logical, imagined or real, men kill each other for money, for hire, for revenge, for greed, for jealousy, or out of the dark compulsion of insanity. In the end, every homicide Jack had ever prosecuted had been committed out of necessity or desperation, passion or premeditation.

If he tried this case right, the jury might be left unconvinced, their thirst unquenched, still asking that haunting question: Why?

Why would Lamb have killed a close friend for none of these reasons?

CHAPTER TWENTY-THREE

Spanning the Mystic River, the Tobin Bridge was in a perpetual state of repair. Workmen painted the underside of the southbound upper deck. Bright orange cones narrowed three lanes to one as Jack inched through traffic toward Mystic. Glancing over the safety rail, he could see the chop of dark waters far below.

Mystic is a dense spit of a city, the smallest in the state, wedged between Revere and Boston. The Treasure Chest was at the tail end of Broadway, a stone's throw from the murder scene.

Jack had always been surprised at how few prosecutors visited a crime scene before trials. Most of the ADAs he'd worked with would try the case off the paper in the file, using photographs of the scene if there were any. Not Jack. No matter how insignificant the case, Jack always went to the scene to walk it, to study it, to feel it before he ever set foot in a courtroom. As a defense lawyer, particularly one with little money for an investigator, this step was critical.

Pulling to a stop across the street, Jack looked at the aging strip joint. The few cars in the parking lot probably belonged to club personnel, the dancers and a few die-hard fans who couldn't tell if it was night or day. When the real entertainment started at sunset, the blacktop would look like an auto dealership on Presidents' Day.

The front door to The Treasure Chest opened. A leviathan of a man in his forties, dressed in a black leather bomber jacket and dark wraparound sunglasses, exited into the sunshine, and staggered over to a pearl-white Cadillac. Firing up the engine, he peeled out of the parking lot, heading north. The clientele didn't look friendly.

Jack hesitated, his pulse skipping. Maybe he should go in, mingle a bit, check out the place. Not today, he decided, and started the car. Just being here, seeing a guy like that, brought back memories of the beating he'd suffered.

Two blocks away, Mystic's public housing projects reared up from a sea of asphalt. The Lambs lived in a four-room unit in Building 4A, one of six squat, three-story red brick structures grouped in an L-shape around a courtyard, only a few miles from the government housing Jack grew up in. The buildings looked identical, gray with age and decay. Nailed to each were round, black-lettered metal signs that said "DRUGS" inside a circle with a red slash through it, its outer perimeter reading: "Paid for by the Governor's Alliance Against Drugs."

Near the side of Lambs' building, there was trash everywhere: old, crumpled newspapers, sales inserts, crushed beer cans, empty foam cups. A strong wind swept many of the items against the wall, the refuse clinging to the brick, the remainder swirling restlessly on the ground in eddies formed by each chilly gust.

Jack continued to survey his surroundings. On the right, an old chain-link fence bordered the housing project. Green-golden wild grass climbed the fence, growing through the rusted links. Beyond this, Jack could make out a railroad bed and railroad tracks.

The metallic squeal of a storm door pierced the silence. Jack turned his head. A little boy, probably about four or five, sauntered out of the building nearest to the fence and the railroad tracks. Tied to his left hand was a small yellow balloon. The sight lifted Jack's melancholy.

The projects seemed deserted, though he sensed people watching him. Dressed in a suit, standing before his BMW, Jack wondered briefly who the residents might think he was.

Not one of them, for sure.

A portion of the fence had been peeled back, providing an entrance to the railroad tracks. Jack walked to the opening, ducked his head, and stepped through the hole, emerging in a field of bramble bushes and more trash.

As he picked his way carefully up the embankment, the wind off the Mystic Creek carried the smell of heavy metals, iron ore perhaps, his eyes watering, his nostrils stinging. He scanned the sky for a plume of smoke that might account for the odor but saw only the rooflines of shuttered factories. After negotiating his way through twenty feet or so of brush, he came to the base of an old railroad bed. Rusted tracks wound east and west, disappearing behind the corner of a factory building.

Overhead, high-tension utility wires hung between old wooden telephone poles, a distinct buzz reverberating off the wires. Every few seconds, the steady hum was punctuated by a zapping sound that pierced the air. That could be the static Lamb had spoken about, the staccato-like hum probably the result of voltage changes in the wires high above him.

Jack breathed easier: he'd finally been able to verify one element of Lamb's account. Of course, that wouldn't matter much to a jury since the site of the murder wasn't in question, but it mattered to Jack. Under the Commonwealth's Canons of Ethics, which he'd sworn to uphold, he owed his client a duty of zealous representation—whether or not Lamb was telling him the truth. Indeed, whether or not he was guilty or innocent. But to Jack, the truth mattered, each confirmation another brick in the moral foundation he needed to build in order to throw his heart and soul into the case.

Across the tracks, maybe two hundred yards away, Jack could see the factory where the Mystic Police had found Tom Regan's body in that abandoned station wagon. He crossed the tracks, carefully walking the area where the crime had taken place two years earlier. What had happened back here? Why had a young father's life been snuffed out? For what? Who wanted to hurt him? Who stood to gain?

A cement embankment at the rear of one of the shuttered factories caught Jack's attention. Approximately eight feet wide, it was the only break in an otherwise bleak landscape. Jack walked over, the stench of urine hanging heavily in the air. The embankment, which sloped at a forty-five-degree angle, was trash-strewn with soiled clothes, old shoes, broken beer and wine bottles. But it was the only spot free of the ubiquitous, choking weeds. If someone lived back here, this is where they'd sleep, Jack thought. Off the dirt. Out of the weeds.

Jack checked his watch. It was almost four o'clock. Soon dusk would merge with the last light of day. Before leaving, he thought he heard faint sounds behind him. The tinkle of glass, maybe. Jack retraced his steps, navigating his way through the bushes, picking through the trash, finally ducking back through the hole in the fence. Still, not a soul in sight.

Emerging from the railroad tracks, Jack froze, staring at his BMW. He'd forgotten to set the damn alarm. The driver's-side window was smashed. Shards of glass lay in a pool next to the car, two of his tires slashed.

Reaching the car, Jack groaned. His briefcase was gone. And a raft of papers relating to the Lamb case had disappeared along with it. His thoughts racing, Jack remembered passing a diner about a half-mile back. Maybe he could use the phone there to call the auto service, perhaps catching a ride with the tow truck or grabbing a cab.

CHAPTER TWENTY-FOUR

The diner was 1950s-themed, a beat-up cross between a genuine railroad car and the hamburger emporium featured in the hit TV series *Happy Days*. Jack waited inside for the tow truck, nursing a cup of coffee at the counter, the smell of fried bacon and sausages permeating the establishment. The few other customers kept to themselves, huddled in booths.

"Tough area around here," Jack said to the proprietor, a squat man with a grizzled white beard. "My car got broken into over near the tracks."

"Goddamn kids," the man said, mopping the counter with a damp cloth, his apron a Pollock of stains. "Mean as hell, too. But believe it or not, twenty years ago, was even worse." As if in response to a question, he said, "Would sell the place if I could. But who's gonna buy?"

"Trains still run back here?" Jack cocked his head in the direction of the tracks.

"Not for a long time."

Jack nodded. "Looks pretty rough out there."

The man shrugged. "Nobody goes back there anymore. Not even the winos. At least not since the murder."

"Murder?"

"Young man got himself killed back there. Hear they have the guy who did it, though. So, things are gettin' back to normal."

"And the winos?"

"Haven't seen any of 'em since the killing."

Jack thought about the acrid smell of urine near the concrete embankment. "Must be a sad bunch."

"Seen a lot of them over the years."

"Did any of them talk about seeing the murder?" Jack had gone over and over the interviews with the dancers and other staff at The Treasure Chest, and they looked pretty thorough. He'd even called a couple of women whose statements seemed iffy. Nothing there, at least nothing they were willing to go on record with. If anyone knew anything about that night and would be willing to talk, it probably wasn't someone inside the club.

"Hell, I don't know," he said, pouring a cup of coffee for another guest. "Not to me anyway."

When the owner returned to the counter after checking a few tables, Jack asked, "Do you know where I can find anyone who might have been hanging around that night?"

"Nah, they came and went. If I had to guess the ones I knew who woulda been around back then, I'd say old Brooks, but he's dead now, and maybe Kenny, no idea what happened to him, and Crazy Nora. Haven't seen her in a while either."

"Crazy Nora?"

"Don't know her by any other name, but she was out there for years. The last holdout. If anyone was still around, it'd be her."

"Think she could've been back there at the time of the killing?"

"Was her home, mister."

"She lived there?"

A nod. "Been an alchy for years. Though the way I heard it, she was stone-cold sober until she lost her kids in a car accident. Turned out, the drunk driver who hit them—well, he might as well have killed all four of 'em. Somehow Nora got it in her head that it was all her fault 'cause she was driving. After that, she put a bottle to her lips and just pulled the trigger." He shook his head. "And kept firing. Owned a stool at every gin joint in the city. 'Course, everyone's got their own bottom. For her, the bottom was the street. Shame. They say she was pretty, once upon a time."

"Why there?" Jack asked, nodding in the direction of the railroad tracks.

"She'd been thrown out of every bar in town. Eventually, she couldn't keep a place of her own. So, she'd go back there to sleep it off. She wasn't hurtin' anyone, and the cops left her alone.

"She used to come around here and beg for spare change. On Sundays I'd open for a half a day, you know, for the church folks, what there was of them. They said Nora would walk into the church to shake hands when it came time to exchange a sign of peace. Not a soul would shake her hand." He shrugged. "So much for 'peace be with you.' Anyway, she'd come out back here, and I'd feed her." He gestured outside, behind the diner. "Looked like hell and smelled to the heavens, but I always gave her somethin' hot to eat. Problem was she couldn't defend herself, and . . ." He shook his head again. "'Fraid some of them tried to have their way with her back there."

"Assault?"

The proprietor shook his head. "Worse. Some local drunks heard she could be taken advantage of, and one night a couple of them thought they'd have some fun with her. Well, Crazy Nora wouldn't go along. Those degenerates couldn't handle the likes of Nora saying 'no.' So they splashed her with some lighter fluid, and—"

Jack caught his breath. "Oh my God."

"Poor girl was burnt bad. When she got out of the hospital, she didn't have to worry about men coming around anymore."

Jack shook his head in disgust. "Sir, I owe you an apology."

"For?"

"My car was broken into, but the reason I'm down here is I'm a lawyer, and I'm looking into the homicide. I was hoping you could tell me where I might find Nora now."

The proprietor eyed Jack warily. "Might depend on whose side you're on?"

"I'm on Nora's side," Jack said. "And those from her world."

The owner nodded. "Mister, I don't know anything about how that young man was killed, but if I can help Nora, I'll tell you what I told the State Police. After that boy was killed, the local police swarmed this place and kicked her the hell outta here. A shame, because that's all she had. I mean, she probably don't have long to go—if she's still with us at all."

"How do you mean?"

"Last time I saw her, she couldn't have been much more than eighty pounds. There's a limit to what a body can take."

An eyewitness, Jack thought. A long shot, but she was his only shot, and if she were alive, maybe she knew enough to pierce the veil of immunity the Commonwealth had awarded Mickey Nolan. A homeless woman, yes. A drunk, sure. But who else would be out by the railroad tracks in the middle of the night?

"Maybe with some luck, I'll find her."

The grizzled diner owner gave Jack a knowing look, nodding toward the train tracks. "Mister, there ain't no luck out there."

Outside the diner, the tow truck driver knuckled his horn. Jack shouted directions to his car over the howl of a wind that had picked up considerably. A yellow cab, its rear bumper bent and hanging inches from the ground, arrived close on the heels of the tow. Exhausted, Jack settled into the back seat and headed home, peering out the rear window at an area of Mystic that God had clearly forgotten.

CHAPTER TWENTY-FIVE

Brad Sears jabbed the intercom on his desk. "Summer, tell everyone I'm gone for the day, okay?" He started packing up.

Summer chimed through from her desk outside his office. "Brad, Assistant District Attorney Lincoln Dawes has been waiting out here for nearly an hour. Says he has to see you."

"Who's Lincoln Dawes?"

"You handpicked him to help you prepare the Lamb case." Summer's voice was low and amused.

"Oh, right. But only with research. What's he want?"

"He won't say. Something important about a report or memo in the Lamb case. Says you'd want to know about it."

"Shit." Sears closed his eyes, then opened them. "Bring him in but call me on the speakerphone in exactly two minutes. When you buzz me, say the DA called and needs me. Understood?"

"Yes."

The door opened to Sears's office and Lincoln Dawes walked in. At 28, he was a handsome slim Black man, his face chiseled, his dark hair shaped perfectly. He looked around, seemingly impressed by Sears's office and ambitious enough to imagine himself there in due time.

"What's up?" Sears asked.

"I heard the defense has been out searching Mystic for witnesses, so I went through everything, and I found something in the file," Dawes said. With a flourish, he placed a memorandum on the glass covering Sears's desk. "I summarized it for you and attached the report I found from one of our local Mystic Police detectives who responded to the Regan murder. I thought we might want to follow up on it."

Sears looked down at the memo and its attachment without touching them. His eyes focused on the attachment, dated two days after the murder of Tommy Regan.

"On this date, interviewed local merchants. Possibility exists that local transient of potentially known identity may have been present in the area at the time of the murder. Recommend follow-up. A female who may answer to the name 'Nora' should be questioned."

Sears stiffened. "Is this the only copy of the Mystic report?"

Dawes nodded. "Only one. I checked the file thoroughly. I was going to call Commissioner Knight to see if he followed up on it or ask one of our State Police investigators to check it out, but I thought I'd talk to you first."

"You did the right thing," Sears said. "There's significant jurisdictional pride involved in matters like this. The last thing we want to do is offend the Mystic Police Commissioner, who I'm sure followed up on this. Leave the memo with me. I'll call the commissioner and make certain that it's been checked out."

"Sure," Dawes said, looking slightly puzzled. "But isn't it Brady material? Should I forward a copy to the defense?"

Sears shrugged. The 1963 Supreme Court case *Brady vs. Maryland* was the bane of prosecutors everywhere. It required them to hand over to defense lawyers any information that might help clear a defendant.

"If there's anything to it, I'll turn it over to defense counsel myself," Sears told Dawes.

His intercom bleated, and he punched the speaker button.

"The District Attorney is waiting for you in his office, Mr. Sears," said Summer.

"Lincoln, keep me advised about any additional developments, especially regarding the murder weapon." After Lincoln Dawes had left, Sears rose from his chair, placed the Mystic Police report in his inner breast suit pocket, and tucked the memorandum under a paperweight on his desk.

CHAPTER TWENTY-SIX

Sears made a dash to the DA's office. "We have a problem with the Lamb case."

"What do you mean, problem?" the DA asked, hanging up the phone.

Sears ignored his tone. Cameron always worked himself into a lather before a press event. Tomorrow, they'd be hosting a press conference, and this case would help them solidify his tough-on-crime stance. Though Cameron went out of his way to appease the media, he considered the press an archenemy, waiting to pounce on him at the first opportunity.

"There may have been a witness to the Regan murder. A street person. I think we can assume it didn't amount to anything, since the commissioner has never said a word about it."

"What's our game plan?" the District Attorney asked.

"Best case, we don't need one. Street people are drifters. This one has probably moved on."

Cameron nodded, his face pensive, his eyes considering.

"But let's just say if it becomes a problem," Sears began, "the memo won't be around for trial."

Cameron said, "Fine but understand two things: One, we've never had this conversation. Two, we can't afford any screw-ups.

None. Check with Knight. Make sure there's nothing to the report. I don't want to give Marino anything to bitch and moan about. You can never predict what Stone will do. The old bastard can turn in a heartbeat."

"Consider this conversation dead," said Sears, trying not to sound stressed. "Worst-case scenario we're talking about some down-and-out wino, and who's going to believe her?"

"Her?" Cameron sounded surprised. He shrugged. "Whatever. Let's focus on our future, not the past. I need to work out my statement. If you sense anything unraveling during the press conference, interrupt me. I'll appear offended, but you go right ahead and correct me. You're a master wordsmith, Bradford. Just make sure whatever you say is accurate. Those bastards would love to catch me in a screw-up."

Sears glanced at the clock behind Cameron's desk. Before he left, he asked, "What about Lincoln Dawes? He knows about the report."

Cameron thought. "Tell him you checked out the report and there was nothing to it. At the same time, give him a raise. Oh. And put our newest rising star on the fast track. Tell him after the Lamb case, he's got the green light to try his first homicide case. Nothing too important. Make sure it involves a no-name victim, where the result doesn't matter."

"Are you sure?"

The raspy laugh again. "How many times have we seen this story played out? Lincoln will keep his mouth shut. Remember, it's that first taste of power that's the most intoxicating."

*   *   *

Alone in Sears's office, Summer checked the time. Almost six o'clock. As was her custom whenever Sears left for the day, Summer rearranged his desk, trying to impose some semblance of order. As she was stacking case folders he'd left scattered on his desk, the name "Lamb" caught her eye. A memorandum referencing something about a possible witness to the Regan murder.

Jack had specifically told her that her boss had said there were no potential witnesses to the Lamb murder beyond the man they gave immunity to.

Moments later, a splash of light from the office copier moved across Summer's face like a time-lapse video of a golden sunrise. When she was done, Summer looked around and doused the lights. With a trembling hand, she locked the door behind her.

CHAPTER TWENTY-SEVEN

"How long did you know Tommy Regan?" asked Jack, settling further into the hard chair in the jail's tiny interview room.

"I don't know," Lamb said. "Five, six years."

"How'd you meet?"

"Met at The Treasure Chest," Lamb said. "I'd come in once in a while for a beer. We just started talkin'. I told him the workers' comp checks weren't cutting it. Turns out, Tommy was on workers' comp, too. Next thing I knew, Tommy spoke to the owner, and I was making a few bucks doing odd jobs at the club. Before long, we just kinda hung out."

"What kinds of things did you do together?" Jack asked, pen poised to scribble along with the conversation.

"The usual stuff, I guess. Fixed each other's cars. Helped each other out. You know."

"Was money tight?"

"Money's been tight all my life. My mother does what she can, plus I try to get as much side work as possible."

"What kind of work?"

"Sometimes I'd help Tommy out on side jobs."

"What kind of 'side jobs'?" Jack asked.

"You know. Cash stuff. We'd button up an addition, redo a bathroom. Whatever it took to make some quick cash."

"Was Tommy working under the table while he was receiving workers' compensation checks?"

"Sure." Lamb shrugged, his gaze sweeping the concrete floor. "It was no big deal. A ton of people do it. Tommy had three kids."

"Yeah, and you had two."

Lamb looked away. "Whatever."

Jack switched gears. "Did you see Tommy Regan the night he was killed?"

"Tommy was at the club when I got there that night, around six p.m. I cleaned the place up, like always, and when I was done, we had a few drinks—me and Tommy and a couple of other people."

"Tell me exactly who was there." Jack leaned forward, his eyes on his client.

"The owner was there, helping at the bar, running the place. Rat was there, but he just sort of kept to himself." Lamb adjusted himself in his seat.

"Who's Roger Ferriter? His name appears in one of the police reports."

"That's Rat. No one calls him Roger. A major league whacko. Everyone steers clear of him."

"Did Tommy stay clear of him?"

"Rat's a tough guy," Lamb said. "But Tommy never backed down from nobody, so they kind of, you know, kept away from each other. At first."

"At first?"

"They got into a jam big-time one night," Lamb said. "Both of 'em were shitfaced, eyeballin' each other across the club. Stupid stuff like that, really, but then Rat kind of like snapped, came off the stool at Tommy like a madman."

"And then?"

"Tommy didn't really want to fight, but Rat looked like he'd kill him. Before you know it, they're breaking each other up pretty bad. Tables crashin'. One point, looked like Tommy was givin' him a run for his money. Till Rat grabbed a bottle off the bar and broke it over Tommy's face. Opened up a helluva gash. Blood everywhere."

"Did the police respond?" Jack asked.

"I can't remember ever seeing the cops at The Treasure Chest, but they came that night. Bunch of 'em."

"David, when did the fight between Rat and Tom take place?"

Lamb thought. "I don't know. At least a few months before Tommy was killed. That's when all the trouble started."

"Trouble?"

"Tommy came out of the fight with a beast of a scar on his face. He started telling the owner, Mickey Nolan, that he was off duty when the fight happened and was going to sue the bar unless he was paid off. Every time I saw Tommy and Nolan together, they were arguing about Tommy's claim that TC's had to pay him money for his scar."

"You mean like a dram shop claim?"

Lamb snorted. "Look, I'm no lawyer. I don't know what they call it. Tommy said the bar had an obligation to protect him because he was off-duty and was a customer at the time and they over-served Rat. Which they did."

Lamb had just given Mickey Nolan a motive. "So, Tommy was trying to shake The Treasure Chest down?"

"Yeah, pretty much. He even claimed he should own part of the club. It got crazy."

"Where can I find Rat?"

"You don't want to. He's a power lifter. A dangerous one. Hangs out at a muscle joint called Tony's Gym."

Jack sat back and watched his client, not certain what to make of it all. But it was enough for today. More than enough. He had third-party motive. He stood up and knocked on the door to signal the correctional officer. Metal clanked, the ever-present sound of keys locking and unlocking. As the heavy door began to move, Jack extended his hand. Lamb took it, his grasp weaker than the last time they'd shaken hands.

"David, you mentioned you were on workers' compensation once," Jack said. "What for?"

"Like I said, I used to do heavy construction. I blew out my left shoulder lifting a gang box out of the back of a pickup truck. I've had two surgeries. My shoulder's junk."

CHAPTER TWENTY-EIGHT

Tony's Gym was on the second floor of an old wood-frame warehouse in downtown Mystic. As Jack pulled into the parking lot, he could see an assortment of trucks parked at the side of the building. On the second floor, behind fogged windows, Jack detected movement.

No doorway or sign pointed to an entrance. But a blue Ford Econoline rolled into the lot behind him. Two men in their twenties got out. Even with jackets on, their bulked-up physiques made them look like walking poster boys for human growth hormone. Gravel crackled under their feet as they lumbered around the side of the building, disappearing from view.

The sight of these giants sent a tremor down Jack's spine. Inhaling sharply, he yanked off his tie, unbuttoned his collar, and walked around the building to the rear. Still no sign, but a lime green door marked an entrance. At the top of the stairs, he yanked open another green door—and stepped into the gym, the odor hitting him like a fist, an unholy mix of sweat, body stink, and testosterone.

Tony's Gym was a no-frills, hard-ass weightlifting joint. A rectangle half the size of a basketball court was jammed with Nautilus and Ironmaster machines, Universal weights, and endless racks of free weights. Nearly twenty 200-plus-pound men converged on the floor engaged in hard-core weightlifting. None of them looked friendly. Steamy, smudged mirrors ringed the room.

There were no women.

In the center of the floor, a herd of blown-up weightlifters circled near the free weights like birds of prey ready to swoop in for a kill. Mammoth biceps, necks, triceps, traps, legs the size of hydrants, muscles so huge they reminded Jack of professional wrestlers. The hard-driving beat of an adrenaline-pumped tune was interrupted by the clatter of steel as large, dense disks of iron were dropped, switched, and hoisted on and off weight bars.

Jack scanned the room for Roger Ferriter. Even without his jacket and tie, Jack felt like a bird in a cage. Near the far wall, a man in his mid-twenties banged out bench presses. Alone. He was bare-chested, clad only in gym shorts and well-worn construction boots. Bottomless black eyes were set in a face that seemed all jaw. His dark brown hair was combed straight back, and a prickly, two-day-old growth of beard contributed to an overall menacing look.

While not as big as some of the men hoisting steel in the center of the room, the bench presser had a smoldering, white-hot intensity, an aura of malevolence surrounding him. He was pressing about three hundred pounds. With ease. No one spotted him. If the weight fell, he was on his own. Everything about him screamed "stay away."

Jack approached, betting this was Rat. From several feet away, he picked up the faint smell of marijuana.

Racking the bar for the last time in the set, Rat sat up on the bench, head and upper body awash in perspiration. He mopped his hands on his shorts.

"You're fuckin' crowdin' me," he said without looking at Jack.

Jack cleared his throat. "Are you Roger Ferriter?"

"That's your second mistake," he said. "No one calls me that. Least of all you."

"Attorney Jack Marino," he said, holding out his card.

Rat didn't take it.

"I represent David Lamb," Jack said, placing the card on the top of the squat rack to his right. "Know him?"

"Thought he was doin' time for killin' Tommy Regan."

"He's held without bail, but he hasn't been found guilty," Jack said. "The trial's coming up soon. Your name's mentioned in some of the police reports."

"So."

"Wonder if you could tell me about Tom Regan?"

Rat looked away almost as if he hadn't heard Jack. Finally, Rat stood up and walked to a pyramid-shaped weight rack. He grabbed two eighties, turned toward the mirror, and began doing standing alternating bicep curls. "The asshole's dead. What's there to tell?"

"I take it you weren't friends."

"Tommy was an asshole," Rat said.

"Police reports say you were at The Treasure Chest the night he was killed."

"There lots of nights," Rat said as he continued to alternate curls, his voice hardly affected by his efforts.

"What was Regan doing that night?"

"Bein' an asshole. Like usual." Sweat poured down Rat's face, neck, and arms as he continued to curl the eighties.

"How so?"

Rat slapped the dumbbells down on the bench. "Same as always. Runnin' off at the mouth. Actin' like the shithead he was. He wanted the dancers to think he was some kinda big deal. Spreading dollar bills all around the stage like he had a million of 'em."

"Where'd he get the cash? Construction?"

"Construction my ass. He was double dipping." Rat stared at Jack.

"Double dipping?"

"Piece of shit was on bongo bucks," he said, as he alternated another set of curls. "Used to brag how he was taking care of his three kids and his old lady by scammin' the comp insurer and makin' another grand a week doing side jobs and working under the table at TC's. I was sick of listening to him."

"You and he ever have any problems?"

Rat didn't even blink. "Caught him staring at me once. Told him flat out: 'Get those lazy mother-fuckin' eyeballs off me.'"

He finished the set and sat on the bench, placing the two dumbbells on the bench beside him. "When he kept staring at me, I opened a beer bottle with his face."

Jack felt a swirling eddy of anxiety. He was out of his league, but he had one more question. "Ever use a handgun before?"

Molten anger flashed in Rat's eyes. Crossing to the weight rack, he grabbed two additional fifty-pound plates. He slid them onto the bar he'd been pressing and sat on the bench. With an enormous effort, Rat lifted the bar off the weight supports, bringing close to three hundred-fifty pounds down to his chest. With a piercing war cry, he heaved the weight up again, his large arms and chest quivering with effort as he racked the bar. Breathing heavily, white puffs of saliva at the corner of his mouth, Rat locked on to Jack's eyes.

"I don't need a gun," he said flatly.

Every one of Jack's nerves tightened. He wondered if Rat might lose control.

"Listen to me, asshole," Rat yelled, his face flushed red. "Don't even think of draggin' me into this. Understand?"

Jack took a step back, his mouth as dry as cotton. Everyone in the gym was watching. Though Jack had prosecuted people like this, even sent them to jail, the always-present security of police, and court officers, had stood between him and the defendant. The only thing between them now was unmitigated 'roid rage.

"If you know what's good for you, get the fuck out of here before I pick your skinny ass up and throw you out the fuckin' window."

Burning with humiliation, his heart pounding, Jack turned and walked out, past the laughs and taunts of some of the X-Men, who formed a gauntlet through which Jack was forced to pass.

*   *   *

Sears sat at his desk and took the call on speakerphone.

"My people turned that area upside down," Commissioner Knight said, his voice booming. "We checked that report out. That was a mistake by one of my men. A false lead. Because it was an error, we destroyed that report. The only people out there that night were the defendant, our witness, and the victim. I wish we had another witness, but unfortunately, we don't."

Sears's grin widened into a smile as large as Massachusetts Bay. Either there really was no witness or Knight was covering up for his incompetent staff, or he was doing Cameron a favor.

"Thank you, Commissioner. We know we can always count on you and your department for a thorough investigation," he said. "District Attorney Cameron appreciates the work you've done on this case and how much you've helped his campaign."

Sears wheeled his chair over to the window, flipped the switch on his new paper shredder, and gently pushed ADA Lincoln Dawes's memorandum, along with the Mystic Police report on which it was based, into the machine, tiny crosscut, metal blades shredding both documents vertically and horizontally into hundreds of confetti-size pieces.

CHAPTER TWENTY-NINE

A dense heavy fog rolled in off Boston Harbor, diffusing the blue strobe of emergency flashers on a parked police car as Jack pulled up outside his Atlantic Avenue condo. The smell of rain and thunder hung in the air as Jack hurried through the lobby and punched the elevator button.

The elevator doors slid open on the 13th floor to reveal people milling outside his doorway. A rectangle of light from inside his home spilled on the carpet in the corridor. For the second time that day, Jack felt a stab of fear. A uniformed Boston police officer in his early twenties, probably right out of the academy, shooed neighbors back to their units.

"I'm Jack Marino. This is my home. What's going on?" Jack asked while his heart thudded.

"Your wife reported a break-in," said the officer. "My partner's with her now."

Jack felt like a wad of gauze was stuck in his throat. "Is she okay?"

"She's okay, sir. Pretty upset, though. Someone made a helluva mess of the place."

Jack crossed the threshold and stopped in his tracks, scanning the living room. Their townhouse looked as if an F4 tornado had hit it.

The larger-than-life saltwater fish tank had been smashed, glass strewn all over the floor, dying fish still convulsing on the carpet.

"Abby?" he called, moving toward the kitchen.

Abby sat at the kitchen table, hugging her own shoulders. Catching sight of Jack, she burst out crying, dabbing her eyes with a crumpled ball of tissues.

Jack pushed past a policewoman to kneel beside his wife. "Abby. Are you okay?" He took her hands in his.

Abby managed only a high-pitched croak. She lifted a wineglass from the table next to her, took a few sips. "Look what they've done to my things," she managed.

Jack wrapped his arms around her, as she began to cry again.

"I came home about an hour ago, opened the door, and found everything ruined."

"Mr. Marino, there's no sign of forced entry," said the policewoman. Her badge identified her as Lieutenant Alverez, Boston Police Department. "Have either of you given a key to anyone?"

Abby shook her head.

It hit Jack. "Shit. My car."

"What is it?" Abby said, looking at her husband.

"It was broken into yesterday when I was out at the crime scene. My briefcase was stolen. I always keep a spare key in my briefcase." His heart sank. "And identification."

"With our home address on it?" Abby's reddened eyes widened. Jack nodded.

"You didn't tell me your car had been broken into. You told me it had broken down."

"It was nothing. I didn't want to worry you, so I took care of it."

"You took care of it all right," Abby said, shifting from scared to accusatory. "Look at this place. This happened because of that goddamn case of yours."

"What case?" asked the lieutenant.

"We're lawyers," Jack said. "I'm defending a murder suspect—but I'm sure this has nothing to do with that. Probably just some kids who grabbed my stuff when they broke into my car."

Lieutenant Alverez's partner stopped scribbling. "Your wife tells us nothing seems to be missing. Just destroyed."

"If they were kids, they'd have taken something, Jack."

"Hard to tell," he said.

By the time the police left their home, Abby had retreated to their bedroom, her face ghostly white, her complexion blotched from crying. If something turned up missing, Jack had promised the officers he'd file a supplemental report in the morning.

Turning away from the door, Jack took stock. Whoever had broken into their home had slashed everything in sight—expertly done so as not to alert the neighbors. Coffee-colored foam padding spilled from the living room sofa. Abby's French abstract, which had hung between the two harbor view windows, lay on the floor sliced into irregular ribbons. Calla lilies that Abby had arranged on the dining room table littered the floor.

Teenage rage? Or a warning? He thought of Rat, the 'roided weightlifter, the crazy look in his eyes. Picking his way through the ankle-deep mess before him, Jack shuddered.

The bedroom door swung open.

"Abby?" Jack said tenderly. "Get some sleep. I'll start cleaning up."

"I don't think so, Jack." Abby walked straight by him, her coat slung over one arm, a small green Fendi travel bag in the other.

"Where are you going?"

"I called Daddy and told him what happened," Abby said. "He wants me to come home for now."

"But this is home."

Abby spun around. "I don't want to be—"

"Go ahead," Jack said. "Say it. You don't want to be with a loser."

"I told you not to take that fucking case. Have you no shame? At least you were a decent prosecutor once. You were putting bad guys away. Now look at you, helping them get off, taking a dime-a-dozen, court-appointed case for some piece of shit. It's embarrassing. And it's placing me in danger. You're in a free fall, Jack. And I don't want to be there when you hit the ground."

"But, Abby, who would I be if I didn't take the case?"

"My husband."

Jack was struck by the absence of sadness or even regret in his wife's voice. He heard some fear, but mostly blistering anger, as if he'd wasted her time these past years. Hell, maybe he had.

Reaching their front entrance, Abby threw open the door. She turned back one last time, her face contorted. "We could have had it all, asshole."

She walked out, her heels clicking loudly on the marble floor, a ting announcing the arrival of the elevator. And then there was nothing.

It was the sound of moving on.

CHAPTER THIRTY

"Let me get this straight, Counsel," Judge Marshal Stone said the next morning from his courtroom throne. "You're asking me to continue this trial because your apartment got broken into?"

"No, Your Honor," Jack said, exhausted. "I'm mentioning that as a circumstance."

"Mr. Marino, do you know how many apartments are broken into in Boston every day? What makes yours any different?" Stone turned to Sears.

Sears smiled so broadly his back molars flashed like traffic lights.

Jack ignored the exchange as well as the painful truth: what made this break-in so different was the fact that his wife had walked out on him and his personal life was a mess. Not to mention any chance of crawling back to the firm. He was on his own. "The reason for the continuance, Your Honor, isn't the break-in. As explained in my motion, I have reason to believe there may be an additional witness available to the defense."

"An eyewitness?" Stone whipped his head up as if he'd smelled wild game. He looked directly at Jack for the first time since the pre-trial conference had begun.

Jack noticed that Sears had stopped smiling, too. "That's the point, Your Honor. I don't know if she's an eyewitness," Jack said, tapping his unread motion and supporting documentation in front of the judge. "As my affidavit points out, she may have been in the area on the night of the murder."

Stone made no move to pick up Jack's motion. "You mean you don't even know if she was present at the time of the murder? What's her name?"

Jack flinched at his lack of specificity. "We don't have a full name—yet. 'Nora' is all we have at the present time."

Stone looked apoplectic. "You don't have a name, but you want to hold this Court up while you go looking for someone whose first name is 'Nora'?"

"That's correct, Your Honor," Jack said in as dry and measured a tone as he could muster. He strangled the impulse to say he'd have the name by now if His Highness had given Jack enough money to investigate the case properly in the first place. "I want a continuance while I look for a potentially material witness in a capital murder case whose first name is 'Nora.'"

The judge turned to the First Assistant DA. "Know anything about another witness, Mr. Sears?"

Sears shifted his weight. "Your Honor, we've given Mr. Marino the names of all the witnesses in our file."

"There you have it, Counsel. The Commonwealth says there's nothing else in its file. What else do you want?"

"Another week, Your Honor," said Jack. "Without additional time, my client will be seriously prejudiced. This is, after all, a murder trial."

"I know what kind of trial this is, Counsel. I also know that we've had a firm trial date a number of times now. I told you when you came into this case, I wasn't going to grant any continuances."

"Your Honor, I've provided this court with a sworn affidavit from an area merchant saying there were certain individuals who lived back there who might—"

Stone cut in, his face twisted into a scowl. "Lived where? I thought this murder took place outdoors, near railroad tracks."

"It did, Your Honor. They're . . . homeless," Jack replied.

Stone looked like a blood-pressure cuff had just burst off one of his arms. "Let me understand this, Counsel. You want to delay this trial so you can go on a wild-goose chase for a derelict whom you claim made her residence near the railroad tracks?"

Sears jumped in, "Your Honor, as this Court knows, Mr. Marino has been on notice of the date of this trial for some time. There has been no showing that any witness exists who has any credible testimony that could possibly bear on this case. Moreover, any continuance at the present time would constitute an extreme inconvenience to the Commonwealth's witnesses, not to mention the victim's family."

Before Jack could speak again, Stone swung his gavel, a loud crack echoing throughout the courtroom. "We impanel Monday morning. Nine a.m. sharp."

Jack didn't move. "Your Honor, I place the name 'Nora Doe' on the witness list."

"You what?" Stone said, raising his voice again.

Jack continued without missing a beat. "Without additional time to find this potential witness, you leave me no choice but to reserve the right to call her should I locate her." Jack looked up at Stone. "That said, Your Honor, I'm still asking this court for more time."

The judge rejected Jack's request with a wave of his hand.

"Note my objection, Your Honor," Jack said to protect the record.

"Of course . . ." Stone hesitated. "If you're asking to withdraw from the case, that might be a different story."

Adrenaline and anger shot through Jack. That hypocritical son-of-a-bitch, who had just claimed there was no time for a continuance, was inviting Jack to withdraw—a withdrawal that would delay the trial, while new counsel would be appointed and get even more time to prepare.

Rage gave away to shame. He was embarrassed to admit it, but the thought of getting out of this damn case brought with it a rush of relief. Jack stifled the urge.

"I'm not quitting, Judge."

As Jack began to turn his back on the bench, the judge asked, "Anything else, gentlemen?"

"Actually, there is," Sears said. "With the Court's permission?"

Jack watched Sears hand a motion up to the clerk.

"The Commonwealth hereby timely files its Notice of Intent to Seek the Death Penalty should the defendant be convicted in this case."

In a single sentence, Jack's world exploded.

CHAPTER THIRTY-ONE

After the bombshell announcement, Jack made it as far as the courthouse lobby where he stood, beset with vertigo, his palms sweaty, his legs like Jell-O. He stared at the statutes that lined the first floor. Rendered in cold marble, a quartet of life-size allegorical figures loomed down from one side of the gallery, representing the cardinal virtues of Temperance, Prudence, Justice, and Fortitude.

Jack would need every one of those qualities in the coming weeks. Stunned by the Commonwealth's intention to seek the death penalty, he pushed his way through a noisy crowd, counting off twelve more statues as he scanned the great hall: Law, Punishment, Guilt, Equity, Right, Innocence, Reward, Wisdom, Religion, Virtue, Reason, and Legislation.

The man the crowd had gathered to hear, District Attorney Cameron, stood directly under the Guilt and Punishment statues, the figure Guilt grasping a dagger, Punishment holding shackles and an axe. The DA beamed. He actually thought this was his building. He might not have a deed to Boston's Temple of Justice, but in his mind, he owned it.

"We don't need less justice," said Cameron, thumping a lectern. "We need more. More mandatory sentences. Tougher parole guidelines. The elimination of work-release."

All the usual campaign themes, thought Jack, but spoken with an enthusiasm he'd never seen in Cameron. He listened as the DA declared he would even cancel funeral passes for nonviolent offenders to honor immediate family: deceased parents, brothers, sisters.

As dozens of supporters cheered him on, Cameron reached a crescendo. "And today, we announce that for the first time in over forty years, the Commonwealth will seek the death penalty in a case against a cold-blooded killer."

More cheers careened off the lobby's walls.

"The public is fed up with the gangs, the killings, the fact that kids can't go to the corner store in Boston without risking being shot. The public wanted the death penalty. The Legislature reinstated it. Now we're going to be the first to use it."

Further cheers, louder still.

Jack attempted to pick his way through the crowd, desperate to get out of the courthouse for some air. In moments, he'd gone from worrying about a continuance to feeling the crushing weight of the State's power to impose the death penalty. On his way out, Jack nearly bumped into Alexa Metranos, the Boston 9 News reporter who had watched him confront Sears at the fundraiser.

With a cameraman beside her and microphone in hand, she said, "Hey, aren't you the defense attorney in the Lamb case?"

TV lights blinded Jack. Several microphones appeared in a flash as other reporters joined Metranos.

Jack put his hand up to shield his eyes.

"Do you still believe the DA gave immunity to a killer?" the Boston 9 reporter asked.

"More than ever," Jack replied.

A press aide to Cameron, who must have recognized Jack, intervened. "Questions about the candidate's positions?" she asked the reporters.

The Boston 9 reporter didn't wait to raise her hand. She looked up at the podium and barked: "District Attorney Cameron, is it true you immunized a murder suspect in your first death penalty case?"

The lobby fell silent as members of the media fixed their attention on the District Attorney.

Cameron was caught off guard. The DA stabbed a glance right through Jack, standing beside the reporter who had asked the question. Cameron pointed at his former Assistant District Attorney and laughed. "Attorney Marino will say anything to free his client, a remorseless killer. Our use of immunity on behalf of a completely innocent witness is wholly justified by the law and the facts in this case."

Murmurs erupted as people jostled for a better look at the men. Jack pressed his way through the swarm of people, ignoring the microphones pointed in his direction. In the uproar, he could barely hear the shouted questions, much less answer them. As he looked out over the crowd, Jack spotted Summer across the hall near the exit, her brown eyes throwing him a lifeline.

Behind him, the campaign wonks dissolved into confusion. Jack made it to Summer. When he reached her, he gestured toward a small alcove.

"Jack, are you okay?"

"I need to talk to you," Jack said.

Summer pointed to the pandemonium around them. "This isn't the best time, Jack," she said.

"Of course. Anywhere but here."

Summer nodded.

Jack told her about the break-in, then asked, "Did you know about the Commonwealth's intention to seek the death penalty?"

"I had no idea. They kept it from the staff, but it looks like they planned it all along. It's already on the radio, TV. It's everywhere."

Jack shook his head. "I don't know what's going on, but the answers to this case aren't here in the courthouse. They're out there—" He pointed. "In the streets of Mystic."

Summer said nothing.

"I can't do this alone," Jack said. "I need help."

"What are you going to do?"

Jack surprised himself. "I'm going to call the only person I've got left. Thing is, I don't even know if he'll take my call."

"Who's that?"

"My brother."

"I didn't know you have a brother."

"I do."

CHAPTER THIRTY-TWO

Three years wasn't that long, Jack thought. Unless it spanned a gulf as wide as the one that yawned between two brothers, once inseparable, now strangers. It took several calls to his brother's parole officer, but Jack finally managed to get a telephone number that worked.

Despite everything, Matt took his call. He asked no questions. Jack's eyes had filled at his brother's clipped response: "I'm on my way."

Jack thought about the last time he'd seen his brother. Jack had wanted to invite him to his wedding. He'd tried calling, but the phone had been disconnected. Jack had tracked his brother to a rooming house so run-down that Abby refused to go in, choosing instead to sit outside in her locked Mercedes. After knocking on several doors, Jack had found his older brother huddled in a single room with no bathroom, stinking of old liquor. Even if Jack could have cleaned him up, Abby's family wouldn't have allowed him at the wedding.

So, Jack stayed away, turned his back on his brother's decline. And not once during their marriage had Abby asked about him. Nor had Jack spoken of him.

* * *

They met at a Mystic coffee shop. "Still with the DA's office?" Matt asked, his brother's once-thick brown hair flecked with gray, dark rings etched below his blue eyes.

"Not exactly." Jack looked down at the steam swirling above his mug. Although the breakfast joint Matt had suggested as a meeting spot was neutral territory, their conversation was anything but.

"I thought that was your life."

"It was," Jack said. "Got myself on the fast track where there was no time for family, no time for relationships, no time for anything. Sad thing was, before I knew it, the prosecutor's office was all that mattered. I actually thought I'd change things by putting the bad guys away."

"Then why leave?"

"Fired, was more like it."

"Why get rid of you?" Matt asked.

"Damaged goods."

He bent his head at an angle. "Heard you were one of the best."

Jack took a deep breath and plunged in. He told his brother about the beating, about being held at gunpoint. He had no other way to explain why he was out of the DA's office. Or even why Abby had left him.

Jack shuddered. "Got to admit, it's taken me a while to begin to climb back," he said. "I've had some issues." He cleared his throat. "The combined influence of my father-in-law and the DA kept the whole incident out of the press. Just another Boston shooting. Among dozens. Anyway, main thing was, Abby wasn't home yet."

"Cops ever find these guys?"

Jack shook his head.

"No leads?"

"Nothing."

"And the DA fired you for that?" Matt asked.

"No," Jack said. "He fired me for giving some stupid interview about the work I'd been doing. My taking a break from prosecuting gangbangers didn't fit with his 'war on crime.' Which was nothing but a wind-up for his campaign for Governor."

"DA's running for Governor now?" Matt asked.

"In the newspapers every day."

"Don't read 'em. No TV or radio either."

Jack looked into his brother's eyes.

"I should have seen it coming," Matt said. "Went the same way for me as it did for Dad. I was drinking in the Marines. The shit I saw . . . I still can't get it out of my head. The drugs didn't start until later. I convinced myself that the drugs were keeping me off the booze, but before I knew it, it was too late. Armed robbery for enough money to get high. I didn't even know where I was. The fuck-up I was with had a gun. Two years for being stupid."

"You know he'd want you to go to AA. Or NA. Because he didn't. How *are* you staying sober?"

"One day at a time. Some harder than others."

"The old man would be happy," Jack said. "So am I."

"Thanks." Matt smiled for a long moment. "You mentioned someone broke in recently?"

Jack described the recent break-in. And, of course, how Abby had walked out.

Matt's steel-blue eyes grayed. "Any idea who might have done it? And why?"

"No."

"Maybe the assholes who attacked you?"

"Doubt it. I'm probably the last person they'd come near. If I ever ID'd them, they'd be looking at armed home invasion and assault with intent to kill. Maybe ten to twenty years, easy. No. I'm pretty sure those guys are history."

"Is there anyone else who might want to hurt you?"

Jack let out a deep breath. "When I left the DA's office, I joined Abby's father's firm to handle corporate matters. Business litigation. That sort of thing. No enemies there. Until my appointment."

"Appointment?"

"Got fired from my father-in-law's firm. For the moment, I'm working as a public defender on a death-penalty case out of my home office. At least until Abby's lawyers take the place."

"A murder? But you've just hung out your shingle."

"Actually, I tried a lot of murders as a DA and won most of them."

"But the death penalty?"

"Didn't have a clue until yesterday." Jack shook his head. "The whole thing has exploded. There isn't a newspaper or television station in the state that isn't ramping up for it." He paused. "I'm over my head. But I can't quit. Not again. Not against the same people who fired me from the DA's office. And the truth is, the further I dig into this case, the more I believe my guy wasn't the shooter."

Matt stiffened. "If you're right, that means there's a killer out there who wants your guy convicted, and my concern is you're the only thing standing in the way."

* * *

Stepping to the right of the black Everlast heavy bag dangling in front of him, Jack threw a hook. Breathless, sweat pouring down his face, he was glad Matt had persuaded him to clear his head at the former boxing gym they'd once attended.

Jack had updated his brother with everything he knew and didn't know about Nora. "I don't even know if she saw it. Or whether she's alive." Jack dug hard into the belly of the bag with another hook as Matt steadied it in front of him.

"Her kind don't die easy," Matt said. "Hey, you still practice, um—what was the martial art that the old man tried to teach us?"

Jack laughed. "Sometimes I think it was the only thing he left us. Forget the name of it. Claimed there was nothing like it . . . anywhere. That he learned it from some guy named Jimmy in California. A Grandmaster. But if you're asking did I use it to stop the . . . attack"—Jack shook his head. "I didn't. Not sure I would have remembered much of it anyway. After Dad died, I never practiced it again."

"At least you stuck with it for a while. I tuned him out."

"Lot of good it did me."

"C'mon, let's see the jab. That's it. Pull it back as quick as you throw it, just like you used to."

Jack flicked out his left hand. The pungent smell of sweaty gloves and headgear came flooding back as Jack recalled the decrepit New Garden Gym located in Boston's North Station, where he and Matt had boxed as kids and practiced a martial art at their father's insistence. He could still hear the ear-splitting squeal of the subway car's steel wheels grinding against the elevated tracks, which ran only a few feet outside the grime of the gym's windows. Once training grounds for world champions like Tony DeMarco, Marvin Hagler, and world-ranked championship contenders like local great Joe DeNucci, the New Garden Gym had become the upscale Boston Karate Club.

"We still have to find her," Jack said, his breath uneven.

Matt peered at Jack from behind the bag. "Got another two minutes in you?"

Jack nodded, a stitch in his side nearly buckling him. He wanted to push down on the pain, but he kept his gloves up, breathing through the discomfort.

"Street people are creatures of habit," Matt said. "If she's alive, she probably hasn't gone far. We both know the area. I'll start down on the tracks, check with some of the neighbors in the projects. I'll scope out The Treasure Chest too. And I'll drop in on this Rat guy."

"Be careful, Matt," Jack grunted, only now thinking of the possible consequences of asking Matt to help. His brother was still on parole.

Matt laughed. "C'mon, let's switch."

Jack reached out and hugged the bag low to give Matt plenty of real estate to hit.

Matt attacked with a succession of lefts, rights, and hooks, the heavy bag dancing from the suspension chains, the blows so powerful they pushed Jack back no matter how he steadied himself.

"It's good to be here—with you," Jack said, his breath catching as he held the bag.

His brother hit the bag with another series of thunderous punches. "Walpole isn't that far away," Matt said.

He might as well have hit Jack with a tire-iron. Sadness, regret, guilt—all mixed together like a Molotov cocktail poured over him. Walpole State Prison was only about twenty miles from Jack's home, yet Jack had never visited his brother. Not once. He thought he had his reasons—if he'd put much thought into it at all. There was Abby. She wouldn't even acknowledge Matt. For her, it was almost as if his brother didn't exist. But even before Abby, there was both shame and pain. Jack had been so embarrassed when he overheard a group of Assistant District Attorneys whispering about the case of Commonwealth vs. Matthew Marino.

Matt had every right to feel angry.

But Jack had his own feelings of bitter loss. Childhood had ended for him on a stiflingly hot, humid summer day. Heart attack, they'd said. It had shocked them all, because Jack's father was only forty-one years old. Forty-one. What would a mother and two children do? No job. No money. No insurance. Tears flowed, but life had to go on. Matt was eighteen, Jack only fourteen. Overnight, the laughter stopped. No more games. Only bills, school, work, and worry.

Then came the second blow. Instead of assuming a larger role in the family, Matt walked away. Joined the Marines. Jack had never understood why his older brother left and never forgot it. His mother's face had been burned into Jack's consciousness, her tired eyes reflecting two enormous losses within weeks of each other. What would they do now—just the two of them?

They'd survive. Jack would make sure of that.

The force of the bag pounded against him. "It wasn't how close Walpole was, Matt," Jack said.

"What then?" Matt asked, still punishing the bag.

"It was how far Vietnam was," Jack said. "Especially for a fourteen-year-old. When we needed you—badly."

The steady percussion of his brother's punches punctuated their conversation. Still breathing easily, Matt said, "Had a long time to think about that. I don't know what the hell I was thinking. I cut and ran. Just in time for one of the first major offensive actions of the war."

Jack understood. For years, he'd been running away himself: focusing on his career to the exclusion of everything else. Intent on creating a new reality, he'd plunged ahead, trying to forget where he'd come from. Problem was, he'd succeeded.

"How do I make this right?" Jack asked.

"You already did," his brother said. "You called me."

"And you came."

CHAPTER THIRTY-THREE

Crisscrossing a maze of corridors under a garish light, the correctional officers ushered Jack toward his client's cell, inmates bathed in shadow yelling from behind steel doors as they passed.

Jack found Lamb atop his bunk in a fetal position, arms wrapped around his sides. This area was reserved for inmates who were segregated from the general jail population. Why had Lamb been singled out for protective custody?

"You all right?" Jack asked.

"Fine."

He didn't look fine. Nor had he moved since Jack entered the small cell. "What happened, David?"

"I fell," Lamb managed at last, still clutching his sides.

"Have you seen a doctor?"

"You kidding. No one sees a doctor in here."

This was a reality Jack had never thought about as a prosecutor. "Why segregation?" he asked.

"Threats," Lamb answered in a flat tone.

"Tell me who, David."

Lamb turned his head. "I've got to live through this to get home to my girls."

Maybe, Jack thought, if they were unable to stop Jack, they'd try to get to Lamb directly.

Jack took a long, hard look at his client. Lamb had passed from skinny to gaunt.

He also smelled foul.

"They letting you out for showers?" Jack asked.

"Once a week. With ankle shackles."

Jack blinked hard. For reasons he couldn't understand, he felt drawn to this young man. Lamb had no understanding of what lay ahead or the weight of the evidence against him. He was fantasizing about walking out with a "not guilty" verdict. But without the missing witness, Lamb was in trouble. Deep trouble.

Jack could put the news off no longer. "I've got something to tell you, David—and it's not good."

Lamb raised his head. "Wendy?"

"No. No. She's doing better."

"Her sister? My mother?"

"This is about you, David."

Lamb breathed hard.

"The Commonwealth has informed the Court it will seek the death penalty if they convict you."

Lamb's eyes rolled back into his head, a wail escaping his mouth.

Jack thought about Judge Stone's comment, an echo of how he used to feel when he was an Assistant District Attorney. Every defendant says he's innocent.

"Look at me, David," he said.

Lamb's eyes were teary, bloodshot. "Why would I kill Tommy?"

"Listen. Here's how the prosecution looks at this. Number one: You were at the murder scene. Number two: you've got a gun conviction and—"

Lamb interrupted. "You know how that went down."

"I do, but now it's your turn to listen. You cannot take the stand unless we convince the judge to exclude that conviction."

Jack watched Lamb struggle to understand. "Can you?" Lamb asked.

It was a question Jack wasn't sure he could answer. "David, I'm here to defend you and to do the best I can with the facts I have."

Lamb looked hopeful. "I heard them say in here you used to be one of the best."

Lamb's jailhouse honesty shook Jack to his core. He hadn't missed Lamb's use of the past tense.

Jack's stomach churned. "There's one more thing I have to tell you."

Lamb barely nodded.

"I've had trouble with this judge."

"Trouble?"

Jack's neck muscles tightened. "When I was a prosecutor, I convicted the son of a former colleague of his, a man he'd served with in the state legislature."

"And now you're telling me?" Lamb shouted.

"No matter what, I'm going to help you, David. I promise."

Jack had nothing left to say.

CHAPTER THIRTY-FOUR

"Brad thinks it's a slam dunk," said Summer, seated across the table from Jack at Adesso, a quiet, upscale Italian restaurant on the banks of the Charles River in East Cambridge. Her eyes shone in flickering candlelight.

"A slam dunk because I'm the attorney? Or because his evidence is so strong?"

Summer hesitated. "They don't think you can try a case anymore."

Her words struck like rounds from a Gatling gun. Jack said, "Maybe they're right."

The waiter appeared with a bottle of wine, a simple Merlot, and poured for both of them.

Summer tasted the wine. "They want to rack up this first death penalty conviction more than you can imagine. The DA has assigned a team of ADAs to help Brad prepare. I've never seen anything like it. They've even got an appellate Assistant District Attorney looking at every possible legal issue that could come up."

As a prosecutor, Jack had been part of the Commonwealth's team, but he'd never felt its crushing weight before. He shook his head. "There must be a hundred attorneys in Boston who could do a better job in this case. Why did Judge McCormack choose me?"

"Why not you?" Summer asked. "You're a great trial lawyer, Jack. That's who you are." She looked down at the table. "No matter what happened to you."

Summer had an easy, relaxed air that had always put Jack at ease, a demeanor he remembered with a smile. "I'm trying to work through some issues. The docs are calling it PTSD. It's like the home invasion is over, but it's not."

"You'll be okay," she said. "I know it."

Jack paused in reflection. "Sounds crazy, but this is also about Abby. About her family. And the realization that we've been pretending."

"Pretending?" Summer asked.

Jack felt himself tense. "Abby left me."

After a lengthy silence, Summer said, "Maybe she'll come back."

"You don't know her."

"I know you."

Jack shifted in his seat, feeling his face flush. "She'd come back if I embrace everything—her father, that damn firm of his, the endless society functions—the whole catastrophe. And this case—I'd have to give it up."

"What do you want?" Summer asked.

Jack looked out the window again. The lights on Edwin Land Boulevard reflected a liquid glow, the night beginning to swirl around them, like mist at the edge of a bad dream.

"I can tell you what I don't want. I don't want to go to another function, another gala, another fundraiser—watching the almighty Thorn family raise money for people they've never met, people who, in truth, they wouldn't spend five minutes with." Jack twisted in his chair. "The problem is you wake up one day and you don't know who you are. But with this case, as crazy as it sounds, I'm someone again. Someone who could save an innocent man's life."

Summer studied him. "What is it?" she asked.

"I'm sorry, Summer. For everything. For hurting you. For walking away. For not having the courage to own up to it all."

Neither of them looked away.

"You broke my heart," she said.

Jack nodded. "And I sold mine." He extended his hand, palm up, across the white linen tablecloth.

Summer placed her hand in his.

Jack leaned toward her, but Summer shook her head.

"You need to win this case first."

Jack nodded.

"But, Jack, don't win it to send a message to Abby. Or to prove something to the Thorn family. Don't even win it for yourself as a way back. Win it for David. He needs you." Summer paused. "I've seen the case file. Find the reasonable doubt."

The restaurant's windows rattled as a gust of wind blew off the Charles River.

Summer laughed.

"What?" Jack asked.

"The wind," she said. "When I was a little girl, my mother used to tell me that the wind had special meaning. A dark wind was an omen of bad things to come. But a good wind was the great unifier— connecting the past, present, and the future. A good wind marks good fortune. A good season."

The clatter of the windows quieted. "Brad had me send out subpoenas for our witnesses for Monday morning," she said. "He's preparing his opening now. Can you find your missing witness by then?"

"Matt and I will be looking for her over the weekend," he said.

"Finding someone who's lost may be the key to your case." She looked at him, leaned in slightly, and said it again.

The hair on Jack's arms stood up. He nodded, never breaking eye contact.

So, she existed. A potential witness was out there.

Had Sears suppressed a witness as Summer was suggesting? It wouldn't be the first time exculpatory evidence had failed to make it out of a prosecutor's file. Cameron was never one to let the law get in his way. And he wasn't alone. For years, the FBI had been cheating in their sworn affidavits for electronic surveillance, keeping federal judges in the dark, telling them half the story. No surprise that certain state prosecutors were no better.

But what could Jack do about it? Did Summer have proof? He hadn't dared ask her. She couldn't come forward anyway. It would violate her status as a confidential employee of the District Attorney's office. She'd be fired. Even prosecuted.

But why? Was it just that Sears was certain he was putting all this behind him and moving on to the Governor's office? Or was it to make sure that Lamb, and no one else, was convicted for the murder of Tommy Regan?

CHAPTER THIRTY-FIVE

"We're getting calls from everybody!" Cameron cursed as he hung up the phone and waved Brad Sears into his office. "The *Tribune*, the *Record*, most of the television stations. And instead of writing about the death penalty, they're asking about immunity. I want Marino slowed down."

"We handpicked him," Sears said. He pulled up a chair in front of Cameron's desk.

Cameron looked like he would boil over. "He's impugned my reputation and the credibility of this entire office."

"Trust me, Jack Marino will unravel just as he did when he worked for us."

"I can't take the chance a week before the election."

"We'll be fine."

"Listen, I've worked my entire career to get to where I am now, and this asshole has nothing to lose. And a man who has nothing to lose is a dangerous man."

"We might be overreacting," said Sears. "Marino has nothing on us."

"I understand that. But think about this. If the unthinkable happens and we lose this case to Marino before the election, the campaign is lost. But if we make sure the verdict is returned after the election, it's all upside for us no matter what the verdict is. As long as the trial is underway, the public will know we're following through with our promise to prosecute the first death penalty case. And if we lose the case after a successful election, who gives a shit? We'll already have been elected, and it won't matter. But if we lose before the election . . ."

"I wish I'd known this earlier. Judge Stone denied Marino's motion to continue yesterday. I could have withdrawn my objection, and Stone would have granted it."

The DA waved him off. "I don't give a shit what you have to tell that old bastard. Delay the start of the trial long enough to ensure the verdict comes in after Election Day."

"And how do you suggest I do that?"

"Get rid of your most valuable witness. It's worked in the past. All we have to do is delay the start of the trial a bit, so it begins before the election but ends after the polls close. We'll look like heroes right up through election eve, no matter what the jury does."

Sears stared at Cameron. "It's risky going with just four witnesses."

"You'll figure it out. That's why you're still on my team . . . and will be on my next one," the DA said with a smile. "And remember, Stone hates Marino's guts. He'll go for it."

CHAPTER THIRTY-SIX

A cool fall breeze and the sound of Boston traffic swept into the open window of Jack's home office. As the city below him scurried about its business, Jack leaned back in his chair.

Some attorneys, no doubt, would convince themselves that the prosecution didn't have much. Even Judge McCormack, who'd appointed him to the case, had implied as much. The government had no gun to place in Lamb's hand. No physical or forensic evidence connected Lamb with the victim.

But Jack refused to take solace in the prosecution's problems. He knew the magic Sears would conjure to beat him.

The biggest problem were the lies Lamb had told the grand jury, lies he'd have to admit to if Lamb had the opportunity to take the stand. Jack could smell the flammable combination of his client's false statements before the grand jury, the fingerprints in Regan's car, and whatever motivation the Commonwealth cooked up. His throat tightened.

And Sears had an eyewitness to say that Lamb had shot a father of three children. In cold blood.

Countless defendants had been convicted on the testimony of a single eyewitness, and scores of others on even less. The Commonwealth's immunized witness was more than enough to convict, unless Jack found a way to take out Mickey Nolan at the knees in front of the jury.

Jack dragged the file out again. It had grown enormously, jammed with documents and potential exhibits that Sears continued to send in discovery.

As he had done so many times in the past weeks, Jack plunged in, thumbing through the file, dictating his thoughts into a Sony micro-cassette recorder he always used. First up were the police reports, the flesh and bones of any prosecutor's case. The initial reports detailed the arrival of the Mystic police officers to the scene, followed by Commissioner Jeff Knight, the preservation and collection of evidence, and the identity of everyone at the crime scene. Crime scene photography and a collection of latent prints were also chronicled.

A document entitled "HOMICIDE UNIT PHOTOGRAPH IDENTIFICATION" described the circumstances—date, time, and location—under which Nolan had identified Lamb as the killer. "Mr. Nolan positively identified the photo of David Lamb as being the person responsible for the death of Thomas Regan."

A two-page memo called an AUTHORIZATION FOR DIS-POSITION OF EVIDENCE described samples of blood, fiber, vegetation, clothing, scalp hair, and sneakers. Jack penciled a circle around the words "fiber," "vegetation," and "human vomitus."

Why would the police gather a sample of bile? Jack snagged the autopsy report and reviewed it. It covered everything, including the tracking or the trajectory of the bullet from the right rear to the left through the victim's skull. Yet the Medical Examiner hadn't made any note that the victim had vomited.

Gradually, as he examined the file, the ex-prosecutor built three piles of documents. "Favorable" consisted of everything that could help him. "Neutral" held everything that neither helped nor hurt.

The third pile was composed of everything that could hurt his client. This one he labeled "Trouble."

By nightfall, Jack turned to the final document in his possession. And there it was. The document that might have sealed Lamb's fate: the Commonwealth's Application for a Grant of Immunity for Mickey Nolan. This was the prize Teddy Smith had negotiated. In it, Nolan asserted his right against self-incrimination under the Fifth Amendment to the United States Constitution as to all matters pertaining to his knowledge of, or participation in, the murder of Thomas Regan.

Jack sat back, fatigue etching dark lines beneath his eyes. He looked at the stacks before him, dismayed. The "Trouble" pile towered over everything else.

CHAPTER THIRTY-SEVEN

A crowd of print and broadcast media types had gathered outside the entrance to the Office of the Speaker of the House. On this Friday before the trial, the smell of victory hung everywhere, drifting toward the scrum of reporters gathered near the pearl-white, fluted marble columns that brushed the vaulted ceiling.

To Brad Sears's left, the entrance to the historic chamber of the Massachusetts House of Representatives loomed in the background, the intricately detailed vestibule gleaming with a timeless patina. Two court officers stood in gold-buttoned, dark-blue uniforms at each side of the entrance, the ornate chamber's dark Honduras mahogany doors hugging themselves in the closed position.

At 2:00 p.m., the legislative session was scheduled to convene. The chamber was off-limits to the public until then, but the Speaker of the Massachusetts House of Representatives, a rock star in the party, had his own private entrance to the chamber.

The Speaker had brought Sears and Cameron up to the historic, elevated rostrum, on the face of which were emblazoned the words of a young President-Elect of the United States, who only ten days before his inauguration, had reminded his fellow public servants, present and future, of the standards by which all public officeholders should be judged.

For of those to whom much is given, much is required . . . our success or failure, in whatever office we may hold, will be measured by the answers to four questions:

First, were we truly men of courage—with the courage to stand up to one's enemies . . .

Secondly, were we truly men of judgment . . .

Third, were we truly men of integrity—men who never ran out on either the principles in which they believed or the people who believed in them—men who believed in us—men whom neither financial gain nor political ambition could ever divert from the fulfillment of our sacred trust?

Finally, were we truly men of dedication . . . devoted solely to serving the public good and the national interest?

John Fitzgerald Kennedy,
President Elect of the United States of America

Sears turned to his right and looked up the hall at the golden glow that radiated from inside the crescent entrance to the highest office in the Commonwealth. A state trooper in full regalia stood at attention to the left of the doorway. Portraits of past governors lined the walls of the corridor leading to the Governor's office.

Thanks to Sears's calls the day before, the media had gotten wind of the meeting between Cameron and the powerful and charismatic Speaker of the House. Bright splashes of light and the hum of 35mm film advancing filled the hallway. Television crews shot videotape for the evening news.

Reporters cornered Cameron at the entrance to the foyer of the Speaker's office. Just that morning the *Boston Tribune* had printed the latest polling results, which placed Cameron dead even with the Governor.

Cameron and Sears couldn't have been happier.

"What do you think of the new poll numbers?" one of the reporters asked the DA.

"Polls don't vote, Cynthia," Cameron answered. "We're taking nothing for granted. We'll be working right up to the hour the polls close."

"Do you think the Governor's criticism of your record on crime is fair?" asked another reporter.

"No one in the Commonwealth can match my record as a prosecutor," Cameron said. "I'm the one in the prosecutorial trenches day in, day out, convicting the guilty, giving a voice to the victims of violent crime." The DA paused. "And I predict we'll be the first to achieve a conviction under the state's new capital punishment statute."

*   *   *

From the front seat of her fifteen-year-old Ford Falcon, Ann Lamb spotted number 215 hand-painted on the front door where Tommy Regan had lived. She pulled around the corner and parked out of sight of the three-family just as her son's attorney had instructed. The moment she cut the engine, the rain began to fall. With no umbrella in the car, she reached over to the glove compartment and withdrew the mantilla she wore at Mass every Sunday.

It was a low-slung row house, three apartments next to each other. The clapboard siding badly needed paint. Mystic was a working-class town: no custom splits, no handsome garrisons, no Cape Cod architecture. The name *Regan* was written on silver duct tape beneath a bell. She drew a breath and rang the chime.

Footsteps ran to the door, which opened to a little girl about nine years old. She wore a pink dress that seemed too big, maybe a hand-me-down. "Who are you?" the girl asked, smiling.

"Hi, sweetheart. My name is Ann Lamb. Could I speak with your mom?"

The little girl scampered back the way she had come, calling "Mommm" in a singsong voice.

What happened next was a jarring blur: Lisa Regan slammed the door shut.

"Please," Ann Lamb called, her voice shaking. "If you would hear me out, you would believe me. My son would never hurt your husband. He's a good young man. As I'm sure your husband was. Please—Mrs. Regan?"

A woman's voice, muffled and angry, shushed her kids, one of whom kept saying, "But, Mommy, there's a lady out there."

As the rain mixed with her tears, David Lamb's mother stood outside and continued to plead her case to a closed door, the soaked mantilla pressed flat to her head so it wouldn't fly away.

CHAPTER THIRTY-EIGHT

Over the weekend, Matt and Jack searched every inch of the old Boston and Maine Railroad, asking everyone they met if they knew of a homeless woman who might have been in the area when the murder of Tom Regan had taken place.

Nothing.

With the trial set for the following morning, sleep was impossible. It was nearly eleven p.m. when Jack clicked off the TV, the flickering images of the Sunday evening news fading into black.

A rap on the door startled him. Guests stopping by this late at night rang from the lobby, then were buzzed in after identifying themselves over the intercom. The last time he'd approached a locked door for an uninvited guest . . . his life changed forever.

He pushed on toward the door in an act of will. He had to overcome this fear. Steeling himself, he left the new chain lock secured and pulled the door open a few inches.

Summer stood in the corridor in blue jeans and a pink cotton shirt. It must have begun to rain, because her hair sparkled under the hall lights.

"Hey," Jack said, unlatching and fully opening the door. "Are you okay?"

She crossed the threshold, extended her hand, and placed her index finger over his lips. The tote bag she was carrying slipped to the floor.

Taking her hand, Jack pulled her further inside, pushing the door closed behind them.

They stood face-to-face for what felt like an eternity, their eyes locked in an embrace, her hand resting on his arm.

He took a deep breath and gave in. He reached out and cupped her face, then kissed her deeply. She seemed surprised. Then she gently pushed him back and looked down.

"I left you behind," he said. "It was the biggest mistake of my life."

"Shhh," said Summer. She pulled his head toward her and kissed him.

Finally, she stepped back. "I guess neither of us managed to wait until after the trial."

He shook his head.

She scanned the condo, which still looked like an ad for catastrophic liability insurance. She raised one eyebrow. "New decorator?"

"You could say that," Jack said. He walked her into the kitchen and pulled out a barstool for her. "Let me make you a drink."

"Thanks. I could use one."

"Bad day?" he asked as he looked in the wine fridge for anything Abby might have left.

"You could say that. The phone was ringing off the hook, and with this campaign, the office is just, well, stressful in a different way. I know I shouldn't be talking about it." She shook her head. "Forget I said all that," she said, looking at the stacks of papers organized into piles on the kitchen peninsula.

"We spent the day at the murder scene yesterday," he said as he uncorked a bottle of Napa Cabernet. "Some of the transients are back. And they all know 'Crazy Nora,' who's my Hail Mary. All I've got. No one will say they've seen her. They're too frightened."

Summer said nothing.

He poured them each a glass of wine. "It would help if I knew her last name."

Summer didn't say anything, nor did she try her wine.

"Am I making you uncomfortable?"

She thought for a moment. "No. Brad is. He put me in the middle when he started cutting corners in this case."

Jack nodded. "Summer, what happened to Brad?"

"C'mon, you've seen it," she said. "Career prosecutors. It's a tough road. He was teetering on burnout, but now he has a mission again. He's become as obsessed as Cameron is with this election. Every case he tries is one less case between him and a place he views as the pinnacle. Blind ambition is a terrible thing."

"No matter how it might have seemed, it was never about that for me."

Summer nodded. "I know." She took a sip of wine. "This is nice."

"But why would he cross the line? What he's doing in the Lamb case is dead-on prosecutorial misconduct. You know it as well as I do."

"First of all, if he wins, he makes history. Second, this case is his last. But either way, Brad is out. There'll be a new DA with a new First Assistant." She hesitated. "And there's something personal going on here. When you were appointed, I actually think he saw some irony in the whole thing. It's his swan song. His crowning glory. A slam-dunk against someone who—and it hurts to say this—he's lost respect for."

Jack shook his head.

"And I thought mine was a simple indigent appointment from a judge who wanted to get me back on my feet again."

"Your timing was never your strong suit," Summer said, smiling. He reached for her hand.

She shook her head. "I can't stay. But soon, Jack. When the trial's over. I just needed to see you."

"Thank you," Jack replied, and kissed her gently on the lips.

* * *

For the first time in years, Jack felt the stir of hope.

It was midnight before he headed for bed. He had to get some sleep. He went to double-check the locks and noticed that Summer had left her bag near the entry door.

Jack bent to pick it up. The tote bag contained a file folder embossed with the words "District Attorney's Office."

What the hell was this?

Jack knelt on his good knee and opened the file.

He couldn't believe it. In his hands was an internal memorandum addressed to Bradford Sears about the existence of a witness to the murder—a document that had never been provided to him during pre-trial discovery, describing a potential witness whose existence Sears had denied in open court.

What had Summer done? And what else was Sears hiding?

Jack let the document fall back into the bag. As an attorney, he was still bound by the Code of Professional Ethics.

Summer had taken an enormous risk, and Jack had pushed her into it. And now as an officer of the court—he had to decide whether to examine portions of his opponent's file—surreptitiously.

He paced the room, the condominium suddenly hot and stifling. He lay on the couch and closed his eyes, but sleep would not come.

At some point, Jack sat up. He had one more thing to do before the sun came up. No matter how exhausted he was.

CHAPTER THIRTY-NINE

As Jack's car approached the projects where Lamb lived—projects that hid the railroad tracks snaking silently behind the look-alike buildings—he neither stopped nor slowed. Instead, without so much as a glance toward the crime scene, he pressed the accelerator, maneuvering the BMW past Lamb's home. At the last building in the complex, he swung a sharp right. Almost immediately, the neighborhood began to change. For the worse.

Not a person in sight: only the occasional car skeleton, stripped to its frame. This part of Mystic didn't even have street signs. Nothing but hollowed-out factories, warehouses, crumbling brick structures that were once multi-family tenements.

Jack slowed. As he crept along, the night grew darker, and there were no streetlights. In fact, the telephone poles no longer supported electrical equipment of any kind. Even the transmission wires were gone. Jack squinted through darkness lit only by the sweep of his headlights. At last, he picked out the faint outline of a cluster of buildings.

Long shuttered, Mystic's first public housing projects stood crippled in total blackness. As Jack pulled into a narrow drive, overgrown with weeds, he could see railroad tracks off to the right, a rail spur that formed one end of the rail line that ran behind both projects.

Finally, Jack brought his car to a stop in front of a large, three-story, cinder-block structure that had once housed thirty or so families. The windows and doors were covered with plywood weathered to a charcoal black.

Cutting the engine, Jack got out of the car. He tugged his collar up tight against the cold and walked to the cement landing beneath two boarded-up windows. The cement landing where he once played with baseball cards and devoured books now sat in pieces, chunks of missing concrete strewn about. Looking up, Jack surveyed the bleak, dilapidated structure.

The place he had called home for most of his childhood. A white minority in these projects, a much younger Jack Marino had watched as Black and Hispanic kids milled around on the corner, humming Motown songs.

Jack shook his head, returning to the desolation. Farther around the corner of his building would be a telephone pole. Number 1711. Flush behind the pole, the chain-link fence separating the projects from an old Catholic school still stood—rusted and bent. A fence he once climbed. Remnants of barbed wire, meant to keep out Jack and the other "project kids," lay limp atop the fence. Beyond, he could make out the outline of an old running track he'd circled countless times. Next to a school he couldn't afford to attend. What was left of the railroad tracks wound silently into the night, overgrown by tall grass and weeds.

Jack stood in a time warp. When he'd climbed over that fence to get to the track, even as a kid, he'd wondered where he was running to. On this night, he understood: he hadn't been running toward anything. He'd been running from everything, just as his brother, Matt, had.

He turned his back on the ghosts of his past and walked toward his childhood home. At the cracked concrete stairs of his building, he stood stock-still, his thoughts clearer than they'd been in a long time. There'd be no more running away. He'd come full circle on the track of life. He was home. Where he belonged. Not in a huge, soulless law firm wedged into four glitzy, brass-detailed floors of a Boston skyscraper.

Above, a jet plane droned through a starless night. The wind whistled. And then from out of the darkness, like a slap in the face, came a voice.

"I knew you'd be here tonight."

Jack's heart slammed against his chest as he jumped back. But he knew the voice.

Through the gnarled branches of a tree Jack had climbed as a kid, slivers of moonlight flickered like arrows, illuminating his brother Matt's face.

Matt nodded in the direction of the splintered wood that covered what was once their kitchen window. "I can still see her face, you know."

"Me too," Jack managed, still rattled by his brother's appearance. Looking up at the darkened facade, Jack half expected to see his mother with that beautiful smile of hers, looking down at them. "You know, she may not have had much in the way of material things to give us, but she showered us with what she did have: love. When I think back on it, she gave us what most everyone here never had—a head start."

Matt gave his brother a sideways smile. "She'd have been proud of you, Jack. Her son, the lawyer."

Jack looked up at his former home. There was something holy about this place. For a fleeting second, he caught his mother's face in the play of shadows. Transfixed, he couldn't help but wonder if there was more to this life than we think. He shook his head. "A few years ago, maybe. Not so much now."

"That bullshit in the DA's office?" Matt said. "Screw 'em. You know something? Even in the joint, I heard about what you can do in a courtroom. I was the only friggin' con in that shithole rooting for a prosecutor. No matter what happened in the DA's office, remember this: You're a kick-ass trial lawyer. And you're going to try the hell out of this case."

A cold wind blasted through the black night, building in strength.

"Truth was, I bailed," said Matt. "You stayed. You became the head of the family when I should have been there for you—both of you. I hope you can forgive me, Jack."

Matt closed the distance between them, crossing time and space to stand before his brother. His voice broke as he wrapped Jack in a backbreaking hug. "I love you, Jack."

Jack returned the embrace fiercely.

Matt looked up at the ruins of their former home. "Tough place to grow up, but not a bad way to grow strong." He cleared his throat. "Nothing will ever change that this was our home."

"Still is," Jack said.

CHAPTER FORTY

Jack woke with a start on the morning of the trial. The speck of sleep he'd gotten hadn't been good. The events of the night before threatened to overwhelm him: Summer's unexpected visit, the taste of her lips, and his late-night return to his boyhood home, where Matt had been waiting. It might all have been a dream, but Summer's scent lingered, along with the memory of his brother's embrace. And Summer's bag remained on the floor, its contents hidden from view.

The clock at his bedside flashed a neon red 5:30 a.m. He hoped a steaming shower would make up for his lack of sleep.

What price would David Lamb have to pay if Jack refused to use the file contents in Summer's bag? What price would Jack pay if he ignored the Rules of Professional Conduct? Goddamn it. Sears would have eaten those documents for breakfast, garnering every strategic advantage he could.

Jack shaved, staring at the face in the mirror. Who was he? Someone who persevered, no matter how tough the task—a lawyer who fought hard and won fairly? Or someone who would cheat to win—in pursuit of the truth? The pounding hot water of the shower brought no answers.

He circled the courthouse, searching for parking. Even at this early hour, the courthouse was a place of frenzied activity. Media news trucks ringed Somerset Street, where the historic Pemberton Square courthouse was tucked behind the horseshoe-shaped Center Plaza Office complex. Jack saw trucks from three local stations—Channels 4, 5, and 7—and another one with the familiar logo of Boston 9 News.

Political protest and civil unrest have always formed the beating heart of Boston, considered the cradle of liberty for its storied role in the birth of a nation. And today would be no different. A death penalty case, the first in decades, had brought out the most passionate believers. Both sides of the death penalty battle pitched their signs and established their camps. Along one side of the entrance to the courthouse, the death penalty opponents had already set up in a long, jagged line. One woman in a wrinkled trench coat held a sign that read, "DEATH PENALTY IS MURDER." The man beside her, in a Boston Red Sox cap, held a poster that stated "THOU SHALT NOT KILL." Two young women, college-age, stood at each end of a long, rectangular sign that proclaimed, "STOP STATE KILLING."

The pro-death penalty forces held their vigil on the other side of the entrance to the courthouse. Their signs read, "DEATH PENALTY IS A DETERRENT," and, "WHO SPEAKS FOR THE VICTIMS?" An old man in his late seventies, wearing a sweatshirt and fatigue pants, had tacked his poster to a stick and held it high above him: "CRUEL AND UNUSUAL LENIENCY." The Boston Police were out in full force, blanketing the courthouse.

Minutes later, a janitor Jack had known for years slipped him into the courthouse through a side door. It seemed like ages since he'd entered a courtroom for a trial. He wanted to sit at counsel table while the room was empty and still. Perhaps some of the anxiety would fade.

Drawing a deep breath, he pushed through the faded-leather doors of courtroom 906, the Homicide Session, entering an arena he'd once thought of as home. A place that had infused him with life, but now loomed as a source of regret and fear.

Jack sat at counsel table and scanned the cavernous courtroom. Overhead, white plaster medallions were arranged in an oval pattern on a cracked blue ceiling, their once-intricate detail hinting at a faded Brahmin style.

Under his feet was a tattered blue carpet, electrical cords running helter-skelter, gray rubber protective raceways covering cords to form a patchwork electrical system. At the front of the room, newel posts supported a dark brown mahogany rail in front of the clerk's bench. Behind the clerk's enclosure was a swivel chair. Towering above it all was an altar-like bench and the judge's high-backed leather chair.

Jack turned toward the witness stand—the crucible where David Lamb's fate would be decided: a simple wooden enclosure elevated five or six inches above the floor. In it stood an empty, beaten-up wooden chair.

A voice Jack didn't recognize broke his reverie. "Jack Marino?" a middle-aged man, dressed casually, asked, entering the courtroom.

"And you are?" Jack asked.

"Constable Chris James. I'm making in-hand service." The man tossed a sheaf of papers on the table before him.

Jack picked up the envelope. *Shit*. Divorce papers. It was the last way he could have imagined the day would start.

CHAPTER FORTY-ONE

By 8:45 a.m., a buzz rose from the now-packed courtroom. Shaking off the calculated emotional assault engineered by Abby, Jack brushed away two years of false starts and a legacy of fear.

His eyes swept the courtroom, as he placed a trembling hand in his left pocket. He was ready—as ready as he could be.

The press had already filled many of the seats in the gallery at the rear of the courtroom. A television pool camera had been set up. Jack recognized many of the familiar faces among the spectators. At the rear of the courtroom a group of assistant DAs gathered, most of whom Jack knew well. All of them, particularly the younger ones, practiced looking important as they gawked at him.

Jack took a breath and steadied himself. Criminal trials were as much about the lawyers as about the defendants. No doubt, all the Assistant District Attorneys had heard a skewed version of the events leading to Jack's dismissal. No doubt, each one hoped to see him fall on his face, humiliated by their champion, First Assistant District Attorney Brad Sears, who unlike Jack, looked like he'd arrived refreshed from a great night's sleep followed by an invigorating morning racquetball game.

He was currently engaged in a hushed but animated conversation with the session clerk. How well Jack remembered the unmitigated self-righteousness of the District Attorney's office, how rigid, how unforgiving its code was. He'd been part of that.

The clerk turned his head toward Jack. "His Honor would like a word with the two of you," he said. "In his lobby."

Jack stopped arranging his "war desk," as he called it. He started toward the door behind the judge's bench. Sears jumped ahead of him. Same old games.

Sears turned and thrust a thin spool of rolled-up papers into Jack's hands. The clerk ushered the two lawyers into Judge Stone's lair.

The judge's lobby looked like a 19th-century study. Two double-hung windows to the right of the judge's desk were shuttered in an attempt to keep the cold at bay. Light shone from an emerald-green desk lamp that rested on a massive desk. Behind it, Stone sat leafing through a mass of papers before him. A clock ticked relentlessly.

"May I take this opportunity to remind the Court about my motion to suppress my client's firearm conviction?" Jack said, before anyone else could speak. A tactical error, he realized at once.

The judge drilled a look at Jack, then referred to the papers before him. "Would you mind telling me what this is all about, Mr. Sears?"

Jack looked down at the unread scrolled papers in his hand.

"Your Honor, this is the Commonwealth's Motion to Continue," Sears began.

"I can read, Counsel," said Judge Stone. "I asked you to explain it. I seem to recall a deeply felt concern expressed only this past Friday that any delay in the trial of this case would prejudice the Commonwealth in the extreme. Do you remember saying something along those lines?"

Sears cleared his throat. "Your Honor," he said, "the Commonwealth is requesting a short continuance because of the unavailability of an expert witness."

"On Friday he was available. Now he's not?"

"I only found out last evening."

"You got a call from one of your experts on a Sunday evening?" Stone peered over his trifocals.

Sears didn't answer.

Stone blinked solemnly. "What's your position on this sudden twist of events, Mr. Marino?"

"Aside from the lack of notice," Jack said, looking down at Sears's papers, "I find it more than a little unusual given the speech I was made to suffer through on Friday." Though part of him wanted to see Sears humiliated as he had been Friday, Jack felt torn. A continuance would give him more time to find his witness, the mysterious Nora, currently his only lead. It would also give him more time to resolve his ethical quandary. "I have no objection."

Stone looked at them both, first Jack and then Sears. "Do you want to give me the full story, Mr. Sears?"

"Judge, as I said, a critical expert witness is not available this week."

"Which expert?"

"The Commonwealth's ballistics expert."

"Can't you put him on the stand, out of order?"

"He's not available for another week, Your Honor."

"Two weeks?" The judge scowled.

"He was called out of state. And unfortunately, that would leave the ballistics expert for the defense as the only ballistics expert who has examined the evidence in this case."

Stone turned to the calendar on his desk, flipping through its pages until he reached the month of November. Stone tapped his finger on the first week of the month.

Sears fidgeted, shuffling his feet during the Judge's silence.

"Counsel, you'll have to put your case in without a ballistics expert." The judge smiled. "Tell your boss his motion is denied. We impanel in five minutes." After a beat, he added, "Notwithstanding the election. And before I forget, it would be reversible error to allow the defendant's firearm conviction into evidence in a case like this. The defendant's motion to exclude his firearm conviction is allowed."

Sears looked as if he couldn't breathe. Almost wobbling, he said, "Your Honor?"

"Five minutes," Stone repeated, cutting him off with a wave of his hand.

Jack stood to leave the judge's lobby.

"Oh, gentlemen?"

Jack turned back toward the judge.

"Given the public interest in this case," Judge Stone said, "I've allowed a pool camera at the request of the news media. I trust you'll conduct yourselves appropriately." The judge faced Jack squarely. "This time."

CHAPTER FORTY-TWO

A nervous energy coursed through the courtroom, as if lightning might strike at any moment.

Jack approached counsel table to shake hands with Lamb, who had been brought into the courtroom by court officers. He looked pale and drawn, despite the suit Mrs. Lamb had managed to borrow for the trial. Jack placed a hand on his client's shoulder.

Then he surveyed the courtroom. As Sears conferred with aides, Jack saw Summer approach her boss and hand him a stack of papers. Jack avoided direct eye contact.

In the gallery, Tommy Regan's wife and three children huddled next to a victim witness advocate, a woman Jack had worked alongside in scores of cases in the past. They'd shared many victories, and Jack considered her a good friend. Today, she avoided his eyes. Just a work friend, not a real friend, Jack thought.

"All rise," a court officer cried. As everyone came to their feet, Judge Marshal Stone entered the courtroom, his black robe flowing behind him.

"Bring in the panel of prospective jurors," Judge Stone said before reaching the bench, intent on wasting none of his precious time. White-haired and scowling, he ascended to his throne.

Jack stood, his legs wobbly. "Your Honor, before the jury venire comes in, I have a motion to permit individual voir dire." His motion would allow him to question prospective jurors individually, a right routinely denied to Massachusetts attorneys, unlike trial lawyers in most other states. Jack needed fair jurors, jurors who would listen, understand, and apply the presumption of innocence, not give it lip service.

"Individual questions? In my Court?" Stone said. "I ask the questions."

"Judge, the law affords the Court broad discretion to permit counsel to ask individual questions of jurors on a case-by-case basis."

"I don't allow individual voir dire," Stone said. "You should know that."

"Other judges have granted this motion." Instantly, Jack realized his mistake.

Stone looked astonished. "Counsel, you're not before 'other judges.' You're before me."

"Your Honor, this is a death penalty case, and the jury questionnaire is nearly useless as a means for the defense to ensure drawing a jury of peers without bias or preconception." On this single-page questionnaire, jurors provided a brief bio and indicated any affiliation with the law enforcement community, involvement in past lawsuits and past convictions.

"It's been more than sufficient for everyone else who has appeared before me," Stone said. "Including you, as I recall."

As a prosecutor, Jack had opposed individual voir dire in the rape trial against the senator's son. "The circumstances are different now, Your Honor."

The judge smiled. "I see they are, Counsel. Much different, it would seem." Stone turned to Sears. "Are you going to weigh in on this?"

"Your Honor, I only received a copy of the motion as counsel was presenting it. The Commonwealth vigorously objects. The information gathered through the jury questionnaire is more than sufficient to gauge the impartiality of the jurors."

"Denied," Judge Stone said, motioning to the court officer. "Bring the jury panel into the courtroom."

"Note my objection," Jack said, as prospective jurors poured in through double doors. His timing couldn't have been worse. Sears beamed as several prospective jurors heard the objection. The last thing Jack wanted was to present himself to the jury panel as the stereotypical defense lawyer, objecting to anything and everything to get his client off.

Jack shrugged it off and reviewed the juror questionnaires. Knowing what kind of juror he didn't want was easy. He didn't want lawyers, doctors, professors, or engineers. At least the ones who thought they knew everything. Blinded by arrogance, they knew little about the human condition and nothing about the excruciating hopelessness of life lived at the margins of society.

No, Jack decided. For this jury, he wanted neighborhood folk, people of color, veterans, the bluest of blue-collar workers. People who'd been cut up by life's sharp edges. People whose wrongs would never be righted. In short, Jack wanted jurors who in life had never gotten their day in court.

But would now.

These were people Jack could relate to. They would allow Jack to play to one of his great strengths—an ability to connect, to establish a heart-link.

But not today. The jurors filing into the courtroom were almost entirely white and particularly well dressed. Jack figured Back Bay, Newbury Street, or Beacon Hill. His stomach started to burn.

Once the panel was seated at the rear of the courtroom, Judge Stone described the selection process, explaining that twelve jurors and four alternates would be chosen in the course of the day. The lawyers could decide some people shouldn't be on the jury without explaining why—a peremptory challenge—or for specific reasons—a challenge for cause.

"Now when the clerk calls your name, say 'here' or 'present,'" Judge Stone said. "At the same time, rise from your seat. When we see you rise, we'll know you're present. But Ms. Gleason, the court reporter, may not see you. She will only take down your spoken word. Thank you. Mr. Clerk, you may proceed."

"Thank you, Your Honor," the clerk began. "Juror in panel one, seat two, Mollie Simmons. Would you take seat number one, please?" Molly was in her sixties. Well dressed and thin, she looked about five-six or five-seven. According to her jury questionnaire, she was a librarian.

And so it continued.

Jury selection moved too quickly for Jack. Both sides traded challenges—first for cause, based on any number of obviously disqualifying factors, and next exercising their peremptory challenges, removing jurors for pretty much any reason. Without individual questioning, it was impossible to get into the heads of these jurors, to glimpse into their lives for insight into how they might feel about this death penalty case.

Jack was out of challenges when Sears used his last peremptory challenge to exclude the one remaining African American. He was in his early fifties, tall and fit, his short-cropped hair turning gray.

Jack bounced to his feet. "Your Honor, may we approach?"

Stone detested sidebar conferences but couldn't avoid them during jury selection. He motioned for them to approach the side of the bench farthest from the jury.

"Your Honor, this is the second time the Assistant District Attorney has struck a minority member from this panel," said Jack, deliberately dropping "First" from Sears's title. "I'd like to know why."

Stone spoke in measured tones. "These are peremptory challenges, Mr. Marino. He doesn't have to provide a reason."

"The Soares case says he does. The Commonwealth cannot use its peremptory challenges to exclude minority representation on this jury."

"The case law, Mr. Marino, states that there must be a pattern in which the party exercising his peremptory challenges demonstrates an intention to exclude a particular race. Where's the pattern here?"

"He's excluded the only two minorities on this jury panel," Jack said, his voice rising. "That's a pattern."

Stone wagged a finger at Jack as the prospective jurors watched. "I hardly think two people constitute a pattern, Mr. Marino." The judge hesitated, undoubtedly thinking about the possibility of getting reversed on appeal following a conviction. His voice grew cold. "That's enough. The Commonwealth's challenges will stand." He turned to the prosecutor. "However, I'm warning you, Mr. Sears, that I'm looking closely at your challenges."

"Your Honor, there's nothing to look closely at," Jack said. "There are no more minorities left on this jury panel."

"Step back," said Judge Stone.

A few minutes later, after the last of the peremptory challenges, the clerk called the name of the last juror: Paul Villano.

"Here." A man in his mid-thirties walked forward. He was clean-shaven with curly black hair.

"Seat number sixteen, please. Watch your step."

Jack looked at the jury questionnaire. Villano was the son of a police officer. Great. He'd never met a police officer who wasn't for the death penalty. "Stone looked to the jurors, "Is the Commonwealth content with this jury?"

Sears smiled as if the jurors were coming to his home for dinner. "Yes, Your Honor. The Commonwealth is very content."

"Is the defendant content with this jury?"

Jack knew any hesitation on his part might be interpreted by the jury as a rebuke. "The defense is equally content," he said.

Stone turned to the court reporter. "The record will reflect that all parties are content."

The judge continued, "Ladies and gentlemen, we have a jury. The remainder of the jury panel is dismissed. On behalf of the Commonwealth, I thank you for your appearance here today. The court officer will give you instructions on whether you are to return to the jury pool or not.

"I note I am three minutes ahead of schedule," he added with satisfaction. "Mr. Clerk, please swear the jury in."

Jack surveyed the jury. He didn't feel like celebrating. Sure, he'd removed the Back Bay and Newbury Street types. But he knew almost nothing about these jurors. Worse, only a few of them made eye contact, and the trial hadn't begun yet.

The ex-prosecutor drew a breath. He'd bring them around.

He had to.

CHAPTER FORTY-THREE

Groaning under his weight, the tired stairs announced Matt Marino's arrival even before he entered Tony's Gym. Not that anyone could hear him over the thunderous clanking of free weights and the raucous jock-banter.

Matt scanned the room. The scent of steroids hung in the air.

"Hey," shouted a muscle-head behind the counter.

With a flip of his hand, Matt waved him off. His quarry was in the corner.

Matt reached his man just as Roger "Rat" Ferriter hoisted the bar back onto the bench rack with an enormous grunt. Rat's upper torso was shredded with muscle that tapered down to a stomach that looked like it was carved out of marble. All 'roids.

Staring at the ceiling, his back reclined on the bench, Rat turned his head and spat on the floor, inches from Matt's feet. "I work alone," he grunted.

"I've got a few questions," Matt said. "Why don't I spot you."

"Only a bitch needs a spotter," Rat said.

"Tough guy?" said Matt.

Turning to his side, Rat stood, revealing himself to be about 6'3", a bit taller than Matt, blue tatts like snakes running down his chiseled arms.

"Tougher than you, fuck-face," Rat said, looking around the gym. "And one word from me, and you're not getting out of here."

Matt smiled. "We'll see. Gym-tough ain't always street-tough."

Three black 50-pound York plates hung on each side of Rat's barbell. Matt took a silent breath and reached down with both hands in an overhand grip. He snatched the weight off the bench. With a low grunt, Matt clean-jerked the bar over his head in a standard military press.

He held the bar motionless for an instant, the enormous weight bending the bar slightly. Then Matt put his head down, threw his right leg back and heaved the enormous weight at Rat without buckling an inch.

The crash at Rat's feet was deafening. Everyone in the gym turned and stared at the two men.

"The fuck!" Rat yelled.

"How'd Tommy Regan end up dead that night at TC's?"

Recognition glinted in Rat's eyes. "You're with that fuckin' lawyer."

"I'd watch your mouth. That 'fuckin' lawyer' is my brother."

"Whatever," Rat said. "Just like I told him, I don't know who the fuck killed Tommy. Don't care, either."

Matt moved over to the dumbbell rack and picked up a shiny hundred-pounder, holding it up high in the air with one arm, hatchet-style.

Rat got the message. He sat back down on the bench.

"Are drugs being sold out of The Treasure Chest?" Matt asked. He lowered the dumbbell to the floor.

Rat's lips compressed. "No fuckin' secret," he said. "Been sellin' shit outta there for years."

"Who sells it?"

Rat shook his head.

Matt looked down at the dumbbell. "I won't miss this time," he said without emotion.

A pained look. "Bartenders handle it."

"Mickey Nolan too?"

"He's in the middle of everything."

"What're they selling?'"

Rat grabbed the sweat rag next to him and threw it on the floor. "Whatever you want. Coke. Smack. Meth. Look, I don't ask questions. No one does."

"And why's that?"

"Fuck," Rat said. "Maybe somethin' to do with the line of Harleys out front. You keep your mouth shut at TC's. Look, man, I don't know who the hell you are, but word gets back that it was me who talked to you, I'm a fuckin' dead man." Sweat dripped down Rat's unshaven face.

"Dangerous guy like you shouldn't have a problem," Matt said. "Second thought, maybe that's why they call you 'Rat.'"

Sweat poured off the man on the bench, his eyes blinking rapidly. Roger Ferriter didn't seem quite so tough anymore. Nor did the rest of the muscle-heads, who silently cleared a way as Matt found his way out.

CHAPTER FORTY-FOUR

"Beyond a reasonable doubt. That's right. In a criminal case, it's up to the Commonwealth to prove beyond a reasonable doubt that the defendant is guilty of the crime charged." Judge Stone approached the end of his fiery pre-charge lecture to the jury, not only laying down the law but also anointing himself as God.

The jurors listened with attention. Judge Stone explained that the Commonwealth would be the first to present its opening statement, followed by the defense counsel's opening unless the defense opted to open after the Commonwealth rested its case. After opening statements, the Commonwealth would present its witnesses, a phase of the trial called its case-in-chief. During direct examination of a witness by either attorney, he said, the attorneys could not ask a question that suggested the answer—that would be leading the witness—but during cross-examination, leading a witness was precisely how it was supposed to be done.

"After the prosecutor rests, Mr. Marino at his option will present his case by calling any defense witnesses." With permission of the court, either side could strike back with rebuttal witnesses, but eventually both sides would rest. The evidence would be closed, and each party would present closing arguments, beginning with the defense.

"Under the law of the Commonwealth," Judge Stone added, "the District Attorney gets the last word." Judge Stone appeared to relish the phrase.

"Alternates will be chosen by random drawing after the Court has instructed you on the principles of law that will apply to this case during your deliberations. Let me emphasize this: Except for the foreman, whom I'll take the liberty of appointing now and who cannot be selected as an alternate juror, we do not know who the alternates will be. All of you should therefore pay strict attention to the evidence since each of you has an equal opportunity to be among the twelve deliberating jurors."

The foreman, to Jack's dismay, was Paul Villano—the cop's son.

After summarizing the charges, Judge Stone nodded in the direction of the prosecutor. "Mr. Sears, you may begin."

Sears stood slowly, buttoning his suit coat as he did so.

Jack felt a knot in his stomach as Sears began. An opening statement was supposed to be an opportunity to tell the jury about the case. Just the facts, no argument. But the opening was a skilled lawyer's first opportunity to prejudice the jury, to subtly argue the facts of a case without getting caught. And no one did that better than Brad Sears.

At last, the trial had begun. And David Lamb's life—hanging in the balance—would be decided.

PART IV

THE TRIAL

CHAPTER FORTY-FIVE

"May I proceed, Your Honor?" asked First Assistant District Attorney Brad Sears.

"You may, sir," the judge responded.

Sears marched to a lectern in front of the jury box. He deposited his notes, fingering them carefully as if he were holding an original copy of the United States Constitution. Every eye in the courtroom—as well as the all-important television pool camera—was focused on him. And he seemed to be savoring every second of it.

"Your Honor. Mr. Foreman. Ladies and Gentlemen of the Jury..."

Sears began by introducing himself, thanking the jurors for the sacrifice they were making, sharing his background, positioning himself as the white knight, the guardian of truth. Justice incarnate.

Then the spider began to spin its web. "In the next few minutes, I intend to give you a preview of the evidence that the Commonwealth will present in this tragic case. Evidence elicited from witnesses who will come into this courtroom and take that witness stand." The prosecutor pointed a manicured finger at the witness enclosure.

Sears wasted no time aligning himself with the jury. He carved out his role as an independent investigator who, along with them, would solve a heinous crime. An easily solved puzzle. Jointly, they would avenge a crime that had left three young children fatherless and a loving wife, now a widow.

"Together, we'll uncover the truth," said Sears. "But when you leave this courtroom, it will be up to you. Only your guilty verdict will make the defendant pay the price for his monstrous act."

Sears strolled before the jury, at ease in his role as teacher, philosopher, righter of wrongs. "During the course of this trial, ladies and gentlemen, the Commonwealth will present several key witnesses. Through them you will learn the facts of this case. Through their mouths you will hear the truth."

Here it comes, Jack thought. The First Assistant would do his best to take the wind out of Jack's sails on the critical issue of immunity.

Slowly, almost gently, Sears explained that in the world of criminal justice there were occasions when—for reasons of intimidation, fear, or concern for loved ones—witnesses were reluctant to come forward. "In such instances, our law in its infinite wisdom provides a way to encourage such witnesses to come forward, to tell the truth, to serve the ends of justice. That special legal protection is called 'immunity.' In this case, the Commonwealth had no choice but to apply for a grant of immunity to protect one of its witnesses."

Sears continued, "We will show through that witness that the victim, Thomas Regan, was simply trying to help out a friend. A friend who, along with Mr. Regan, happened to work at an exotic dance club, The Treasure Chest, located in Mystic. Not a place where Thomas was particularly proud to work. But a job, nonetheless. It was there that he befriended the defendant, David Lamb, who along with Mr. Regan was hired to clean the bar, trash the empty bottles, and do whatever needed to be done to keep a place such as that clean.

"Sometime during the evening of August tenth, into the morning of the eleventh, a bit over two years ago now, something went wrong.

Terribly wrong. It began when David Lamb approached the victim and offered to sell him cocaine."

There it was: the Commonwealth's attempt to establish a motive. When the prosecution has nothing, it always falls back on drugs. A modern-day taboo, a hot button issue, that could be counted on to inflame the passions of jurors, many of whom went home every night wondering if their kid would be the next to fall victim to the allure of illicit drugs.

Sears continued to weave his tale. "Thomas Regan was a family man. He refused Lamb's offer. The two men argued, and in the heat of passion, Thomas threatened to tell management that Lamb was selling drugs. That, ladies and gentlemen, would not only have cost Lamb his job, but would have exposed him to arrest and prosecution. And that sealed Thomas Regan's fate."

Consulting his notes, Sears looked up. "Because, as you will learn, shortly after closing the establishment, Lamb, who had driven Mr. Regan to work that night, told him that his car had broken down behind the building and that he needed help. Alert to the tension between the two men, the owner of the club, Mr. Mickey Nolan, followed the men outside to the rear of the property, which abuts an unused railroad line, which you'll see when we take a view of the scene.

"As the defendant led the victim out to what would turn out to be his execution, Mr. Regan turned to ask where the car was. Without warning, the defendant pulled out a gun. In shock, Mr. Nolan yelled to stop, but it was too late. The defendant shot Thomas Regan through the head. In cold blood. The defendant, who hadn't even realized that Mr. Nolan was present, then pointed the gun at Nolan and told him that if he were ever to breathe a word of what had happened, he and his family would end up like Regan. At gunpoint, Mickey Nolan was then forced to drag the body of Mr. Regan into the bushes, where they left it. With a gun to Nolan's head, they retrieved the victim's car using keys they'd taken out of his pocket. Then they dragged the body into the car and drove it to a nearby maintenance shack, for the police to discover the next morning."

Sears paused. He looked at the jury. He glanced at Lamb. "Because of the obvious threat to his life and the life of his family, Mickey Nolan denied any knowledge of what had happened to Thomas Regan that night. And despite the best efforts of the Mystic Police Department, he remained silent. It was only when the Commonwealth extended an offer of immunity and protection for his family that Nolan broke down and told the truth of what had happened."

The jurors listened, sneaking surreptitious looks at Lamb.

"Now that," said Sears, "merely outlines the evidence you will hear in this case. Together, we will prove that when the defendant was spurned and threatened with disclosure that night at The Treasure Chest, he decided to murder Thomas Regan. And, in fact, that's what he did, executing Mr. Regan by shooting him in the back of the head alongside the railroad tracks where he thought no one would see him. Where he thought he could get away with a deliberately premeditated murder with malice aforethought."

Sears paused to emphasize the words "with malice aforethought." He drank in a long breath, surveying his charges, his allies in his fight against crime. In a tone that blended notes of solemnity and dignity, Sears ended his opening as he always did. "I am confident that you will return a verdict of guilty of murder in the first degree against this defendant," he said, turning with a flourish to jab a finger at Lamb. Facing the jurors again, he gathered his notes and swept the jury with his best prosecutorial gaze. "Thank you for your service and sacrifice."

The courtroom fell silent.

Stricken, Lamb sat next to Jack, diminished by the overwhelming power and might of the forces that had gathered to commandeer his fate.

As Sears sat down, Judge Stone turned to Jack. "Mr. Marino. You have the right to waive or reserve your opening. Of course, you also have the right to address the jury now should you choose to do so. What is your desire, sir?"

Jack could see several jurors staring at both him and his client. Judge Stone's comments had piqued the jury's curiosity, doubling their expectation that Jack would open now. Damn the judge. He should have instructed the jury—in his pre-charge—that opening statements aren't evidence. Told them it was their duty to draw no conclusions regarding guilt or innocence until all the evidence had been heard and the trial concluded. Had Judge Stone done so, Jack could have deferred his opening, garnering critical insight into Sears's strategy.

"Thank you, Your Honor." Jack rose.

CHAPTER FORTY-SIX

"My name is Jack Marino," the onetime prosecutor began. "And I consider it a privilege to appear before you today representing my client, Mr. David Lamb, who sits beside me today and whose mother, Ann, and one of his twin daughters are seated in the gallery at the rear of the courtroom."

Jack struggled to gather his thoughts, the floor seeming to tilt beneath his feet.

"What I have to say to you today and in the days that follow will not be easy to hear. It will challenge your ideals, your beliefs, even your confidence in the very nature of our judicial system. It will be painful. I know it will be for me. As a former Assistant District Attorney in this very county, indeed as a former colleague of Mr. Sears, it will trouble me to expose an ugly truth."

Sears shifted in his chair.

"You see, I agree with the First Assistant District Attorney that a horrendous crime was committed," Jack continued, "a crime that has left a family without a father and without a husband. Except for one thing: the person who killed Tommy Regan was not his close friend David Lamb."

Jack dropped his eyes. "The ugly truth is that the person who killed Tommy Regan is none other than the Commonwealth's chief witness—Mickey Nolan. My client witnessed him murder Tommy Regan, and the only reason he's not the one with the immunity deal is that Mr. Nolan struck first, hiring an expensive lawyer in order to pin the crime on David Lamb."

An energy seemed to animate the jurors, their attention riveted on Jack, who spoke with gathering force.

"That's right. The Commonwealth, desperate for a conviction in a long unsolved murder case, which has now become a death penalty case, has extended immunity—absolute immunity—to the actual killer of Tommy Regan, the Commonwealth's star witness—indeed its only witness—against David Lamb."

Sears kept his head down, reviewing his paperwork.

Jack continued, making eye contact with each member of the jury.

"A second crime was committed in this case." He slowed his delivery, punching with each word. "And, members of the jury, I will prove it."

Sears looked up.

"The second crime I speak of is obstruction of justice. A crime committed by the prosecutor, Brad Sears, and his boss, District Attorney Trevor Cameron." Turning on his heels, Jack pointed straight at Sears.

Several jurors looked shocked.

Sears started to rise as if to object but Jack just rolled on.

"What was this crime?" Jack asked. "The prosecution had a witness to this murder—an unbiased witness—and failed to disclose the identity of this witness as required by law, effectively keeping that witness from me. And from David Lamb. But most importantly, from you."

Sears did stand, but again before he could speak, Jack was talking.

"That's right. The Commonwealth tried to deceive you and me by concealing the existence of a key witness. And now, instead of admitting to the truth of what they've done, in their cowardice, they're going to compound this tragedy by attempting to convict— and then execute—an innocent man for a crime he didn't commit."

"Your Honor," Sears finally managed, slamming his open hand against the top of the table, causing several members of the jury to jump. "Objection!"

Jack turned toward the prosecutor.

"Sidebar," Judge Stone said. "Now."

*　*　*

"Your Honor, this is outrageous," Sears said. "I have never, in all of the years I've been a prosecutor, seen or heard anything like this. I demand to know what possible basis defense counsel has for making these outlandish, unsupported allegations."

Judge Stone needed no convincing. "Mr. Marino, have you forgotten what it is to practice in a criminal courtroom?"

Jack stood silently, looking the judge in the eye.

"Identify the good-faith basis upon which you rely to make these scandalous charges," Judge Stone said. "Now."

"I'm sorry, Your Honor," Jack said. "At this point in the trial, I can say only that I have a good-faith basis for everything I've put on the record."

"I'll ask you again. What is your basis, sir?"

"I can't say."

Judge Stone bore down. "Mr. Marino, you don't make an allegation of prosecutorial misconduct of this magnitude without providing more than a bald assertion of a good-faith basis. Not in my courtroom. Now, I won't merely ask you, I'm ordering you to explain your conduct."

Jack held Judge Stone's gaze without interruption. "As an officer of the court, I can only represent that I have a good-faith basis, though I'm afraid I cannot say any more."

The judge snorted and tapped his chin. "Very well, Mr. Marino. Have it your way. For now. But listen to me carefully. If you don't introduce admissible evidence to support these allegations of yours, I will not hesitate to hold you in contempt of this Court. Then it will be you who will need a defense attorney. A good one."

Jack didn't blink.

"You're on notice, Mr. Marino." Judge Stone turned toward the prosecutor. "In the meantime, are you requesting a special instruction to the jury, Mr. Sears?"

"Yes, Your Honor. I ask that defense counsel," the words rolling off his lips with derision, "be admonished in the strongest possible terms, and further, that his highly offensive remarks be stricken from the record and the jury be instructed accordingly."

"So ruled," Judge Stone said. He looked down at Jack. "Not another word, Mr. Marino. Your opening is finished. Return to your seat. And be thankful you still have a chair inside the bar enclosure."

*　*　*

Jack remained in his seat, head bowed, waiting for the last of the spectators and court personnel to file out of the old courtroom on this abbreviated first day. The courtroom grew quiet. The judge had instructed the jurors with brutal clarity, doing his best to ensure that each juror knew that the defense had done something terribly wrong. Through it all, Jack felt the jury's collective gaze settle on him, scrutinizing him, wondering about him.

In the stillness of the empty courtroom, Jack could feel his heartbeat as he surveyed the judge's bench, the witness stand, the empty jury box. Though he'd tried dozens of major felonies in this same courtroom, his memories seemed to belong to someone else. A prosecutor who had once fearlessly charged the witness stand with in-your-face cross-examinations. A prosecutor who had challenged jurors to cast their rigidity aside, to walk in the shoes of the victim, to feel Jack's outrage. To fight back. To chase away the darkness of crime with the light of truth. Once, long ago, Jack had been able to do all those things. But that was another time. Sitting here now, he'd never felt so utterly out of place.

His opening statement had been strong and would lead the media's coverage of the trial's opening day. That had been his goal. But it placed him in a dilemma. As a defense attorney, he was obligated to represent his client zealously. And knowing that the Commonwealth had committed a constitutional violation by destroying potentially exculpatory evidence, he was obligated to pursue it. In doing so, he would destroy Summer.

Part of him wished she'd never left behind the file that had changed the defense of his case. But she'd known all she was risking. And still she did it.

Judge Stone had prejudiced Lamb's case with his rebuke of Jack in front of the jury. Jack wondered if he'd been fair to his client. Maybe he should have refused to take the case as soon as he'd learned who would preside. He shook his head at all that lay before him; he was facing two prosecutors, and one of them was wearing a black robe.

The jury's view of the murder scene, which would take place in the morning, would go much better. It had to.

David Lamb's life depended on it.

CHAPTER FORTY-SEVEN

The rented yellow school bus rumbled into the Mystic housing projects near where Tommy Regan had met his fate. The brakes squealed, jarring Jack, the vehicle shuddering to a stop not far from the break in the fence that divided the projects from the railroad tracks. A few residents appeared at their doors, curious about the spectacle, about a busload of strangers who didn't live there, settling in on their doorstep.

Disembarking, the jurors, judge, and court officers filed past Jack. He watched each juror closely, aware that he needed to mend whatever damage his opening statement had caused. He needed to reestablish his professionalism, and—with luck—develop a rapport with these jurors.

During the bus trip, he'd caught some furtive glances from jurors who seemed to regard him with curiosity. He watched them survey a neighborhood they must have felt thankful not to live in. He hoped they wouldn't pass judgment on his client because of the world David Lamb had been born into.

As Jack stepped off the bus, a court officer waved the jurors through a narrow triangle of grass. A gaping hole in the fence would take them to the railroad tracks.

The ground was uneven, marked by holes and debris. Judge Stone, the jurors, the court officers, the stenographer, and the lawyers gathered as a news helicopter hovered above.

Jack looked around. The sparse gravel of the railbed was so strewn with broken bottles, paper, tires, garbage, and other detritus that it was hard to imagine trains chugging down these tracks.

What a terrible place for a kid to grow up in, Jack thought. Yet—amid all the debris—a crudely fashioned tree house hung suspended from a maple tree next to the chain-link fence. An old railroad tie formed its main support. Broken boards with rusted nails poking out of them made up the rest. Was it still in use? Hard to tell, but it was a vivid reminder of the power of a child's imagination.

One of the jurors, an impeccably dressed middle-aged man with salt and pepper hair and expensive shoes, bent down and picked up a broken bottle. He heaved it over to the side. The gesture, so futile amid the mess, puzzled Jack.

The group began to walk. As a child who had walked these tracks often, Jack could never have imagined he'd return here so many years later, a lawyer with a jury in tow. Fighting for the life of a man he believed in his heart was innocent.

Brad Sears, who would get to address the jurors first, was leading all of them to the spot where Tommy Regan had left this world. The chief prosecutor looked every bit the part, pointing out this and that with great flourish and authority. Walking the prosecutor-walk, speaking the prosecutor-talk. Great for the courtroom, perhaps. But out here, he looked and sounded out of place. Jack wondered if the jurors sensed it too.

Standing near the spot where Regan was killed, Jack tried to estimate the distance to the back of the club. The walk from the strip club to here would take only a minute or so. Despite the short walk, it was a desolate place, the wind gathering around them, the jurors and the others shrinking against the fall chill. It was the perfect place for a murder.

As Sears rambled on, Jack's eyes followed the tracks until he could see them no longer. As a kid, he'd often wondered where these tracks—powerful symbols of the freedom he dreamed of—ultimately led.

Judge Stone's voice broke Jack's reverie. "Mr. Marino? Counselor, have you anything to say to the jurors?"

Jack cursed himself for missing whatever it was Sears had focused the jurors' attention on. It was his turn to direct the jury's attention to areas of the crime scene that could be significant to the defense of David Lamb.

He pointed out the place where Lamb had said that Regan and Nolan confronted each other on that fateful night. The foreman seemed uninterested, but two of the women jurors nodded as Jack asked the jurors to examine certain things that might come up later at trial. One of the jurors, a heavyset woman with a round face and upturned nose, caught her sweater on a thorn bush.

Jack seized the opportunity. "Let me help you," he said as he unhooked her. He asked each juror to look closely at the bushes—at the large thorns, razor-sharp and ubiquitous, growing up and down the tracks, the same thorns he remembered cutting himself on as a kid. The juror who'd gotten herself tangled up in the thorns nodded and asked, "Are the thorns important?"

"Critical," Jack responded.

"But why?" the foreman asked.

Before Jack could utter another word, the Judge cut him off. "This is an opportunity to view the scene of the crime. It's not an opportunity for presenting legal argument. We need to return now."

As they turned to go, Jack caught a glimpse of some newer-looking empty beer cans and a wine bottle under some brush.

Had Nora or anyone who knows her been out near the tracks recently? How many nights had she spent in these fields trying to survive one more day? What had she seen that night, and where was she now? Was she even alive?

As the bus lurched away, Jack glanced one last time through the window at the projects. Once again, he was leaving, this time headed for the courthouse where his client's life would be decided. Yet not before he'd learned a strange truth about himself, something that he hadn't fully realized until this day. Jack felt more at home in the streets of Mystic than he did in the halls of justice.

CHAPTER FORTY-EIGHT

The bus reached the County Court in time for the luncheon recess. Instructing the jurors to return promptly for the afternoon session, Judge Stone retreated to his chambers. As the courtroom emptied, Jack was relieved to see Matt waiting for him at the back of the gallery.

"Let's grab lunch," Matt said. "Somewhere we can talk privately."

Only weeks ago, defeat had hovered over Matt like an apparition. But since then, color had crept back into his face. He seemed infused with the energy Jack remembered from their youth and, later, from a rare visit Matt had made to Mystic as a taut, young Marine grunt. For the first time in years, Jack experienced the felt presence of a brother.

"The Steaming Kettle restaurant. Lots of people, lots of noise."

"Something's going on at The Treasure Chest," Matt said, as they slipped into a booth. At the courthouse across the street, the protesters still chanted: "Murder cannot be abolished by murder."

"How do you mean?" Jack asked.

"I parked behind the club yesterday. As soon as night fell, they started rolling up."

"Who?"

"Bikers."

"Outlaws?" Jack asked.

"The worst."

"How can you tell?"

"It's not hard. It's in their walk. The way they look at you. I saw it in the joint. They operate on the lunatic fringe. Some even wore their colors." Matt paused. "Jack, these guys are fucking reptiles. How far do you want to take this?"

Jack didn't flinch.

Matt nodded. "Okay."

A waitress walked over with a notepad.

"We still need a minute," Jack said. When she was out of earshot, he turned to Matt. "So, what are they doing there?"

"I think they're moving drugs through the club. Coke. Heroin. I can smell it. But there's something else too. I called a knife fight into the police station from a pay phone. Said there were serious injuries. Sat in my car for near forty minutes. Took the police that long to come. And even then, no lights. No one in a hurry. Cops sauntered in. An hour later, they drifted back out."

"A potential life-threatening felony, and the cops take almost an hour to respond?" Jack said.

"I need a closer look," Matt said.

Jack took a breath. The terms of his brother's parole would prohibit him from carrying a weapon.

"Not now," Jack said. "I've got another lead I need you to follow up on. Tommy Regan had a lawyer who represented him in his workers' comp case. Tommy may have consulted him about injuries he suffered during a fight he got into at The Treasure Chest when he was off duty. See if you can locate him and find out if there's any truth to Lamb's claim that Regan was going to sue the club and the muscle-head he had a beef with, that guy Rat Ferriter."

"What's the attorney's name?"

"David T. Sherman. Out of Mystic. Here, I have his address from the Lawyer's Diary." Jack ripped a page from his notepad and handed it to Matt. "Any luck with Nora?"

"Shortly after the murder, someone definitely saw a homeless woman talking to the cops. It might have been her."

Jack shook his head. "Sears has known all along there's a potential witness to this murder. That's the memo he's sitting on." Jack shot Matt a sideways look. "I told the jury in my opening there's an eye-witness to the murder, and the DA himself is knee-deep in a cover-up."

Matt gave him a wide grin. "You're at your goddamn best, Brother, when your back's against the wall."

"Must be in the gene pool," Jack said and laughed. Matt hadn't called him "brother" in a long time.

Matt turned serious. "If she's still out there, I'll find her. You know that, don't you?"

Jack nodded. "I do. And in a worst-case scenario, we've got the corroboration requirement on our side."

"Come again?" Matt said.

"The Commonwealth can't convict solely on the testimony of an immunized witness," Jack said. "The government has to produce some independent evidence to corroborate the testimony of an immunized witness. That's the law here in Massachusetts, and I don't see them introducing anything. But unfortunately, it's Judge Stone who's going to decide that one. Not me."

CHAPTER FORTY-NINE

"Call your first witness," Judge Stone intoned.

Practically leaping from his seat, Sears strode to a podium positioned near the far corner of the jury box.

"Your Honor, I call Police Commissioner Jeffrey Knight to the stand."

The commissioner had been sitting in the first row. Now he stood and walked to the stand, his bearing marked by dignity and self-righteousness.

"Please tell the court and jury your name and occupation," said Sears, laying his notes on the podium.

"Jeff Knight. Police Commissioner. City of Mystic Police Department." The commissioner sat straight as an arrow within the witness enclosure.

The First Assistant District Attorney marched the commissioner through direct examination—his questions relaxed, confident, authoritative. Hard to screw up a direct examination, Jack thought. When all was said and done, it boiled down to, "And what happened next?"

Seamlessly, Sears moved to the date of Tommy Regan's murder. "Directing your attention to August eleventh a bit more than two years ago, do you recall that date?"

"I do."

"What happened on that day?"

"Early in the morning, I received a call from one of my patrolmen that a body had been found in a car near the former Boston & Maine railroad tracks."

"Did you personally go to the scene?"

"I did." The commissioner looked calmly at the jury then back to Sears.

"What did you do once there?"

"I secured the scene and called detectives to photograph the victim and the car. I also met with your opponent." He nodded at Jack. "When he was the head of your urban gang unit."

Sears changed the subject as the remark seemed to pique the interest of several jurors. "What else did you do?"

"After I spoke with Mr. Marino, I called the coroner."

"Did you call anyone else?"

"We called the State Police as a matter of investigative protocol. And they sent out a forensics team."

"What was the condition of the victim?"

"He'd suffered a single gunshot wound to his head."

"At some point did you continue your investigation?"

"Yes, sir. We obtained a list of his friends and associates from his wife, or widow I should say, and we began interviewing those individuals."

"And what did you learn?"

"Mr. Regan was seen working the night before he died at The Treasure Chest, an adult entertainment club in Mystic."

"What else?"

"Well, the more questions we asked, the more it became clear that no one was talking."

"And did that include David Lamb?"

"It did."

"By the way, do you see David Lamb in the courtroom today?"

"I do."

"And for the record, would you point him out and describe what he is wearing."

The commissioner pointed at Lamb, taking pains to describe his clothes as if he were a leper dressed in rags. It was a necessary but foregone ritual, repeated countless times in criminal courtrooms throughout the Commonwealth.

As if drawn by the strings of a puppeteer, the jury followed the commissioner's finger to David Lamb, who sat rock still beside Jack, a look of fear pressed onto his face by the sheer enormity of the accusation. Commissioner Knight had been here before. The jury hadn't.

Sears announced the obvious. "Your Honor, may the record reflect that the witness has identified the defendant, David Lamb."

Stone stared down at Lamb. "It may."

Sears made it sound as though he'd cracked the case in the first several minutes of direct examination, like a modern-day Perry Mason. Beside him, Jack could feel Lamb shudder.

"At some point, Commissioner," Sears asked, "did a break occur in your investigation?"

The commissioner looked at the jury, then turned to Sears. "After Mr. Nolan was assured of protection, he decided to come forward to tell what had happened to Thomas Regan."

"Now, when you say protection, are you referring to the immunity that was conferred on Mr. Nolan at the request of District Attorney Trevor Cameron?"

"It's my understanding that he was given immunity, yes."

Jack laughed to himself. It was common practice for a trial lawyer to take the wind out of an opponent's sails by exposing the weaknesses in one's own case. But would Sears be foolish enough to think he'd neutralized the defense with his fleeting reference to immunity?

"What happened next?" Sears asked.

"Once Mr. Nolan agreed to testify, the case came together quickly. In short order, the grand jury returned murder indictments against the defendant."

Jack shook his head. From here on, Sears would be sure to call David Lamb "the defendant," never again using his proper name.

Sears gave the jury a satisfied look, suggesting an open-and-shut case, as if the indictment itself proves guilt. "By the way, Commissioner, did the defendant testify during the grand jury's investigation?"

"He did."

"And what did he say?"

"That Mr. Regan was a close friend. And that he left the club before him and knew nothing about his murder."

"But he did, didn't he?"

"A whole lot."

"What else did you learn, Commissioner?"

"Based on our investigation, and on statements of witnesses as well as the work of the grand jury, we learned that at about one a.m. on Saturday night, August eleventh after The Treasure Chest closed, the defendant shot Thomas Regan in cold blood."

"What was the motive?"

Jack rose to his feet. "Objection, Your Honor. The question calls for speculation and hearsay."

Judge Stone looked at Sears as if to say, "Nice try," and sustained the objection.

"Your Honor, I offer the defendant's grand jury testimony into evidence as a party admission."

Judge Stone looked at Jack. "Any objection?"

Jack started a slow burn. His client's previous testimony was a party admission. An exception to the hearsay rule. The transcript would come to haunt them both. "None, Your Honor."

Sears looked at the jury. With a flourish, he handed the document to the clerk. Exhibit One.

At the conclusion of the direct examination, Sears was in control, the commissioner, relaxed—the consummate law enforcement officer.

"No further questions, Your Honor," said Sears.

Prosecution, one. Defense, zero.

CHAPTER FIFTY

"Your witness, Counselor," said Judge Marshal Stone.

The jury already looked tired, so Jack had to be on his game.

"So, we meet again, Commissioner?" Jack began as he approached the witness.

"We do."

"As I recall, you supervised the crime scene and were present throughout the field investigation?"

"Except for the fingerprints."

"But you received the fingerprint report, right?"

"Yes." Commissioner Knight nodded.

"In fact, you received all the investigative reports in this case, isn't that true, Commissioner?"

"Of course."

"Including the photographs of the decedent, right?"

"Uh-huh."

"You need to answer 'yes' or 'no' for the court reporter," Jack said.

"Yes."

Sears frowned.

"And the toxicology reports?"

"Yes."

"The coroner's report?"

"Yes."

"And eventually the ballistics report and the print results?"

"That's right."

"And as the head of the investigation into the murder of Tommy Regan, is it fair to say that you reviewed all these reports very carefully?"

The commissioner straightened up. "Of course."

"And you would agree with me, Commissioner, would you not, that not one of the findings contained within these reports connects David Lamb with the murder of Tommy Regan?"

A long pause. "No. I wouldn't agree with that."

Jack saw a smile bloom on Sears's face.

"Well. Let's take it point by point. Nothing in the photographs connects David Lamb to this crime, isn't that right?"

The commissioner hesitated.

"You didn't see my client, or anything even associated with my client, in any of those photographs, did you?"

"No."

"And there's not a single finding in the toxicology reports that connects Mr. Lamb to the death of Mr. Regan, is there?"

The commissioner paused for one beat too long. "No."

"Then is it fair to say, sir, that the only connection between David Lamb and the murder of Mr. Regan is the testimony of an immunized witness?"

Sears stood. "Objection, Your Honor, that's for the jury to decide."

"He may have it."

"Thank you, Your Honor," Sears said, as if the judge's adverse ruling was a favorable thing.

"That's not for me to decide," said the commissioner.

"Well, Commissioner, let's return to whether the physical evidence in this case in any way connects Mr. David Lamb to this murder. Was the gun used to kill Mr. Regan ever traced to David Lamb?"

"I believe you know we never recovered the murder weapon."

Jack walked over to the counsel table, next to Lamb. "So, is it fair to say that no weapon can be tied to this young man?" He placed his hand on his client's shoulder.

"We've recovered no weapon," the commissioner repeated.

"So—so let me get this straight—nothing in the Medical Examiner's report, nothing in the ballistics report, and nothing in the toxicology reports implicates Mr. Lamb in this homicide, correct?"

Sears stood. "Objection. The reports speak for themselves, Your Honor."

"Sustained. Mr. Marino, the reports were pre-marked and placed in evidence by agreement."

Jack stiffened. "Your Honor, I have a right to cross-examine this witness as I see fit. If you deny me that right, you deny my client the right to present an effective defense."

"Sidebar. Now," snapped Judge Stone. He dropped his voice as the lawyers approached. "Mr. Marino, you haven't been with us for a while now. Perhaps you've forgotten a few things. I don't permit speeches in my courtroom. Am I clear?"

"What's clear is that this court is restricting my right of cross-examination," Jack said. "And if you continue to do so, and my client is convicted as a result, I'll flip this case on appeal."

Judge Stone seemed to seethe as he considered this. Like all judges, the one thing he feared was the embarrassment of appellate reversal. Particularly the state's first death penalty case in decades. His voice bumped up an octave. "Mr. Marino, you may rephrase your question. But I warn you, do not make another speech in this courtroom. Now step back."

Sears strolled past the defendant back to his chair as slowly as he had approached the bench. Lamb's look of relief had vanished.

"You would agree, would you not," Jack continued, "that not one thing in all these reports connects David Lamb to the murder of Tommy Regan?"

The commissioner paused.

"Go ahead, Commissioner," Jack said. "You have 'yes' written all over your face."

The jury was no longer looking at Jack. They were watching the commissioner.

"No, sir. That is not correct. The defendant's fingerprints were found throughout the victim's vehicle."

Sears smiled.

"But, Commissioner," Jack said, "you would expect to find Mr. Lamb's fingerprints in his friend's car—a car they both drove in frequently—wouldn't you?"

"Not necessarily."

This time it was Jack's turn to smile. "Do you know what time Mr. Regan arrived at The Treasure Chest on Saturday night, August tenth?"

"Excuse me. I'm a police commissioner, not a timekeeper in a strip joint."

"You seem to harbor a certain disdain for The Treasure Chest?"

"Counsel, The Treasure Chest is a blight on my city, but it was licensed long before I became police commissioner." The witness let out a long sigh. "Unfortunately, I'm stuck with it."

"Do you get many calls from The Treasure Chest?"

"Calls?"

"Problems. Crime reports. That sort of thing?"

"Surprisingly, there's not much trouble. They know who they'll have to deal with."

"That would be you, right?"

"You got that right."

"On those few occasions when your department does get a call, do you respond as quickly as possible?"

"Immediately."

"And you investigate fully?"

"Of course."

"As your department failed to do when my client's daughter was nearly killed in a recent hit-and-run that occurred in your jurisdiction?"

"Objection!" Sears screamed.

Stone rapped his gavel against the solid mahogany bench. Once. Twice. Three times, the sound echoing throughout the courtroom.

"The objection is sustained," the judge bellowed. "Both the question and the answer are stricken from the record. The jury is to disregard them. Mr. Marino. You have five minutes of cross left with this witness. That's it."

Sears sat.

Jack waited a beat. "Now, were you the first person on the murder scene?" Jack asked the commissioner.

"Not exactly. Two patrolmen and some bystanders were there when I arrived. But nothing at the crime scene was compromised."

"But when you got there—if I heard you correctly—you made observations of the victim, didn't you?"

"Yes."

"And you watched the victim being photographed?"

"Yes."

"And you watched as the body was eventually removed by the coroner, didn't you?"

"I did."

"Did you watch closely?"

"Hard not to, Mr. Marino."

"What did the victim's face look like?"

"It had a bullet hole in it," the witness said.

"Actually, Commissioner, he was shot in the back of the head. I'm asking you what his face looked like."

"It wasn't pretty."

Jack retrieved a sheaf of crime scene photographs and reports from counsel table. "Were there any scratch marks?"

"I'm sorry?"

Jack dropped the reports and photos before the commissioner. "You don't see any scratch marks or lacerations on the victim's face, do you?"

The commissioner looked down at the photos. "I guess not."

"Commissioner, how many suspects did you have one year from the date of the murder?"

"We talked to a number of people."

"Let me ask you this way. How many people had you considered placing under arrest in this case?"

"One."

"How many people did you indict?"

"One."

"And that was David Lamb."

"That's right."

"At any time during the first year you spent investigating this case, did you talk to a Roger Ferriter, who'd had a fight with the victim on the premises of The Treasure Chest shortly before Mr. Regan's murder?"

"Offhand, I don't recall the name."

"But if someone, in fact, had a fight with Mr. Regan—a fight that left Mr. Regan with permanent facial injuries—shortly before his murder, wouldn't you agree that it might be important to speak to that person?"

"If my detectives didn't speak to him, I'm certain there was no reason to do so."

"You haven't answered my question, Commissioner. If Mr. Regan had been involved in a fight before he was killed, would it be important to speak to the other person?"

"It would depend."

"Well, what did your investigation consist of?"

"We interviewed the people who found the body, his family, and friends."

"Did you interview the people who were at The Treasure Chest on the night he died?"

"No one saw anything. It happened after hours."

"Did you take a statement from the owner?"

"Sure. One of my detectives took Mr. Nolan's statement."

"I'm curious. When did you first meet the immunized witness—Mickey Nolan?"

The commissioner paused. "I met him briefly at the station house when he gave us a statement."

"In this case?"

Another beat passed before he answered. "Yes."

"Did he tell you about how David Lamb murdered Tommy Regan?"

"No. He did not."

"In fact," Jack said, "he told you he knew nothing about the murder, which just happened to be the same thing David Lamb said when you questioned him, right?"

"Nolan was frightened."

"I didn't ask you about his mental state. I asked you if what the immunized witness told you matched what David Lamb told you."

"Pretty much the same."

"So, the only thing you have now—that you didn't have then—is the story you got after the Commonwealth dealt Mickey Nolan an immunity deal. Am I right about that?"

"Yes, we have the testimony of an eyewitness now—Mr. Mickey Nolan."

"Right," Jack said. "Speaking of eyewitnesses, a number of transients and street people take shelter in the area of the murder scene, correct?"

"There's no shelter there." The commissioner's reply came too quickly.

"Really?"

"That area consists of an abandoned rail line sandwiched between factories that closed years ago. There's nothing out there."

"Commissioner, you wouldn't mislead the jury, would you?"

"Of course not."

"That's interesting. I grew up not far from there. And for well over twenty-five years that area has been used by the homeless, by alcoholics, by the addicted. And as I recall, you and I observed a group of transients who had gathered there on the very day Mr. Regan's body was discovered."

Sears jumped to his feet. "Objection, Your Honor. If he's suggesting he's a witness, maybe he shouldn't be trying this case."

"Leave your life story out of this, Counsel, and try the case before you," said Judge Stone.

Jack turned to the witness. "Is it your testimony that the homeless have never been known to frequent the area in the vicinity of Mr. Regan's murder?"

"No. I'm not saying that," Knight said. "But we checked that area out. There was no one down there at the time of the murder."

"Actually, there was."

"I beg your pardon?"

"You know who I'm talking about. A member of your department learned that a homeless woman, who might use the first name Nora, may have been present at the murder scene, and for that reason, recommended further investigation."

"That turned out to be a false lead."

"I remind you, Commissioner, that you are under oath."

"Objection," Sears said. "Defense counsel hardly needs to remind one of the most respected law enforcement officials in the Commonwealth that he is under oath."

"All right, Mr. Sears," said Stone. "Your objection is sustained. Mr. Marino, next question."

"Have you ever heard of a homeless woman in Mystic whose name is Nora?"

"Don't believe so."

"You've never heard of 'Crazy Nora,' as she's called by some of the folks still doing business in that area?"

"No."

"How many years have you been commissioner?"

"Near seven now."

"Then you must remember a woman who was set afire at that same spot about six or seven years ago? You were leading the force then, weren't you?"

"That's what I said."

"And you've never heard of a homeless person who was torched by several men when they attempted to sexually assault her?"

"I'd have to check our police logs."

"Well, when you check, you'll learn that she survived that attack. But, of course, you already know that. Because you also know that she was present at the time of Tommy Regan's murder, right, Commissioner Knight?"

A loud murmur rose from the gallery.

"I don't know what you're talking about."

"A detective from your department took a report about her."

Sears leapt to his feet. "I strenuously object, Your Honor. This is preposterous. Mr. Marino knows he has to have a good-faith basis to ask such a question."

"Sidebar. Both of you."

Sears practically ran to the bench, while Jack took his time.

"Mr. Marino," Judge Stone began, his voice cold and unforgiving. "You might recall we visited this issue in your opening statement. If you have a good-faith basis for your questions, you may ask them. Otherwise, you're in deep trouble."

Jack stared at the judge. "I withdraw the question."

"Mr. Marino," Stone said, "get back to your seat and sit down. Mr. Sears, call your next witness."

CHAPTER FIFTY-ONE

With each step, the jurors felt Lisa Regan's grief, the widow's long walk to the witness stand hammering home her suffering. She wore an oversized jacket with padded shoulders over a dated black pantsuit. Though she was in her early thirties, her face reflected years she hadn't yet lived. Someone shattered this woman's life and the lives of her children. And someone had to pay.

Of course, most of the time, it was the defendant who did the paying. Beside him, Jack could hear his client's irregular breathing.

Not this time, though. Not in this case. Only this morning, Matt had handed Jack an envelope containing a copy of a lawsuit filed against The Treasure Chest, plus copies of workers' compensation checks made out to Thomas Regan. The lawsuit sought a hefty sum: $100,000.00 for failure to protect an off-duty Regan against the violent attack of a drunken patron. An attack, the lawsuit alleged, that could have easily been prevented because the establishment knew of the customer's violent tendencies, yet served him an excess of alcohol, nonetheless. An attack that had left a permanent, ugly razor slash tattooed on Regan's face.

The witness took her seat. A splash of late-fall sun spilled through the courtroom's oversized windows and lit her face. Dust motes floated in the air, the moment infused with a sense of surrealism.

Her head was unbowed, her emotions constrained, dark half-moons etched under her blue eyes.

Hearing a shuffle from the back of the courtroom, Jack turned in unison with the jurors as a victim-witness advocate from the DA's office ushered the Regan children out of the courtroom. It was a move timed for maximum impact. Just the opening salvo, Jack felt certain. Sears's questions would have one purpose: to engender overwhelming sympathy for the victim. And it wouldn't be hard to do.

"Mrs. Regan, could you tell us how long you were married?" Sears asked.

"Almost ten years," said Lisa Regan. She pressed a scrunched-up tissue to her eyes.

Haltingly, she answered Sears's questions, describing how she and her late husband had met, the birth of their children, her husband's employment history, well-selected anecdotes illustrating Tommy's generosity, his dedication to his children.

"The Friday night before he was killed, he took the kids and me for ice cream. And afterwards, we took a ride to Revere Beach. The kids loved it. Tommy was a good father," she added.

"How are you and your three children managing today?" Sears asked.

The question was objectionable, wholly irrelevant and intended to prejudice the defendant. Yet standing to object would only paint Jack as an insensitive shark intent on keeping the full picture from the jury.

The tears came hard and strong, the courtroom becoming deadly still, the silence assuming a heavy syrupy quality. Even Judge Stone sat quietly, his customary impatience suspended in recognition of Lisa Regan's loss.

"The defendant said he and your late husband were great friends. Is that true?"

"They knew each other." She shot a look of betrayal at David Lamb. "At this point, I wouldn't say 'great friends,' no."

Even Jack couldn't blame her for not considering Lamb a friend after what he'd been accused of. Sears returned to his seat. He didn't need to say another word.

CHAPTER FIFTY-TWO

Most skilled defense attorneys would pass on cross-examining the widow of a homicide victim. Jack wasn't one of them.

"Mrs. Regan, I'm sorry for your loss and I apologize, but I must ask you some difficult questions." Jack's voice was soft, understanding, empathetic.

"What was your husband doing at a strip club, on the night of his murder?" he asked.

Sears sat back in his seat.

"He was trying to earn some extra money," she said. "I wasn't happy about it."

"Prior to your husband's murder, had he filed a workers' compensation claim?"

"Yes. He'd hurt himself on a construction job."

"Was he still on workers' compensation on the night he was killed?"

The witness shifted in her seat. "No. His benefits were over."

Jack walked to counsel table to retrieve a stack of paper. He turned to the bench. "May I approach?" he asked.

Judge Stone nodded.

Jack spread the paperwork on the witness stand. "I am showing you certified copies of workers' compensation checks dated up through the end of the week during which your husband was killed."

Lisa Regan stared at the copies without touching them.

"Do these checks refresh your recollection as to whether your husband was still receiving workers' compensation for total disability at the time of his death?"

"I guess he was," she replied, her voice colder.

"Mrs. Regan, do you know it's considered fraud to collect workers' compensation for total disability and work at the same time?"

"I'm not a lawyer, Mr. Marino," she said with a flash of fierce intensity.

Sears grimaced.

"Your Honor, I offer certified copies of these business records into evidence, establishing that Thomas Regan was illegally receiving workers' compensation benefits at the time he was working at The Treasure Chest up and through the date he died."

Stone looked at Sears, who mumbled, "No objection."

"They may be admitted," said the judge.

"Most respectfully, ma'am, can you tell us if you and your husband paid taxes on his earnings from The Treasure Chest? Or was he working under the table?"

She hesitated. "I'm not sure."

"Mrs. Regan, were you aware that your husband planned to sue The Treasure Chest for injuries he'd suffered at the hands of a drunken customer?"

Sears closed his eyes.

"I wasn't aware of it."

"Not something he talked to you about?"

"No."

Jack shot a look at Lamb, who wore a scowl.

"Your husband had a razor cut on his face that resulted in a permanent scar, didn't he?"

"He did."

"How did he get that?"

"He was attacked by some guy at The Treasure Chest."

"But you don't know anything about the lawsuit that was prepared on his behalf, Mrs. Regan?"

"There was no lawsuit. I would have known about it."

Jack paused. He glanced down at his legal pad to gather his thoughts. "Forgive me, ma'am, but I need to ask one final question."

Mrs. Regan stiffened.

"Did your husband use drugs?"

"My husband never used drugs," she answered without hesitation. "Ever."

Walking to counsel table, Jack scooped up another document. "Your Honor, I offer as a defense exhibit the Commonwealth's autopsy report, which establishes the presence of cocaine in Mr. Regan's blood at the time of his death."

Handing the document to the clerk, Jack let his question, the witness's denial, and the incontrovertible evidence of drug use register with the jury. Only the light tapping of the stenographer's fingers capturing the last few sentences punctuated the silence.

"No further questions."

CHAPTER FIFTY-THREE

Jack slammed a right cross into the old leather heavy bag, which his brother, Matt, held in place. "Keep banging away," Matt said.

"Trying," Jack said, breathless.

"I mean in the courtroom like you did today."

Jack laughed. He hadn't realized his brother had been in the courtroom.

"Who's the big guy attached to the commissioner's hip in the gallery?" Matt asked. "You can't miss him."

"I'm pretty sure he's one of the commissioner's lieutenants," Jack said.

"I think I've seen him in the parking lot of The Treasure Chest," Matt said.

"Really?" Jack tried to pick up the tempo, jabbing the heavy bag, the chains jangling with each punch.

"Talk to Abby recently?" Matt asked his brother.

"Only through her lawyers. Temporary divorce orders out of Probate and Family Court say no direct contact between the parties." Jack sighed.

"Talked to a divorce lawyer?"

Jack shook his head. "No. I'm not interested in her money. Looking back on it, I was just window treatment. Whenever I was with the Thorn family, it was as if I were hired help."

Matt dug his shoulder into the bag while Jack pounded it with a succession of blows.

"It'll be over soon," Jack said, breathless. "She wants an expedited hearing. Her lawyers claim our marriage has suffered an irretrievable breakdown." Jack laughed. "At least they got that right."

CHAPTER FIFTY-FOUR

"The Commonwealth calls Mickey Nolan."

Jack watched as David Lamb's blue eyes zeroed in on Nolan as he stood to approach the witness stand. Pushing back in his chair, Lamb sat upright, rigid as a steel girder.

Would Nolan's testimony, which was the second of Brad Sears's one-two punch, mark the beginning—or the end—of his client's torment? Come what may, Jack was determined to reveal an ugly truth about the use and abuse of legal immunity. That a witness on whom immunity had been bestowed had nothing to lose. Worse, once conferred, immunity could never be withdrawn, not even if new facts emerged. And that immunity could trigger unthinkable injustice in a murder case.

Jack wondered about Teddy Smith, who was sitting in the gallery to hear her client's testimony. What made her so willing to twist the law? Was it just money for money's sake? Jack had been wooed by security and prestige, and prayed he'd never fall under that spell again.

As Nolan, took his seat on the stand, expectation filled the air. This was the man Jack had accused of murder in his opening statement. The jurors sat attentively, all eyes on the witness, the pool camera humming. Even Judge Stone seemed alert for a change. Jack could hear the demonstrators outside, a mournful lament rising and falling like prayers at a graveside.

A muscular man dressed in an ill-fitted suit, Mickey Nolan wore his dye-job, jet-black hair swept straight back above dark eyes that gave away little. The owner of The Treasure Chest had an unmistakable air of danger about him, and Jack was hoping the jury would sense it.

"Mr. Nolan, are you the owner of The Treasure Chest?" Sears asked after the usual opening questions.

Nolan stirred in his chair, evincing the shrug of someone for whom life held few remaining surprises. "I am."

"Do you see the defendant in the courtroom today?"

"Yes."

"Please point him out for the members of the jury."

Nolan raised his arm and pointed at David Lamb.

Judge Stone beat Sears to the punch. "The record will reflect that the witness has identified the defendant." Like a Roman procurator, he waved his hand, signaling Sears to continue.

"How do you know the defendant?" Sears asked.

Nolan cleared his throat. "He worked for me."

"What did he do?"

"Odd jobs mostly. We serve pizza. Sandwiches. Dave would do the dishes. The trash. Errands for the girls. Whatever needed to be done."

"Did you know Thomas Regan?"

"Knew him well."

"How did you know him?"

"Worked for me, too."

"At the club?"

Nolan nodded.

Judge Stone cut in. "Sir, you must answer verbally, so the stenographer can record your response."

Nolan glanced up at the judge in a practiced manner. "Sorry, Your Honor. Yes. At the club."

"And what did he do?"

"Tommy did much more than Dave. Dave was a gofer. Tommy was the doorman. Checked IDs. Called the cops if there was trouble. Stuff like that."

Judge Stone interrupted, addressing the jurors directly. "Mr. Foreman, ladies and gentlemen of the jury. This might be a good time for the court to instruct you on the use of this witness's testimony. Mr. Nolan is an immunized witness. He enjoys 'transactional immunity,' which means he cannot be prosecuted for any crime arising out of the death of Mr. Regan."

The judge looked sharply at Jack, then turned back to the jury. "You are allowed to consider the testimony of an immunized witness. You may give that testimony whatever weight you wish—that is, you may accept or reject it, in whole or in part, just like the testimony of any other witness. But you must keep in mind that the witness's testimony is being given in exchange for a grant of immunity, meaning that Mr. Nolan cannot be prosecuted unless he commits perjury by lying under oath."

Jack grimaced as he listened to the judge. Normally, it was the prosecutor who would broach the controversial subject of immunity to blunt the impression that the Commonwealth had forged a deal with the devil. But once again, the judge was doing Sears's dirty work. All the same, Jack noticed a few furrowed brows among the jurors.

The judge having illuminated his path, Sears wasted no time finishing the journey. "Mr. Nolan, at some point after the murder of Mr. Regan, did you consult a lawyer?"

"Yes."

"Why?"

"I was friggin' scared."

"We'll get to why you were scared shortly. But first, as a result of your consulting with your lawyer, did you ultimately agree to come forward to tell the police what you knew about the murder of Thomas Regan?"

"I did."

"Did you know anything about immunity at the time?"

Nolan shook his head. "No. My lawyer handled all that."

This last remark, Jack thought, seemed to conceal something beyond an expression of ignorance.

Sears stepped closer to the witness. "Mr. Nolan, directing your attention to August tenth and eleventh, a bit more than two years ago now, do you recall those dates?"

Nolan shrugged. "I do."

"Were you working then?"

"I work every Saturday night. I was at the club from about three in the afternoon 'til closing at one and beyond," he said, leaning against the chair back.

"Was the defendant at the club that night?"

"Worked the same shift as me. Three to one."

Nolan's tone was dry, practiced. Too practiced, Jack thought.

"Could you describe the relationship between the defendant and Tommy Regan?"

Nolan folded his arms. "I would say it was competitive. I think Dave resented—"

Jack jumped to his feet. "Objection," he said. "The question is intended to elicit improper opinion testimony by asking the witness to do the impossible: discern the mental impressions of another person who is unavailable for cross-examination."

Sears didn't wait for a ruling. The prosecutor rephrased his question. "Mr. Nolan, confining your answers solely to what you either saw or heard, what do you mean by competitive?"

"Dave complained a lot to me that he didn't want to do the, ah, you know, the grunt work. One night about a week before Tommy was killed, Dave said he was sick of workin' like a dog. Said he wanted to do what Tommy was doin'."

Jack watched his client shake his head.

"Were you able to accommodate him?" Sears asked.

"We didn't need two doormen. I told him that."

"What did he say?"

"We were in my office, and he kicked a stool clear across the room," Nolan said. "I should have fired him, but I didn't. I felt sorry for him but told him not to pull a stunt like that again or he was out."

"Why did you feel sorry for him?"

Jack sat poised to object again, but hesitated, hoping that whatever Nolan was going to say might generate some sympathy for his client.

"Well. He's always been—I don't know. Slow, I guess I'd say. I know he had trouble holding down a job. That's why I gave him the job in the first place. That and the fact he's got kids to support."

Sears continued. "Directing your attention to about one thirty in the early morning of August eleventh, did something happen at the club that evening?"

"Dave was cleaning tables, and we were closing up. But I could tell he was jawin' something to Tommy, who was over at the door. Tommy ignored him, but Dave kept yelling over. It got the attention of some of the customers, so I went over and told them both to shut up."

"And then what happened?"

"I didn't even know they'd left, but at some point, I realized they were gone. So, I went out front to look for them."

"And what did you find?"

Nolan folded his hands, staring down at them as if engaged in deep thought. "At first, nothin'. I remember goin' over to the side of the building, checking the parking lot, and I still couldn't find them."

"What did you do next?"

"I went out back. The way it is, the back of the club faces the railroad tracks, and we've got some floodlights that light the place up real good."

"Did you find them?"

"I heard voices around the corner where the tracks run. So, I approached and there they were."

Sears nodded. "What were they doing?"

"They were beyond the floodlights where it was much darker. But I could feel trouble."

Sears looked thoughtful. "Was anyone else out there?"

Nolan shrugged. "Didn't see no one."

To Jack, the way Nolan phrased his reply seemed telling. Sears and Nolan had worked on this response. They knew someone was out there that night. Nora was out there. That much Jack knew for sure. As sure as the fact that Sears covered it up. But why?

"Could you tell the jury more specifically what you saw?"

"Well. Tommy's a big guy. But he was kneelin' on the ground. Like he was begging."

"Could you hear anything?"

"Tommy kept sayin' 'Please,' over and over again."

Sears pivoted on his heels, looking meaningfully at each juror in turn, then extended his open hand, palm up, toward the jury like an invitation. "Did he say anything else?"

Nolan turned, too, facing the jury for the first time. "Tommy said, 'Please, Dave, I have three little kids.'"

Jack studied the jurors. One juror placed a tissue to her eyes. The others sat rock still. It was a devastating answer, part of a plan to upset and anger the jury.

Compounding the impression, Nolan cradled his head between two hands.

Sears remained quiet for a moment, then resumed his questioning, leaning forward with renewed purpose. "He begged, didn't he?"

Jack sensed that his former colleague was beginning to taste blood. As the Commonwealth's most experienced prosecutor in first-degree murder trials, Sears truly believed he was unbeatable. With luck, his conceit might be the only mistake Jack needed.

"Yes," Nolan said, his tone resolute.

"And what did you do?"

"I froze. Didn't know what the hell to do." Nolan looked at the judge. "Excuse me, Judge." He cleared his voice. "I could hear myself yell—I don't even know what I said—but just as I did, there was a loud crack."

Sears let the answer linger. "A crack?"

"Yeah. You know. A gunshot."

"And then what happened?"

Nolan looked grave. "I saw Tommy go down."

To Jack, this was preposterous. Could the jury possibly believe that Tommy Regan was murdered because of the petty resentments of a coworker?

As if Sears had read Jack's mind, he looked at Jack, their eyes meeting momentarily before he turned to the witness again. "You say you yelled. Did you think the defendant heard you?"

"Oh, yeah. He turned immediately. Had a wild look in his eyes. As soon as he saw me, he walked over to me, put the gun to my head, and said, 'Do you want to die too?'"

"What did you do?"

Nolan took a quick, shallow breath. "I freaked out." Nolan paused and shook his head slowly, his voice beginning to weaken. "I said, 'I didn't see anything.'"

"Did the defendant respond?"

Nolan shot Lamb a look. "He said, 'That's right. You didn't see an eff'n thing.'"

"That's bullshit," David screamed.

Judge Stone wasted no time. "Mr. Marino, I would have expected you to have educated your client on the rules of decorum. Another outburst and he'll be removed from the courtroom."

"I'm sorry, Your Honor," Jack said.

"What happened then?" Sears continued.

"Dave ordered me to help him drag the body into the bushes."

Sears rested one hand on the prosecutor's table. "Was the defendant still pointing the gun at you?"

"Right at me."

"What hand was the gun in?"

"Ahh—it was his right hand."

"What happened next?"

"Dave told me to come with him to get Tommy's car from the lot."

"Where did Lamb get the keys?"

Nolan shook his head. "No idea."

"What happened then?"

"We got Tommy's car and drove it up to where we left him."

"Who drove?"

"Dave drove."

"And then what?"

"Same thing. Dave and me dragged the body back out of the bushes."

Beneath Nolan's testimony, Jack could feel the subtle force of hours of preparation, the practicing and coaching Sears usually did with his witnesses. Which wasn't surprising—every prosecutor and defense attorney coached key witnesses—but Nolan's testimony was perjury. Unfortunately, as the ex-prosecutor knew too well, even that wouldn't matter unless Jack could prove it.

"Did the defendant say anything to you at that point?"

"Once we got Tommy to the back of the car, Dave just said . . ." Nolan turned to the judge and jury and apologized. "'Grab his fuckin' legs and we'll put him in the back of the wagon.'" Nolan's voice grew louder.

"What did he do with the gun while you lifted Tommy?"

"He put the gun in his waistband while we lifted him into the car."

The prosecutor took several steps toward the witness. "What was your state of mind at that time, Mr. Nolan?"

The witness cleared his throat again. "To be honest, I was shakin' head to toe. I remember thinking he was gonna kill me because he knew I saw everything. Then I figured he was keepin' me alive just long enough to get Tommy's body back into the car and then he'd shoot me."

"After the body was placed in the car, what happened?"

"He came over to me. Told me to kneel down."

Lamb let out a low moan, his head bowed. "Lies," he said in a whisper barely audible even to Jack. Jack felt himself tense. The faces of the jurors had turned hard.

"Did you?"

"Yes."

"Then what happened?"

Again, Nolan looked at Lamb as if Jack's client were a caged animal. The jury, Jack saw, had begun to follow Nolan's gaze. "He put the gun in my mouth and said, 'I'll fuckin' kill you and your whole fuckin' family if you ever say a word.' He said, 'Tommy was an asshole and had it comin.'"

Sears paused long enough to allow the jury time to visualize the terror Nolan must have felt. He stepped forward. "How were you feeling at that point, sir?"

"All I kept thinking about was my wife and kids."

Sears let a moment pass. "Mr. Nolan, could you tell us what happened next?"

"We walked back to The Treasure Chest. The place was empty. Dave told me that if the police asked me anything, all I knew is that Tommy took a break and never came back."

"He told you to say that?"

"Yeah. That Tommy took a break and never came back."

"And is that what you told the police?"

"The cops interviewed all of us, and I told them exactly what Dave told me to tell them."

"Why?"

"Look . . ." Nolan straightened. "I saw the guy kill someone in cold blood. I got family, too."

"Why did you finally come forward some two years later?"

Nolan glanced at Lamb, the jurors following his stare like a beam of light.

Lamb sat rigidly, the knuckles of his folded hands bleached white.

"I thought about it a long time before I could bring myself to do it. They told me they wouldn't let anything happen to me or my family. And I knew, it was just a matter of time before Dave was going to come after me or one of my kids."

"Who did you call?"

"My lawyer. And she called your office."

Sears paused. "Mr. Nolan, one more question. Do you keep a firearm behind the bar?"

"Sure. We keep one there—in case of trouble."

"Did the defendant have access to the handgun behind the bar?"

"Didn't need it."

"And why's that?"

"He had his own."

"Own what?"

"Gun. I saw him with it about a week before the murder. Semi-automatic, too."

"Objection," Jack shouted, startling the jury. "This is outrageous."

"Come up here now," said Judge Stone, waving the attorneys toward him.

Reaching the sidebar, Jack seethed, "Judge, the prosecutor is purposefully and irreparably prejudicing this jury. This court excluded Mr. Lamb's prior convictions, and the defendant has relied on that ruling. And the Commonwealth ignores it? He was coached to say that. The Commonwealth is introducing through the back door what it can't get into evidence through the front door."

"Your Honor," Sears said. "Mr. Nolan said nothing about a conviction. Massachusetts law states that evidence of prior unconvicted bad acts is admissible to show, among other things, a common scheme, identity, intent, motive, or state of mind."

Jack snapped back. "It's admissible only during impeachment of a witness. This isn't impeachment. Nolan is his witness. This is reversable error. The danger of prejudice clearly outweighs the probative value of the evidence."

"Mr. Marino, I'm going to allow the question and the answer to provide a context for the shooting, without which the killing might appear to the jury as an inexplicable act of violence."

"Judge, this is a naked attempt to paint the defendant as someone who carries a gun in a case where the Commonwealth can't connect the defendant with any gun—much less the gun used to shoot the victim. You can't do this."

"Counsel, I just did. In point of fact, the evidence is highly probative of the defendant's familiarity with and access to firearms. Not to mention it demonstrates a logical relationship between the prior bad act and the crime charged. In a few moments and at the conclusion of the trial, I will instruct the jury on the limited purpose for which they may consider it. Your objection is noted."

Jack placed his arm on the side bench. "I'm demanding a mistrial, Judge. The defendant can't get a fair trial after a remark like that, and you know it."

"First, you'll address the Court appropriately. Second, remove your arm from my bench. And third, your motion for a mistrial is denied."

Sears turned away, but not before Jack saw a prosecutor who was absolutely convinced he'd destroyed any chance David Lamb had for an acquittal.

The courtroom fell silent, Jack acutely aware of everything and everyone around him. Judge Stone, his wild white brows knitted, stared at Lamb in condemnation. Lisa Regan, sitting alongside a victim witness advocate, could be heard sobbing. The jurors seemed to stop breathing, several of them appearing overwhelmed by the eyewitness account of the murder of Tommy Regan.

Jack sat limp, his palms moist. Looking at his client, who sat help-less beside him, Jack could only imagine the fear that was engulfing him.

Jack took a breath. To expose Mickey Nolan as the liar that he was, Jack's cross-examination would have to be perfect.

CHAPTER FIFTY-FIVE

"You say you witnessed a murder firsthand, Mr. Nolan. That you were the only eyewitness who saw Tommy Regan shot. Yet you refused to speak to the police in this case?"

Jack stood scant steps from Nolan, crowding him much closer than he had any other witness.

The Commonwealth's chief witness shot Jack a cool look. "I was afraid."

"So, instead of telling the truth, you retained one of the most experienced criminal attorneys in the Commonwealth. Do I have that right?"

Nolan continued to appraise Jack. "I hired an attorney. Yeah."

"And you paid her fifty thousand dollars so you wouldn't be prosecuted, didn't you?"

Before Nolan could answer, Sears was on his feet. "Objection, Your Honor! Attorney-client privilege."

"Your Honor," Jack said, "the prosecutor doesn't have standing to raise attorney-client privilege."

"Then I'll raise it, Mr. Marino," growled the judge. "I have all the standing I need to protect one of the oldest common law privileges. Next question."

Jack resumed his questioning of the witness as if there'd been no interruption.

"Mr. Nolan, isn't it true that you agreed to tell the truth only after the DA guaranteed that you wouldn't be prosecuted?" He didn't wait for the witness to respond. "And as a result, the investigation in this case stalled out for about two years?"

"I told you, I was scared."

"Instead of telling the police what you knew about the murder of Tommy Regan, you waited until your lawyer struck an immunity deal with the prosecutor's office, didn't you?"

"I did what my lawyer told me to do."

Jack turned briefly to Lisa Regan, making eye contact with her before facing the witness again. "So, for two years, because you wouldn't speak, Lisa Regan and her children had no idea who murdered Tommy, isn't that fair to say?"

"I told you I was frightened."

"Maybe I'm just a bit naive," Jack said, "but why would you need a criminal defense lawyer like Ms. Smith if you didn't commit a crime?"

Nolan's eyes were chilly. "I got a right to a lawyer."

Jack stood straighter. "So I understand you correctly, what you're telling us is that you were simply present when Mr. Regan was killed, is that it?"

"That's right," Nolan said with a smirk.

"Just the three of you out there that night?"

"You got it."

"And it's your testimony that you didn't aid or encourage the crime?"

Nolan shifted in his chair. "No way."

"In fact, more than that," Jack continued, turning to the jurors, "you want the members of the jury to believe you're a victim in this case?"

"I am."

"But you didn't need a lawyer as a victim. You only need a criminal lawyer if you're a suspect, right?"

"I was being threatened," Nolan said loudly, his eyes slits, the smirk gone.

"By him?" Jack gave a short laugh and pointed to his client, who seemed anything but a threat. "You're the owner of a strip club that outlaw bikers frequent. You've got bouncers the size of tree trunks. And you were afraid of him?"

David Lamb stared at the jury, looking gaunt in his oversized suit.

Nolan looked defiantly at Jack, without answering.

"Since you were so terrified, did you ask the police to protect you from the frightening threat that's sitting over there next to me?"

Again, no answer.

"I'm asking you, sir, did you ask for protection?"

"No."

"But wouldn't you agree that a person who's being threatened would ask for protection, not immunity?"

Nolan swallowed. "If you say so."

"Mr. Nolan, it's not what I say, it's what you say. You would agree that immunity doesn't protect you from threats?"

A stabbing glance. "I don't know."

Jack stepped closer. "Are you telling this jury that you don't know that a grant of immunity protects you from prosecution, not threats?"

"I told you I don't know."

"You keep saying 'I don't know,'" Jack said, "but you heard Judge Stone explain immunity to the jurors, didn't you?"

"I heard the judge."

"So, you know that immunity means you can never be prosecuted for the murder of Tommy Regan?"

"I guess."

"Mr. Nolan, you wouldn't *guess* about something like that, would you?"

"Well, I'm not a hundred percent on the details."

"But you know that you're in the clear as long as you testify, correct?"

A look of suspicion flashed across his face. "I don't understand the question."

Jack glanced over at the jury. "Sure, you do," he said, leaning forward. "The DA gave you a free ride—absolute immunity—and because of that you sit here without fear of prosecution for the murder of Thomas Regan?"

"Ask my lawyer."

Jack's voice rose considerably. "I'm asking you, sir."

"I don't know how I'm supposed to answer that question."

Jack threw up his hands. "How about truthfully."

"Objection, Your Honor," Sears said.

Jack didn't wait for a ruling. "You want this jury to believe you sought absolute immunity for protection from threats, when in fact the only protection you wanted was protection from the consequences of what you did out by the railroad tracks that night?"

Sears was on his feet. "Objection, Your Honor. He's arguing with the witness."

"Mr. Marino," Judge Stone said, "keep your voice down and ask another question."

Jack looked over the yellow notepad he held in his left hand. After a short silence, he resumed. "Now you say you hired Attorney Theresa 'Teddy' Smith to cut your immunity deal with the government, is that right?"

"I hired her as my lawyer to protect me," Nolan said, as if repetition equaled credibility.

"So, I see." Jack pointed to the rear of the courtroom. "And she's here today at the back of this courtroom, still protecting you?" Marino asked.

The witness didn't answer.

The jurors stirred, turning to appraise Attorney Teddy Smith sitting in the gallery at the rear of the courtroom.

"Just so we all understand, Attorney Smith is supposedly here to protect the only witness who cannot be prosecuted for any crime arising out of the murder of Thomas Regan, right?"

"I don't know how to answer your question."

"Mr. Nolan, you were scheduled, along with David Lamb, to testify before the grand jury in this case, weren't you?"

Nolan squinted. "We were scheduled to testify on the same day."

"You didn't have your attorney with you when you arrived to testify that morning, did you?"

Nolan seemed puzzled. "I don't remember when my attorney arrived."

"But you drove to the courthouse that morning with Mr. Lamb, didn't you?"

"I may have."

Jack pushed harder. "But during that ride you didn't tell Mr. Lamb that you had an attorney, did you?"

The color seemed to drain from Nolan's rugged face. "My attorney told me that was private."

"And you never told David Lamb that you had called your attorney from the pay phone at the courthouse a number of times that morning?"

"I don't recall."

"And after one of those calls, you told David you'd testify, but that he should testify first, correct?"

"I didn't care who testified first."

"And you told David to lie and say the same thing you would say when you testified after him: that neither of you knew anything about the murder, right?"

Nolan's anger flashed. "That's bull."

Jack bore in. "So, it's your testimony that Mr. Lamb just happened to go into the grand jury room first?" He paused. "And while Lamb was in there testifying," he continued, "Attorney Smith just happened to waltz into the same courthouse where you were waiting to testify. Is that what you want this jury to believe?"

"That's what happened."

"And after David testified, you just happened to refuse to testify, is that right?"

"I testified."

Striding to counsel table, where David sat scowling at the witness, Jack scooped up one of the thick black binders that held the grand jury minutes. "Oh, you testified all right." Jack fanned through Nolan's sworn grand jury testimony. "You testified long enough to invoke your Fifth Amendment right not to incriminate yourself in response to every question asked of you except your name, age, and address."

Nolan eyed Jack with intense suspicion. "I did what my attorney told me to do."

"And was that because you and your attorney sat down with Mr. Sears prior to your appearance before the grand jury?"

"I did what she said to do," Nolan repeated.

"Mr. Nolan, had you ever met First Assistant District Attorney Bradford Sears before you testified before the grand jury?"

Nolan remained silent.

"Your Honor, I ask that the Court instruct the witness to answer the question I asked."

"Objection." Sears stood.

"Your Honor, conversations with the Assistant District Attorney don't come under attorney-client privilege," said Jack.

Judge Stone turned to Sears. "He's right. It's cross-examination. Answer the question, Mr. Nolan."

"I met with him."

"And during those meetings you discussed what you would say today."

"It came up."

"And after those meetings you understood that all you had to do was stick to the agreed-upon story and you were home free?"

"I have to tell the truth."

"And that's because Mr. Sears explained to you that, once immunized, the only crime you can be prosecuted for is perjury?"

"Can't recall exactly what he said."

"And didn't he also tell you that a conviction of perjury carries a very harsh sentence?"

The witness shrugged.

"Well, you don't have to worry about that now, do you?"

"I don't have to worry about perjury because I'm telling the truth."

"You don't have to worry because the only perjury conviction you're afraid of is the one Brad Sears threatened you with if your testimony deviated even slightly from the story you and he agreed to, correct?"

Sears leapt to his feet. "Objection. Your Honor, this is outrageous."

"He may have it," Stone responded.

Sears sat.

"He told you that if you change anything, they'll indict you for perjury and prosecute you, didn't he?"

"He told me that if you asked me what we talked about, to say that he told me to tell the truth."

"But you're not here to tell the truth, are you, Mr. Nolan? Aren't you really here to save yourself so you're not prosecuted for the murder of Tommy Regan?"

"I don't have to save myself from anything," Nolan said.

Jack moved forward. "Because you've been granted absolute immunity." He put his hand on his waist. "By the way, Mr. Nolan, how many times have you met with the prosecutor prior to today?"

Nolan's eyes shot in the direction of Teddy Smith, who couldn't help him this time. "I'm not sure."

"More than five?"

Nolan hesitated. "Maybe."

Jack allowed a brief silence. "And on one of those occasions, he took you into his office and told you that a trial is nothing more than theater?"

Slowly, Nolan said, "Something like that."

"And the witnesses nothing more than actors?" Jack added with the confidence of one intimately familiar with the County District Attorney's office, and more particularly with Sears's personal—and up to this point private—protocol for preparing a key prosecution witness.

"Don't recall the exact words."

Jack looked steadily at the Commonwealth's witness. "And as in theater, he told you that the best actors are the ones who practice their roles, isn't that right?"

"Told you. I don't remember."

"And he told you the best place to practice was in an actual courtroom, didn't he?"

Nolan shrugged. "Maybe."

"And the best courtroom would naturally be the one in which you would give your testimony, right?"

"I don't understand the question."

"Let me ask you this way, Mr. Nolan. This isn't the first time you've been in this courtroom, is it?"

Nolan glanced at Sears, his face ashen. He shook his head.

"You can say it, Mr. Nolan. You've been here before, after hours when the courthouse is closed, haven't you?"

"Yes."

"And you sat exactly where you're sitting right now, haven't you?"

"Uh-huh."

Judge Stone peered down at the witness. "You're required to respond yes or no, Mr. Nolan."

"Yes."

Jack's jawline set. "And you did this at night because Mr. Sears's office is in this building, and he arranged for you to use public property after hours at the public's expense, isn't that right?"

"I don't know how he arranged it."

Jack pointed to the witness enclosure. "How many times have you taken that stand before today, Mr. Nolan?"

Nolan hesitated, retreating a bit in the witness box. "I'm not sure."

"You practiced and rehearsed your testimony right here on three separate occasions?"

"Went over it, yeah," Nolan parried.

"And during one of those practice sessions, Mr. Sears told you that at some point during his direct examination, he'd give you a signal, didn't he? When he opened his hand and motioned to the jury, that was your signal to turn to the jury as you did and tell the part about Regan begging for his life?"

Sears stood. "Your Honor, I object to this entire line of questioning. These aren't questions. It's a speech."

The judge looked annoyed. "This is cross-examination. He may have it."

Jack looked in the direction of the jury before resuming. "That's something he told you to do, right?"

Mickey Nolan's chest heaved a bit. For the first time, the witness appeared rattled. "He told me to tell the truth."

"And then tell them that David Lamb shot Tommy in cold blood, right?"

"He told me to tell the truth," Nolan repeated, his face reflecting the fatigue that was settling in.

"And he told you that if anyone on that jury began to weep, to put your head down and cradle it in your hands, to channel that emotion, didn't he?" Jack's voice echoed throughout the courtroom.

"I'm not sure what he said," Nolan said again.

As one, the jurors stared at the witness.

"And you did exactly what he told you to do minutes ago—when Mr. Sears turned to the jury and opened his hand, right?"

"I don't know what I did. I was upset."

"Because he told you to be upset."

"That's not true." Nolan's changed tone suggested a primal, deep-seated contempt for Jack Marino.

"So, you practiced, and you rehearsed after hours in a closed courthouse at the taxpayers' expense. And here you are today for the final performance, right?" Jack moved toward the witness, cutting the distance between them sharply. "You saw Tommy Regan earlier on the night he died, didn't you?"

Nolan considered him. "Sure. I saw him. He worked at the club."

"And you had a conversation with him, didn't you?"

"Of course."

"And one of the conversations took place outside The Treasure Chest, didn't it?"

"Not sure."

"You don't remember Tommy asking you to step outside?"

"He could have."

Jack cocked his head. "And you argued with him out there because Tommy said he wanted money or even a slice of ownership in the club."

Nolan shook his head.

"Isn't it true, he'd been after you for months to transfer a piece of the action at The Treasure Chest to him?"

Nolan chuckled. "Ownership? Tommy was broke."

"So broke that there was no reason in the world Tommy could think he could buy into a portion of the club, right?"

"No way."

Jack phrased his next question with care. "Unless, of course, Tommy had something to hold over your head?"

Nolan's face paled. "I'm . . . I don't follow."

Jack stood straighter, ignoring the witness's answer. "Unless Tommy threatened to go to the police about some of the things he saw at the club."

"I don't know what you're talking about."

"Mr. Nolan, isn't it true that Tommy Regan tried to blackmail you on the night of his murder?"

Nolan folded his arms again. "That's crazy."

"He didn't just want an ownership interest in a strip club, he wanted a piece of the action, didn't he?"

Nolan slowly shook his head. "I told you. I don't have a clue about what you're talking about."

"Sure, you do. The action he wanted was a piece of the lucrative drug trade at The Treasure Chest—drug dealing that he witnessed each and every day he worked there? Drug dealing that you're a part of."

"Objection," Sears cried.

"Sustained," Stone said.

"Tommy Regan knew you were dealing drugs at The Treasure Chest, didn't he?"

"Objection, Judge." Sears was on his feet again. "Mr. Marino needs a good-faith basis to ask a question like that, and he doesn't have one."

Stone bared his teeth. "Have you forgotten what 'sustained' means, Mr. Marino?"

Jack looked at David Lamb, his demeanor animated, his eyes unblinking, focused on Mickey Nolan.

Nolan straightened in the witness enclosure. "I run a clean operation at TC's."

Jack shot a look at the jury, then turned to the witness again. "So clean that Tommy Regan told you he wanted ten thousand dollars to keep his mouth shut about the drug dealing, right?"

"Already told you that's not true."

"Do you know a customer who goes by the name Rat?"

"Yeah, I know him."

"And isn't it true when you refused Tommy Regan's demand for ten grand, Tommy told you he was going to sue the club for much more than ten thousand dollars over the injuries he suffered in a fight with Roger 'Rat' Ferriter when Tommy was off-duty?"

"Never happened."

"And, in the course of the lawsuit, his lawyer would be asking all kinds of deposition questions of you and others under oath—questions that you wouldn't want asked. Isn't that right?"

Nolan stared at Jack. "Never happened."

"In fact, Tommy told you his lawyer had already gone ahead and filed the suit against you, didn't he?"

Nolan shook his head.

"But Tommy said he'd drop the case in exchange for ten thousand dollars in cash."

"I don't know anything about no lawsuit."

Jack stood, the courtroom hushed, the jurors riveted on Nolan, the former prosecutor trusting they'd turn on him as soon as they saw the lawsuit.

At length, Jack continued. "And it was after Tommy Regan tried to extort you, that you told David Lamb not to leave the club that night without telling you?"

"No," said Nolan.

Jack pointed at the defendant, his face contorted and purpled with anger. "You told David Lamb repeatedly not to leave without you, didn't you? And less than twelve hours after that conversation, Tommy Regan was found dead."

"I told you, I never told him not to leave."

"By the way, did you see Mr. Regan use cocaine while he was at the club on the night of his murder?"

"No."

"Really? Had you ever seen him use cocaine or any other controlled substance?"

Nolan shrugged, looking away. "Never."

"Are you aware that the autopsy establishes that there was cocaine in Thomas Regan's blood?"

Nolan seemed rattled. "No."

"You sold him cocaine that night, didn't you?"

"No."

One of the jurors straightened, several others leaned forward.

"You've sold lots of people cocaine at The Treasure Chest, haven't you?"

"I've already answered that question."

Jack strolled back toward counsel table, adopting a bemused tone. "Mr. Nolan, you're familiar with handguns, correct?"

"I'm licensed," Nolan replied. "You have to be in a place like that."

"You said on direct examination that you keep a gun behind the bar at The Treasure Chest in case of trouble, isn't that right?"

"Yes."

"But you've never used it, because The Treasure Chest has never had any trouble, wouldn't you agree?"

"It's a safe establishment."

"Mr. Nolan, would you agree that Tommy Regan was a big guy?"

"Good size. Sure."

"And would you agree, as noted in the autopsy report, that at the time of his death he weighed two hundred and seventy-five pounds?"

"Sounds about right."

"Yet if I heard you correctly, it's your testimony that David Lamb, who weighs about one hundred and sixty pounds, helped you drag Mr. Regan's body into and out of the bushes before you both placed him into the back of Mr. Regan's station wagon?"

"That's what happened."

The defendant shook his head emphatically. Jack turned and held up a finger, a reminder to his client to control himself.

"And David dragged him with his left hand while he held the gun in his right hand. Is that what you're saying?"

"Yep."

"And you're telling us that the gun was pointed at you, right?"

"That's right. Yeah."

"Now, Mr. Nolan, when you told this jury that Mr. Lamb dragged this two-hundred-and-seventy-five-pound man with his left arm, were you aware that David Lamb underwent extensive reconstructive surgery on his left shoulder only two months prior to Mr. Regan's murder?"

Nolan shifted his weight. "I don't remember no operation."

"Well, you must recall that he was out of work when he had the operation, right?"

"We—I'd have to check my records. I don't remember when he started with us."

Jack ambled to counsel table and grabbed a sheaf of papers. "There's no need to check your records, Mr. Nolan." Turning to the court, he said, "Your Honor, I move to introduce Mr. Lamb's certified hospital records under General Laws, chapter 233, section 79. The records establish that my client had major reconstructive surgery on his left shoulder only two months before the murder."

Sears stood. "Objection."

"What's your objection, Mr. Sears?" Judge Stone asked.

"Relevance."

Stone waved off the objection. "The records will be admitted."

Jack handed the records to the clerk and asked the clerk for the autopsy photographs that had been admitted into evidence. He shuffled through them and asked, "Was Tommy faceup or facedown when, as you say, you and Mr. Lamb dragged him in and out of the bushes."

"Facedown."

"So, the victim was dragged into the bushes with his face and torso facing down. Is that your testimony?"

"Yeah. That's what happened."

"By the way, was Mr. Regan dragged in and out of the bushes by his hands or feet?"

"We dragged him by the hands into the bushes and dragged him by his ankles on the way out."

"So, the last position Mr. Regan was in was on his stomach being dragged by his ankles to the car, right?"

"That's right."

"And these are the same thorn bushes the jurors saw for themselves when they visited the crime scene?"

"I guess."

"May I approach the witness, Your Honor?"

Stone nodded.

"I'm showing you the autopsy photos previously introduced into evidence by the Commonwealth. Mr. Nolan, do you see any scratches whatsoever on the torso or face of Mr. Regan?"

Nolan stared at the photos without responding.

"Mr. Nolan, you need to respond."

"I don't see any."

Jack paused, long enough for the point to be driven home. "Mr. Nolan, are you sure you were alone out there on the railroad tracks?"

"We were alone."

Jack gave Nolan a long look of disbelief. "You didn't see or hear anyone else out there, huh?"

"No."

"By the way, Mr. Nolan, where was David Lamb standing when he supposedly shot Mr. Regan?"

"He was standing to the left of Tommy, behind him."

"How far back?"

"At least three or four feet."

"Are you sure?"

"Positive."

Jack paused and looked around the courtroom. "You killed Thomas Regan, didn't you?"

"Your Honor, do I have to answer this question?" Nolan asked, beseeching the court.

Stone took his glasses off, shooting Nolan a sideways look. "Oh, I can assure you, Mr. Nolan, you do."

"I didn't kill Tommy Regan," he said emphatically.

"You killed him because he was trying to blackmail you, isn't that right?"

"Nothin' to blackmail me about."

"Your Honor, may I approach?"

"I'm placing before you a certified copy of a civil complaint filed in the Mystic District Court on behalf of Thomas Regan one day before he died, seeking damages against The Treasure Chest for failing to protect him from a drunken patron who scarred him for life. Do you recognize this complaint?"

Nolan stared at the lawsuit as if it were radioactive. He stuttered, "I don't know. You—you have to ask my lawyer."

Jack turned to look at the jurors. "We don't have to, Mr. Nolan. You've told us everything we need to know." Waving the complaint in the air, he said, "Your Honor, I move to admit the complaint along with a Certificate of Service that proves that a constable served a copy of this complaint on a liar whose name is Mickey Nolan."

The jury box stirred, a murmur like the buzzing in a beehive rising from the jury box, as the judge admitted into evidence documentation of Tom Regan's lawsuit against The Treasure Chest.

Sears didn't dare look at the jurors.

CHAPTER FIFTY-SIX

By the time Sears finished leading the Medical Examiner through his background, Dr. Neil J. Backman sounded like the next Surgeon General of the United States. A graduate of Harvard Medical School. Five years of post-grad work at Massachusetts General Hospital. Certified in forensic pathology by the American Board of Pathology.

Jack rolled his eyes, willing Sears to jump ahead.

"In the course of your career," asked Sears, "how many autopsies have you performed?"

"Over a thousand."

The jurors stirred with interest, heads craned to look closely at a man who had picked apart so many human beings.

"Doctor, have you been qualified as an expert in the field of forensic pathology by the courts of the Commonwealth?"

"Yes."

"Approximately how many times?"

"Nearly five hundred."

"And out of approximately five hundred cases, how many involved gunshot wounds?"

Jack straightened, waiting for the answer.

"The majority," Backman said.

"Dr. Backman, could you explain to the jurors what a pathologist is?"

"Basically, a pathologist studies disease. More specifically, he analyzes human tissue to make a diagnosis. He also conducts autopsies to determine a cause of death."

The jury had been reeled in neatly, Jack realized. They respected this witness and hung on his every word. Jack had noticed a chink in his armor, though: Backman was old school. He spoke as if every pathologist were male, breezily dismissing the fact that women comprised a growing number of medical school enrollments. Jack scanned the jurors, hoping to detect some recognition of this. He saw none.

"Doctor, did you have occasion to perform an autopsy on the body of Thomas Regan?"

"Yes."

"Where did that occur?"

"At the Boston Regional Office of the Chief Medical Examiner, 284 Massachusetts Avenue."

"Prior to the autopsy, was the decedent identified?"

"Yes. By his wife."

Sears waited enough time for the jury to consider what it might be like to identify a loved one in a morgue.

The jury foreman's face blanched.

Sears moved on. "Following the identification of the victim, did you conduct an internal and external examination of the body of the deceased?"

"I did."

"Your Honor, with the Court's permission, may the witness leave the stand and approach the illustration affixed to the chalkboard to help explain his testimony for the jurors?"

Judge Stone nodded.

"Thank you, Judge," Sears replied.

The Medical Examiner stood to point to an easel holding a diagram.

"Beginning with the head of Mr. Regan," Sears prompted, "please tell us the results of your examination."

"The victim's head showed a single gunshot wound. Marked by an irregular entrance hole in the mid-to-right occipital region, in other words, in the middle to right side of the back of the head."

"Were there other wounds?"

"Yes. There were multiple skull fractures. There were also multiple abrasions and contusions of the nose and right eye. The upper lip was contused, too."

"Anything more?"

Backman checked his notes. "The jaw was fractured."

"When you conducted your internal examination of the head of Mr. Regan, did you find any bullets or metal fragments within his skull?"

"Yes."

"What was the caliber of the bullet?"

"Nine-millimeter."

"And where were these found?"

"Various fragments were found embedded in the front of the skull and the rest within the brain itself."

"You may resume the stand, Doctor."

Sears glided to counsel table and snatched a group of photographs. Jack braced himself.

"May I approach the witness, Your Honor?"

Judge Stone nodded.

Sears moved toward the witness, holding the photographs in his French-cuffed hand. He placed them on the rail of the witness stand.

"Dr. Backman, I've placed before you a series of photographs and ask you to review them, please."

Backman surveyed the photographs. Jack's stomach squeezed down as he recalled the scent of death from the autopsies he'd attended as a prosecutor.

"Do these photographs fairly and accurately depict the condition of the decedent's body at the time of your examination?"

"They do."

"Your Honor, the Commonwealth moves that these photographs be admitted into evidence."

"Sidebar, please, Your Honor," said Jack, shooting a protective glance at Lamb, who seemed frozen. He had to do something, anything, to keep the photos out of the jurors' sight. "Judge, these photographs are ghastly. They show a man who has been cut into pieces. What possible relevance could they have for anyone other than medical professionals?"

"Let's see them." Stone beckoned with an outstretched hand. Fanning the photos out, he eyed them dispassionately before turning to Sears. "I assume your position is that the photos would assist the jury in understanding the Medical Examiner's testimony?"

Jack could feel his temper spike. Stone was coaching Sears. "Your Honor, the man is dead: that's why we're here. How will photographs of the inside of Mr. Regan's brain help the jurors decide who killed him?"

"Mr. Marino, the Court well knows why we are here. It only hopes you do."

Jack fought to ignore Judge Stone's rebuke, stealing a peek at the jury, his anger giving way to alarm as several jurors avoided eye contact. "Judge, please, these photographs can only be meant to prejudice the jurors by playing on their sympathies—and in a death penalty case, the prejudice is irreparable."

Judge Stone turned to his session clerk. "I find that the evidentiary value of these photographs outweighs any danger of prejudice.

They may be admitted into evidence. Mr. Sears, you may publish the photographs to the jury."

Jack fumed. What the jurors were about to see, they'd never forget.

Jack shot a sideways look at the jurors as they examined the photographs, silence settling upon the courtroom, several jurors covering their mouths as if to mute a cry.

When every juror had seen the photos, Sears continued his direct examination. "Doctor, as a result of your autopsy of Thomas Regan, did you form an opinion as to his cause of death?"

"Yes."

"And what was that?"

"He died of a single gunshot wound intentionally inflicted to the back of his head."

"I have no further questions."

Jack watched as Sears returned triumphantly to his seat. He'd legally established that a man had been murdered, cut down in the prime of his life.

The only remaining question was who killed him. David Lamb, sitting shell-shocked at Jack's side, seemed the odds-on favorite.

CHAPTER FIFTY-SEVEN

"The hole where the bullet entered the rear of Mr. Regan's head was irregular. Is that what I heard you say, Dr. Backman?" Jack asked on cross-examination.

"Yes. The hole was irregular."

"In your experience when a bullet is fired into a human body from a short distance, the gunshot produces gases, does it not?"

"Yes."

"And these gases stretch the underside of the skin, causing the skin to blow outward, am I getting that right?"

Backman hesitated, his mouth set. "That's possible."

"And when the skin blows outward, an irregular entrance hole is formed?"

Another beat. "It's possible, I suppose."

Jack turned to the judge. "Your Honor, I move to strike the witness's answer as unresponsive. This is cross-examination. I ask that the witness be instructed to answer the question 'yes' or 'no.'"

Judge Stone shook his head. "It's cross-examination of an expert, Mr. Marino. If your question delves into an area beyond the common experience of the jury, the witness will not be required to answer 'yes' or 'no.'" He turned to the Medical Examiner. "Doctor, if possible, answer counsel's question 'yes' or 'no.' However, if defense counsel's question calls for an answer involving aspects of forensic pathology, you may fashion your answer as you please."

Sears smiled. "Thank you, Your Honor."

Judge Stone glanced down at Jack. "You may ask the question again, Counsel. If you wish."

Jack changed the question. "If a bullet were fired from twenty feet, you wouldn't expect an irregular entrance hole, would you?"

"Not generally. No."

"So, you would agree this was a close contact wound Mr. Regan suffered?"

Backman considered his response. "The entrance hole was consistent with a close contact wound."

"Doctor, were you able to form an opinion as to how long Thomas Regan could have survived such a gunshot wound?"

"Yes."

"And what is that opinion?"

"He died instantly."

Jack continued. "Doctor, you've testified about the victim's head wound. Did you examine the rest of his body?"

"Of course," Backman answered.

"Did you examine his chest and stomach?"

"His entire upper torso."

"And what did you find?"

"My findings were unremarkable."

"Meaning?"

"We observed nothing of significance."

"Can you tell us if the victim had any abrasions on his upper torso?"

"I'd have to look at my report."

Jack approached the witness stand. "I'm placing before you a copy of your autopsy report."

The Medical Examiner studied his report, taking his time.

"Any mention of abrasions on his upper torso?" Jack repeated.

"None that I noted."

"Any scratches or cuts of any kind?"

"None."

"And you would have noted them in your report, if there were, right?"

"Of course."

"Any vegetative matter anywhere on the victim's body? Plant material of any kind?"

"May I look at my report again?" Backman asked.

"Of course, Doctor."

"There's nothing in here about plant material," Backman said.

"Well, let me show you the autopsy photographs."

"I've seen them."

"Then it won't take but a second."

Jack snatched the photographic exhibits from the clerk and handed them to the witness, who shuffled through them with the indifference of a casino blackjack dealer.

"Any cuts or scratches on Thomas Regan's upper face, chest, stomach—anywhere on his body?"

"No."

Sears tapped a finger against his lip. David Lamb sat silent at counsel table, his eyes falling to his hands, Jack feeling grimly pleased.

"Thank you, sir," Jack said. "I have no further questions for this witness."

CHAPTER FIFTY-EIGHT

In the United States, the burden of proof always rests with the prosecutor. Even to get the case to the jury. The government must introduce enough evidence to permit a jury to find every element of the crime charged beyond a reasonable doubt. Otherwise, the case is dismissed, wiped clean from the books without a defense attorney ever needing to introduce a scrap of evidence. And the defendant can never be prosecuted again. Double jeopardy, the law calls it.

So before resting its case, the Commonwealth had better be damn sure it had put everything it had into evidence. As a prosecutor, Jack had learned this lesson the hard way.

"Your Honor, the Commonwealth rests," Sears said. Earlier that morning, on redirect examination of Mickey Nolan, he had established that the constable who had served the lawsuit on the club had done so through "last and usual" service, meaning that the complaint was simply dropped off at the club, not served directly on Mickey Nolan. It gave Nolan the wiggle room to claim that he'd never seen the complaint and was unaware of it on the evening of Regan's murder.

Taking measured steps, Sears walked back to the prosecutor's table as if he were the lone survivor of the Alamo.

Jack leaned over to David. "They know they're in a fight," he whispered.

Lamb closed his eyes and breathed out audibly.

Now it was all up to Jack. But before presenting Lamb's defense, Jack would submit a Motion for a Required Finding of Not Guilty, shorthand for arguing that the evidence was insufficient for the case to go to the jury. Before the defense proceeded, Stone would be required to rule on whether the government had met its initial burden.

Sears—likely distracted from the shitshow his star witness had put on—had ignored the corroboration requirement, an obscure but critically important legal principle. In cases involving immunized testimony, the Commonwealth must introduce independent evidence corroborating the testimony of an immunized witness. Knowing this, Jack had sat through the prosecution's case, waiting, watching, hoping. No corroboration, no conviction.

"Counsel, do you wish to be heard?" Judge Stone said, a hint that he expected Jack to file his written motion for a required finding of not guilty and waive oral argument so as not to waste his time.

Not a good sign. It meant the judge hadn't spotted the corroboration issue either. He reached into his briefcase for the motion and thick memorandum he'd prepared.

"I very much wish to be heard, Judge."

Judge Stone leaned forward to dismiss the jurors, who weren't permitted to hear these arguments. "Perhaps this might be a good time for coffee," he said.

As the door closed behind the last juror, Stone looked over at Jack. "I'll hear you briefly, Mr. Marino. Very briefly."

Jack passed his motion and memorandum to the clerk, who placed it before the judge.

"What's this?" Stone asked, glancing at the memo.

"Given the importance of the corroboration requirement, I briefed the issue for the Court."

"I'm listening," Judge Stone said.

"As this Court well knows, in every case involving immunized testimony, the Commonwealth is legally obligated to introduce sufficient, independent evidence to show that the defendant committed the crime charged—apart from the immunized testimony."

"The Commonwealth has clearly failed to do that here. Instead, it relied solely on Mr. Nolan's uncorroborated testimony."

The judge turned to the prosecutor. "What do you say about this, Mr. Sears?"

Sears hesitated, the first hint of his uncertainty. When he spoke, though, his voice betrayed no concern. "Your Honor, the Commonwealth introduced more than sufficient evidence corroborating the commission of murder in this case."

"Judge, there wasn't a shred of corroborating evidence that David Lamb murdered Thomas Regan other than the testimony of a man who owes his soul—and his freedom—to the government in exchange for immunity."

Jack studied the judge. Stone had a problem with no way out. Yet he appeared unfazed, staring out the windows into a gray sky, the din of the capital punishment demonstrators, an elegy of sorts, continuing to invade the courtroom.

After an unusual delay, the judge spoke. "Mr. Marino, it seems clear to me that the Commonwealth has introduced through the Medical Examiner more than sufficient evidence corroborating that a killing took place."

Jack's mouth dropped open. Even Sears seemed surprised.

"Judge," Jack snapped. "Obviously, a killing took place. We hardly needed a Medical Examiner to tell us that the victim is dead. That's why we're here."

"Mr. Marino, I don't need you to tell me why we're here," Stone said.

Jack drew a deep breath and let it out slowly. "Fine, Your Honor, but the Medical Examiner didn't connect the death of the victim to this defendant. No one besides Nolan did."

A dark light flashed in Judge Stone's eyes. "I've heard enough, Mr. Marino." He turned to face the stenographer. "Let the record reflect that this Court does not interpret the corroboration requirement to require that the Commonwealth must prove entirely by independent means that the defendant murdered the victim as has been suggested by the defense."

The judge hardly took a breath. "Rather, this Court finds that the corroboration requirement merely requires that the government introduce some independent evidence on any one element of the crime charged." It was Stone's turn to show his disdain. "That's exactly what the Medical Examiner's testimony established: that a human being was killed. And that's all the Commonwealth has to establish under the corroboration requirement. Defense counsel's motion is without merit." Jack's fastidiously prepared memorandum sat on the bench, untouched and unread.

Jack struggled to fathom Stone's inexplicable—and unprecedented—interpretation. Surely the judge's ruling couldn't possibly be upheld on appeal. The sole reason for the corroboration requirement was to protect against what could happen here: a conviction based solely on immunized testimony.

But Jack wasn't interested in appeals. He needed a not guilty verdict, and this motion had been his best shot.

"Your Honor, the corroboration requirement was created by the Legislature because it recognized the terrible danger inherent in prosecuting someone solely on the basis of the testimony of an immunized witness. It would have no meaning at all if the

Commonwealth need only show that someone was murdered in a murder case. Someone is always murdered in a murder case."

Judge Stone hammered his gavel against the bench, the clap of wood-on-wood booming throughout the courtroom. "Mr. Marino, this Court has made its ruling. In the event you didn't hear me the first time, your motion is denied, and—"The judge glanced at the clock—"Court is adjourned for the day."

* * *

The entire courtroom seemed to shudder. Lamb was mumbling something, but Jack couldn't make it out. The pitched battle between two estranged, former colleagues had become triangular. Each time Jack gained a momentary advantage, Judge Stone snatched it away. Jack had to calculate every move not only to beat Sears, but also to make an end-run around a vengeful judge.

Jack watched as Sears chatted it up with a group of younger Assistant District Attorneys at the rear of the courtroom, celebrating the denial of his motion. Amid muted laughter, Jack heard Sears say something about Jack quitting.

Jack knew the type of attorney Sears was comparing him to. Club fighters. Easy enough to beat, looking for a soft place to fall down. Jack might have lost the promise he once had—and maybe even his nerve—but a club fighter he wasn't. David Lamb wasn't going down without the fight of Sears's life. Or Jack's.

* * *

Jack sank into the green cushioned sofa in what was left of his living room, the stress of the day oozing from muscles wracked with spasm.

He sipped black coffee and watched Boston 9 TV reporter Alexa Metranos on the television screen.

"The countdown has begun as both candidates make their final swings through the state," she said. "To the surprise of the pundits, District Attorney Trevor Cameron has pulled dead-even in a race where few predicted he could credibly challenge the Commonwealth's popular governor."

The camera segued to Cameron standing before a cheering horde at City Hall Plaza, the city's powerful and vote-delivering mayor standing and smiling at Cameron's side.

"Most experts believe that the DA's surprising surge is due to a strong law and order campaign. After months of candidate rallies, advertising, and debates, it all comes down to this: a ground war at the grassroots level and the result of the state's first death penalty prosecution."

Jack's telephone rang.

The reporter continued, "Only one thing is certain: The race is so close at this point, even the experts can't predict a winner."

The phone bleated a second time, then a third.

"At Boston City Hall Plaza, this is Alexa Metranos reporting for the Boston 9 Ten O'clock News."

Jack snatched the phone.

CHAPTER FIFTY-NINE

"She's alive," Matt said. "Someone saw her two days ago, wandering near the tracks a mile or so north of the murder scene. Near our old building."

"Funny that the projects would someday become an advantage for us," Jack said.

"I'll be following up a couple of leads tomorrow. My hunch is she'll stay close to what she knows best—the railroad tracks."

"I'll stall as long as I can, but I don't have a lot of witnesses."

"How's it going?" Matt asked.

Jack sipped his coffee. "My motion was tossed, but I still think I've got reasonable doubt. The Commonwealth's case rises and falls on Nolan's testimony. And I can't believe the jury's going to believe that piece of shit. He's dirty. I'm certain the jury can see it."

"I'll keep looking. But, Jack?"

"Yeah?"

"Can you talk slowly for once. I need time."

* . *

Ballistics expert Jonathan Hayes wore a faded blue shirt under a tweed sport coat and khaki slacks. A scraggly beard hung from his face, wire-rimmed glasses failing to hide the dark furrows under the eyes of Jack's first witness.

"Could you please state your name, Doctor?" Jack asked.

"Dr. Jonathan W. Hayes," the witness replied.

"Mr. Marino. Sidebar," Judge Stone snapped.

Jack turned with a look of incredulity. "Your Honor?"

"That's right, Mr. Marino. Sidebar," Judge Stone barked again.

Sears and Jack ambled to the side of the bench, their shoes making brushing sounds in the quiet of the courtroom.

Judge Stone looked down at defense counsel. "Is Mr. Hayes a medical doctor?"

"Ph.D.," Jack said.

"Unless he's a medical doctor, you'll refer to him as Mr. Hayes, is that understood?"

"Your Honor, he's devoted a lifetime to the study of ballistics," Jack said. "He's earned his doctorate—and the title."

"He's 'Mr. Hayes' in my courtroom. Is that understood?" Stone looked away.

Sears smiled.

"Note my objection," Jack snapped and walked back to the far end of the jury box.

"Sir, having examined the scene, the ballistics evidence, and other forensic reports, are you here today to provide the jury with your opinions regarding the murder of Thomas Regan?"

"Yes, sir. I am," Hayes said.

"Is it your testimony that Mr. Lamb could not have shot Mr. Regan from the distance Mr. Nolan testified to?"

Sears stood. "Objection, Your Honor. Counsel is leading his own witness."

"Sustained," Judge Stone said. "Ask the question another way, Mr. Marino."

"Sir, you stated you have an opinion in this case. Could you tell us that opinion, please?"

Sears squirmed.

"My opinion is that Mr. Regan could not have been shot from the distance described by Mr. Nolan." He added, "Or in the way Mr. Nolan described."

"Objection. Your Honor, this witness is improperly commenting on the credibility of another witness, and counsel is prompting him to do so."

"Sustained. Mr. Hayes," Judge Stone said. "Confine your answers to whatever opinions you're here to offer."

Jack asked, "Sir, could you tell the jury what you mean when you say the victim could not have been shot from the distance the Commonwealth has alleged?"

"It's clear beyond doubt that Thomas Regan was shot at close range."

"How can you be sure he was shot at close range?"

"It's actually very easy. I examined the photographs of the entrance wound carefully. There are unmistakable powder burn marks on the skull of the victim."

Jack approached the witness with the autopsy photographs and autopsy report. Jonathan Hayes morphed into the community college professor he was, explaining, educating, demonstrating, and persuading until the matter was clear in the minds of the jury.

"By the way," Jack asked, "did you hear the Commonwealth's medical examiner mention anything about powder residue on the victim's skull?"

"I did not."

"Did you hear Mr. Nolan testify that the victim was not only shot from a certain distance, but from the left rear of the victim?"

"Yes. I heard him say that."

"Based on your examination of the forensic reports in this case, the physical evidence, including the clothing of the victim, as well as the testimony rendered in this case, do you have an opinion as to the entrance angle of the bullet that killed Thomas Regan?"

"Yes, I do."

"And what is that opinion, sir?"

"The victim was shot from behind from his right to the left."

"And what is the basis of your opinion?"

Hayes picked up the autopsy report that had been placed before him. "The autopsy is clear: the bullet tracked from right to left. Had he been shot from the angle Mr. Nolan described, the trajectory would have traveled left to right."

"Sir, as part of your examination, were you able to examine the bullet fragments taken from Mr. Regan's body?"

"Yes, sir. They were made available to me . . . after repeated requests."

"And could you tell us," Marino continued, "as a result of your examination, if there is any connection whatsoever in this case between Mr. Lamb and the bullets that killed Mr. Regan?"

"There is absolutely no physical connection of any kind between the two."

"What makes you say that?"

"There is no evidence showing the existence of any gunshot residue on Mr. Lamb."

Jack turned back to his witness. "Sir, did you have an opportunity to examine the murder scene?"

"A number of times."

"And when did you last do that?"

"Yesterday."

"While you were there, did you examine the area closely, including the bushes in and out of which Mr. Nolan claims David Lamb dragged the bare-chested body of Tommy Regan?"

"I studied those bushes carefully."

Judge Stone interrupted. "Mr. Marino, how much longer will you be?"

"Judge, this is an important witness for the defense," Jack said.

"Mr. Marino, you've had ample time with your 'important witness.' I suggest you wrap up your examination soon."

Slowly Jack turned to the jury, exchanging glances with several jurors, as if to say, *all I ask for is a fair trial.*

"And can you tell us what you observed in those bushes?"

"Thorns."

"Thorns?" Jack repeated.

"There are thorns everywhere on both sides of the tracks, including throughout the brush that Nolan described as the place where the victim's body was dragged in and out of."

"How many thorns did you observe in the area where Mr. Lamb is alleged to have dragged Mr. Regan's body?"

"Countless."

Jack returned to counsel table to scoop up a sheaf of photographs and approached the witness again.

"Sir, I've placed before you photographs of the victim's body already admitted in evidence by the Commonwealth. Do you see any scratch marks on the victim's face, chest, stomach, or abdomen—the exact areas Mickey Nolan testified were exposed as Mr. Regan was supposedly dragged into and out of the bushes next to the tracks?"

"None at all," the witness answered.

Sears rose to his feet, sweat trickling down his face.

"Objection. Your Honor, this 'expert' is not a medical examiner. I object to any attempt by this witness to render medical testimony."

"Your Honor, the witness is not providing medical testimony," Jack said. "He is simply describing whether or not there are any scratches on the body of the victim. In any event, the photographs are already in evidence, and as I recall, it was the Commonwealth who offered these exhibits in evidence."

Judge Stone glared down from the bench. "Mr. Marino, this witness has been qualified by me to testify on matters relating to ballistics and gunshot wounds. He is not a medical doctor as we've discussed. More to the point, his testimony is cumulative. The Commonwealth's objection is sustained."

"Judge, I'd like to approach."

"No," Judge Stone barked.

"Judge, I have a right to protect the record. And I insist on a sidebar conference. Now."

Judge Stone's face flushed with anger. "Quickly, Mr. Marino. Very quickly."

Jack leaned on the bench. "Judge, as you may recall—"

"Counsel, I've told you, don't ever touch my bench," Stone barked. "I insist on a particular decorum in my courtroom."

Jack recoiled, yanking his hand away as if he'd touched a lighted barbecue grille. It was one of Judge Stone's idiosyncrasies that he kept forgetting about. "Judge, this witness can testify to anything he relied on in forming his opinions. And he relied on his observations of the autopsy photographs as well as his observations at the crime scene."

The judge turned to the jury. "Ladies and gentlemen, you have heard testimony regarding certain conditions at the murder scene and the condition of the victim's body. The Commonwealth has objected to this testimony as is its right, and I have sustained that objection. Accordingly, I instruct you to disregard any testimony relating to the presence of thorns at the murder scene."

But each and every one of the jurors had seen the thorns for themselves, and even Judge Stone could not unring that bell.

*   *   *

Jack had barely settled into his seat at counsel table when Sears approached the witness.

"Mr. Hayes, you stated during direct examination that you examined the bullet fragments?"

"Yes."

"What caliber bullet were those fragments from?"

"Nine-millimeter."

"And can you identify the gun that discharged those bullets?"

"I can't identify the exact make and model, but a nine-millimeter bullet in most cases can only be fired from a semiautomatic handgun."

Jack winced as he recalled Nolan's fabricated testimony that he'd seen David Lamb with a semiautomatic weapon before the killing.

"Sir, are you a member of the National Association of Forensic Scientists?"

"No. I am not."

"Have you ever been a member?"

Hayes hesitated. "At one time."

"Isn't it true that you've been suspended from the association?"

Jack didn't even bother to stand. "Objection," he roared.

"Because you haven't paid your dues?" Sears continued over his objection.

"Objection," Jack repeated. "Your Honor, if this witness chooses to drop his membership in a private association, that's his business. The District Attorney is trying to make it look like a crime."

Judge Stone banged the gavel. "Move on, Mr. Sears. The jury will disregard the question and answer."

Feigning contrition, Sears backed away from the witness stand dramatically. "You've testified previously in murder cases, haven't you, Mr. Hayes?"

"I have."

"In fact, you've testified some thirty-four times in murder cases, haven't you?"

"If you say so."

"Of those thirty-four times, you've testified for the defense each and every time, is that true?"

"Just as your Medical Examiner has done for the prosecution."

Sears looked up at Judge Stone. "Objection, Your Honor, and I move to strike the witness's response. The question calls for a simple 'yes' or 'no.'"

"Answer 'yes' or 'no,' Mr. Hayes," Judge Stone instructed.

"Yes."

"In fact, you've never once testified for the Commonwealth in a court of law, have you?"

"Correct."

Sears spent the next half hour arguing with Jonathan Hayes, Ph. D., pursuing anything and everything except admissible evidence. When it was over, Sears sat down, his fingers rubbing the fatigue from his eyes.

Jack noticed that the jurors were staring at the First Assistant District Attorney, skepticism painted on their faces. The moment was electric with potential. One thing was certain: if Jonathan Hayes was right, Nolan had lied about how Tommy Regan had been murdered. If that were true, maybe—just maybe—he'd lied about who killed him as well.

Jack smelled opportunity and wondered whether the jury smelled deception.

CHAPTER SIXTY

"What the hell do you mean you won't testify?" Jack slapped his hand on the cement wall, his eyes laser-focused on Lamb, who sat on the edge of the bunk in the lockup behind the courtroom.

Ten minutes earlier, after Lamb had begun to murmur that he couldn't testify, Jack had requested an early recess. Judge Stone hadn't been pleased, but the hour had grown late, so he allowed it. As usual, a phalanx of court officers had escorted Lamb into lockup to await transportation. But this time Jack had asked to be locked inside with the defendant, instead of standing outside his cell in the corridor speaking through steel bars.

Jack stared in disbelief at his client, whose head hung down. He unbuttoned his shirt and loosened his tie. He wasn't sure if it was the change in events or a touch of claustrophobia, but his breath was labored as he stood inside the puny cell.

"David? Why won't you testify?"

Lamb slumped on the edge of the bunk. Without answering Jack's question, he began to sob, melting down before Jack's eyes.

Jack grabbed him by both shoulders. "David. Listen to me."

Lamb refused to look up.

"Why'd you let me turn myself inside out to exclude your prior conviction so you could take the stand? What was that all about?"

"I'm sorry," Lamb mumbled, shaking his head from side to side. "I'm sorry."

"Sorry? What do you mean you're sorry? We've prepared for this."

Lamb cried, "You don't understand."

"Understand? I understand we made a promise to these jurors. We told them in our opening statement that we'd tell them what really happened out there the night Tommy died. So far, there's no sign of the missing witness. So, you're it. You're the only one who can tell them what they need to know." Jack cleared his throat. "Make no mistake: if we don't follow through with that promise, you could pay for it with your life."

Lamb buried his face in his hands.

"David." Jack was yelling. "Look at me."

Lamb raised his head. He looked exhausted, eyes bloodshot, his hair a greasy mess, his court clothes damp with perspiration.

Jack pointed toward the courtroom. "The jury is waiting for you. Everyone in that courtroom is waiting for you. They want to see you take that stand out there and tell them you didn't do it."

"If I'm innocent, how can the jury find me guilty?"

Jack shook his head. "Look. The Constitution says you're innocent until proven guilty. And the judge is going to tell the jury exactly that. But you know what? For some jurors, you're guilty until proven innocent.

"Let me tell you a story. Several years ago, I was called for jury duty. They usually bounce attorneys from jury service as fast as a Nolan Ryan fastball. But somehow, I was selected for a criminal case. No one else on the jury knew I was a lawyer. At the end of the trial, we went to the jury room for deliberations. Do you know what the first words spoken by a juror were? 'Is this when we convict him?' That was the first sentence out of that juror's mouth. It's my job to prove you're innocent. And goddamn it, I'm going to do it. But I can't do it alone. You have to help me."

David held his head between the palms of his hands as if it would explode. "My kids."

"Your kids?"

"Don't you see? I can only protect them if I'm sittin' in here."

Jack stared at his client. His words made no sense.

Did Lamb actually believe he had to sacrifice himself to safeguard his kids?

"Protect them from what?" Jack asked, incredulous.

Lamb shook his head. "You don't understand what these people can do."

"Tell me," Jack said.

"You think the hit-and-run on Wendy was an accident? It was a message. On top of that, twice now, someone's approached her sister, Katie. Once in the park. Once on the way home from school."

"Who?"

Lamb shook his head again, his blue eyes opaque. "Don't know. Some guy. Twenties. Maybe early thirties."

Lamb looked wild. "Do you understand where I live? There's no hidin' in the projects. There's no safe place."

"I know that," said Jack softly.

"How can you know that?" Lamb snapped. "Look at you."

"David, I'll tell you how I know. I know cinder-block buildings just a couple of miles from where you live with thirty families squeezed into every one of them. I know sleepless nights because the interior walls did nothing to deaden the constant squabbling from the people next to us. I know what it feels like to be afraid to turn on the lights because I knew what might skitter across my bedroom floor. I also knew parents who bought cats and risked eviction because of the no-pets policy—all to keep the rats away from their kids." Jack sighed. "Ever follow the tracks up to the old projects?"

"No one goes up there."

Jack paused. "Unless you lived there."

"You?" Lamb asked.

Jack nodded. "Born and raised." He let that settle for a moment. "Look, David, the best way to protect your kids, no matter where you live, is to stand on the highest mountain you can find and scream the truth for all the world to hear—and that means you take the goddamn stand."

Lamb seemed like he was pushing down a ball of fear.

"Listen to me. If you don't testify, they're going to convict you. How're you going to protect your kids by dying in the electric chair?"

Lamb stared at him.

"The only way to take care of your girls is to come home, David." Jack's voice echoed off the walls of the small cell. Usually, it was a defense attorney's job to convince a client not to take the stand. Instead, here he was insisting that Lamb give up the most fundamental constitutional right of a criminal defendant—the right to remain silent.

Jack took a deep breath and tried to clear his head, the tiny cell shrinking around him. He called for the court officer, who arrived just as the claustrophobia threatened to overwhelm him.

As the cell door clanked shut behind him, Jack wiped his neck. He turned back to his client. "You've got the night to decide."

CHAPTER SIXTY-ONE

Jack struggled to stay awake as he lay in bed watching the late news. It'd been a long day, and tomorrow—the day he would rest his case—would be even longer. He needed to sleep. In the morning, Sears would do his best to destroy David Lamb.

The television anchor turned to the political news of the day.

"We've got breaking news in the Governor's race, and here to tell us about it is Boston 9 reporter Alexa Metranos, who has been following this race closely."

"Thank you. In a major development, a new Suffolk University poll has District Attorney Trevor Cameron overtaking the incumbent governor with only seven days until the election. A spokesperson for District Attorney Cameron issued a statement urging voters to get out to the polls on Tuesday, November second, to vote in what the spokesperson predicted would be a historic upset victory. In response, the Governor's campaign representatives say the only poll that counts is the one that occurs on election day."

Jack clicked off the TV, leaned over, killed the lamp, and fell back into bed.

Sleep came fitfully, but when it arrived, the railroad tracks loomed before him, a freight train pulling away from him, the earth beneath the tracks rumbling from its enormous weight, its steel wheels crying in the night. Through a gray mist, a lone figure, head bowed and shrouded in shadow, walked slowly down the center of the tracks, following the train. Jack was certain he was looking at Nora for the first time.

He called out, but she continued to move away from him. He called again. Without turning, Nora marched on.

Jack broke into a jog. Oddly, there was no pain in his knee from the gunshot wound he'd suffered. If he could catch her, he could speak to her. And finally learn the truth.

As he closed the distance between them, she turned, stepped off the tracks, and melted into the waist-high, wild grass.

Jack began to run. When he reached the spot where she'd disappeared, he looked in every direction. With his arms, he beat back the grass in wide arcs in an effort to find her. It was as if the night had swallowed her whole. "Nora," he screamed. "Nora—"

He wasn't sure how long the phone had been ringing. Jack looked at the alarm clock. It was two thirty in the morning.

He stumbled across the mess that had been his and Abby's bedroom. As he snatched the receiver, Jack heard Summer's voice trail off. "Jack, I . . ."

"Summer?" Jack said. The line was quiet but remained open. Jack rushed head-on, trusting that she remained on the line. "Summer, I'm so sorry. For everything I've done. The lost time. The pain I caused you.

"I was stupid, and . . . scared. Scared I'd always be the kid from the projects. From the wrong side of the tracks. Then I realized that's exactly who I want to be. You've helped me realize that."

He brushed away a tear. "I love you. I never stopped loving you," he said to silence. "I'm trying to find my way back. I'll never give up on us again. If only I had a second chance . . ." The line remained silent, as he gently placed the phone back on the cradle.

*   *   *

Early the next morning in the courtroom, Jack loosened his collar, a legal pad in his left hand, a pen in his right, and drank in a view of his client on the witness stand.

"Mr. Lamb, how would you describe your relationship with Tommy Regan?" Jack asked.

Lamb grabbed the rail of the witness enclosure to steady himself, his body weak and gaunt from jail life. "We were friends. Good friends." His answer was hollow sounding.

"How long were you friends?"

"Years. Maybe four or five. Right up till he died."

Jack paused long enough to cause several jurors to look at him. Then he walked calmly toward his client. Stopping short of the witness stand, Jack asked, "David, did you have anything—anything whatsoever—to do with the murder of Tommy Regan?"

Lamb's chest began to heave. "No," he said, shaking his head. "I had nothin' to do with what happened to Tommy."

Jack noticed Sears inch up fractionally in his chair.

"David, were you present when Tommy Regan was killed?"

Lamb's voice was a choked whisper. "Yeah."

Several jurors straightened in their seats.

"Can you tell us what happened the night Tommy was killed?"

Lamb's tone softened. "Tommy and me were working that night. Around nine, I noticed Tommy left the door where he was checking IDs. I would've covered for him, but I'm not allowed on the door—so I went lookin' for him. So he wouldn't get in trouble."

"Can you tell us what you did to find him?" Jack asked.

"I checked out back. Sometimes the strippers go out there for a smoke."

"What did you see?" Jack asked.

"Saw Tommy and Mickey Nolan out there."

"What were they doing when you first saw them?"

"They were gettin' into it real hard."

"How do you mean?"

"Arguing."

"What were they arguing about?"

Sears stood. "Objection. Your Honor, counsel's question clearly calls for hearsay."

The judge turned to the defense attorney. "Mr. Marino?"

"Your Honor, first, the defense is not offering the conversation for its truth. We don't care about what was said or whether it was true or not. We're offering it solely to show that an argument took place. Second, the defendant has a right to present a complete picture of the circumstances of Thomas Regan's murder under the Completeness Doctrine."

Before Sears could be heard, Judge Stone waved off his objection with another brush of his hand. "You may have it, Mr. Marino."

Sears sat down, shaking his head so the jury could see his scorn.

"Proceed, Mr. Lamb," the judge said.

"Tommy kept saying, 'Where's my money? Where's my ten grand?'"

"What did Mickey say?"

"At first, Mickey was makin' fun of him. Callin' him a loser. Said something about how he wouldn't pay him ten cents. Finally, Tommy said, 'Hey, don't matter anyway.'"

"And then?" Jack asked.

"Mickey got real quiet and said, 'What do you mean?'"

"And Tommy said, 'Even if you'd paid me the ten grand, I was gonna sue you and the eff'n club anyway.' Said he'd seen a lawyer. Knew his rights."

"Sue the club?" Jack asked.

"Yeah. After Tommy got hit with a bottle and scarred up pretty bad, he got it in his head he could sue The Treasure Chest. Somethin' about the club continuing to serve the guy after he was drunk and not protectin' Tommy from the assault. Every time Tommy brought it up, I told him to forget it, but he kept going on and on about it."

"If you know, would that have been Roger Ferriter who assaulted him?"

"That's the guy. They call him Rat."

"And what happened after Tommy indicated he would sue the club?" Jack asked.

"Micky said, 'Sue? For what? That eff'n zit on your face?'"

"And what did Tommy say?"

"Well, that's when the shit . . . sorry. That's when it all fell apart. Tommy was screamin' now. Said he wanted a piece of the place. Part ownership. And if he couldn't get it his way, he'd sue the bar and, in the process, blow the cover off the whole joint."

"The cover?"

"That's what he said. 'The cover.'"

"How did this confrontation end?"

Lamb leaned back. "Not good. Nolan was laughin' but not really. He pointed to the club and said like real calm, 'Get the fuck in there. You're lucky to have a fuckin' job.'" Lamb turned to face the jurors. "I'm sorry, but that's exactly what he said."

"That's all right," Jack said. "What else was said?"

"Tommy shot back and said, 'It'll cost you more than a job.'" And Nolan said, 'The fuck's that supposed to mean?' That was when Tommy started screamin' like crazy, 'Ya think I'm a fool. That I'm blind. You think I don't know what's goin' on here. The drugs. I've seen everything.'"

Several jurors leaned forward in their seats, tension simmering throughout the gallery.

"What happened then?" Jack asked.

"Nolan shut down. Almost like, I don't know, like he was a different person. He said to Tommy, 'Wait for me after work. Maybe we can work things out.' Just like that."

"Did either one of them know you were there?"

"I don't think so."

"Did you speak to Mr. Nolan later in the evening?"

"Yeah. Mickey told me he needed me to work late. I told him I had to get home, but he kept sayin' he needed me."

"What did you do?"

"I stayed after the one o'clock close like he said. Then Mickey said he and Tommy needed some help outside."

"And then what happened?" Jack asked.

"I followed Micky out back after everyone was gone."

"Can you describe for us what occurred next?"

"Mickey told Tommy he thought they could work out, you know, a deal. But before I knew it, they started arguing again in front of me."

"What did you see next?"

"Outta nowhere, Mickey pulled out a gun." Lamb lowered his head and began to sob.

"A gun? What kind of gun?"

"No clue. I couldn't tell you."

Sears squeezed his temples.

"What happened next?"

"Mickey ordered us both to walk out to the tracks."

"What did you do?"

"What I was told."

"And then what?"

Lamb had started to rock back and forth on the witness stand, the jury riveted.

"Mickey told me to kneel down and put my face in the dirt."

"Can you describe your state of mind at this point, David?"

"Excuse me?"

"What were you thinking at the time?"

"As soon as I saw the gun, I thought he was gonna kill both of us. I just kept thinkin' of my girls."

"What was Tommy doing?"

"He was freaking out. Could hear him sayin' over and over he was only kiddin' about suing the bar. You know. That he didn't mean it."

"What, if anything, did Nolan say?"

"He said, 'The fuck were you thinkin'—that we were gonna hand The Treasure Chest over to a piece of shit like you?'"

"Excuse me. Are you sure he said 'we'?"

"Definitely said 'we.'"

"What happened next?"

"Everything went down real quick. My face was still in the dirt, but I could hear Tommy begging."

Jack scanned the jury.

"And then what happened?"

I heard Tommy yell, 'Please help me. Thank you. Thank you.' I remember he kept sayin' 'thank you.'"

"And then what?"

"Nothin' at first. Then I heard some other voices."

"How many?"

"Not sure. Two, I think."

"Did you see them?"

Lamb shook his head. "No. Don't know who they were. Had my head down like I was told, but then someone said, 'Do it.'"

"And then what?"

"I heard a shot."

"Did you hear Tommy after that?"

The defendant swallowed hard. "No."

"When you heard the shot, what were you doing?" Jack continued.

"Like I said, had my head in the dirt. I could taste it."

"So, you didn't see anything?"

"Couldn't."

"How were you feeling then?"

Embarrassment flashed across the defendant's face. "I couldn't breathe, and I—" Lamb hesitated. "I peed my pants."

Jack waited long enough for the jury to wonder if this really sounded like the testimony of a murderer. Or of another victim.

"Did something else happen at that point?"

"There was a muffled noise, like someone coughing or heaving, and then I heard the men's voices again. One of 'em said, 'Shit, there's someone else out here.'"

"Whose voices were these?"

Sears watched the defendant consider his answer.

"I don't know. It wasn't Mickey. Whoever it was—they were speaking to Mickey. One of 'em was the one who said 'do it.' Then he said, 'Find who's out there.'"

"Objection, Your Honor," Sears said, a bead of perspiration dotting his brow. "I move to strike any reference to these unidentified individuals supposedly speaking to Mr. Nolan in the middle of the night. This witness clearly isn't sure what he heard and, in any event, concedes that he didn't see anything."

"Objection sustained," Judge Stone said. "That portion of the testimony is stricken from the record."

Jack continued, undaunted. "Without regard to what was said, are you positive the male voices you heard did not include Mr. Nolan?"

"Positive," Lamb shot back.

Sears flinched.

"And then what?"

"I heard them walkin' through the brush."

"Anything else?"

The defendant squinted. "I heard some kind of electrical sound."

"What do you mean?"

"I'm not sure. Like a high-voltage crackle."

"Could you make anything out?"

"Not really. Just that strange sound. And the voices."

"The same male voices you heard before?"

Jack glanced at the jurors, who were rapt.

"Same voices," Lamb observed, sliding his hand through his greasy hair.

"Mr. Lamb, what did you do when you heard the shot?"

"Prayed I wasn't next." He took a quick breath. "After a while, Nolan told me to get up."

"Did you see anyone once you got up from the ground?"

Lamb hesitated. "Just Mickey. The others were gone."

"Can you describe exactly what you saw?"

"Saw Mickey with a gun in his hand. And Tommy on the ground, his body draped over one of the tracks. Not moving."

"What happened then?"

"It was pitch dark and no one was around, so we left him there and went and got Tommy's car."

"Did you help Mickey Nolan drag Tommy's body in and out of the bushes?"

Lamb shook his head. "No. I couldn't drag anyone anywhere. I'd just had surgery on my shoulder. Tommy weighed at least two hundred and fifty pounds. Maybe more."

"Are you sure Mr. Nolan didn't ask you to help him drag the body into the bushes?"

Lamb shook his head. "Very sure. All the bushes down there have thorns sharp as knives. You can't get in the bushes without cuttin' yourself to pieces."

"Objection," Sears said from the prosecutor's table. "Improper opinion testimony."

Jack said, "Judge, I can establish the basis for his testimony."

The judge nodded, allowing the question.

"How do you know about the thorns on the bushes?" Jack asked.

"I grew up there. Played on those tracks all my life. If someone hit a ball into the bushes, the game was over. Nobody would shag it."

"At some point, did you get Tommy's car?"

"Yeah."

"Where did you get the keys to the car?"

"Mickey told me to take them outta Tommy's pocket."

"Then what did you do?"

"Drove it to where Mickey told me."

"Did he go with you?"

"Yeah."

"And who drove?"

"He told me to drive, while he sat in the passenger's seat."

"Where did you drive to?" Jack asked.

"He told me to leave the car behind one of the old warehouses. Said the drunks would get blamed for it."

"What happened then?"

"Mickey told me if I said a word, I'd end up just like Tommy."

"Anything else?"

A long pause.

"He said if you want your eff'n kids to live—you do exactly what you're told."

"So, what did you do?"

Lamb paused. "I thanked him."

Jack stopped in front of the witness stand. He was talking to his client but looking at the jury. "David, why didn't you go to the police?"

"I was afraid they'd hurt my kids."

"You say 'they.' Who do you mean?"

"I'm not really sure," Lamb said. "I mean, Mickey said flat out he'd hurt my kids. But there were other men out there that night that were part of this thing, and there was always a lot of outlaw bikers at TC's. They were real friendly with Mickey." Lamb paused. "Any of these people would kill you as quick as look at you."

"Objection. Your Honor, he can't speculate—"

"Sustained. Ask another question, Mr. Marino," Judge Stone barked.

"Were your kids ever threatened?"

"Lately some guy's been comin' up to one of my daughters after school. Just starin' at her. Scared her bad though. And me too," Lamb said. "Recently her twin sister, Wendy, was struck by a hit-and-run driver."

"How is she?"

"She's going to make it, but my mom told me she's never goin' to be the same."

"And by the way, have you ever carried a handgun anywhere at any time?"

"No. Of course not."

"Mr. Lamb, have you testified about this matter previously?"

"Yes. I have."

"When was that, sir?"

"Before the grand jury."

"And did you tell the truth on that occasion?"

Lamb shook his head.

"I need a response."

"No," he admitted, his face a mask of pain.

"Can you tell us why?"

"We came to the courthouse together. Mickey and me. He told me what to say, but said it'd be better if I testified first. That way, his story would back up mine. So that's what I did. But when I came out of the grand jury, there was a woman standing with Mickey. I started to walk over to him, and the woman put her hand up and separated us."

"Do you know who it was that separated you?"

"Attorney Teddy Smith."

"Did Mr. Nolan testify after you as planned?"

"No. Somethin' about the Fifth Amendment, and later, they gave him immunity."

Jack looked at his client, then turned directly to the jury. No one turned away. Finally, he said in a loud and clear voice, "So they gave absolute immunity to someone you know killed another human being, is that right?"

"Objection," Sears said.

"I withdraw my question. Your witness, Mr. Sears."

CHAPTER SIXTY-TWO

Sears rose slowly as was his custom, stationing himself at the very end of the jury box, farthest from David.

"Mr. Lamb, is it your testimony that you had nothing to do with the killing of Mr. Regan?"

Lamb seemed relieved to hear the question. "Yes."

"In fact, you told the jury a minute ago that you didn't even see the murder, let alone commit the murder. Isn't that what you said when Mr. Marino asked?"

"I told them what happened."

"And you said that because it's the truth, is that right?"

Lamb nodded in agreement. "It is the truth."

Sears's voice resonated. "And you told the truth because you took an oath before this court and this jury, right, Mr. Lamb?"

"Yes."

"And telling the truth pursuant to that oath is important to you, isn't it?"

"Yes."

"And it's important to you because you know that when you raise your right hand and take an oath, the criminal justice system depends on your telling the truth, right?"

Jack had been waiting for this. Sears was lecturing the jurors who were once again sitting in his classroom.

"Yes."

"Would you also agree that this court depends on witnesses, like yourself, who take an oath to tell the truth?"

"Yes," Lamb answered more warily.

"Would you agree that each of the jurors sitting on this case needs to hear the truth, the whole truth, and nothing but the truth?"

"That's right."

"Mr. Lamb, having said all that, you testified before the grand jury in this case, didn't you?"

"Yes."

"And before you testified in front of the grand jury, you took the same oath you took today, didn't you?"

Lamb nodded.

Judge Stone hunched his shoulders forward. "Mr. Lamb, you need to answer yes or no."

Lamb sat straighter. "Yes."

"Yet you lied to each member of the grand jury, didn't you?"

"I was afraid. Mickey told me to say that."

"In fact, you told the grand jurors that you weren't even present when the victim died?"

"I did."

The prosecutor gathered himself. "Now, as I understand your testimony, you say you were close friends with the victim. Is that true?"

"It is."

"Had you ever been over to Tom and Lisa Regan's house?"

Lamb fidgeted. "We didn't double date, if that's what you mean."

"Well, then, let me see if I have this right. Your close friend was murdered, and you never went to the police about it?"

"I wanted to."

"You were concerned about your close friend's wife, weren't you?"

"Sure."

"But not concerned enough to tell the police what happened to her husband, is that right?"

"I told you—"

"You were concerned about your close friend's three kids, weren't you?"

"Yeah. I was, but I was worried about my kids too."

"But again, not concerned enough to call the police and tell them the truth, were you?"

Lamb fought back tears. "I'm sorry."

The prosecutor pressed on.

"Instead, you let your close friend's wife and kids wonder about what happened to a husband and father, didn't you?"

Lamb didn't respond, his head bowed.

"As I recall, Mr. Lamb, you were disabled when Mr. Regan was killed, were you not?"

Lamb nodded. "Had surgery on my shoulder."

At the table, Sears picked up a series of standard-size checks and thumbed through them. "In fact, you were collecting workers' compensation, weren't you?"

Lamb tried to catch his breath as Sears approached the stand.

"Weren't you?"

"I was hurt. Yes."

"And you were collecting workers' compensation because you were supposedly totally disabled?"

"Well—"

With a loud, dramatic slap, Sears dropped a stack of checks on the rail of the witness stand. He thundered, "Isn't that what you told the Industrial Accident Board, so they'd send you all these checks while you were working?"

Lamb appeared dumbstruck.

"So that the jurors understand this correctly, at the same time you were collecting workers' compensation you were working under the table at The Treasure Chest Exotic Dance Club."

"I had to."

"But you knew that was wrong, didn't you?"

Lamb looked over at Jack.

"Objection, Your Honor," Jack said in an effort to purchase some time for Lamb to compose himself. "These are excludable prior bad acts."

"He may have it," Stone said.

"In fact, you knew that was against the law, didn't you?"

"I'm not sure what the law is. People do it. Tommy was doing it too. He told me it was no big deal."

"Yes or no—you knew it was illegal to be working at the same time you were collecting workers' compensation, didn't you?"

Lamb snapped back, in tears, "I needed money for my family."

"In any event, today for the first time, you tell a story about Mr. Regan threatening to sue the bar?"

"That's absolutely true."

"Mr. Lamb, did you tell the same story to the grand jury under oath?"

"No."

"In fact, today was the first time that you publicly told anyone about this conversation that you now say you're sure took place. Isn't that true? Yes or no, please."

"I told my lawyer."

"Other than your lawyer."

"Yes."

"Mr. Lamb, do you have any proof such a conversation even took place?"

"Just myself. As far as I know."

Sears strolled to the clerk's desk and snapped up the Commonwealth's fingerprint exhibits. "By the way, you're not suggesting to this jury that these fingerprints, which were found on the steering wheel of Mr. Regan's car, are not your fingerprints, are you, sir?"

"My fingerprints were already in the car. I drove Tommy's car every week."

"Likewise, you're not suggesting that these are not your fingerprints that were found on the keys, are you?"

"They're mine."

"So now you say that you were at the crime scene, yet you have no idea who killed Mr. Regan."

"I know who killed Tommy."

"But didn't you say you had your head in the dirt and couldn't see anything?"

"After the shot, when Mickey said I could get up, I saw him holding a gun with Tommy on the ground. And the others were gone."

"And where were the men whose voices you described?"

"I don't know."

"And you want the jurors to believe they just disappeared?"

"That's what happened."

"Tell me, Mr. Lamb, which version of the truth do you want this jury to believe today, the one you told the grand jury or the one you told today?"

Jack stood. "Objection, Your Honor. Argumentative."

"Move on, Mr. Sears," Stone said.

"Mr. Lamb. Part of the reason you're so confused about the voices and what really happened is that you were on cocaine on the night of Tom Regan's murder, weren't you?"

"We all were. Mickey. And Tommy, too."

"That wasn't the first time you used drugs, was it?"

"Objection," Jack shouted.

"Sustained," Judge Stone announced. "Mr. Sears, you know better."

"Thank you, Your Honor. In any event, Mr. Lamb, you used cocaine because it made you feel powerful."

"No."

"You liked the feeling that cocaine gave you, right?"

"It's stupid, but yeah, I liked it."

"In fact, it made you feel like you could do anything at all, didn't it?"

"No. It made life bearable."

"And while you were under the influence of cocaine, while you were feeling as if you could do anything in the world, you put a gun to the back of Tommy Regan's head and pulled the trigger, didn't you?"

"No."

"And that's how he died?"

"That's not how he died."

"And after you killed him, you told Mickey Nolan if he ever said a word about what happened out there, you'd kill him too, didn't you?"

Lamb was shaking his head, back and forth. "Mickey was the one who said that."

Sears said, "The Commonwealth is finished with this witness, Your Honor."

*   *   *

Jack wondered where the jurors stood. He had no more witnesses to help sway them. Lamb had denied ever possessing a handgun. But that didn't matter. The damage had been done. Had he done enough to earn a not guilty verdict? Maybe. If the jurors were his people.

Folks who'd grown up as he had. From neighborhoods like his. They'd be able to see through the Commonwealth's case. They wouldn't take Lamb away from his kids and put him to death on this evidence.

But he had to find Nora. Then Jack could prove the DA's office knew she'd witnessed the crime, yet it chose to hide her existence. If Jack could argue to the jury that Sears purposely didn't look for her—or worse, suppressed her existence—he wouldn't have to second-guess himself: the verdict would surely be not guilty. But that was one hell of an *if*.

Somehow, Jack had to convince this jury that a witness was out there, someone who could shed light on whether one friend killed another in cold blood without any reason, without any credible motive. He had promised as much in his opening. But could he do that without sacrificing Summer? If he produced his copy of the Lincoln Dawes memorandum, Sears would know that she'd leaked confidential file material. At a minimum, she'd lose her job. Worse, she'd almost certainly be charged with a crime.

Jack shot a glance at the ancient black-and-white clock at the rear of the courtroom. Two o'clock. Maybe there was a way. Jack would ask the Court for one last chance to find Nora. Matt had said he was close. All they needed was a little more time. How could Stone deny a request to adjourn for just a few hours in a case where a man's life hung in the balance?

CHAPTER SIXTY-THREE

Jack felt spent.

"Mr. Marino," said Judge Stone. "Call your next witness."

Jack glanced at his yellow legal pad without responding.

"Mr. Marino, are you resting your case?" Judge Stone asked, his voice louder.

"Your Honor, may we approach?" Jack asked.

"Counsel, is this necessary?" Stone sounded exasperated.

"It is."

"Approach."

Sears stood and followed Jack to the judge's bench, while the jurors fidgeted.

"Your Honor, the defendant respectfully requests a brief continuance—until Monday morning," Jack said.

"A continuance? On what grounds?" asked Stone.

"Your Honor, we're very close to locating a critical witness. The same witness I spoke about previously."

The judge snorted. "Counsel, you've had more than enough time to find this so-called witness of yours. I will not lock this jury up over the weekend while you trot around Mystic looking for a . . . phantom."

Jack leaned forward, shifting his weight, and spoke softly. "I only need this one continuance."

"No," Judge Stone said, shaking his head. "Enough. You've been talking about this witness since the beginning of the trial. You've produced nothing, no evidence demonstrating to this court that such a person even exists. I specifically instructed you after your opening statement that I will not permit you to come into my court-room and make bald, unsupported allegations. I trust you under-stand that."

Jack said, "I want to state for the record that this court is refusing to grant me a short continuance in a death penalty case where—even if I rest—jury deliberations, not to mention closing arguments and the court's instructions, will push us well into Monday anyway."

Judge Stone let out a long sigh. "Mr. Marino, this is as far as I will go: In the very unlikely event your mystery witness shows up and the jury is deliberating, I will hold a hearing and listen to what she has to say. If the jury returns a verdict of not guilty, you've got no problem. On the other hand, if the jury comes back with a guilty verdict and the testimony of this witness demonstrates that justice may not have been done, I will entertain a motion for a new trial forthwith. Otherwise, you're out of luck." Stone turned away.

Sears turned and backed away, leaving Jack frozen, standing alone at sidebar, stricken to the bone.

When Jack reached the defense table, Judge Stone asked again, "Does the defense rest?"

Jack felt the burden of the jurors' expectations.

A tinge of regret born of a shared past tugged at Jack's face. "I do have another witness, Judge." He paused. "I call the District Attor-ney, Trevor Cameron, to the stand." Jack turned and pointed at the DA sitting in the gallery, a buzz rising from the audience and

Cameron's retinue, Jack's eyes locked on the man who had fired him when he was most vulnerable, the District Attorney's ever-present campaign smile gone.

*   *   *

"This is a courtroom, not a romper room," Judge Stone said. He motioned both lawyers back to the bench, then covered his microphone. "Mr. Marino, what kind of stunt is this?"

"Your Honor, the District Attorney has granted immunity to a killer, and I intend to ask the DA about it under oath."

Stone stared down at Jack in disbelief. "You may not care that you are making a spectacle out of yourself. Nor can I do anything about the fact that you're not the lawyer you once were, but if you want to continue to be any kind of lawyer within the Commonwealth of Massachusetts, you will not make a mockery out of my courtroom."

"I also believe that the District Attorney's office is suppressing the existence of a key witness," Jack said. "In fact, I know it is."

"Mr. Marino, if you persist, I'm going to order that you be examined by the court clinician. Take a moment to gather yourself and finish this trial. Do we have an understanding?"

Jack turned away from the judge.

Judge Stone's voice boomed again. "Mr. Marino, does the defense rest?"

Jack remained silent. With his back to the judge, he huddled in conference with his client, the chants from the capital punishment demonstrators outside penetrating the courtroom like a funeral dirge.

Judge Stone stood. The pressure of a long trial and his deep-seated resentment of Jack Marino exploded. "Mr. Marino, I'm inquiring of you again. What are your intentions? Do you rest or do you have another witness?"

Sears looked over at the jurors, who seemed unsettled.

Finally, Jack looked up. "Your Honor, the defense has no other witness available at this time. The defense—"

A gentle but resolute voice floated up from the rear of the courtroom. "Make me a witness."

* * *

Jack watched as Summer St. Cloud slowly made her way to the front of the courtroom, pausing momentarily as she reached the bar enclosure. Stunning in a gray business suit, Summer extended her hand and pushed through the dark mahogany gate of the enclosure, through which only lawyers and witnesses were allowed to pass.

The gate squealed behind her as she began to walk to the witness stand.

"Stay where you are, young lady," snapped Judge Stone, holding up his hand like a traffic cop. "Would you mind telling me what's going on here?" He looked from Jack to Sears.

"Your Honor, I deeply apologize," Sears said, his chest heaving as if he were hyperventilating. "This is my secretary, Summer St. Cloud. I'm at a complete loss as to what she's doing here." Sears turned toward his assistant. "Summer, I'm ordering you to leave this courtroom immediately."

Summer ignored him. Instead, she stood, clutching a document in her hand, her arm and its explosive cargo extended toward Jack.

Sears blinked.

Summer motioned again for Jack to take the document.

Jack looked past Summer's outstretched hand. Instead, he peered down at his client who sat rigidly, looking as bewildered as everyone else. Finally, Jack turned back to Summer with a sad smile.

"Make me a witness," she said again, her gaze fixed on Jack, her eyes moist with tears.

Judge Stone smashed his gavel against the bench. "Mr. Marino, if you're behind this, I'll have you disbarred."

Jack ignored the judge.

"Your Honor," Sears said. "I object to this outrageous stunt. I don't know what defense counsel is doing here, but I ask this Court to instruct Mr. Marino to rest his case."

Judge Stone stood. "Mr. Marino, I'm talking to you. Do you plan to call this woman as a witness?"

Jack remained silent, looking only at Summer.

Jurors exchanged glances with one another and then focused their collective gaze on Summer and Jack.

Judge Stone smacked the gavel against the bench again, drawing all eyes to himself. "Mr. Marino, answer this court at once, or I will hold you in summary contempt."

Jack neither moved nor shifted his gaze from Summer.

Finally, he turned to the Court. He stared beyond the judge, back at his client, Lamb returning Jack's stare as if his attorney's words and skills were a life raft in a hundred-year storm.

"Judge," Jack said, his voice clear, resolute, unwavering. "The defense rests."

CHAPTER SIXTY-FOUR

Pandemonium reigned for one endless minute.

"Clear the court," Judge Stone demanded. Wielding his gavel like an axe, he slammed it down repeatedly. "Jurors, I order you to disregard everything you saw and heard after the defendant left the stand. Everything! None of it is admissible. Counsel, be prepared to conduct a voir dire examination of Ms. St. Cloud immediately. And shut the pool camera."

Why had Summer thrown everything away? Odds were that Judge Stone wouldn't have allowed the Dawes memo into evidence anyway. Jack had rested his case to save Summer's career and to adhere to the Rules of Professional Conduct. But with Judge Stone's decision to conduct an examination of Summer under oath, Jack's decision to rest his case had backfired in every possible way.

Summer sat within the witness enclosure, the courtroom cleared of jurors and spectators, her face flushed, her complexion blotchy.

Jack approached her cautiously and asked his first question, his voice, at once, both an apology and a caress.

"May I have the document?" His fingers brushed against hers as he took it from her hand. "Please describe it to the Court."

"It's a memorandum from Assistant District Attorney Lincoln Dawes to First Assistant District Attorney Brad Sears." Summer's voice was a whisper.

"Have you seen this document before?"

"I have," she answered.

"Can you describe the circumstances by which you obtained this document?"

A pause. "I first saw the document on Mr. Sears's desk." She caught herself, looking toward Brad Sears.

"Please, it's all right," Jack said.

Summer cleared her throat. "You had told me that the prosecution claimed there were no third-party witnesses to the Regan murder. So, I was surprised to see a memo that mentioned the existence of a potential eyewitness. It worried me. That afternoon, I made a copy of the memo when I was copying other documents. Later, after Brad returned to his office, I noticed the original was gone. When I checked the file, it wasn't there either."

"Did you ever ask Mr. Sears about the document?"

"No."

"Why not?"

"I was concerned he might have destroyed it."

Sears stood. "Objection!"

Stone waved him off. "Mr. Sears, this is voir dire. There are no objections. Continue, Mr. Marino."

"What did you do with your copy of the document?" Jack asked.

Summer was silent for a long while. Then she lifted her chin. "I gave it to you."

Jack took an audible breath. "Why did you give the document to me?"

"I thought it was the right thing to do. I knew you suspected there might be a witness to Mr. Regan's murder, yet the time for

disclosure of witnesses had passed. Brad hadn't told you about it."
She caught herself, "And a man's life was at stake."

"Did the document ever leave your possession before you provided it to me?"

"No."

Jack turned to Judge Stone. "Your Honor, I move for a dismissal
of the charges against the defendant—or in the alternative, that you
declare a mistrial based on evidence that the prosecutor's office intentionally withheld exculpatory information, which I believe
would tend to prove the innocence of the defendant."

Judge Stone ignored him. "Mr. Sears, cross-examination?"

Jack knew his opponent would need very few questions.

"May I, Your Honor?" asked Sears.

"Proceed."

Sears walked straight to the witness. Uncomfortably close.

"Ms. St. Cloud, you say you obtained the document in question
in the course of your position as my confidential secretary, is that
correct?"

"I—"

"Yes or no, Ms. St. Cloud?"

"Yes."

"And after you claim to have stolen this document, you gave it to
defense counsel, my opponent?"

"I gave it to him. Yes."

"You have access to blank memorandum forms, like the one this
memo appears to have been typed on, do you not?"

Summer removed a tissue from her black leather pocketbook.
"You know I do."

"Is it fair to say you're familiar with the names of all the people
mentioned in this memorandum?"

"I know them."

"And that would of course include Mr. Marino, with whom—shall I say—you're acquainted, correct?"

"Yes."

"And as my secretary, you can obviously type?"

"Yes."

"Just one last question, Ms. St. Cloud," Sears said. "Isn't it true that you were involved romantically with Mr. Marino when he worked with us here in the District Attorney's office?"

Jack jumped up. "Objection, Your Honor."

Sears continued. "And isn't it equally true that you're sleeping with him now?"

"I've heard enough," snapped Judge Stone.

"Judge, this document is nothing but a copy of something that Ms. St. Cloud could easily have typed up in my absence," Sears said. "Not only is it inadmissible under the best evidence rule, but Ms. St. Cloud may very well be guilty of obstruction of justice and fraud upon this Court."

"Mr. Marino," Judge Stone said, his face purple. "I find this witness inherently unreliable. Given the circumstances, I assume you would prefer that I not comment on her credibility, not to mention her bias and self-interest in connection with you. Accordingly, after voir dire, I hereby exclude her proffered testimony and whatever this unsupported document is as wholly immaterial and irrelevant to this trial."

Sears smiled.

"Your Honor," Jack said, "at least let me bring in Lincoln Dawes? Assistant District Attorney Dawes will no doubt establish that the document is genuine and that he wrote it."

Judge Stone squinted, an odd gleam in his eye. "The fishing expedition is over, Mr. Marino. Another incident like this one, and I will not only hold you in summary contempt, but this Court will refer you to the Board of Professional Responsibility for disciplinary action against you for obstruction of justice."

Jack slammed his fist against the defense table. "I had nothing to do with this witness coming forward. In fact, I rested my case so as not to involve her. At a minimum, the memorandum establishes there is a missing witness, and I again ask for a continuance until Monday to find that witness." Jack tried to steady himself as the judge remained silent. "Fine, if this court chooses to look the other way in the face of clear prosecutorial misconduct, then so be it, but just in case something happens to it—yet again—I want the memorandum marked for identification and made part of the permanent record for appeal—though I'm confident there'll be no need for an appeal."

Judge Stone smiled and said, "Closing arguments begin in five minutes, Mr. Marino."

CHAPTER SIXTY-FIVE

When Jack rose to speak, he did so knowing he was fighting the full weight of the Commonwealth's expectations: District Attorney Trevor Cameron, who expected the first death penalty case in decades to catapult him into the Corner Office beneath the gold-domed State House; a horde of Assistant District Attorneys—Sears included—who had hitched their legal futures to Cameron's rising star; ambitious campaign staffers poised to snatch victory from an incumbent governor. And every one of their dreams teetered, then crashed as Jack's words resounded across the courtroom, the pool camera memorializing it all.

"This wasn't a prosecution of David Lamb. It was a campaign promise."

Looking at each juror in turn, Jack spoke in measured tones.

"The Commonwealth needs a conviction badly. And, sadly, it will do anything to convict David Lamb. Because not to convict him means they've immunized the wrong man, the real killer. In an election year. And they would rather have you convict an innocent man than admit that terrible truth."

Sincere and resolute, Jack scanned the jurors before him. Gone was the tension that had infected his trial performance.

"The DA was being criticized for having too many unsolved murder cases on his watch. Compared to the Governor, the District Attorney looked soft on crime. At least that's what the newspapers were saying. So, what did they do? The high-profile cases were too risky. No sure suspects. Intense media coverage. Plenty of it unflattering. Might as well leave those headaches for the next incoming District Attorney. So, before the DA leaves office, he and his campaign manager, Bradford Sears, decide to go for a sure bet. A case where they know there'll be no dream team for the defense. No jury consultants to advise the defense on what you jurors like and dislike, think or don't think, eat and don't eat." Jack pointed at District Attorney Cameron, seated in the gallery, and then at Sears. "A case where they know that an innocent young man may die because of nothing more than their ambition—and the defendant's nothingness.

"So, what do they do? They meet with Teddy Smith, a prominent defense attorney who promises to give them exactly what they want: a suspect who can easily be convicted."

Outside, anti–death penalty protesters chanted, their words continuing to penetrate the thin glass panes of the courtroom's arched windows. Jack paused to let the jury hear them. "Murder cannot be abolished by murder."

"This prominent defense attorney, with whom Brad Sears had dealt many times before, sat in secret meetings with the District Attorney's office. Meetings that David Lamb, who had no attorney, didn't know about. A deal was struck. In exchange for a grant of absolute immunity, Mickey Nolan—who had refused to help the police up until then—would suddenly claim to know the truth about the death of Thomas Regan and the DA would get a high-profile conviction."

Jack observed Sears shift in his seat, the jury looking solemn and attentive.

"What happened in this case was nothing but a footrace," Jack continued. "A one-hundred-yard dash toward a grant of immunity: whoever could get to the DA first with a willingness to turn on the other would win. Problem was, David Lamb had never heard the word 'immunity' before. And he certainly didn't have a fancy, expensive lawyer to tell him what it means. He's a nobody who now has only me. A perfect fall guy, born and raised in the projects. He knows no one. Unlike Mickey Nolan who knows lots of powerful people. People who had a plan.

"First, Nolan would get David to lie before the grand jury. That would be a layup. David depended upon his job at the dance club to support his children. Nolan knew Lamb would do what they told him to do. Second, once David lied under oath, Nolan would get total immunity. And the Commonwealth had exactly what it wanted: a defendant who'd already lied under oath. A slam-dunk." Jack let out a breath, his argument teetering on the razor's edge of impropriety.

Turning, Jack pointed at Mickey Nolan in the gallery. "Having made a pact with the devil, the Commonwealth's case now rises and falls on the testimony of Mickey Nolan alone. Mr. Sears wants you to convict someone of murder on the testimony of a person who, but for a grant of immunity arranged by a politically connected attorney, would be the chief suspect himself.

"Make no mistake. The Commonwealth's case now depends upon a man who has gotten away with murder. Because he was granted absolute immunity, Mickey Nolan will never be prosecuted for a murder he planned and committed as long as he turns on the only other known suspect—David Lamb, an under-educated, nameless young man from the projects.

"Do you want to know what the dark side of the criminal justice system looks like? Look no further than the use and abuse of a grant of immunity." Jack pointed again to District Attorney Trevor Cameron in the gallery. "That's a part of their system they don't want you to think about, that they don't want you to understand.

"They don't want you to know that testimony from an immunized witness is inherently unreliable, that immunized testimony is outrageously susceptible to abuse. So much so that the Legislature requires any prosecutor relying on immunized testimony to provide independent corroboration that the crime occurred. Evidence that, by itself, establishes the defendant's guilt."

Jack looked at Sears, then back at the jury. "What happened to the corroboration requirement in this trial? Mr. Sears had the nerve to look at each of you and suggest that the Commonwealth has somehow corroborated the immunized testimony on which its entire case is based. That's rubbish. Not a shred of physical evidence connects David Lamb with this crime. Nothing. All they have are the bald, self-serving allegations of Mickey Nolan—a killer—whose testimony, I would suggest, has been bought and paid for."

Jack drifted in the direction of the defense table, where David Lamb sat, his head bent down, hanging on his every word. "The Commonwealth has told you that you can't believe anything that David Lamb tells you. That instead, you should believe its immunized witness, Mickey Nolan."

Jack nodded at the defendant. "David Lamb isn't proud of his testimony before the grand jury. It was false. No question about that. But consider this before you decide who to believe now."

He extended his arm, pointing again to Mickey Nolan, who sat in the gallery near Lisa Regan, the victim's wife. As he did so, Jack inched closer to the jury box, eyeing the jurors with earnestness.

"It was Mickey Nolan who told the central lie in this case. Nolan didn't say a word on direct examination about the meeting he had with Tommy Regan on the night of his murder, about Tommy's attempt to extort him. The Commonwealth hid that from you. But David Lamb told you about it.

"There was something else the Commonwealth didn't count on. And that was the lawsuit against The Treasure Chest." Jack brought a hand to his heart. "I showed it to you. You didn't hear about it from the Commonwealth, and I'll tell you why. Because that meeting and the lawsuit reveal the only motive for murder that exists in this case: the preservation of the status quo—whatever that is—at the exotic dance club known as The Treasure Chest. Yet, incredibly, the Commonwealth wants you to believe that even though Tommy had filed a lawsuit against the club—and threatened to expose whatever nefarious activity goes on at The Treasure Chest—his death immediately thereafter is a coincidence?"

Jack carefully surveyed the jury.

"It was no coincidence. Tommy Regan is dead because the meeting between him and Nolan was about the ten thousand dollars that Tommy demanded from the club in exchange for withdrawing his lawsuit. Problem was that the owner of the club wasn't going to give it to him. That was bad enough, but what happened next cost Tommy Regan his life. In a fit of rage, Regan told Nolan that even if the club gave him the money, he was going ahead with the lawsuit anyway. And in the process of that lawsuit—the depositions, the interrogatories, and all the rest—whatever illegal activity is going on at The Treasure Chest would come to light. Do you think the strip club wanted that? And that, members of the jury, left only one option.

"And it was the ruthless exercise of that last option that brings us here today."

Jack turned to look over his shoulder. Mrs. Regan was weeping.

Jack bore down. "You've seen a lot of things in this trial: objections, rulings that went against my client, my being reprimanded repeatedly by this Court. But no ruling by any Court can take away your common sense. In deciding the defendant's fate, you are the sole judges of the facts in this case. And in deciding what those facts are, thankfully you can use your own God-given common sense."

Counting on the fingers of his outstretched hand, Jack ticked off point after point.

"One, does it make sense to you that David could have placed a handgun in the elastic band of his sweatpants, as Nolan claimed he did? Wouldn't a gun made with heavy steel have fallen out of his running pants as he was supposedly lifting a man who weighed more than two hundred fifty pounds into the rear of a station wagon?

"Two, while we're talking about this gun, which we've never seen, did it strike you as galling that Mickey Nolan, the man who has the most to gain from David Lamb's conviction, claimed he just happened to see my client with a gun shortly before the murder? A tad convenient given that the prosecution never found the murder weapon in this case. But they want the next best thing: they want you to think that if Lamb had a gun in the past—and there's no credible evidence he did despite the judge's ruling—he must have had one on the night of the murder.

"Three, does it make any sense to consider David Lamb's fingerprints as evidence of guilt if David admits to having used Tommy's car every week?

"Four, how much sense does the Commonwealth's case make when Nolan himself places David to the left rear of the victim, yet the ballistics expert testified that the bullet traveled through the skull from the opposite direction, right to left?

"Five, does it make any sense that David Lamb, who weighs about one hundred sixty pounds and had had left shoulder surgery shortly before this tragedy, could drag a man who weighed more than two hundred fifty pounds using his injured left arm while he held a gun in his right hand?

"Does any of that make sense?"

Jack looked over at his opponent who stroked his forehead with a handkerchief.

"Sometimes in life, it's the little things that count, that illuminate the truth," Jack said. "Ladies and gentlemen, do you remember your visit to the scene of the crime? At one point, I asked you to look closely at the bushes in the area where the body was found. Do you remember that?"

Jack paused and looked down at his own extended hands. "To be sure, nothing much changes in the projects. I can tell you that. And when you're a kid and the railroad tracks are your only playground, you can cut yourself badly in those bushes." Gathering himself, he looked at each juror. "As you saw for yourself, all of the bushes down there are spiked with countless thorns. It's always been that way. Long, sharp thorns growing wild everywhere on both sides of the tracks.

"Now think about this. David and Nolan are dragging the body of Tommy Regan on his stomach, as Mickey Nolan would have you believe, in and out of those same thorn bushes. And they're doing all this with Tommy's shirt rolled up and his stomach and abdomen and face fully exposed. If that were true, wouldn't you expect to see bloody thorns embedded in Tommy's skin? At a minimum, don't you think there'd be scratches on Tommy's body? Yet, the autopsy report and photographs, as gruesome as they are, makes clear that there isn't a single scratch on his torso." Jack raised his voice. "That—members of the jury—is reasonable doubt.

"There's yet another problem the Commonwealth doesn't want you to think about. Motive. True, the Commonwealth doesn't have to prove motive. But, again, use your common sense. Can any one of you imagine waking up one morning and deciding to kill a good friend for the hell of it? The only motive in this case was Nolan's desire—or the desire of those he's associated with—to eliminate a threat that wouldn't go away. And that threat was Tommy Regan."

Jack had hit cruise control. "Two crimes were committed in this case," he said, his eyes blazing. "The first was the murder of Tommy Regan. That was horrific beyond words. But the second crime is still in progress."

He slapped his fist against the podium. "Right now, right here in this courtroom, the Commonwealth is knowingly trying to convict—and then sentence to death—an innocent man for a murder he didn't commit based on nothing more than Mickey Nolan's word. And that second crime, should you permit it to occur, would be as tragic as the first."

Jack drew himself up to his full height. "I believe in the innocence of David Lamb. Twenty-six. Father of two beautiful young girls. His only guilt is being born and raised in the wrong place and suffering the injustice that too often goes with it."

The room fell silent. Jack searched the eyes of the jurors. They searched his in return, one juror dabbing her eyes with a tissue.

"The prosecution will ask you to decide whose story you believe more, but that's not actually what you have to decide. Only one man is on trial for his life. The issue is not whether you believe my client—though I suggest you should. The only thing you must ask yourself is—are you certain beyond a reasonable doubt that David Lamb should be convicted and possibly executed on nothing but Mickey Nolan's uncorroborated word? Members of the jury, either justice or injustice awaits David Lamb. The choice is yours," Jack added, without losing eye contact. "Please choose justice."

CHAPTER SIXTY-SIX

"David Lamb is a liar," said Sears to the jury. "A damnable liar."

The courtroom was packed to overflow for the prosecution's closing argument. Nonstop media coverage of the Commonwealth's first death penalty case in decades had reached a crescendo. The trial was no longer a prelude to the election; it was the election. In addition to the usual assemblage of reporters, the gallery was teeming with a who's who of Boston's legal community. Everyone who was anyone had scrambled for a seat on this last day of the trial.

As he scanned the courtroom, Jack saw a congregation of ghosts from his past: former colleagues, former friends, his former boss, the DA himself, the police commissioner, and one other he never expected to see: his wife, Abby Thorn. She looked stunning. Jack caught her eye just as he turned to focus on Brad Sears.

Standing before the jurors, Sears nodded as if he understood their dilemma. "Ladies and gentlemen, this is a very simple case. The only question before you is who's telling the truth."

Jack tensed. The Commonwealth's closing would be predictable and powerful. Sears would ignore the deficiencies in his own case and try instead to convince the jury that the defendant's entire case rested on one irrefutable fact: David Lamb was an admitted liar. If

the jury believed this, nothing Jack might say or do could rehabili-
tate his client in the eyes of the jurors.

"In recent days, you've heard two versions of the facts that are so
wildly different they cannot possibly be reconciled. You must believe one or the other."

Sears took a breath. "Mickey Nolan, an eyewitness, told you with
frightening accuracy exactly how the defendant shot Tommy Regan
in cold blood. He provided you with details so specific that they are
self-authenticating. He told you when, where, and how. And—make
no mistake—Dr. Neil Backman's testimony provided the necessary
corroboration for this testimony.

"From the defendant," Sears continued, "you heard a tale about
barroom fights, threats of lawsuits, and dangerous midnight liaisons
where bribery turned murderous. And the defendant tried to sell
you even more: a crazy story about drug trafficking so ridiculous
that even I can't make sense of it all. This melodrama stems from one
source: a man who will not hesitate to lie under oath. Does the defendant offer a scintilla of evidence from any independent source to
support these fantastic claims? He does not. He cannot. Because the
evidence doesn't exist. It's all fantasy.

"The evidence from which you must decide this case," Sears told
them, "is the testimony you heard from the lips of the witnesses who
appeared before you. Nothing else. Not rumors. Not wishful thinking. Not imaginary witnesses."

Jack stirred at the not-so-subtle reference to Nora, a subject he'd
been prohibited from mentioning in his closing argument.

Sears spread his hands. "The defendant would have us believe that
he doesn't know anything about guns. Does that sound consistent
with the fact that the defendant was seen with a handgun only a
week before Tom Regan's murder? A gun of the same type we know
was used to kill Tommy Regan in this case."

Jack studied the jurors carefully. Each returned Sears's gaze without commitment. So far, no one had shot an accusing look at Lamb, a sign, perhaps, that these men and women weren't buying what Sears was selling—yet.

Sears continued to beat the prosecution's war drum. "Mr. Marino would have you believe that you shouldn't convict his client just because Mr. Nolan was granted immunity, or maybe because Mickey Nolan didn't go to the police as he should have. But Mr. Nolan had been threatened. He's not proud of his silence, his initial failure to cooperate, but he did what he had to do to protect himself."

Sears took a breath. "What Mr. Marino won't tell you is that immunity is commonly granted in appropriate cases, like this one, where the interests of justice demand it. Without the incentive of immunity, countless crimes would go unpunished. Without immunity, witnesses would remain intimidated, frightened, unwilling to come forward." Sears paused for emphasis. "Just as Mr. Nolan once was."

Sears, his face deadly earnest, looked at each of the jurors. "One thing is clear here. It wasn't a grant of immunity that killed Tommy Regan. It was David Lamb."

Sears pressed on. "David Lamb is the only man whom we know was upset at management and the only man who was seen shortly before the murder wielding a handgun.

"And now he wants us to believe he was friends with Tommy Regan." Sears threw up his hands in mock disbelief. "'Why would I kill my friend?' the defendant asks incredulously. But Tommy Regan's wife didn't think they were such good friends."

Jack straightened as several jurors turned to engage him in eye contact. Another attorney might have looked away. Instead, he returned their gaze openly.

Sears shifted gears. "Mr. Marino would have you believe that you cannot convict without a complete understanding of motive. But it's not your responsibility to delve into a mind so twisted that even a trained forensic psychologist couldn't understand it. We don't know why people commit terrible crimes. If we did, we could prevent crime. But we can't because we'll never fathom all the reasons people kill and maim and rape.

"What we do know," Sears continued, "is that on the night of Tommy Regan's murder, David Lamb was, by his own admission, high on cocaine. And based on the Commonwealth's credible evidence, you can conclude that he tried to sell cocaine to Mr. Regan, who refused. And you can further find that when Tom Regan threatened to let the club know that Lamb was selling drugs, Lamb turned on him.

"If Mr. Marino wants to talk about motive, I would ask, what motive does the defendant have to lie at this trial? The defendant has a very good motive. He already lied previously under far less onerous circumstances: when he wasn't a suspect, when he faced no punishment. Now, he's accused of a crime. A monstrous crime. And the punishment is severe."

Sears asked harshly, "What do you think he would do now?"

Jack cursed. No one better understood the power of a lie than Brad Sears. One of his consummate skills was that he himself could wrap, twist, and bend the truth, and at the same time hang a defendant on the string-size strength of one small lie.

Sears moved closer to the jury box, his voice dripping with contempt. "What happened that night is clear. I would suggest that on that terrible night, the defendant was out of control. He was out of work, that is to say real work, honest work. He was not only high on drugs, but he was selling them. He had a gun, and he knew how to use it. Tom Regan threatened to tell the management of The Treasure Chest that the defendant was selling cocaine on the premises. And the defendant had no way out. Except one."

Sears's air of patrician equanimity was gone now, stripped away by Summer's revelations only an hour earlier. The First Assistant District Attorney was laying it all out on the line, as if his own life, not Lamb's, depended on it. This would be Sears's last closing argument in County Court. The outcome of the trial wouldn't change that. Nor would the outcome of the election. After this case, District Attorney Trevor Cameron would cede his position to a newly elected District Attorney, whose first task would be to select his own First Assistant.

"Ask yourselves this," said Sears, his alligator eyes guileless. "Why should we now believe that suddenly the defendant is going to tell the truth when he lied under oath to the grand jury—made up of jurors like yourselves, who were simply trying to get at the truth?"

Jack tensed even more. Beside him, Lamb seemed to hold his breath, eyes darting as he absorbed all that was being hurled at him.

"He tried to fool the grand jurors in this case, and once again, he's trying to fool you. He wants you to believe he only lied that one time, to protect his family. Really?"

Jack swallowed hard. Perspiring heavily, Lamb was slumped in his seat. Jack leaned over and whispered, "Just breathe. The prosecution's closing is always the worst."

Jack looked up in time to see Sears stand at attention, his back as straight as a soldier's, his bearing resolute, his job finally done.

Sears then swung into the winning refrain he had used in front of hundreds of jurors during his long and celebrated career. "Ladies and gentlemen, the word 'verdict' comes from the Latin *veritas*, which means the truth. I ask you to speak the truth, and find the defendant, David Lamb, guilty of murder in the first degree."

CHAPTER SIXTY-SEVEN

The lock shot home on the courtroom door. Nothing would interrupt the hour it took for Judge Stone to deliver his instructions to the jury—part speech, part homily—on the law they were to apply in the case of Commonwealth vs. David Lamb.

As the jurors filed out to begin deliberations, Jack looked up at the clock at the rear of the courtroom. It was just after three o'clock. He surveyed the courtroom, which was again opened to the public. A deeply satisfying feeling of relief washed over him. For the first time since his beating, and later his firing, Jack could feel the deadweight of fear lifting. He felt like the lawyer he'd once been: confident, bold, in control. Leaning over, he spoke quietly to David. "All we need to do is establish reasonable doubt," Jack said.

David Lamb sat crumpled in his chair, exhaustion written on his face. As if he could hardly believe that his nightmare might actually be over soon, David whispered, "Thank you."

Two court officers approached to offer Jack their congratulations. "Like the old days," one of them said, shaking his hand.

Smiling, Jack hid his pride. Some of the ADAs in the gallery nodded, as if he were still their golden boy.

"We need to take him now," the other court officer said, gesturing to David.

Jack nodded as David was handcuffed and led to his holding cell.

As the jury deliberated, Jack spent time with Lamb's mother. They talked about the case, analyzing and reanalyzing the evidence; about how worried she was about her son; about how weak the Commonwealth's case had been.

"What happens now?" Ann Lamb asked, her eyes stenciled by dark circles, her bent frame wracked with fatigue.

"We wait." Jack checked his watch. "They've only had—what? —less than two hours, and it's late in the day." He touched her shoulder gently. "I'm sure they've just begun wading through all the exhibits, reports, demonstrative aids, everything. On Monday, they'll have a full day of deliberations."

Ann Lamb extended her hand. "Thank you," she said.

Another court officer approached the two of them and motioned for Jack.

Jack nodded.

"There's a guy on the pay phone downstairs, says his name is Matt. Says it's urgent. Something about Nora."

Judge Stone's words came hurtling back. *Find her and I'll hold a hearing.* Clearly, there wasn't a second to waste.

"Mrs. Lamb, excuse me," said Jack.

Jack rushed out of the courtroom. Downstairs, the lobby was crowded, filled with the sights and sounds of the pursuit of justice. Next to a concession stand operated by the Massachusetts Commission for the Blind, a telephone receiver dangled from the cord of a pay phone.

Jack grabbed the receiver. "Matt."

"Meet me at the projects."

"Lamb's?"

"No." Matt hesitated. "Ours."

"Ours?"

"Nora's there. The police are looking for her too. They've blanketed the streets. Threatening everyone. Making clear no one's safe until they find her."

"My God, Matt," Jack said, shooting another look at his watch. It was already a bit past 5:00 p.m. "In a few minutes, Stone will dismiss the jury until Monday. I'll clear the building a minute or two after that." He drew an erratic breath. "That gives us the weekend to find her."

CHAPTER SIXTY-EIGHT

A helter-skelter of nervous chatter greeted Jack as he reentered the courtroom. The gallery had filled again. Jack wondered why as the courtroom doors shut behind him.

He saw Judge McCormack in a seat at the back. He caught her eye, and if he wasn't mistaken, she was beaming. He felt grateful she'd pushed him to get back into criminal law rather than hiding in corporate. He hoped her faith in him was warranted, that he'd been the right attorney for this case.

He moved in her direction but was interrupted by Ann Lamb who hurried toward him, her eyes fearful. "They're back."

"Who's back?" Jack asked.

"The jury," she said. "They've reached a verdict."

Astonished, Jack stared at her. "That's impossible," he said. "They've been out for less than two hours."

Jack tried to calm himself. Early verdicts almost always favored the defense. He'd learned to fear them as a prosecutor. Could he allow himself some hope?

Jack entered the bar enclosure and made a beeline to counsel table. A probation officer came into the courtroom and took a seat at the probation table. A gauntlet of court officers ringed the courtroom.

Court officers escorted a disheveled David Lamb to the defense table, his face dark with confusion. Jack hadn't prepared him for an early verdict, let alone a nearly instantaneous one.

Jack's instinct to ease his client's fears overcame his reluctance to speculate. He placed his arm on Lamb's shoulder. "Early verdicts are almost always a good sign, David."

Lamb never looked up.

"All rise," the court officer cried.

The door to the jury room opened.

The jurors marched in with military efficiency, filing back into their assigned seats. Jack studied them with hope—and fear.

Judge Stone entered and took his seat, his robe billowing up behind him.

"Be seated," said a court officer.

No one moved. No one spoke.

Surrounded by lawyers, court officers, and expectant spectators, Jack could not conceive of a lonelier place. One of the alternate jurors, who hadn't participated in the jury's deliberation, looked at Lamb. All the deliberating jurors stared straight ahead, their faces betraying nothing.

"Mr. Foreman, has your jury agreed upon its verdict?" Judge Stone asked.

"Yes. We have, Your Honor," said the foreperson.

The jury foreman leaned over and passed the verdict slip to a court officer who in turn handed it to the court clerk. Without looking at it, the clerk passed the verdict slip to Judge Stone.

Unblinking, Judge Stone stared at the verdict. At length, he handed it back to the clerk, who addressed the jury.

"What say you, Mr. Foreman? Is the defendant guilty or not guilty, of murder in the first degree?"

Jack couldn't breathe. Lamb sat motionless beside him—somewhere between heaven and hell.

"Guilty," said the foreman.

The courtroom erupted. Lamb collapsed in his seat. In the gallery, Assistant District Attorneys high-fived one another. The victim witness advocates hugged Lisa Regan. The District Attorney beamed as the police commissioner shook his hand.

Judge Stone tried vainly to gavel the courtroom into order.

Nausea overwhelmed Jack. How could they throw away someone's life in barely two hours? Less, if you subtracted out the time for coffee and small talk. He stared at each member of the jury. Not one would look back.

Jack ached to scream at each juror. It was impossible to review the testimony—and all the trial exhibits—in little more than two hours. As far as Jack was concerned, the jury, like the judge, had abdicated their responsibility. They had a constitutional obligation to consider all the evidence before arriving at a just verdict, and they didn't do it.

Judge Stone asked the jury, "Do you find beyond a reasonable doubt that the defendant did kill one Thomas Regan? So say you, Mr. Foreman?"

"Yes."

"So say you, all members of the jury?"

"Yes," the jurors replied as a chorus.

Jack realized Sears was standing. Jack tried to speak, but the words wouldn't come out.

Judge Stone continued, "Having found the defendant guilty of murder in the first degree, has the jury reached a unanimous verdict on the sentence?"

The jury foreman spoke directly to Judge Stone. "Your Honor, after a careful consideration of the sentencing factors as per your instructions, we could not come to a unanimous verdict on the punishment to be imposed."

Sears stood. "The Commonwealth accordingly moves that the defendant be sentenced by the Court."

"Your Honor, I move for a mistrial on the sentencing phase," Jack managed, his feet unsteady, his eyes stinging.

Judge Stone waved Jack off. "Mr. Marino, the Legislature changed all that. Judicial override. Read the statute."

The juror who had dabbed her eyes during Jack's closing began to sob.

"Mr. Lamb, please rise," said Judge Stone, looking directly at the defendant for the first time during the trial.

David Lamb sat as if nailed to his seat, crying helplessly. Jack helped him to his feet.

"You will hearken to the sentence the Court has rendered against you," Stone said.

"Your Honor," Jack interrupted. "The statute will never pass constitutional muster."

Judge Stone continued as if he hadn't heard him. "In light of the deadlock, the Court having duly considered your offense, as well as relevant aggravating and mitigating factors, it is ordered, by this Court—"

"Please, Your Honor," said Jack. "I'm begging you. At least stay the sentence while I attempt to locate the missing witness."

Judge Stone held up his hand. "—that you be put to death by Order of this Court in accordance with the law of the Commonwealth.

"Mr. Court Officer, kindly place the defendant into custody for transfer to the Commonwealth's maximum-security prison to await execution of his sentence."

Several court officers descended on Lamb, who stood, still weeping. One bent down to fasten heavy black iron leg shackles around his ankles, tightening them until he yelped.

Lamb turned toward the jury, Jack, and then to his mother. "Please . . . please."

"David," Jack stuttered. "The state supreme court will reverse this. I know it." Whatever Jack was saying didn't matter. Lamb didn't have a clue what "reversible error" meant, anyway.

Two deputy court officers stepped forward, ready to escort Lamb to the holding cell and then later to death row.

Red-faced and out of breath, the court officer who had fastened the leg irons on Lamb turned to Jack, regret flashing across his face. "Jack, it's late. The transportation people are tired. They either get on the road now, or they'll be sitting in traffic for hours."

At that, Ann Lamb broke down. She extended her hands toward her shackled son. "Please, let me see my son."

"Can you stall them?" Jack asked the court officer.

The court officer wiped his brow with the cuff of his shirt. "Jack. You know the rules. Property of the state now."

Jack placed his hand on the court officer's wrist. "It won't take long."

A few moments later, accompanied by Ann Lamb, Jack followed the court officer down the narrow corridor behind the courtroom. Turning left, they found David kneeling in the holding cell in front of the toilet, retching.

Ann Lamb covered her mouth.

Jack turned to the court officer. "Can she be with him?"

"Jesus, Jack, my job." The court officer hesitated. Then a bark to his subordinates. "Goddamn it. Open the door and lock her in. Just a few minutes. The mother only."

A decade and more of practicing criminal law hadn't prepared Jack for what he saw as he turned to leave mother and son alone.

In the 4' by 4' holding cell, David Lamb knelt on the floor, elbows on knees, tears streaming off the tip of his nose, dripping into the stainless-steel toilet below his head. His mother bent over him, hugging him, cradling him in her arms, rocking her son.

*   *   *

Preparing to leave for the last time, Summer surveyed the DA's office, where a makeshift post-trial party was underway. Summer barely recognized her own office. People she'd worked with for years snubbed her, leaving her standing against a wall, an observer among strangers.

Moments earlier, she'd emerged from the District Attorney's office following a hastily convened exit interview. There, Cameron and Sears had discharged her and sent a state trooper from the CPAC unit to clean out her desk. The District Attorney was almost giddy as he announced his intentions.

"After the election," Cameron had said, "charges will be filed against you. And if I were you, I'd retain a real lawyer. Someone who understands the law. Unlike your boyfriend."

In the main area of the DA's office, cases of beer were stacked against a moveable partition that formed a spare conference room. Individual beer bottles lay in a cooler of ice, Assistant DAs and staff crowding around to scoop up cold brews.

The public relations officer, doubling as campaign press agent, appeared. Quieting the chatter with a whistle, he raised his glass to propose a toast.

"To Trevor Cameron, in honor of his distinguished career as County District Attorney and in recognition of his dedication and selfless service to the citizens of our county."

Whoops of jubilance all around.

"If there were a Hall of Fame for District Attorneys, Trevor should be in it. But before that, we have one more place for him to go. The Governor's office." A crescendo of applause threatened to drown him out.

"Wait a minute. Please," he said as the applause died down. "And to Brad Sears. The single best First Assistant District Attorney in the Commonwealth. For your leadership and uncompromising legal and ethical standards, we salute you as the state's winningest prosecutor who proved today, once again, that lesser mortals are no match for him. Brad, we all wish you the very best—we trust—in assuming your new duties in the Governor's office."

Another ovation rolled through the crowd.

"Hey," someone yelled, punctuating the cheers. "Listen to this." Summer watched as a young A.D.A. hefted a portable television set atop a vertical filing cabinet

The room grew hushed as all eyes focused on the TV.

"In breaking news," a television anchor began, "a new poll shows District Attorney Trevor Cameron pulling away from the incumbent governor. This just after his office made news by achieving the state's first death penalty conviction in decades. As the countdown to election day enters the final seventy-two hours, the challenger is surging ahead as undecided voters begin to choose between candidates. The District Attorney has run on a get-tough, law-and-order campaign platform many believed could not be successful against the incumbent. Be sure to stay with us, as we continue to bring you up-to-the-minute election coverage."

As Summer turned to leave, applause reverberated throughout the DA's office. The jubilation in her now-former office gave way to chaos as she stepped into the throng outside. Word of the guilty verdict had whipped the mob into a frenzy. Across from the pro–death penalty folks, the death penalty foes had grown in number and were shouting in anger. The Boston Police, who had beefed up their ranks, struggled to keep the two factions apart.

Summer scanned the crowd and finally saw the one person she needed to be with, as he, too, left the courthouse alone.

PART V

HOME

CHAPTER SIXTY-NINE

In time, all roads lead to home.

As Jack sped north alone, a darkening sky closed in. He barely remembered leaving the courthouse, though he could still feel Summer's heart beating against his chest as they met and embraced for one long moment before separating. Whether it was her humiliating termination or the chill sweeping off the harbor, Summer had shivered as he held her, fixing her focus beyond him on the horizon.

"What do you see?" he had asked her. She paused, stuck somewhere between the present and the future. "A storm's coming," she answered, tears filling her eyes.

The iron struts of the Tobin Bridge dropped behind him in a blur of steel. Turning the wheel, he drove into Mystic, past a brightly lit billboard featuring a giant image of a smiling District Attorney Trevor Cameron. Under Cameron's picture, the billboard proclaimed, *Strong on Law and Order. The People's Candidate for Governor.* The election was only days away.

Jack pressed the accelerator, as the last vestige of daylight slipped below the horizon.

His childhood home loomed ahead, as haunting and dark as the memories tied to it: an unfinished childhood. A father's premature death. A mother's toil. A brother's abrupt departure.

Jack pulled his car in by the hole in the fence. Matt's car was already wedged behind the thorn bushes he'd hoped would figure so prominently at the trial.

Once out of the car, he looked around. Above him, the sky was a mass of dark violet, the temperature dropping, the storm gathering. He took off his tie and tossed it in the back seat of his car. Scrambling up and over the fence, Jack landed on both feet with a thud, his injured knee throbbing with pain. The deserted buildings of Mystic's first public housing projects loomed before him, silent and crumbling. Not even the homeless gathered here.

The only sound Jack could hear was the shrill whistle of wind from the Mystic Creek and beyond it the Mystic River. Was this the dark wind that eventually came to every man?

Jack hurried around crude barricades that gangbangers once used to block police vehicles. Matt would be at their old home, waiting for him. Sure enough, drawing closer, he eyed a solitary figure standing near his building.

Approaching Matt, Jack nodded, a silent apology for being late.

"Heard it on the car radio," Matt said.

"It took the jury not more than two hours to convict him," Jack said.

The brothers stood together, the wind, like a knife blade, nipping at each of them.

"I scoped the place out," Matt said. "Two buildings up from here, a piece of plywood has been pulled away from a window at street level. The opening's big enough for someone to crawl through."

They plunged deeper into the dilapidated projects. When they reached the opening, the old, discolored plywood surrendered easily, falling to the ground. Carefully, the two brothers climbed in through the open window, entering a world of shadows neither had visited in decades.

The interior stank of wine and fetid air. Narrow columns of dusty moonlight streamed around the edges of the battered plywood covering the windows, revealing years of neglect: open floorboards, exposed plumbing, dead insects, rodent droppings. Like every unit in the projects, this one was identical to all the others. Social engineering run amok. The first floor would consist of a kitchen, hallway, and living room. Upstairs were bedrooms and a bathroom.

Could Nora actually be here? And if so, did she actually witness the murder? Swatches of plaster walls had peeled away, old wooden lathes and patches of mold exposed. Having grown up in an identical unit, Jack understood that this place had once been a home to someone's family, that these scarred walls had formed the borders of someone's childhood. He shook his head. The city should have bulldozed this place into the ground years ago.

As they picked their way from the kitchen to the living room, an unnerving blackness gnawed at Jack. Whether it was the gloom that surrounded him or the shock of Lamb's conviction, his limbs felt heavy, as if he were walking in water. But he pushed on.

In the living room, shallow pools of rainwater dotted the floor. If Nora were here, she'd be upstairs. Jack looked up at the ceiling. Scratchy, scampering noises overhead suggested that the second floor was still home to something.

As they reached the landing at the top of the stairs to the second floor, the brothers paused.

"Did you hear something?" Matt asked quietly.

Jack stopped, straining to hear. He thought he heard a weak moan, coming from a back bedroom.

When they reached the first bedroom, they found the door closed. Matt pushed it open, the door squealing on rusted hinges, a gush of foul air slapping Jack in the face. He blinked, his eyes straining to adjust to the darkness, his heart beating like a jackhammer.

In the dark of the far corner, curled into a fetal position, lay Nora. At long last.

A long black overcoat hid her diminutive body, her gray hair, a matted tangle of knots, splayed around a gaunt face. She was stone-still, her hands curled around a dark, jade-green bottle.

Gingerly, Jack knelt on one knee beside her. Bending closer to whisper her name, he recoiled at the acrid smell of urine. Matt crouched next to his brother, seemingly unfazed by the odor.

Jack shook her gently, but she didn't rouse. He prayed he wasn't too late. Memories of the day he'd found his father flashed before him. He shook her again.

"Nora!"

A low, scratchy wheeze.

"She's alive," said Jack, letting out a breath. He lifted her head slightly and brushed the hair out of her face.

Nora weakly pushed her hands up as if to protect herself.

"It's okay," Jack said. "We're here to help you."

"Please," Nora pleaded, her breath labored and irregular.

Leaning closer, Jack gently placed an arm around her shoulder, cradling her head off the wooden floor. "Nora, we're here because of the murder."

She nodded. "Night . . . that night."

"What do you remember, Nora? What happened out there when the young man was killed?" Jack asked.

She seemed to drop off, then mumbled, "Bad, real bad."

"Do you remember a thin man with oily black hair? He had a gun, didn't he?"

She nodded.

"And a blond man. Younger?"

"Young," she said anxiously. "Pushed his face in the dirt. Held the gun . . . to head."

"What about the other? A big man, maybe up near three hundred pounds."

"Yes."

"Did someone shoot him?"

She moaned, flicking a look at Jack. "'When they came."

"Who?" Jack said, an alarm going off in his mind. "Who came, Nora?"

Nora was struggling, one hand clutching the bottle, the other pressed to her stomach. "Police."

The words hit dead silence.

"The police were out there that night?" Jack asked.

"Yeah. Cops there."

"Maybe she's confused," said Matt. "Maybe she means the cops who responded to the discovery of the body the next morning."

"Nora, when were the police there?" Jack asked. "The next morning?"

"No." Nora shook her head. "Night."

"How do you know they were police, Nora?"

"Blue. One in uniform."

"Did the police try to help, Nora?"

"No." Nora began to cry. "Police say everythin' be all right. Could hear 'em."

"Then what happened?"

A moan—"They shot him."

Jack felt a wave of apprehension. "Who? Who shot him?"

"Thin man. Black hair."

Jack and Matt exchanged baffled looks. How could Mickey have shot anyone with the police there?

"Nora, did the police take the gun away from him?"

Nora looked up at both brothers. "No." Her breath was coming in short gasps. "Police—told him to shoot."

Nora's words hung in midair, then dropped, like an axe, into the pit of Jack's stomach. He turned to Matt, who stared back, his face betraying shock and bewilderment.

"Oh my God," Jack stammered. "The police were in on this kill."

"Do you think Cameron and Sears are part of this?" Matt said.

"They're up to their necks in it. But not like this. No. Their sin isn't murder; it's blind ambition."

Jack shook Nora again, gently. "Where was the blond man when they shot the big man?"

Nora's breathing slowed. "Still kneelin'. Sorry. Nothin' could do."

"How did they know you were there, Nora?"

"Tried cover my mouth. Threw up."

"They came after you, didn't they?"

"Mmm." Nora's breathing was almost imperceptible now. "Crawled. Crawled into creek and stayed quiet."

The creek. Jack thought back to the Mystic Creek, the sewage-filled stream of sludge that ran the length of the railroad tracks for miles. As kids, Jack and his friends used to throw sticks and trash into the creek, betting on how long the stuff would take to sink. Some of it never did. It was like black quicksand. He couldn't believe she'd crawled into that cesspool.

"Couldn't find me."

"Nora, do you remember what the police officers looked like?"

Her strength failing, Nora described the Mystic Commissioner with uncanny accuracy, leaving no doubt.

"The police are still looking for you, aren't they?" Jack asked.

"No . . . Not angry. No more."

Jack felt a jolt of apprehension. "Have they been here?"

"Friends now." Nora's voice grew fainter, as she drew her knees up toward her stomach and clutched her bottle tighter. "More tonight, they said."

"Nora, we need to take you from here," Jack said, his voice shaking. "We'll get medical attention."

Nora looked up at Jack. "No. Please."

Jack reached for her hand. "Let me help you. We're going to take you to a hospital. You'll be safe."

She didn't reply, a single tear spilling down her face.

Jack shook her, without response. "Nora?"

Silence.

Jack lifted her into an upright position.

"Shit," Matt said. "What the hell is this?" Several bags of heroin packaged in tied-off plastic baggies fell onto the floor. Matt scooped up at least six or seven bags of the brown powder. "There's enough here to kill someone. Look at this," Matt said, pointing to the floor. Not inches away, Matt grabbed a used syringe.

Jack recoiled, examined her arms. "Look, there's no track marks. She may be an alcoholic but she's not a heroin user. She doesn't have a penny to her name. She couldn't buy a single bag, much less all of this."

Matt pressed his finger to her neck. "Fuck. I can't find a pulse. Help me." In the shadowy grime, Matt began feverishly administering CPR, precious seconds stretching into minutes.

Finally, he stopped, his skin hot and slick with sweat. Dragging his shirt cuff across his forehead, he slumped against the wall. "She's gone. Bastards gave her a hotshot. Tried to make it look like an overdose. Or suicide. By any name, it's murder by heroin."

Jack cradled Nora's body, his nervous system pulsing with adrenaline. Why is justice denied to those who need it the most? In the stillness and filth of that room, he whispered a prayer for Nora's soul. As the words tumbled from his mouth, he had to believe that she was going to a better place than the one she'd left behind.

They sat in silence.

"No one will believe this," Matt said.

"They might," Jack said. Drawing a breath, he held out his micro-cassette recorder. "It's all here, Matt. Everything she said. Should be admissible in evidence under the dying declaration exception to the hearsay rule."

"No more rules, Jack."

"What do you mean?"

"Jack, these guys are coming for us. We're the only thing in their way."

Jack was silent, the realization nearly paralyzing him: he and Matt were marked for death just as Tommy Regan once was.

"Jack," Matt said, "you've played by the rules your whole life. And I get it. In your world, there's a lot of rights and wrongs. But you know what? Sometimes the only way to get justice is to break the rules. And make your own."

Jack nodded. Matt was right. Jack had spent his whole life following the rules. As if his pursuit of perfection and falling in line were an antidote to the poverty and scarcity of his youth. Sure, he'd gotten to the front of the line. He'd been named the chief of the DA's gang prosecution unit. He'd been somebody. But that somebody no longer existed. What brought Jack this far had served him well. But not anymore. There were no rules in the area surrounding the Mystic Creek. No laws, statutes, regulations, or fancy titles could protect him here. So, Jack decided to do something he'd never done before. He'd toss the rules and make his own.

"No more rules," Jack said to his brother. "But we gotta go now. C'mon, help me move her. I've got an idea."

Carefully, the brothers carried Nora into the next bedroom and placed her into a closet, her coat draped over her.

Jack held up the cassette recorder. "If I can convince the Mystic Police that Nora's alive and can testify against them, they'll panic, and the first thing they'll do is start moving product out of The Treasure Chest. Then, they'll come for her."

"I can get to TC's in fifteen minutes," Matt said. "If I see what I think I'm gonna see, I'll call it into the State Police. As soon as the state troopers see the magnitude of the operation, I'll tell them about Nora. They'll have no choice but to send a cruiser. Or more. I'll circle back and meet you here with backup within the hour."

"I'll light a fire at the Mystic PD but tell the State Police no sirens. That way, we'll both be here with the State Police when the police commissioner arrives."

Amid the gloom of the apartment and their worsening circumstances, Jack could still make out the smile on his brother's face.

"What?" Jack asked.

"Semper Fi," Matt said. "We stick together this time."

CHAPTER SEVENTY

Jack cursed as he punched the accelerator, fingers wrapped tightly around the steering wheel. Everything began to fall into place. Tommy Regan had threatened more than a strip club. He threatened a local crime syndicate. He'd tried to extort money from a club in which Police Commissioner Jeff Knight had a controlling interest. Talk about a perfect cover. Mr. Law and Order. A hardline adviser on criminal justice to District Attorney Cameron, the man-who-would-be governor. Who would ever suspect?

It was beyond incredulous. A corrupt cop or two, yes—but a police commissioner and his top lieutenant? Acting as joint venturers to a murder, hiding a witness, then killing her? Surely Sears and Cameron weren't part of this. But they didn't have to be. The problem with the prosecutor's office was its blind acceptance of everything the police said, true or not, no questions asked.

Jack swallowed hard. In the end, he wasn't sure the tape would be admitted in evidence. He couldn't prove that the voice on the tape was Nora's. Hell, he didn't even know her last name. And now that she was dead, he had no voice exemplar against which to compare the tape. Worse, the District Attorney's office would convince the court of the obvious: disjointed and subject to gross misinterpretation, the tape never identified the specific cops involved.

Only a successful motion for a new trial could reverse the verdict, and the burden of proof was on Jack. But Stone would never consider the tape sufficient evidence to justify a new trial. To free Lamb, Jack had to get the commissioner to convict himself—to admit that he'd poisoned Nora. That he was part of the hunting party that killed Tommy Regan—and then covered it up with another murder.

He slowed the car, rumbling past a series of boarded-up stores, searching for a pay phone. Nothing. This section of Mystic was lifeless.

Cursing, Jack banged the wheel. Matt would be at The Treasure Chest by now. For his own safety, Jack should have followed Matt back to The Treasure Chest, instead of planning to meet him again at the apartment that held Nora's lifeless body. For now, Jack was on his own.

He slowed down. Nearby, he heard the sound of bottles crashing on pavement. He turned left at Union and Blackman, spotting several street people. A block beyond, a telephone booth stood like a sentinel in front of a former clothing shop. Skidding to a stop, Jack sprang out of the car. He grabbed the receiver and dropped a dime into the coin slot.

No dial tone.

He jumped back in the car. Taking a chance, he made a sharp left, spotting another pay phone in front of a former barroom. He put two wheels up on the sidewalk and stopped. He got out of the car, ran to the phone, and grabbed the receiver.

Jack took a breath as he squeezed a coin into the slot. A dial tone. Thank God. He dialed a number he'd memorized years ago as a young prosecutor.

"Desk Sergeant, Mystic Police Department. This line is being recorded."

His hand shaking, Jack held the tape machine to the mouthpiece of the phone. He took a breath, squeezed the Play button, and once again listened to the words of a lost soul, who even in death could save an innocent man.

Hanging up, Jack's chest tightened, and his stomach dropped. That would flush the commissioner out. Just as Nora claimed, Nolan hadn't acted alone. What had Nora said? "Cops." And "Cops told him to shoot."

Jack fought the urge to run as fear began to consume him. These men were capable of anything. And neither he nor Matt was armed.

An idea hit him: a way to establish the commissioner's guilt and Lamb's innocence all at once, without dying himself or, worse, getting his brother killed.

Where there's darkness, shine a light. He pushed his last dime into the coin slot.

*   *   *

A cassette tape landed on Commissioner Knight's mahogany desk.

Knight looked up from a mound of paperwork. "The fuck is this?"

"I just pulled it off the 9-1-1 line," said Lieutenant Garetti. "Anonymous hang-up. Listen."

The commissioner stared at the tape and didn't move.

Garetti slid the cassette into a tape recorder on the commissioner's desk and hit Play. It was a woman's voice, a voice both Garetti and the commissioner recognized.

"Thought the police would help him," the woman said in a halting, hoarse voice. She struggled, her breathing sporadic and weak.

"Nora, did the police take the gun away from him?" a male voice asked.

Commissioner Knight recognized that voice, too.

"Police . . . told him to shoot."

Knight slammed the palm of his hand on his desk. "They fucking found her. Goddamn it. They found her alive. How is that possible?"

Garetti shook his head. "We gave her enough heroin to kill half a pro football team."

"Apparently, she needed more," the commissioner shouted. "Issue a BOLO for Marino and his brother. If one is in Mystic, the other one is, too. Descriptions and vehicles only. No names."

"What about the tape?" Garetti asked.

"If we hurry, the tape will come to us. But first get over to the club, and clear everything out. I don't need the State Police up my ass now." The commissioner checked his watch. "I'll meet you at the projects in an hour."

CHAPTER SEVENTY-ONE

The U-Haul truck arrived shortly after Matt parked his car outside The Treasure Chest, the low-deck freight carrier rolling to a stop, its headlights snuffed out, an armored car pulling up directly behind it. How much cash could strippers generate?

Moments later, a gang of men—bikers, from the looks of them—appeared, hauling cartons, boxes, and crates marked with drug codes Matt recognized from prison. A kilo press machine suggested the scope of the operation. Joining them at the scene, his hands gesticulating wildly, was Lieutenant Anthony Garetti. Matt recognized him as the man sitting beside the police commissioner in the gallery at the trial.

Matt continued to stare at the pandemonium unfolding before him, the size of the drug trafficking operation mind-boggling, proof positive that Jack had managed to get through to the Mystic Police, those running the Treasure Chest in all-out panic mode.

It was all coming together now. Unknowingly, Tommy Regan had risked exposing the local police when he'd threatened to have the club investigated.

Matt needed to reach the State Police. Once they saw this, they'd dispatch troopers to Nora and Jack in minutes. There was a pay phone a few blocks away. Matt pulled onto Broadway and gunned the engine. At this hour, there would be nothing between him and that phone.

A block down the road, Matt revved the engine faster. A Mystic blue-and-white pulled out from a side street. In a roar, the cruiser sped past him, its blue lights flashing, its siren wailing. Matt relaxed, letting out the breath he didn't know he was holding.

A block ahead of him, cherry-red brake lights blinked on. The police car fishtailed, swerving into Matt's lane, its brakes squealing, forcing Matt to a stop.

Matt slammed the transmission into reverse, his heart sinking. Another Mystic cruiser screeched to a stop behind him, bumper to bumper with the rear of his car.

In an instant, several Mystic cops surrounded his car, weapons drawn.

From all directions, orders flew. "Get the fuck out of the car! Hands where we can seem 'em! Get on the ground!"

Matt locked the doors, searching for a way out. An ear-splitting explosion shattered the driver's window, jagged shards of glass shredding his clothes and skin, as police dragged him out of the window.

As he hit the ground, he watched helplessly as a long, ugly police baton arced above him. In an instant, everything turned blinding white in a way that reminded him of incoming ordnance that had lit up a night sky long ago in a remote and unforgiving jungle in Southeastern Asia.

Then nothing.

CHAPTER SEVENTY-TWO

An evening wind swept in from the Mystic Creek, as an angry rain began to fall, the night sky a reservoir of black ink.

Clutching cold steel, Jack clambered to the top of the fence again, teetering there briefly. He hit the dirt hard, an involuntary groan escaping his lips as pain shot up his left leg. Inhaling sharply, he hurried toward the building where he would find Matt and Nora. He hoped he wasn't too late.

The night seemed darker, more desolate. Jack struggled to see through a gathering curtain of wind and rain. He could see nothing: no police, no Matt, no one. He considered remaining outside, but it was too dangerous. If the police arrived, they'd spot him easily. He hoped Matt had hidden his car and was waiting for him inside.

Jack threw one last glance over his shoulder. Seeing no one, he heaved the dripping plywood aside and slipped silently back into the apartment.

Inside, Jack waited for his eyes to adjust to the darkness, the rhythmic percussion of wind-whipped rain the only sound. Gradually, he peered deeper into the apartment. Though he'd stood in the same spot less than an hour earlier, this was a different, more frightening place. Shadows danced off the walls, and an unsettling darkness shrouded the abandoned home. The occasional flash of lightning and clap of thunder served only to punctuate a palpable sense of danger.

Feeling his way against the kitchen wall, Jack crept toward the stairway that would lead upstairs to Nora. He hoped Matt was with her. Squealing treads mocked his efforts to remain silent. Once upstairs, he turned toward the room where Nora's body lay hidden.

Jack paused. As far as he could tell, the second floor was as deserted as the first. Nonetheless, he proceeded slowly. He cursed himself for not bringing a flashlight, but the night had unfolded too quickly for him. Passing the room where he and Matt had found Nora, Jack felt his way to the next bedroom and slipped inside. He picked his way in the dark toward the closet where they'd hidden her body.

Jack cracked open the closet. Nora lay undisturbed in deep shadow. Jack tried to crouch by her, but the pain in his left knee forced him to sit. He was alone. Of that he was certain. At least, no one had come for her. Not even Matt. Yet.

He hung his head between his hands, silently promising Nora that he and Matt would hold her killers accountable. Soon, the commissioner would return to make sure Nora was dead. But this time, his visit would be caught on film by the Boston 9 film crew Jack had called with his last dime.

"Nora," Jack murmured, "I should have saved you."

Downstairs, a jarring creak pierced the silence. He strained to listen. Maybe it was the wind. A floorboard. Or Matt. Jack held his breath, not daring to call out.

He thought he could make out the murmur of conversation, his heartbeat racing. It couldn't be Matt. His brother would be alone. He'd have no one to talk to.

A crackling sound cut the silence. Jack whipped his head toward the stairway, trying to figure out what the sound was and where it came from. His heart sank with the realization. It was the sound Nora and David Lamb had described hearing on a dark night two years ago. The night Tommy Regan was murdered.

The sound on that fateful night hadn't been the humming and crackling of high-tension wires at all.

The sound was static squelch from a police radio.

*   *   *

Only hours earlier, Commissioner Knight had been slapping backs in a courtroom, warmly congratulating Brad Sears on David Lamb's conviction, beaming at District Attorney Cameron as the Commonwealth's first modern-day death row inmate was whisked away.

The commissioner would act much differently now, Jack thought. Gone were the secure trappings of the court. Instead, Jack was on a killer's turf. The potential for catastrophe swirled about him.

How many men had entered the apartment? Jack could make out voices, one of which he knew well.

"What makes you think she's still here?" said the commissioner.

"Unless she was taken out on a stretcher, she'd be too sick even to move."

Jack cringed as he heard the first footfall on the splintered steps leading to the second floor. And to him.

"I want her dead this time," said the commissioner.

"Understood."

"And then we'll deal with the Marino brothers."

Jack stopped breathing on hearing his name. He felt as if someone had swung a baseball bat at his head and barely missed.

Old fears swept over him. He squeezed further into the closet alongside Nora's body, tendrils of panic beginning to lick at him. Where was Matt? The State Police? And the Boston 9 TV crew?

Everything had gone wrong, no one could help him, and he had no way out.

CHAPTER SEVENTY-THREE

"Marino said the projects, right?" Alexa Metranos asked her cameraman. She looked out the windshield through sheets of rain.

"Yeah. I took it right off the tape. Said he'd be near the tracks, but I don't see anything around here."

"Play it again," Alexa said.

"Sure." Rich punched a series of buttons on the console of the Boston 9 mobile news truck, a marvel of high-tech communication equipment.

Jack Marino's voice filled the van, repeating that he would be at the old Mystic projects.

"Wait a minute," Alexa exclaimed. "Shit. Hear that?"

"What?"

"He said the 'old' projects. Aren't the original projects up near the mouth of the Mystic Creek? You're from around here, right?"

"They've been shuttered forever. What would he be doing there?"

"Let's get the hell up there and find out," Alexa replied, dialing the State Police on the van's converted marine-band satellite phone.

* * *

One room away, Jack heard the men yank the closet door open.

"Jesus!" said the commissioner. "She's not here. Could she have made it out of here alive?"

"No fuckin' way," said Garetti. "I told you. She couldn't even make it down the stairs. She's here somewhere."

Terrified, Jack listened, the impulse to run nearly overwhelming him.

"She'd fucking better be," said the commissioner.

The footsteps were closer and heavier, the beam from a flashlight dancing through a crack at the bottom of the closet door.

Seconds later, the door flew open. Jack froze, his pulse thumping in his neck. It was the commissioner and Garetti.

"Our lucky day after all," Garetti said. "Two birds with one stone."

*   *   *

"Playing musical chairs with the dead, Marino? That's sacrilege," said the commissioner, the beam of his flashlight lighting up Nora's body.

Jack deflected the intensity of the light with a splayed hand. "What would you know about sacrilege? Now that you've killed two people?"

"The once great Jack Marino."

Jack shut his eyes momentarily. *Where the hell was Matt?*

"Now that Crazy Nora has fallen asleep for good, the only loose ends left, by my count, are you and your ex-con brother," said the commissioner.

"Who will be here any minute," Jack said.

The commissioner spat on the floor. "Your brother's sitting in my jail. That is, if he's come to yet. I own him. And shit happens in jail. Especially when it's mine."

Jack shivered. He had to buy some time. Maybe the commissioner was lying about Matt. Maybe, he prayed, the TV crew was on its way.

"I'm curious. Why me?" Jack asked. "Why was I appointed to this case?"

"We all knew you'd take the case. You were on your ass, tossed out of the DA's office like junk. Only mistake we made was thinking you were smart enough to lay down and stay down. We were wrong about that. You didn't know any better. You just kept getting up."

"C'mon, let's do him and get it done," Garetti said, standing at the threshold of the closet.

Jack struggled to breathe, his chest heaving, his blood pulsing in his temples.

"Easier to kill him outside," the commissioner replied. "Gotta take him out anyway."

"Better than dragging his body downstairs." Garetti reached for Jack. "Don't worry, asshole. It only takes a second to die."

Jack looked at Garetti. Up close, the commissioner's lieutenant was a giant of a man, his muscled chest and shoulders pressing against the rain-spotted fabric of his uniform. As Garetti inched into the closet, clawing his way toward Jack, the panic came, black and howling. Flashes of the armed home invasion, of Summer, the woman he loved, of his brother—and all that he still had to say to both of them.

"Let's go," Garetti shouted, reaching further into the closet to grab Jack.

In an instant, Jack recalled that in this and every other project apartment, a panel at the back of the second-floor closets concealed a crawl space where someone—a young boy, perhaps—could hide or even sneak out of the house by exiting through another room or even another apartment. "Wait." Jack pointed at Nora, lying on the floor next to him. "I'm not leaving without her."

The commissioner laughed. "What do you give a shit about her ugly ass for? Another fucking drunk who drugged herself to death—just like your father."

Something shifted in Jack. He felt it move with glacial force. Old rage. A loss and pain so powerful that it had no name. So hurtful that until now he'd buried it under years of hurt, of shame, of feeling like he didn't measure up—all culminating with his humiliating fall from grace in the DA's office.

But this time, Jack would fight back. He no longer needed to be part of his old office—or any office—to know his own self-worth. "You bastards," Jack screamed. With all his strength, he kicked the door onto Garetti's hands.

The commissioner's henchman screeched like a wounded feral beast. A gun clattered to the floor. A shot rang out, a deafening roar piercing the night, the smell of gunpowder filling the small closet.

Heaving himself backwards, Jack dove through the cheap panel at the rear of the closet. It collapsed, and Jack found himself behind the closet beneath roof rafters, scrambling toward the next room.

Pulling an identical panel away, Jack crawled into the closet of the abutting room. Once there, his chest heaving from the exertion, Jack willed himself to keep perfectly still as he listened to the commissioner and Garetti grow frantic.

"Give me your flashlight," Garetti yelled. "Christ. He's gone. She's the only one in here. What the hell? There's a hole back here."

"Check every goddamn room up here," the commissioner screamed. "I'll cover downstairs. Whatever you do, don't let that prick out of here alive."

Jack forced himself to think. Maybe Garetti would go in the other direction first, giving Jack a chance to escape.

But he had to act. Jumping up, Jack bolted out of the closet toward the door to the bedroom. At the threshold, his heart nearly stopped.

He was looking directly into the eyes of one of Tommy Regan's killers.

In an instant, Garetti broke through the shadow of the hallway, coming at Jack like the hunter he was. Jack leaped backwards, escaping his grasp by mere inches.

Jack fought the impulse to freeze.

Garetti snarled in a low, guttural voice.

The contest was uneven. Garetti could tear Jack apart with his brute strength alone. Except for one thing. This place of darkness and shadows—where his past and present were colliding—was once Jack's world. A dark carbon copy of his boyhood home. A place where Jack needed no light to find his way.

Somewhere in the dark ether of that moment, Jack gave in to and was swallowed whole by the monsters of his past. Outgunned and outweighed by the savage looming before him, Jack would run no more. When Garetti plunged toward him, Jack attacked. It was his father's San Soo that came back to him. Or never left him. Quick, deft strikes, born from cold fury and the drills his father had burned into his memory. The volley rocked Garetti on his heels.

Garetti seemed shocked. Like all bullies, the alpha-predator never imagined his victim would fight back. But with shocking speed, the giant man's elbow emerged out of the blackness and caught Jack evenly in the face, shattering Jack's nose.

Blinding pain coupled with the metallic taste of his own blood turned Jack's stomach. He shot a left four-knuckle punch between

Garetti's ribs, slowing his charge enough to buy a precious few seconds, then slipped further into the darkness, circling his opponent. Digging down deep, Jack swept his right elbow in a high, powerful arc, swinging up and left. As it crashed into Garetti's face, Jack heard the unmistakable sound of facial bones fracturing.

"Officer down! Officer down!" the commissioner screamed into his police radio from a vantage point in the hallway. "The old Mystic projects. All personnel."

Blood still pouring from his nose, Jack circled to Garetti's left in the dark and struck a hammer fist to his temple. Swiftly, Jack moved away, leaving a stunned Garetti wondering from which direction the next blow would come. With every strike, Jack inflicted more damage. His father had once warned him: San Soo was not a fighting art. It was an ancient Chinese death art, and Jack was reaching a point of no return. The point of San Soo. Summoning all of his strength, he willed himself to stop.

Garetti lay motionless on a filthy floor.

Soaked in perspiration and blood, Jack fell to one knee in exhaustion. He held the crook of his arm to his nose to stem the flow of blood. Almost giddy to be alive, he couldn't believe what had happened. Slowly, he dragged himself up. As he did so, his heart nearly stopped again. He felt the cold barrel of the commissioner's gun flat against his temple.

"I don't give a fuck if I kill you here or outside."

The words hung over him like a knife.

Jack slumped, his remaining resolve sucked out of him.

"Get up," the commissioner yelled, stepping back to flick the flashlight beam directly at Jack. "And not a fucking move. Nice and slow."

Blinded by the light, Jack tried to engage his tormentor.

"I've got Nora on tape," Jack said, breathlessly. "Anything happens to my brother or me, you'll find yourself in the same prison where you sent David Lamb."

The commissioner laughed again, but not as heartily. Leaning down, he propped the flashlight on the floor, at once illuminating a slice of the room and plunging the rest into darkness. "That tape is garbage. Besides that, you called the station house less than an hour ago. My bet is you haven't even had time to hide it. In fact, I'll bet you're so stupid you brought it here with you and not a soul knows it exists."

"You mean this?" Jack said, holding up one of the empty tapes he'd placed in his pocket at the beginning of the night. "I've got you and Garetti admitting to the murders of Thomas Regan and a homeless woman, known as Nora. And there's more. I taped it all."

The commissioner leveled the barrel of his semiautomatic directly at Jack's head, his voice boiling with rage. "Give me that fucking tape now."

"You want the tape. Here, you can have it." Jack tossed the tape over the commissioner's shoulder into the darkness.

Hearing it land, the commissioner reflexively turned to locate it. "You fucking . . ."

It was the advantage Jack was waiting for. He lunged for the commissioner, tackling him at the knees. The commissioner's gun fell to the floor, his flashlight skittering away. The two men rolled in the darkness, Jack straddling him, pinning him to the floor, pushing his knee hard into his chest. Then Jack nailed the commissioner with a vicious blow to the face.

Spitting blood, the commissioner coughed out words. "You have no idea what I'm capable of. Half my force will be here in minutes, each one of them with a bullet for you."

Jack struck him again.

"Wait," the commissioner gasped, spewing more blood. "There's still time to work this out. What do you want? I own the fucking Treasure Chest. And the fortune that goes along with it. Part of that could be yours."

"The same share you offered Tommy Regan?"

"Don't be a fool, Marino. No one's going to believe anything you say."

Suddenly, countless streams of light flooded the apartment like a meteor shower, pouring through crevices and cracks. Outside, tires screeched, and doors slammed. "My men are here," the commissioner said. "You're fucked now."

"No—you are." Jack grabbed the commissioner and dragged him downstairs, stumbling through the darkness.

When Jack pushed aside the splintered plywood one last time, a surreal sight greeted him. The Boston 9 News truck was parked directly in front of the project, its powerful lights illuminating the building's facade like a Friday night football game.

Alexa Metranos ran up to Jack. "We assumed you meant the other projects. On the way here, I called the State Police colonel and played the tape for him." Next to the news truck, a State Police cruiser skidded to a stop. Two troopers, already briefed by their colonel, jumped out, Smith & Wesson, double-action revolvers in their hands.

Shooting an exhausted look at Alexa, a state trooper at her side, Jack placed his microcassette recorder in her hands. Loaded with the real tape. "Play that on the ten o'clock news tonight. A complete confession from the Mystic Police Commissioner and one of his lieutenants to the murders of Thomas Regan and a homeless woman. Her body is upstairs." Jack turned to the state trooper. "Be careful. His accomplice is up there, too, and he's armed."

"You can't get that into evidence," the commissioner blustered, twisting away as a state trooper detained him.

"Sure I can," said Jack. "It's called the rule of law, asshole. Something you wouldn't know a damn thing about."

Alexa turned to her cameraman. "Jesus, Rich, crank up the satellite dish. Tell 'em we're breaking in with a live feed for the News at Ten. Do it now. This is big. Really big."

Jack limped toward the overgrown grass opposite the house, his face—his whole body—throbbing unmercifully. A state trooper helped him lean against the old oak tree, the pulse of flashing blue lights lending a dreamlike quality to the area around him. A biting rain continued to fall, the wind bending the branches, their weight creaking loudly above him.

"You okay, sir?" the trooper asked.

Jack nodded, his clothes covered with blood. His? Garetti's? The commissioner's? He didn't know. But what he did know was that he'd finally fought back: the ghosts of the gang attack he almost didn't survive were in retreat, the brokenness inside him beginning to heal. More emergency lights flashed as several other State Police vehicles roared up as three Mystic Police squad cars did the same. Briefly, the two jurisdictions clashed, but it was no contest. The State Police took control in minutes.

Jack started to fade, but a clear, practiced voice brought him back. Still leaning against the tree, he turned to his right.

Standing in an unrelenting rain before mobile lights and a television camera, Alexa Metranos began her live report.

"Tonight, an exclusive on twin murders and corruption in Mystic, Massachusetts. At the center of the case is Mystic Police Commissioner Jeff Knight, top campaign adviser to the nominee for Governor, Trevor Cameron. Sources suggest that the commissioner and at least one other police official will be charged in the murder of both Thomas Regan, formerly of Mystic, and an unidentified homeless woman who witnessed Regan's killing two years ago. They also face charges for the attempted murder of defense attorney Jack Marino, who once worked as a senior assistant district attorney for Trevor Cameron. Boston 9 News will continue to bring you live coverage from the scene."

CHAPTER SEVENTY-FOUR

Early on Monday morning, the day before the election, Jack hurried across the courthouse plaza toward a bedlam of news trucks and crowds of reporters. He and Summer had planned to file David's motion for a new trial together. Judging from the crowds, he thought with weary satisfaction, David Lamb would make every news broadcast and paper across the Commonwealth.

A damp wind blew off Boston Harbor and enveloped him, kicking up dirt and litter that flew across the plaza. When he spotted Summer hastening toward him, Jack felt lighter with each step he took. It meant everything to him that she would be there to see David's conviction overturned.

"I called you all night," Summer said.

Taking her arm, Jack moved toward the courthouse. "Sorry. The press was relentless. I took the phone off the hook." Jack patted his briefcase. "Made some last-minute changes on my motion for David's immediate release."

"Jack." Summer tugged him back.

"What's wrong?" he said.

"Hey, that's Jack Marino," a reporter yelled.

"It's David," Summer said, her customary equanimity gone. "He's dead. An inmate killed him in lockup last night." She hesitated. "They're trying to determine if it was linked to the police commissioner."

Jack's world shattered into a thousand pieces. Summer extended her hand, but he felt so unsteady he didn't dare reach for it for fear he would fall to the ground.

He looked up, trying to clear his head, a swarm of reporters rushing him, each yelling questions, the chaotic sea of faces resurrecting feelings of claustrophobia. Out of the corner of his eye, he thought he recognized Alexa Metranos, but everything else dissolved into a watery blur.

Unable to breathe, Jack clenched his fists. He leaned over, his hands on his knees as he tried to force some air into his lungs.

Beneath his feet, the architects of the Pemberton Square renewal project had embossed select words of the Constitution of the United States on brass-covered cobblestones placed strategically in front of the courthouse. Though he'd crossed the plaza countless times before, he'd never once stopped to read them.

Electronic camera flashes blinded him, video cameras whirring all around him.

Jack stared at the Preamble on the cobblestones beneath him, his tears blurring words that had crafted a new and better world.

"We the People of the United States, in Order to form a more perfect Union, establish Justice . . ."

EPILOGUE

Over the weekend, Trevor Cameron's gubernatorial campaign collapsed. Voters awoke each day to newspaper headlines and live news reports about a web of police corruption reaching into the District Attorney's office. On election day, the incumbent Governor was handily re-elected. He announced that the first priority of his second term would be a complete review of the Bay State's criminal justice system.

In the days and weeks that followed, the *Boston Tribune* and the *Record* ran extensive follow-up exposés that picked apart the case against David Lamb. The House Speaker promised a vote on the abolition of the death penalty during the next legislative session. A blue-ribbon commission would take up the issue of the use and abuse of witness immunity.

Lawyers for Commissioner Knight and his lieutenant busied themselves begging the newly elected District Attorney for a plea to murder in the second degree. The recently sworn-in District Attorney, a square-jawed, former standout halfback for Harvard College who had run on a strong law and order platform, refused. Instead, because all three men shared the same felonious intent, the new DA charged Commissioner Knight and Lieutenant Garetti with murder in the first degree as joint venturers. Due to the Commonwealth's immunity deal, the actual shooter—Mickey Nolan—could only be charged with perjury.

For intentionally suppressing evidence favorable to the defense, an expedited disbarment hearing was scheduled for former First Assistant District Attorney Brad Sears. The most damaging witness scheduled to testify against him: Assistant District Attorney Lincoln Dawes, whom the newly elected DA chose to be his First Assistant.

The new acting police commissioner of Mystic, working in tandem with the mayor, shut The Treasure Chest down.

With the pittance the state paid him for defending David Lamb, Jack buried Nora White, a former ER nurse, in a leafy cemetery in Mystic, high on a hillside amid a stand of New England oak trees, her headstone looking down upon Boston Harbor, which fed the ancient rivers, streams, and tributaries that came to an end like so much else at the Mystic Creek.

The Court found David Lamb not guilty, posthumously. Judge Stone, forced to conclude that a terrible injustice had occurred, would tender his resignation, but not before the Commission on Judicial Performance disciplined him with a stinging public censure and rebuke.

Leaving the courtroom after David's posthumous acquittal, Jack pushed through a crush of press, lawyers, courthouse employees, and others to reach the front entrance. He stayed close to Summer, so he wouldn't lose her in the crowd. Matt, heavily bandaged but intact, walked ahead, blocking for them.

"Jack," called a familiar voice.

Jack turned to see Abby Thorn, her hand extended out to him. For an instant, Jack's eyes met Abby's, as he took her hand. "Still one of the best damn trial lawyers in Boston," she said.

Then he released her grip, turned, and walked into his future.

*   *   *

The wind churned and spun and raced down Congress Street, whipping around and between the labyrinth of buildings that made up the financial district of downtown Boston, as Jack and Summer left the worldwide headquarters of Fidelity Investments.

"A king's ransom," Jack said, thinking about all that had come to pass, holding the envelope containing the $100,000.00 check from his divorce settlement, all he was due thanks to the pre-nup.

Without a word, Summer turned to Jack and beamed, the unusually bright, early winter sun illuminating her face and her glowing complexion. For a magical moment, everything was perfect.

The couple turned to cross Franklin Street and waited for a break in traffic. As they were about to cross, Jack stopped and gently pulled Summer back onto the sidewalk. He pressed his forehead to hers as lovers sometimes do. "One last thing," he said into her ear.

As Summer looked on, time began to slow. Jack pulled a stamped, pre-addressed envelope from his suit pocket along with a pen. Against the palm of his hand, he endorsed the settlement check as it fluttered in the wind, slipped it inside the envelope, and sealed it.

Jack turned toward Summer but said nothing. He didn't have to. The first flush of surprise on her face gave way to wonder, then to the most beautiful, luminescent smile he'd ever seen in his life.

The blue corner postal box opened with a jarring squeal. Jack looked up at the imposing facade of Fidelity Investments, the quintessential symbol of American wealth and establishment, to which he was neither born nor would ever share in, and then turned to look one last time at Summer. Without moving or speaking, Summer gifted Jack the space he needed to reach his journey's end.

Slipping through his fingers, the envelope fell silently into the mailbox.

Mailed to a Mystic address—one Jack would never forget—the settlement check was endorsed in trust to the twin daughters of David Lamb.

"A head start," Jack said, as he returned to Summer.

Radiant, Summer drew Jack tightly against her.

Jack turned the collar of Summer's coat up against her bare neck, shielding her from the cold, stinging wind. Entwined in each other's arms, the city all but disappeared around them. With Summer's hair swirling about her face, Jack gazed into Summer's eyes, then kissed her softly on the lips, as he folded her collar back down.

Summer smiled. "Everything's going to be all right, Jack." Looking up at a perfect, cobalt-blue December sky, she whispered in his ear. "It's a good wind."

AUTHOR'S NOTE

Long-form writing of any kind is challenging. Writing a novel is even more so. It takes inspiration to keep going and to get up and dust yourself off if you've put the manuscript down. I found my inspiration in the attorneys—defense lawyers, prosecutors, and their civil counterparts—as well as my colleagues, all of whom I've had the privilege to know over these past many years. Each day, I have the opportunity to observe these dedicated professionals, who bring to life the promises of our civil and criminal justice system for the people they were intended to serve.

On the subject of the criminal justice system, a few words about the dedication. I had the great good fortune of working in the Massachusetts Legislature and attending the evening division of Suffolk University Law School with Paul McLaughlin, and I remember with affection when he greeted me on my first day as a prosecutor in 1983. The world turned dark with Paul's passing, but we remember and continue to aim for the ideals that he personified: Paul McLaughlin was the consummate prosecutor and will always remain the model for what a prosecutor should be both in Massachusetts and throughout the nation—dedicated to seeking justice, dedicated to the communities he served, and dedicated to the legal profession's highest calling.

I thank former longtime Suffolk County District Attorney Dan Conley and his predecessor and successors, for keeping Paul's legacy alive within the Office of the Suffolk County District Attorney. I urge prosecutors everywhere to learn more about Paul McLaughlin's life and legacy.